Wulfnoth
Thegn of Compton

Peter Wilcox (signature)

Peter Wilcox

**Grosvenor House
Publishing Limited**

This book is published by
Grosvenor House Publishing Ltd
Link House
140 The Broadway, Tolworth, Surrey, KT6 7HT.
www.grosvenorhousepublishing.co.uk

A CIP record for this book
is available from the British Library

ISBN 978-1-83975-829-4

To my family for their tolerance:
To Margaret, Elizabeth and Mark for their proof
reading and frank criticism
And to Ruth for her technical assistance

England and France in the year 1000.

Main Historical Characters

The Cerdics

King Aethelred II	King of England	(978-1016)
Queen Aelfgifu	first wife of King Aethelred	
Prince Athelstan	eldest son of King Aethelred	
Prince Edmund	second son of king Aethelred	
Queen Emma	second wife of King Aethelred	

The Ealdormen

Aelfric	of Wessex	(982-1016)
Aethelweard	of the Western Provinces	(956-998)
Aethelmaer	of the Western Provinces	(998-1015)
Aelfhelm	of Northumbria	(982-1006)
Eadric	of Mercia	(1007-1017)
Uhtred	of Northumbria	(1009-1016)

The Thegns

Wulfnoth	of Compton
Beorhtric	of Shrewsbury
Siferth	of the Five Boroughs
Morcar	of the Five Boroughs
Thurbrand the Hold	of Holderness
Ulfkytel	of East Anglia

Place Names

Only in relatively modern times has the spelling of place names become fixed. My own village of Barnburgh for example has had a variety of spellings down the centuries. Beornsburh may have been its original form, but it appears variously as Barneburg, Berneborc and Berneburg in the Domesday Survey, Beornburg, Baronburgh, Bernesburghe and Barnburghe in the Middle Ages and even Barmboro in the nineteenth and early twentieth century.

I have, therefore, generally used the modern place names of most of the larger towns for ease of reading. However, I have indulged in the use of what I feel are more appropriate Anglo-Saxon forms for some smaller settlements such as Cyningesburh (the king's burh) for Conisbrough and Barnburh for Barnburgh where the Anglo-Saxon 'burh' signifies a fortified place. Similarly modern Southampton reverts to Hantone (domestic dwelling) and Sandwich to Sandwic (the dwelling on the sand).

I hope such inconsistencies do not detract from the reader's enjoyment.

Contents

Portents

"Here the star comet that is 'the haired one' appeared"

Anglo Saxon Chronicle

The Manor of Compton July 996

Blood......Blood......Blood! There had been enough blood in his life already. Yet even in the heat of battle when the broad-edged and steel-hardened axe-blades bit deep into bone Wulfnoth had always remained ice cool. Steadfast in the shield-wall, he had been impervious to the carnage and suffering around him until the death-blow had finally silenced his enemies and stilled their twitching limbs. Such was the brutality of battle.

This was different. This was torture. And he was powerless to intervene.

He winced as repeated gasps and howls of pain struck the fragile bone structure deep inside his ears, each piercing sound like the surge-pain of a rotting tooth. No matter how hard he pressed his fingers into his ears he could not shut out the suffering. Only as each strident cry subsided did he relax, but then lay back exhausted, floundering in a leaden sea, knowing that in a few moments he must brace himself in anticipation of the next shriek of anguish. How on earth, he thought, could another human-being endure such pain!

Suddenly, he was aware of blessed silence and moments later heard the lusty cries of an infant waking up in an alien world demanding that his need for warmth, comfort and above all sustenance be addressed.

Relief spread across the thegn's face and his steely-grey eyes lit up in the realisation that his long vigil was over and his beloved Ragnild had finally given birth.

Minutes seemed to drag by. Wulfnoth could bear it no longer and forced his way into the room. At first he could only stand and gaze in amazement at his young wife as she lay suckling their first-born child still glistening with amniotic fluid yet grasping her hard nipple and pulling vigorously as he greedily consumed his first breastful of milk.

For a moment, Ragnhild's face seemed to glow with a radiance he had not seen before and she smiled at him and whispered "Wulf, our son."

"He took his time, but now he seems impatient enough to get on with life," said Wulfnoth, the relief clearly showing in his voice.

"He is a strong boy like his father."

The thegn stroked the boy's cheek gently. "And what are we going to call this little seawolf?"

"You must call him Godwin for he will be a good lord to his people, just like his father."

"But, it is a Christian name."

"He is the son of a Christian."

"But his mother is a Dane, who still clings to the old gods," Wulfnoth said smiling.

"He is their gift to you. He will remind you of me when I return over the searoads."

"But you cannot return to Denmark. You are my wife. Your home is here now. "

"Yes, my love, but I'm tired now and must sleep."

Her eyes certainly seemed heavy and he noticed now how drawn her face appeared. As he turned to leave he became aware for the first time of the amount of blood that saturated the bed sheets. He had seen plenty of it in battle, yet had not realised that so much was lost in childbirth. Somehow its profusion there seemed obscene, but Estrith hurried him from the room before he could question her. Alone again, slumped in a chair he closed his eyes.

His childhood had been peaceful enough growing up in the tranquillity of Compton, the Sussex manor granted to his father Biorn for services to the household of the king's cousin. He had known no other home. It comprised one hide of land with a rent of four shillings a year.

Then he recalled that dreadful day when he had returned home at the age of fifteen to find his own parents savagely hacked to death by a Danish raiding party. From that moment the course of his life had changed forever. Bent on vengeance he had joined the army of Ealdorman Edwin of Sussex where his ruthless courage in the thick of the fighting was noted and reported to King Aethelred, who had summoned him to Winchester.

Arriving at the Cathedral he had found the King in high spirits attending a Mass of Thanksgiving for the safe delivery of his son and heir, Prince Athelstan. There in the Chapel of St. Swithun Athelred had rewarded him with the title of King's thegn and granted him additional lands tripling the size of his estate at Compton. Over the shrine holding the saint's bones he had willingly sworn his allegiance not only to the king, but also to the aetheling.

After that he had confronted the Danes both on land and sea at every opportunity and his body had the scars to prove it. He never seemed to have stopped fighting, he thought, vaguely aware that under the direction of Estrith the women had been ferrying basins of hot water. There had been that time when a raiding party had been sighted entering the channel between the islands of Hayling and Thorney. Wulfnoth had taken the unusual and risky strategy of ordering the harbour settlement of Warblington to leave their homes and retire to the chalk hills, letting the invaders land unopposed. Sweeping round the headland, he had surprised the handful of Danes left on guard and burnt their ships as they lay beached on the shore. The smoke was the signal for the men of Warblington and neighbouring settlements to attack from the north while he and his sailors marched from the sea. Together they had fallen on the half-drunk Vikings as they celebrated their sacking of the deserted village with the jars of ale and mead so conveniently abandoned by the inhabitants.

There had been plenty of blood then. Iron-hafted battle-axes had been swung in the name of the king and the sea-pirates had been cut down to bleed on the coast they had come to plunder. None asked for mercy: none received any; and in a small way blood served to expiate the indignities previously suffered.

Among the Danes guarding the ships had been a group of women who had fought bravely alongside their menfolk and like their menfolk they had succumbed to the axe. However, a young child had been found alive behind the mound of death. Trussed up like a suckling pig he was dumped beside the pile of weapons stripped from the dead to await Wulfnoth's sentence.

The Danechild was brought to Compton, but he would not or could not communicate and when his hands were untied he made a dash for freedom and was half way across the open field before he was caught by Cerdic who helped manage Wulfnoth's stables.

"Be gentle with him," ordered the thegn, "but lock him up for the time being. With warm food inside him he'll be more amenable."

At suppertime Estrith sent one of the servants down to the barn with warm stew and two hunks of rye bread, but the boy had cowered somewhere in a dark corner, so the bowl was left inside the door which was locked for the night. In the morning the food had been eaten and the bowl wiped clean, but no-one caught sight of the boy. It was the same with lunch and supper.

Meanwhile Wulfnoth had been occupied with tackling the vulnerable coastal defences, assessing the natural harbours and exposed beaches between Portchester and Chichester taking particular note of the various vantage points along the chalk downs.

Surprised on his return to find that their diminutive captive was still imprisoned Wulfnoth decided to try his luck. He placed a bowl of hot leek and ham soup on the floor of the barn and pretended to leave, but while Cerdic slammed the door shut from outside he concealed himself in the shadows. Minutes later he heard someone moving cautiously through the straw. After watching the slight form of the captive as he knelt gulping down the contents of the bowl and mopping up the last few precious drops, Wulfnoth leapt forward and wrapping his powerful arms round the Danechild called for Cerdic to open the door. He could smell the sweat of fear and once outside was shocked to see just how filthy the young urchin was and how matted and tangled his long greasy hair.

"Fill a trough with water," he ordered. "We'll give our little heathen seawolf a wash."

Fresh water was brought from the well and the trough was filled, but when the Danechild realised what they intended he began to twist like an eel.

"Hold him, my lord," laughed Cerdic, "while I pull off his tunic."

They struggled for a moment, but the filthy garment was finally drawn over his head and then suddenly to his amazement Wulfnoth found himself holding not a boy, but a young nubile girl who was pounding his face with clenched fists.

"Cover her, you fool, and fetch Estrith and the women," he remembered shouting and held the prisoner close to him so that he could not look at her naked body, but then suddenly she had stopped struggling and was weeping uncontrollably.

It was a considerable relief when Estrith had gently taken the girl from him, but still he had felt like a naughty boy again as his old nurse had driven him and all the other men out of yard.

Some hours later when he was sitting alone studying his plans for a line of new beacons there was a knock on his door and Estrith entered leading a stranger by the hand. Wulfnoth was stunned by the transformation. Before him dressed in a clean simple white tunic was a young woman whose hair shone like gold and whose blue eyes, deep as rampion, opened wide as they took in the richness of her new surroundings, but when they rested on him and she realised he was looking at her they immediately focused on the ground in obvious embarrassment.

"Tell her she is welcome here and will be well looked after. Tell her.... she will be treated with honour and.....," Wulfnoth stammered, "..... that I apologise for her former treatment. Tell her...."

"Hold hard, my lord. She does not speak our language. She is frightened, but I think she feels safe with me and will not let go of my hand, so with your permission, let her sleep with me tonight."

Several days later two strangers had arrived at Compton. Despite their appearance and the quality of their retinue, the servant had asked them to wait while the master was informed of their arrival.

The taller of the two smiled his acquiescence. He had been told that Wulfnoth was not a man to be caught at a disadvantage and given the state of the world admired his prudence.

"Is the king's messenger to be kept waiting while this rustic thegn puts on a clean tunic?" demanded his companion, a sharp-featured Mercian with exceptionally long arms.

"Don't disparage him because he doesn't spend his time buzzing around the palace at Winchester," observed the more affable of the two dryly. "He served his time at Court, but now has important work to do guarding the coast of Sussex and remember he's the first man to destroy a Viking raid since Ealdorman Byrhtnoth's disastrous defeat at Maldon."

"A lucky gamble by all accounts," acknowledged the other grudgingly.

Wulfnoth, who had overheard this exchange, appeared in the doorway and quickly sizing up his visitors, addressed the taller man, "Welcome to Compton. Your apparel betrays you for a northerner, sir, but your retinue suggests you come from Court."

"You are perceptive, Wulfnoth. I am indeed the king's messenger and my home, as you rightly surmise is in the Danelaw. I am Siferth of the Five Boroughs and this is Beorhtric of Shrewsbury. We bring you the grateful thanks and congratulations of King Aethelred on your recent success against the Vikings."

"The king is generous, but I did no more than my duty to my king and to the people for whom I am responsible."

"Your modesty does you credit, Wulfnoth, but the king is anxious to build on success and wishes to know at first hand if your victory can teach us how to deal with future incursions.

"Then I shall not disappoint him. The work here is already in hand. We are clearing headlands and plan to link the ports by a line of beacons."

"You are a man of foresight and when the king hears of your plans he may well want you to extend them to include the whole of the south coast from Sandwic to the mouth of the Exe."

"You overreach yourself I think, Siferth. Such a task would require someone of ealdorman rank, not a mere country thegn," snorted Beorhtric.

Wulfnoth refused to react to the insult, but led his visitors inside where Beorhtric was clearly taken aback by the rich wall hangings and array of battle trophies.

Siferth took the opportunity of whispering, "Our Mercian friend is jealous of the king's favours and sees everyone who catches the royal eye as a personal threat to his own advancement."

"Sussex air and the smell of the sea suit me best, but I'm at the king's service. Our friend is welcome to court life."

"He's no great danger on his own, but his brother is a man to avoid, a cold calculating fellow and unfortunately cultivated by our sovereign lord."

As Beorhtric caught them up, Siferth changed the subject, "How many Vikings were in this raiding party?"

"We buried over seventy of them," replied Wulfnoth.

"I hope you didn't let any of the enemy escape," said Beorhtric, probing to see if he could find grounds for belittling Wulfnoth's achievement. "We can't afford to have those vermin roaming the countryside."

"None escaped me I assure you," said Wulfnoth carefully.

"The only good Dane is a dead one," declared Beorhtric, with menace. "They think because we tolerated their settlements in the Danelaw, there are easy pickings here." He had the good grace not to look at Siferth as he spoke.

Wulfnoth's suggested they stay the night and visit the local harbours the following day, but Beorhtric, who was anxious to return to court as quickly as possible, declined to join them and left Compton. The others were delighted to see the back of their unpleasant companion.

After supper discussion centred on the problems faced by the people of the north during which Wulfnoth heard himself ask rather deliberately, "Do you still speak the Danish tongue after so many generations?"

"Enough," said Siferth." Why do you ask?"

"Well, I have a Danish prisoner."

"I'm relieved you didn't mention it earlier. Beorhtric would have been delighted to interrogate him. He likes that sort of work."

"My prisoner is unusual and I would not have placed her in that animal's clutches, I assure you."

"Her?" repeated Siferth, raising an eyebrow.

"You shall see," added Wulfnoth enigmatically and sent for the girl. "So far we have not been able to get a word out of her."

When Estrith returned with the girl, she still refused to look up and kept tight hold of the housekeeper's hand. Realising that he towered over her, Siferth knelt down and spoke softly in a language that Wulfnoth recognised, but could not understand.

After about ten minutes he rose and sat beside his host. "Her name is Ragnhild," he said, "She is the daughter of Godfred brought to England to marry one of his henchmen, who planned to settle on conquered land. She thought she would be sacrificed when you celebrated your victory, but I have told her that she has nothing to fear and that you are a man of honour and will protect her from harm if she submits to your authority. I think I have reassured her."

"I am indebted to you, Siferth, but I must ask you keep her existence a secret from the Court. Much as I serve the king I do not trust that she will be safe even under his protection."

"I'm sure you are right. You may count on my silence."

The young woman was watching their faces carefully and when they had stopped talking she came forward and kneeling before Wulfnoth laid her head against his knee.

Instinctively, he had put his hand on her head and then against her cheek. Then he lifted her to her feet and kissed her lightly on the cheek before Estrith came forward and led her away.

Since the arrival of Ragnhild new life had been breathed into the whole household. Estrith undertook the duty of training her in its ways and she was an eager learner, rapidly picking up the English tongue, willing to take on all manner of tasks, both inside the house and on the estate, whether it was helping in the kitchen, serving at table, tending the herb garden or carrying messages.

It was as if a cloud had been lifted from the shy young Danish hostage and she radiated a warmth and light that gradually illuminated the lives of all at Compton: the household guards smartened up their appearance, the servants went about their chores with more enthusiasm and the village cottars would fumble with their woollen caps when she passed. The whole house rang with laughter and even the bread baked by the cook seemed to smell better.

The months that followed were among the happiest Wulfnoth could remember and he could hardly bear to tear himself away to inspect the progress of the new ships and the completion of the early warning system and when he did he would waste no time on his return pushing his horse into a sustained canter until he could see the smoke rising from the manor hearth.

When family bereavement had necessitated Estrith's absence, the housekeeper had proposed that Ragnhild should be given the keys. "You'll not even notice my absence," she had assured him and it had been true. Life at Compton seemed to glide effortlessly through the water like a sea-going vessel, manned by a well-trained and highly skilled crew. Ragnhild ran a tight ship, but her touch on the helm was light as a breath of wind and the ship's complement willingly sailed under her captaincy.

Wulfnoth began to look forward to her arrival each evening to discuss household arrangements. At first he expressed his complete satisfaction and could think of nothing else that he required, so she would smile, curtsey and leave him and he would spend a lonely evening. After two or three days he found himself trying to devise ways of detaining her. Eventually he hit upon the idea of seeking her opinion about anything and everything.

The next night he spread out his plans to extend the manor, so that it seemed natural to ask her advice as to the advantage of various arrangements. "Should the new bakehouse back onto the existing hearth? How far away should they build the wood store? Where should the bolting of the wheat take place? What could be done to improve the storage of dried beans and salt-fish? How could they speed up the processes of preparing meat and vegetables?"

The following week he showed her the design of his new ships and asked her how they compared with the current vessels used by her countrymen. Although her knowledge of construction methods was scant, she had a good eye and could draw detailed sketches of both the narrow warships and broad-beamed cargo vessels used by both Danes and Norsemen.

The two hours after dinner each evening had seemed to race by and as the days shortened they frequently lit the rush lights until the smoke became unbearable and then reluctantly Wulfnoth would kiss her lightly on the forehead and let her go.

On the 28th of October a comet had appeared and both had left the manor to watch it blaze its way across the heavens. They stood together gazing up into the night sky for well over an hour until a keen breeze sprang up. Wulfnoth noticed that Ragnhild was shivering in her thin tunic, so he put his cloak around her shoulders and led her back inside to get warm by the dying embers in his room. That night was the first time they shared a bed together.

Thereafter every morning she would slip out of his room well before the cockerel clamoured to be released and life at Compton sailed on in much the same way even after Estrith returned. His housekeeper accepted the new arrangement as if it was the most natural thing in the world and deferred to Ragnhild in all matters concerning the household and took to referring to her in front of the other servants and any visitors as "the young mistress." By Christmas Ragnhild thought she was pregnant and by the beginning of March she knew.

Wulfnoth vividly recalled a Spring day when they travelled to Bosham to trial the first of his new ships with its single-timber keel stretching from the stern to the great stem post carved with the head of a wolf. The sleek shape of the craft told even the untrained eye that that this was a ship that would glide proudly through the roughest searoads of the world and so it had proved. Ragnhild had wanted to join him, but he'd refused promising her that after their child was born the two of them would sail her alone out into the channel that separated England from the Great Continent.

Satisfied with the way she handled, he congratulated the shipwrights and ran back up the beach to Ragnhild grinning like a young boy.

"She's magnificent," he cried.

"She handles well. But what will you call this new mistress of yours?" she added mischieviously.

"*The Ragnhild*, of course. Did you not recognise the goddess with the long hair?"

Ragnhild smiled for she had already noticed the carving of the Danish goddess Freya, which graced the sternpost.

He recollected his recent visit to Winchester to buy birth-gifts for his wife and child from Torgrim the fourth-generation Danish silversmith and moneyer whose mint stood at the junction of Goldsmith's Street and the High Street. On arrival he had found the stockade gate firmly shut for Torgrim's premises held considerable quantities of silver and newly minted coins. Wulfnoth pulled the bell rope and waited until the spy-hole panel was slid back and he could be recognised. Then he heard the oak beam withdrawn and the gate opened to reveal the half-naked, sweaty, muscular frame of the bellows man.

"Hard at work I see, Eric," grinned Wulfnoth as he tied his horse to an iron ring while the man secured the gate.

"Ahh, Mah Wuffnah," he wheezed out of his misshapen mouth. He was a man of few words and those barely distinguishable since a sword had sliced through his jaw and left only the stump of a tongue in his mouth, but he had the strength of two men and never seemed to tire, despite the hamstring injury sustained in the same battle. As they passed a stack of charcoal he effortlessly gathered an armful of billets, without interrupting his shambling gait.

"Lord Wulfnoth, a pleasure to see you," called Torgrim from the smoky atmosphere of the mint where they found the moneyer snipping away at small squares of sheet silver until he had a pile of near-perfect blank discs and a heap of scraps which his daughter, Hild, swept onto a triangular board and tipped neatly into a crucible.

"We can't afford to waste any silver," observed Torgrim, "or the king will accuse us of cheating him," and he carried the blanks over to the minting table. Slipping a blank on top of the standard die bearing the royal head the mint-master struck it deftly with a single blow from the mallet, before placing the trussel die with the hand of benediction on top and delivered a second strike. Hild then trimmed and polished each new coin.

"An excellent piece of workmanship," observed Wulfnoth. "Aethelred's still a fine looking man."

"They're new dies sent from London. It's a symbolic image of course. He wants to be seen as father of the nation with his sceptre and on the back his hand blessing the people like a priest," said Torgrim somewhat ruefully.

"You don't like him, then?"

"I don't like some of his new Mercian friends. Every time there is news of a Viking raid they stir up trouble and we suffer intimidation and abuse, but enough of my problems. How can I be of service to you?"

"I'm looking to buy some jewellery."

"Did you have something particular in mind?"

"No, but I shall know when I see it."

Torgrim unlocked a side door leading into another room with a solid wooden floor. To Wulfnoth's surprise he got down on his hands and knees and using his nails withdrew four wooden pegs before prising two of the boards up and reached down into a void. Seconds later he lifted out a plain wooden box and placed it on the table. Inside individually wrapped in cloth he revealed an assortment of armlets, bracelets, necklaces, brooches, pendants and rings made of gold, silver and bronze and decorated with garnets, glass, red and yellow amber and even amethyst. Wulfnoth felt spoilt for choice, but eventually selected a gold chatelaine, a blue glass bead necklace, a garnet cloak brooch and a plaited ring of silver threads for Ragnhild, and a wild boar's tooth mounted in silver for himself. Finally, even though he knew it was tempting fate, he couldn't resist a simple cowhorn spoon for his unborn child.

Torgrim returned the box to its hiding place before unlocking the door.

"Come again, my friend. It's always a pleasure to do business with a man of such good taste," Torgrim laughed as Wulfnoth remounted.

"I can't afford to make a habit of it," the thegn replied smiling. As he left and turned for home he heard the mint-master close the stockade gate and slide the bar back into position.

Making his way homeward at a comfortable canter Wulfnoth felt exhilarated at the thought of the pleasure he would see in the lovely eyes of his attractive young wife – a pleasure he was determined to resist until they could celebrate the birth of their first child.

July came and the sun seemed to shine endlessly until at last the waiting was over and his beloved Ragnhild was in labour.

His reverie was brought to an abrupt end when he felt the hand on his shoulder.

"Come quickly, my lord," whispered Estrith. "My lady is unwell and we cannot stop the bleeding."

Suddenly wide awake he leapt up and ran to the bed-chamber where his young wife lay. He was vaguely conscious of one of the women carrying a pile of bloody sheets past him. Ragnhild, her eyes closed, was covered with a clean linen sheet. She looked dreadfully pale and her skin had an alabaster quality that left little doubt in his mind that she was slipping away from him.

"Don't leave me," he pleaded, kneeling beside the bed and touching her cheek.

For a moment the lids flickered, then opened and her blue eyes smiled sadly at him.

"He is beautiful, Wulf. Tell him his mother loved him."

"But you will recover."

"No, my love. I feel so cold. Bring him to me so that I can hold you both."

The woman who was nursing the baby brought him over to the bed and placed him between them and he kicked and gurgled, which made Ragnhild smile again, but Wulfnoth looked utterly defeated for he had seen that blood was beginning to seep again through the sheet.

"I can't live without you," he whispered.

"You will and you must for our son," she replied. "Remember to call him Godwin. He will bring our people together; and, Wulf, promise me you will return me to the wine-dark sea."

"I promise," said the thegn with resignation and shut his eyes.

When he opened them again Ragnhild had drifted into a coma and by midday she was dead.

Wulfnoth refused Estrith's offer of help and closed the door. Then he removed the sheet knowing that bleeding always ceased with death. She seemed so small and vulnerable. Taking fresh cloths he washed her entire body with the gentleness that he had explored it on the night when the fiery-tailed star had promised so much as it crossed the night sky. Finally he dressed her in the simple white tunic she had worn that night, took the presents he had bought from his strong box, placed the beads round her neck and the ring on her finger.

The moon was well up in the sky when they left the landing place and he lent on the blade-shaped oar and swung the *Ragnhild* eastward down the quiet creek trailing a second vessel behind her. As they passed the grey stone Saxon church of Bosham, built where Christianity has first been preached by Paulinus to the South Saxons, he knew the strengthening current would soon carry them into the outer harbour and thence between Hayling and West Wittering to the deepest water of the channel that separates England from France. Bringing the oar back so that it trailed behind the stern, he lashed it down securely, before checking the sail and lighting the torch.

Ragnhild lay at his feet on the raised aft deck under which he had piled a quantity of charcoal and dried timber together with all her possessions save the garnet brooch he had purchased in Winchester. Bending down he kissed her lightly on the eyelids and the lips for the last time. Then he plunged the torch into the kindling. For a while he watched as sparks ignited then died in one place only to break out again in another before returning to the sternpost where he stood in silent vigil listening to the hiss and crackle from the splinters of wood until tongues of flame licked through the blacken planks to embrace her young body and claim her spirit for Freya's fastness.

Satisfied that all was as it should be, he lowered himself into the water, unhitched the tow and swam to the trailing vessel, surrendering his young wife to the keeping of the sea.

Alone in mid channel the fulfilment of his final promise to commit Ragnhild's body to the care of the unfathomable depths of the sea in accordance with the ancient pagan rites of her people had sustained Wulfnoth through the first hours of his loss, but as he sailed back, cold as hoar-frost, he was filled with a sense of emptiness.

Back on shore in the early hours of the morning he cast a solitary figure as he left the beach, untethered his horse, dragged himself into the saddle and lost in the void of grief let the beast carry him the ten-mile journey back to Compton, where he retired to his room and collapsed onto the bed.

In his absence, Estrith had given orders that the room was to be aired and scrubbed clean; the bed remade with fresh linen; and everything returned to its customary place. Cerdic's sister, Asa, whose recent child had been stillborn, was to be hired as a wetnurse for Godwin and his crib placed in the kitchen so that he would be kept warm by the fire and Estrith herself could keep an eye on him.

Wulfnoth, however, was oblivious of these arrangements since he withdrew completely from life at Compton and kept to his room during the day, venturing out only after dark to relieve himself and to pass an hour or two staring up into the night sky. Instinctively he sought isolation as a protective membrane between himself and reality.

He picked at the food Estrith brought for him, but hardly noticed what was on his plate and when she came to clear away he would dismiss her with a nod to indicate that he wished to be left alone. The fire from his light grey eyes, that had never been known to have lost their bright twinkling intensity even in the midst of battle, seemed strangely extinguished. The old nurse did not intrude on his grief knowing that only time would gradually erase the pain.

For several months a curtain of gloom seemed to hang over Compton broken only by the cries or gurglings of the hungry or satisfied Godwin who was fussed over by all who visited the great kitchen. Outside its thick walls the inhabitants went about their daily household duties in managed silence, whispering only in suppressed snatches, as if afraid to disturb the fragile air like desperate parents for ever listening beside the bed of a sick child in dread for the breathing to falter or in hope for the fever to break.

The smoke from the Portsdown beacon was the catalyst and Cerdic was the harbinger of impending disaster who burst unannounced into Wulfnoth's room one morning in late spring the following year.

"My Lord, the Danes have been sighted!"

"What did you say?" demanded the thegn dragged back to reality from semi consciousness of his private world by the urgent appeal of the young man.

"There's black smoke rising above the hills."

"From which direction?"

"From the southwest."

"Above the Roman fort?"

"It's bound to be one of those overlooking the great harbour, Sir."

"Then God help old Nothhelm and his family, if they have been surprised." Instinctively Wulfnoth had buckled on his sword. "Saddle up all the horses and tell Swithred, Oswy, Osmund and Alfred to be prepared to ride immediately," he said as he bent down to lace up a pair of cowhide shoes.

Minutes later he strode into the kitchen, dipped a hunk of black bread into the pot over the fire and was about to eat it when he was conscious of Asa sitting breast-feeding a healthy-looking blond-haired infant.

"He's a fine boy," he said as he gently ruffled the blond hair. "She would have been so proud. Take great care of him and bring him to me when I return."

A few minutes later Cerdic arrived with the horses only to find that one of the men was laid up in bed stricken with a fever. Seizing his chance he dashed into the kitchen and confronted the thegn. "Osmund is sick, sir, but I can ride and know the area well. May I not take his place?"

"I need every man I've got, so grab your axe and be quick about it." Taking a last look at his son, Wulfnoth nodded to the rest of his servants, strode out of the kitchen and mounted his waiting horse. Then he, Cerdic and three heavily armed men cantered out of the gate.

"Thank, God for the Danes," murmured Estrith with relief as she watched the cloud of dust travel along the road to the coast.

Small groups of thegns, and men who had served in the fyrd had gathered in every village alerted by the pall of smoke so that by the time they reached the chalk hills above Cosham their numbers had swollen to over a hundred and fifty. They knew that the people of the coastal settlements would join them with axes, knives and an array of land implements that could wreak a terrible vengeance on the flanks of an enemy faced with a well-disciplined force of Sussexmen.

Meanwhile Wulfnoth's fleet at Bosham had put to sea and four ships had sailed north of Hayling and taken up station on the Langstone end of the Hillsea waterway, while the other five had sailed south to block the great harbour entrance effectively bottling up the intruders beneath the old Roman fort. Wulfnoth could afford to wait for there seemed to be only six enemy ships and his army was growing by the minute as men from Fareham, Rowner and Alverstoch joined him while others gathered on either side of the great harbour mouth. The net was closing and the mesh was getting thicker all the time.

Viking longboats could carry up to forty men so he had estimated that the invaders comprised two hundred and forty at most but in reality he knew they probably amounted to about two thirds of that figure. As he looked down from a vantage point on the chalk hill he could see that they had landed, entered the enclosure of the disused shore fortress and set fire to the old wooden church. Probably they had stripped it of its meagre treasures, sacked the aisled hall and slaughtered the inhabitants. Now it appeared that they were preparing to make camp within the walls before venturing further inland for richer pickings. While the gates were in a sorry state and would prove little problem, they were narrow and the walls still stood at a considerable height so if properly manned the old fort presented a formidable defensible position. However, Vikings rarely fought defensive battles preferring to rely on naked aggression, a strategy that usually wrong-footed and demoralised their opponents.

Complete surprise was impossible since the beacon spoke eloquently to friend and foe alike, but at least Wulfnoth knew the ground and was determined to conceal the arrival and exact size of his force. Time was on his side. As reinforcements continued to arrive the thegns dismounted and deployed their forces in various wooded areas that had grown up around the disused Roman fort. Cerdic and one of the household guards were sent to spy out the land and returned just before midday when Berthun of Hantone arrived with fifty well-armed men gathered from the settlements along the road from the west setting the odds decisively in the English favour.

"We saw the beacon and came as soon as we could," panted Berthun as he slipped heavily out of the saddle. "Where is Nothhelm?"

"He's not been seen. I fear the old man was taken by surprise."

"Very probably. He's not the man he once was. I thought Aelfric would have replaced him long before this. The defences haven't been maintained these past ten years."

"Then I doubt anyone in the household remains alive," observed Wulfnoth with sadness. "Sea raiders take no prisoners."

"True enough," nodded Berthun with resignation. "By now the Danes will be digging in to consolidate their position. How do you propose to attack?"

"I'd like to separate them from their ships first, but my spies tell me that they lie on the narrow beach below the walls sheltered by two of the round bastions north of the watergate and can easily be defended by a handful of Danes."

Berthun scratched his head. "Then we'll have to wait for the tide to turn."

"Not necessarily," said Wulfnoth thoughtfully. "We've a couple of hours or so before high water and the wind is onshore. Perhaps we can smoke them out."

"But we can't get close to the curtain wall on the seaward side. You said a handful of men could hold that strip of land."

"I know, but I have an idea and what's more I have just the man who might manage to pull it off." He drew Cerdic to one side and, having explained his plan, sent him off to one of the nearby settlements.

Selecting some forty battle-hardened fighting men, he split them into two groups and ordered them to conceal themselves about a quarter of a mile beyond each end of the fort and as close to the sea as possible. Behind them he positioned the rest of the Sussexmen.

Meanwhile Berthun sent his men into the woods facing what used to be the land gate and the army of coastal settlers hid in undergrowth close to the north and south posterns. Then they waited.

Just before high tide three small shallow-drafted fishing vessels edged their way along the shore from the west keeping about a hundred and twenty yards from the shore. Each held a single oarsman who bent doggedly to his task apparently ignorant of the warships lying half in half out of the water under the great stone walls. The Danish guards, seeing no danger watched with amusement as the fishing boats struggled to maintain their course and some were tempted to launch a warship. However, they were under strict orders and the rewards were hardly promising, so they satisfied themselves by unleashing a couple of arrows, but these fell short.

The fishermen, who were now passing directly in front of the fort, responded by shaking their fists and shouting abuse at the Danes. Then two of them quickly lashed their vessels together, hauled up their sails and began to row furiously towards the shore.

The incredulous Danes, who could neither believe their luck nor the foolhardiness of the West Saxons, grabbed their axes and waited at the water's edge.

Shielded by the sails in front of him Cerdic in the third boat had lit two torches and plunged each into the containers of dried grass, tar and old rope in the sterns of the leading boats. As they burst into flame he laid branches of freshly cut laurel on top, stepped back into his own boat and slipped her line. As the smoke billowed out the other two fishermen shipped their oars, dived over the side and swam back towards their comrade.

At first the dumbfounded Danes hefting their axes in expectation of easy pickings, but as a great black cloud of swirling smoke enveloped the fishing boats and swept towards them indecision and panic broke out. The enemy had disappeared and they did not know whether to wade out to meet him, pull the warships clear of the water or send a warning to their leader who was somewhere behind the curtain wall. In the matter of a few seconds, however, they were themselves stumbling about in the dense acrid fumes. At that moment a hail of arrows rained down on them and as the smoke was drawn up over the ancient stones carefully chosen men with wet cloths wrapped round their noses and mouths fell on them from either side. The well-honed edges of the Sussex axes swiftly dispatched those Danes who were still on their feet and a reverse swing mashed the unprotected heads of those crouching in a paroxysm of coughing and retching on their knees. Within seconds the narrow shingle beach ran with brains and blood.

The first sign of smoke above the walls had been the signal for Berthun's force to stream out of the woods to attack through the land gate while Wulfnoth following hard on the heels of his shock troops led the rest of the Sussex thegns and fyrdmen along the beach and through the water gate. Despite having little or no warning, the main body of the Danes instinctively sprang into battle mode and prepared to engage the enemy on both fronts in the only way they knew by charging headlong into the teeth of the attack. The resulting clash of opposing forces rocked both sides for a brief moment and then hand-to-hand fighting saw men beaten to their knees and hacked into blood-soaked bundles of human flesh. The ferocity of both sides might easily have led to total annihilation had not the men from the coastal settlements streamed through the east and west gates and attacked the Danish flanks bludgeoning them to the ground with all manner of weapon, ripping them to death with the scythe-blade and seax. The battle ended as suddenly as it had begun. No Dane remained alive and the victors collapsed exhausted where they stood. A number of the Sussex men had fallen and Alfred, one of the Compton men had suffered a serious flesh wound, but Wulfnoth, Cerdic and the others from the estate had fought with such single-minded determination that none had sustained serious injury. Berthun and his men had stood their ground and lost less than a fifth of their number. Above all the system of beacons had proved its worth.

The collection and redistribution of weapons, armour, clothing, rings, brooches and combs and the disposal of the bodies began that evening and took up the whole of the following day. Wulfnoth and Berthun divided the undamaged warships between them, but each man left alive was given a share in the spoils appropriate to his rank or by virtue of his contribution to the victory. Cerdic, in particular, was singled out and presented with a broad two-edged sword with a damascened blade and inlaid hilt for his part in the ruse of the fire ships. It was a weapon that was to serve him well during a long and distinguished career under three generations of masters. After the thegns had had the pick of the remaining weapons, Wulfnoth insisted that his household guard should choose before the rest of the fyrdmen and settlers.

Meanwhile the wounded received what little help their comrades could offer and if their injuries were such that they were unable to travel they were left to the care of the women from the nearest coastal settlement, who reset limbs, stitched open wounds with horsehair and did all that they could to nurse them back to health, but saw nothing wrong in pocketing their meagre belongings if they happened to die. Nothing would go to waste. Cerdic's mother took charge of Alfred and his wound was cauterised to prevent further bleeding. Then she prepared a poultice of feverfew, nettles and various herbs and taught him the charm that had to be recited whenever the poultice was applied. He declared himself fit and eager to return to Compton with the others.

On the third morning Berthun and the men of Hantone took their leave and, once he had checked the beacon and watched his ships head for the harbour entrance, Wulfnoth was anxious to return home.

Apart from the burnt-out church and the disturbed earth over the burial pit nothing remained to show that a bloody battle had taken place and that some two hundred and sixty men had been hacked to death. The remains of the fishing boats had been reclaimed by the following tide, but the blood-soaked soil would have to wait for a period of prolonged summer rain before it was washed clean and the trampled grass revived. An hour before noon Wulfnoth and men of Compton rode out of the land gate in sombre silence and left the ancient fort in the capable hands of Berthun's son until Ealdorman Aefric had chosen a successor to Nothhelm.

By the time they reached home, however, their mood had lightened. There were no empty saddles; they brought no bad news; the estate had lost no one. The warriors could look forward to an evening of feasting and celebration and a long night in the arms of their wives and lovers. Although Wulfnoth could not share that final solace he was back in the real world and longed to hold his son in his arms.

Word of the victory had preceded them and Estrith had given orders for two suckling pigs to be killed and skewered on the spit. The new season's beets, leeks, peas and beans were gathered, along with wild mushrooms, onions and wild garlic leaves. Finally an amphora of Wulfnoth's favourite Rhenish wine, pitchers of mead and the last two jars of the previous year's fruit and nut crop preserved in honey were brought out of the store just as the troop entered the court yard.

As soon as they arrived the men unsaddled and then rubbed down their sweating horses before stripping off their own soiled clothes and washing in the millpond. Half an hour later Wulfnoth, in a well-worn but comfortable dark tunic, lifted his sleeping son out of his cradle and sat nursing him like a mother beside the kitchen fire. The thegn's eyes were closed and only Asa noticed the tears that leaked onto his cheeks. The healing process had begun.

When the men began to gather outside the kitchen Wulfnoth opened his eyes and finding Asa close by handed Godwin to her and, blinking away his tears, feigned interest in the new spit arrangement and proposed that he should carve the meat. Selecting the largest metseax he began cutting succulent pieces of glistening roast pork and distributing them to his followers as they lined up holding their thick slices of barley bread. Then Estrith ladled out helpings of cooked vegetables from the stewpot before they made their way to the benches on either side of the trestle table that had been set up outside the kitchen in the open air. Eating with one hand they were all able to manage the drinking horns that Asa kept topped up from a pitcher. Having regained his composure and a large trencher of food, Wulfnoth took his place at the head of the table and the warm summer evening was spent swapping recollections of the battle and lamenting the sad state of many of the old shore forts.

* * * * *

Beorhtric, attended by a couple of men at arms, arrived two days later to find Wulfnoth stripped to the waist and working alongside two farmhands as they tried desperately to save an old ox cow that was lying half in and half out of the stream that fed the mill race. The cow had obviously been labouring to give birth for a considerable time, but there had been some blockage or obstruction and needing to slake her thirst before making one final effort, the confused animal had slipped on the bank. Fortunately she had been discovered and when Wulfnoth had arrived he had seen that the calf's front legs were protruding, but that there was no sign of the head. While the other two prevented the cow from slipping further down the bank in her struggles, Wulfnoth forced the legs back, put his arm inside and found the head, which he managed to pull down and bring forward so that the muzzle and legs were both visible. Suddenly, there was a squelching sound and the calf was swiftly expelled onto the muddy grass. Instinctively the exhausted cow rolled over knocking the two farmhands into the water before regaining her feet and struggling up the bank to stand bemused as Wulfnoth cleared the remains of the caul from the calf. Seconds later the ungainly creature staggered to its feet and was nuzzling its mother's udder, while the three men stood around grinning.

"Is that really you, Wulfnoth the scourge of the Danes, wallowing in all that mud like some village ceorl? I doubt I will be believed back at court when I say how I found you," the supercilious voice sneered.

"Ah, the Shrewsbury courtier! A cow is a valuable creature and a live female calf with several years of milk in her an even greater prize. We Sussex folk have to be thrifty." Then leaving the serfs to keep an eye on the two animals, he escorted his visitor back to the manor.

"I'll not keep you waiting while I wash and change," he said affably, rinsing his hands in a bucket of clean water at the back door and added, "I know you don't like being away from court too long, so we'll take something in the kitchen while you deliver your message and then you can be on your way."

Beorhtric raised his eyebrows and looked round in disbelief when they entered partly because of the grandeur of the new building and partly because no one acknowledged the thegn's arrival with more than a nod or a smile.

Amused, by the man's obvious disapproval, Wulfnoth remarked, "We're a busy family down here. Everyone has important work to do, so we don't stand on ceremony, I'm afraid, but if your business is private we'll take a bowl of stew and step out into the courtyard."

Estrith smiled sweetly at the disconcerted Beorhtric and offered him a steaming bowl and hunk of black bread, while Wulfnoth spoke softly to Asa and let Godwin grasp hold of his finger. The thegn would have let the child play for a while, but an impatient cough from his visitor drew his attention.

"I like to spend time with my son," he heard himself say proudly and then for no apparent reason he wished he had bitten his tongue.

"A fine boy, such blond hair and blue eyes. I did not realise you were married. Will you not introduce me to your wife?" asked Beorhtric.

Wulfnoth said nothing.

"A fine raven-haired Sussex girl, if I'm not mistaken."

"You are," said Wulfnoth curtly. "But you come on the king's business, sir. I must not detain you with simple family matters."

"Of course", sneered Beorhtric. "The king wishes to acknowledge your second success against the Danes," he said grudgingly and then paused.

"But?" asked Wulfnoth intuitively.

"Well," continued his guest. "Without wishing to detract from your victory, Ealdorman Aelfric is concerned that you not only took it upon yourself to place a beacon on his land without permission, but that you led a party of Sussex thegns into his territory without authority."

"I had thought that my first duty as a thegn was to serve the king and protect his realm. The Danes had landed and if I had waited for an invitation there could have been widespread butchery."

"Yet, you failed to save Aelfric's friend, Thegn Nothhelm. He and his whole household were slain!"

Wulfnoth bristled with indignation. "That was hardly our fault, sir. We rode with all haste as soon as my beacon gave warning, but by then the Danes had easily overrun that ill-maintained fort."

"Do you criticise Thegn Nothhelm for failing in his duty?"

"That poor old man had grown senile and should have been replaced years ago."

"Then you blame Lord Aelfric or perhaps the king. Have a care, sir."

"I blame no one, sir. It is the nature of things," said Wulfnoth, back on his guard.

Beorhtric switched tack. "Why could you not have attacked at once?"

"It seemed prudent to wait for more men and I had word that Berthun of Hantone was on his way. A foolhardy attack would have lost more lives. I trust the king would not have wished that."

"Of course not," said the wrong-footed Mercian sharply. "I'm sure you were right to wait for reinforcements. He will understand your caution, but," he added quickly trying to regain the initiative, "he was surprised not to receive some tokens of your victory, some of the captured weapons and equipment perhaps."

"There was little of value," said Wulfnoth guardedly. "I'm sure our sovereign Aethelred would not begrudge his brave thegns and fyrdmen the spoils of war. His generosity is acknowledged throughout the kingdom."

Beorhtric could hardly disagree with that. "Well," he said brusquely, "I've delivered my message. I shall return to court with your answer."

Good riddance too, thought Wulfnoth, but said, "Tell the king we Sussex men pledge to defend his kingdom against all its enemies, Dane or English."

Leaving the black bread untouched Beorhtric bowed stiffly to Wulfnoth and seeing Cerdic coming out of the stable shouted, "Bring us our horses, slave, and be quick about it."

As he rode furiously out of the yard, Wulfnoth confided, "Cerdic, I neither like nor trust that upstart. Take heed you never fall foul of him."

Osmund did not recover from his fever and died three days later. Miraculously, however, Alfred's wound healed cleanly and did not fester, but whether that was owing to the cauterisation, the poultice or the incantation no one could be certain. He was soon back at work, but with the loss of Osmund arrangements would have to change. The next morning the thegn called Swithred, Oswy, Alfred and Cerdic into his private room and told them what was on his mind: Cerdic would replace Osmund, but remain responsible for the stables and horses; Alfred would act as his reeve and liaise with the village craftsmen; Swithred, who came from the coastal region to the south of Lindsey, would be responsible of the maintenance of the beacons and Oswy would be his link with the fleet. Cerdic was to be trained by the others in weaponry and he would teach the others the arts of the sea. All would serve as estate guards and defend the manor in time of danger.

"We live in harsh times," Wulfnoth said, "and I must have men about me whom I can trust."

"Do you expect the Danes to return?" asked Swithred.

"At some time or other, if not for land, then for the geld. Aethelred has shown he is willing to pay. But remember it's not just the enemy without, but the enemy within that we may have to face."

"Like the man from Shrewsbury?" asked Cerdic.

"Yes, like him. If Siferth is right there's a new breed of men at court who seek to feather their own nests and there may be dark times ahead."

Before they left each placed his hands between those of Wulfnoth and swore to serve the thegn loyally.

During the following weeks Wulfnoth threw himself into life on the estate, rising early to ride out and inspect the boundaries. Then he would spend most of the day discussing a variety of farming matters: making arrangements for the harvest; supervising repair work on the stables and storehouses; and planning the cultivation of more scrubland. He hoped to plant an orchard of continental apple and pear trees the following year. There were also the annual tasks of selecting the cattle for keeping over winter and overseeing the slaughter of all of the rest, so that Estrith and the other women could hang or salt the carcases. Once or twice a month accompanied by Oswy or Swithred he would visit Bosham or the coastal defences, but for the next year all was quiet in the Solent, the estate prospered and Wulfnoth was able to spend more and more time with his son.

But all that was to change.

PART ONE

The Mintmaster's Loss

"If a moneyer is found guilty, the hand shall be cut off with which he committed the crime and then fastened up on the mint. But if he is accused and he wishes to clear himself, then he shall go to the hot iron and redeem the hand with which he is accused of having committed the crime."

Athelstan's Second Code of Law

Wulfnoth was summoned to attend a meeting of the
Witan on the Feast of St. Benedict to discuss the
latest Danish incursions. His initial reaction had been
one of irritation, but then he remembered that there
were a number of items he needed for himself and the
estate. He normally liked to support the local cottars,
but in the great walled city of Winchester the range of
goods was far greater and the quality often far better
and he was more likely to find exactly what he wanted,
so he could kill two birds with one stone. Therefore, at
first light on the day prior to the feast he left Compton
accompanied by Cerdic in good spirits and without the
slightest apprehension.

Simplicity and practicality had always dictated his
choice of clothes at home and he saw little reason to
change, and with the keen March winds and a louring
sky both wore plain leather tunics and carried woollen
cloaks tied behind their saddles against a sudden drop in
temperature. At midday they trotted through Warnforde
and after a further two hours, during which they heard
only the calls of native birds and the rat-a-tat-tat drum
roll of the occasional spotted woodpecker above the
sound of the horses' hooves and their own voices, they
reached St Giles Hill. At the top of the rise Cerdic looked
down in amazement at the three great minsters that

obscured the palace and towered high over the narrow wooden houses laid out in a neat grid pattern between the high stone city walls. It was a picture of splendour and order in which the insect-like inhabitants seemed to be participating in some sort of religious procession half making its way up one side of the main street while half was coming back down the other.

Once they reached the old flood plain they found themselves facing a line of wagons and packhorses laden with sacks of flour, bundles of fleeces or piled high with skins trundling inexorably out of the city, before turning north for London or south for Hantone. Trotting past them they found progress increasingly difficult as they approached the narrow funnel of St Swithun's Bridge, passed the great water wheel of Athelgeard's Mill and entered through the East Gate. Cerdic, who had been chatting with excitement ever since his first sight of the city, was suddenly struck dumb by the sheer volume of people who thronged Cheap Street. More used to the pace of life in rural Sussex he found himself struggling to follow Wulfnoth through a seething tide of human activity reminiscent of refugees fleeing the hoards of Ragnar Shaggy Breeches.

It was market day. Sellers were shouting their wares, buyers were haggling over prices and satisfied customers were heading towards the gate, their backs bent under bulging sacks and freshly slaughtered carcases. Women laden with armfuls of household implements and earthenware pottery were clutching reluctant children who wanted to stay and play tag in and out of the crowd, while dogs foraged slyly for scraps among the forest of shod and unshod feet that trod in all directions along the dusty thoroughfare.

Eventually they reached the Nunnaminster resplendent in its greensand ashlar blocks of stone and flint and could hear the hammers of the metalworkers in the forges of the abbey foundry. Here a foul stench drifted down from Tanner Street where the cattle hides were being softened with excrement and steeped in tanks of pungent liquids, so they hurried on until Wulfnoth led Cerdic up a narrow street to the right where he dismounted and entered the shop of a shieldmaker. Inside some workmen were covering the shields with leather while others were riveting the metal bosses and handgrips into place. The thegn preferred the greater manoeuvrability of the lighter wicker-framed shield and chose two before rejoining his servant who had remained tending the horses.

Further up the street he bought a set of bone needles for Estrith and then they made their way along the northern walls to return via Shoemaker Street where he was measured for a new pair of shoes that were promised for the following day.

Back at the High Street they crossed to the southern side where they arrived outside Torgrim's stockade just as his workers and apprentice were leaving in order to reach home before dusk. Eric as usual was on duty at the gate and recognising Wulfnoth held the door open for him. Torgrim was delighted to see the thegn and led them into the house.

"So, Lord Wulfnoth, what brings you to Winchester, more presents for your wife perhaps?" he asked cheerfully and was about to describe some of his recent designs when he saw the look of pain on his guest's face and realised that he had innocently reopened an old wound.

"My wife is dead, sir," said Wulfnoth simply.

"How could I have been so insensitive? Please forgive me, Lord Wulfnoth." Torgrim was desperately trying to repair the damage of his unfortunate blunder.

"Nothing to forgive. You were not to know and I have come to terms with the loss. No, this time my business is with the King's Council which meets in the morning, but I doubt there will be accommodation for us in the palace so we seek a friendly house where we can share the roof for two nights."

"You are always welcome in my house, Lord Wulfnoth. It is my pleasure. Hild, we have guests tonight. We shall need a good supper."

"Of course, father," the girl nodded and disappeared.

"And how, my friend, is life in Winchester?" asked Wulfnoth after Torgrim had brought extra stools and placed them round the fire.

"Not the happy place it used to be in my father's time. I grew up in a friendly community and we were well respected. Our jewellery was sought after and the income from the mint provided even greater security. Three years ago I was elected to represent the other mintmasters on the council of city burghers and held a place of honour in the meetinghouses, but now there is a campaign to make me an outcast and many of my former friends have been advised to avoid contact with me."

"Who's behind this campaign?" said Wulfnoth indignantly.

"There is a new gang from Shrewsbury that swaggers about the town and they have made it clear that they don't like Danish settlers. I have been attacked in the street and my daughter has been called a whore. Even my workers have been threatened with beatings if they don't find employment elsewhere. I've lost two and can't find decent replacements that I can trust. Now they want to take over my business under the pretext that it should be run by a government official! Recently there have been two break-ins, although nothing has been stolen. I think it is all part of an attempt to drive us out."

"But surely," asked Wulfnoth, "you have complained to the King's Reeve?"

"Oh yes. He's an honest enough fellow, but can do little without proof. They work for powerful thegns who have the king's favour. If I make too much of a fuss they will produce witnesses to proclaim their innocence. No it is better to avoid trouble and Eric is always on hand and can accompany Hild if I am not with her."

"I shall speak with Ealdorman Aelfric," promised Wulfnoth. "I'm sure he and the king know nothing of this and will put a stop to it."

"It's kind of you, my lord. For myself I am not afraid, but my daughter is all that I have since her mother died and she rarely smiles these days. But enough of my troubles. Let us go in and see what she has prepared for us.

* * * * *

Beorhtric was among the first to arrive at the New Minster the following morning and made his way behind the two vast organs where three shifty individuals stood whispering. They were all migrant foundry workers from Mercia and recent recruits to the seventy strong team of organ bellowsmen who under the instructions of a monk would feverishly work the mighty arms of the twenty-six bellows that filled the great wind chest.

When they saw the thegn they fell silent and kept their eyes on the stone flags of the floor.

"Well, Porthund?" Beorhtric demanded.

The shortest of the group, a furtive stocky little man stepped forward, glanced quickly in both directions and swallowed hard before bowing to the thegn and confiding, "We followed your instructions, my lord, and pretended that the coins you gave us were given to us by the foundry master and we said at once that they felt too heavy."

"What did he say?"

"That they were a new issue, but agreed the weight seemed wrong so he took them back and said he would consult the King's Reeve."

"He has done so and what of the other coins?"

"We took them to the market as you said and bought things at various stalls."

"Did no one challenge you?"

"No, my lord. We chose our moments well when there were others clamouring to buy. They hardly glanced at us and didn't weigh the coins lest they missed a customer. No doubt some of the merchants discovered by nightfall that they had been swindled and have demanded action from the authorities. Have we done well, my lord?"

"It would seem so, but others have done well too. All week there have been rumours of a great fraud."

"When are we to be paid, my lord?" asked Porthund warily.

"As soon as you have done me one more service."

Porthund looked disappointed, but knew better than to question the thegn further.

"My lord?"

"The man I point out to you must not leave the Cathedral until nightfall."

"We'll see to it, my lord. You can rely on us."

Suddenly, voices could be heard in the nave heading towards the organ.

"It's the bellmen and the rest of the bellowsmen, my lord. They have to wake the dead and we have to begin making wind."

Beorhtric ignored the remark and as soon as he had identified Eric he made his way swiftly round the recess behind the altar and out through a side door. He arrived at the gates of the Palace just the city was summoned to life.

* * * * *

Cerdic leapt off his straw sack convinced that the day of judgement had arrived when the bells of the Old Minster, the New Minster and the Nunnaminster rang in hideous competition with each other urging all the inhabitants of Winchester to rise and attend the Mass in honour of St. Benedict.

Soon he and his master joined their hosts and were hurrying down Great Minster Street their eardrums painfully complaining of the dreadful assault. Once inside the Cathedral there was blessed relief for the sound was partially absorbed by the floors of the tower and the fabric of the building.

Cerdic had never been in such a huge place and could hardly believe that the roof would not come tumbling down crushing them all. He imagined that this must be what it was like in some great beehive or anthill and that the townspeople were an army of insects, each rushing to perform his own business yet each part of a great battle plan.

Torgrim drew them to one side where a group of pilgrims had already formed a line to shuffle past the shrine of St Swithun whose reliquary was a blaze of gold when shafts of sunlight streamed through the windholes and struck its house-shaped mortuary box. They marvelled at its embossed gilt sheets decorated with acanthus leaves and pious saints behind the grill through which the crippled and infirm could stretch their arms in the forlorn hope that physical contact with the saint's casket would evince a miracle and make them whole again. Neither Wulfnoth nor Cerdic had remembered to offer a prayer before they were swept past by the tide of eager petitioners that followed them.

The current carried them down to where two teams of Winchester's finest were bathed in perspiration as they toiled like galley slaves to provide the wind for the great organs. Eric grinned as he spotted them, but dare not wave and upset the rhythm of his fellow bellowsmen. At that moment two Benedictine monks simultaneously struck the letters painted on the keyboards and four hundred pipes shattered the relative peace of the Cathedral to announce the entry of King Aethelred who walked slowly down the aisle to take his place on the left of the altar.

Before the second organ blast which heralded the arrival of the abbot, Torgrim led them towards the back of the Cathedral where they found places to stand among the more prosperous inhabitants of the city and from where they could follow the Mass without suffering permanent deafness.

At the end of the service, once the royal and ecclesiastical dignitaries had retired, a spontaneous hubbub of noise broke out as the merchants gathered in conspiratorial groups. Torgrim shrugged his shoulders and suggested they leave. Wulfnoth couldn't help but notice that a pathway seemed to open up before them as they made their way towards the great west doors and if his host made eye-contact with anyone they quickly looked away as if embarrassed. Clearly Torgrim had not exaggerated his problems and once in the open air the mintmaster expressed his determination to take his daughter straight home leaving Wulfnoth, who was due to attend the Witan, and Cerdic to make their way across to the Royal Palace.

Before they reached the gates it was agreed that Cerdic would spend the afternoon in Foundry Lane where the metal workers plied their trade to buy a new coulter for the plough and an assortment of iron artefacts required on the estate. Then he would collect the thegn's new shoes before returning to the mint. The thegn would attend the council and return as soon as it was over.

Wulfnoth was challenged but allowed to pass through the gates and began to walk up the incline towards the steps of the Great Hall when he was hailed by a voice from the past.

Wulfnoth was delighted to see the thegn from the Five Boroughs, with whom he had developed a close friendship since that memorable day at Compton, when he had learnt the name of his little Danish hostage. "It's good to see a friendly face," he said.

"I thought it was you, Wulfnoth," said Siferth with equal pleasure, "but I heard that since your great loss you had buried yourself in deepest Sussex and only came out to fight Vikings."

"It's true I prefer the quiet life, but no one can refuse the king's summons."

"Ah! Yes. Well you may have me to blame for that, I'm afraid. I told Ealdorman Aelfhelm that if anyone knew how to tackle the sea robbers it was you and he put you on the list. I trust you will forgive me."

"On this occasion," smiled Wulfnoth, "but don't make a habit of it. I have a son to rear and he takes all of my time."

"I know the feeling. My son Sigewith is about the same age. How is young Godwin?"

"He's a fine boy. He has his mother's looks and grows fast, thank God."

"I'm pleased for you, but let me introduce my brother Morcar and this is Thurbrand of Yorkshire."

The introductions over, Siferth led them into the Great Hall where Councils were held when the king was resident in the great capital. They found benches on the outer circle obliquely opposite the empty chairs reserved for the royal party.

The king entered almost immediately with his two eldest sons Athelstan and Edmund walking behind him. He already had six children and rumour had it that that the queen was pregnant again. Lucky man thought Wulfnoth, but then, noticing Aethelred's look of resignation, remembered why he had shunned the court and found fulfilment in his Sussex estate and the freedom of the searoads.

The business of the day began with the witnessing of a diploma authorising the conversion of Sherborne Abbey to Benedictine rule and granting the new establishment various land in Devon and Dorset. One after another the names of the members of the Council were called and a scribe entered them on the parchment. A tedious process thought Wulfnoth and wondered how often those parcels of land had changed hands at the whim of Saxon kings.

Of the old guard appointed by Aethelred's father, only the frail and gaunt Aethelweard still held office as Ealdorman of Wessex beyond Selwood and the sound of his voice suddenly jolted Wulfnoth back to the present and the main reason for the gathering of the Witan.

".....leaving Watchet in flames. Then they sailed round to the Tamar and sacked the rich silver mines at Lydford before they burnt down Ordwulf's monastery at Tavistoch, slaughtering nuns and priests alike in their quest for treasure. No one is safe from these sea raiders who line their boats at will with our gold and silver." He paused and seemed uncharacteristically at a loss.

The king looked round to see who was prepared to venture a solution.

"It's no good wringing your hands, Aethelweard. Can you not concentrate your forces and provoke a major battle?" suggested Ealdorman Aelfhelm of Northumbria.

"Easier said than done," said the old man. "We do not know where they will strike next. They control the channel and the coast is full of creeks and coves unlike the long beaches of the north." Aethelweard looked round for support.

"It's all right for you people of the Danelaw," remarked Ealdorman Aelfric, of Central Wessex acidly. They do not attack you since you are of the same rootstock."

"Scratch a northerner and you'll find a Dane," said a familiar voice and Wulfnoth saw Beorhtric among a group of West Mercian thegns he didn't recognise.

"Our allegiance is to King Aethelred," snapped Thurbrand. "We are not traitors who deal secretly with the enemy, like some I could mention,"

Aelfric shot him a venomous look.

"If the king wishes to call out the fyrd we are ready to share in the defence of the whole kingdom, providing the army is commanded by the king himself or by someone we can respect," declared Aelfhelm.

The king looked wary and Aelfric was apoplectic.

"Such a mobilization would take weeks, during which time the Danes will strike all along the south coast and plunder every monastery and manor from St. Michael's Mount to Canterbury. We must raise a new geld from the whole of England and buy them off. It's a strategy that worked with Olaf Tryggvason and will work again."

There was fury at Aelfric's proposal from the northern thegns and when the furore died down Siferth rose and addressed the council. "It's true Olaf Tryggvason has not returned, but the Danegeld is an invitation to every adventurer to try his luck on these shores in the belief that we will pay them tribute rather than fight to defend our land. Perhaps Wulfnoth of Sussex can offer an alternative strategy. After all, he is the only one present who has successfully repelled Danish attacks this decade."

This suggestion produced an initial outburst of whispered questioning and then silence as members of the council craned their necks to identify this unknown champion.

Wulfnoth had been taken completely by surprise and rose to his feet with the eyes of everyone in the Council Chamber upon him. He felt uncomfortable as he rose in his leather tunic but cleared his voice.

"My lords, I do not believe in giving way to the enemy. Siferth is right. The Danegeld is a strategy for disaster that will only give heart to our enemies."

The king visibly bristled at this, but Wulfnoth pressed on. "We must offer him the axe and the edge of the sword on every occasion he sets foot on our shores, unless he agrees to live in peace and obey the laws of our land. If we tax our people let the money be used to build a fleet of ships based in every river and at every coastal settlement so that we can intercept him on the searoads before he reaches our shores. That would be my advice to your lordships."

He had not meant to say a word in the Council and knew that having been forced to he had probably said far too much so he bowed formally to the king. As he resumed his seat he was surprised to hear a spontaneous murmuring of approval for his proposal.

Seconds later Aelfric was on his feet. "Brave words from an opportunist who has won a few minor skirmishes, but has no regards for authority, lets good men die while he waits for reinforcements and then claims a victory that was only made possible by the intervention of the Thegn of Hantone," he said savagely.

"Can we trust the word of a seaman who spawns a son out of a Danish whore and favours the Danish long ship?" asked Beorhtric and added with undisguised cynicism, "Perhaps the Thegn of Compton plans to continue to expand his empire of vessels at the nation's expense."

Wulfnoth had drawn his seax, was half out of his seat and would have rushed at Beorhtric in his fury had not Siferth held him back. "Don't let that animal provoke you. You're playing into his hands and would be cut down by that bunch of thugs from West Mercia before you reached him," Siferth hissed.

For a moment there was consternation in the Chamber until Aelfhelm's voice could be heard above the din. "The Danegeld was a necessary evil after the defeat of Byrhtnoth and when treachery led to the debacle of the king's fleet the following year. The king and Council acted wisely then, but we have squandered the time that tribute bought us. Wulfnoth is right. It must not be thought that England is a soft touch. Like your ancestor, the great King Alfred, my lord, you must build a new fleet to protect our shores and we must call upon the expertise of seamen like Wulfnoth of Compton to help lead it, not sink to personal attacks bred out of spite and envy by lesser men."

Wulfnoth still struggling to recover his composure could not but admire the statesmanship of Aelfhelm who had turned a potentially dangerous situation to his advantage. The king smiled at the contrived complement and for a moment looked like his former self, then shot a warning glare at Beorhtric who was livid that his attempt to discredit Wulfnoth had failed.

"Perhaps," said Aelfric, eager to limit any damage that references to treachery might do to his own reputation and to regain the initiative, "we should consider another of your forebear's innovations and reintroduce the split levy so that we can maintain a standing army that can be called upon at all times."

He was interrupted by the distant bells of the Nunnaminster calling the Black Nuns to their midday prayers and waited until there was silence again. However, when he attempted to expound on his idea the king had raised his hand for silence and addressed the assembly, "I am indebted to the full council for its opinions and will give consideration to your proposals. We shall retire, therefore, for refreshment after which you will learn of my decision." Without looking at anyone in particular he rose and swept out of the chamber.

As the meeting broke up Wulfnoth's first thought was to catch up with Beorhtric so that he could settle his score with him, but as he pushed his way through the press, Ealdorman Aelfhelm appeared at his side, took his arm and steered him away from the crowd.

"He's not worth it and this is neither the time not the place for private squabbles and revenge. There are more important matters to address."

"True, but one day that man will pay for his foul and malicious insults to me. So, my lord, what happens next?"

"The king will consult with those he currently favours."

"Surely, my lord, your advice will be heeded and the king will build a fleet."

"He's half convinced, and your victories cannot be ignored. He's grateful, but others envy you your success and seek to poison his mind. Aelfric, despite his past failures, is still a powerful voice and you have hurt his pride. As for my influence it still rankles with the king that since King Edgar's time we of the Danelaw are autonomous in laws and social customs. It is the price his father paid for our loyalty and there is still resentment and a lack of trust. We shall soon see the direction of the wind."

"If Aelfric has his way there'll be no fleet. He loathes me and will not support it."

"You made some dangerous enemies today, young man, but many friends too. Be assured you will always find a welcome in the Danelaw especially if you ever have need of a bolthole."

Wulfnoth was amused at being called 'young' but he supposed that the Ealdorman was old enough to be his father, a fact that excused the familiarity. "I am indebted to you, my lord, for your kind words and offer of friendship."

"Believe me. It is not altruism that drives me. That quality is a luxury that few men can afford. My brother, Wulfric, has it, but alas I do not. We all have need of friends. Let us join the others and slake our thirsts."

* * * * *

After Mass the stocky bellowsman had told Eric that he was needed in the church tower to help lift one of the bells that had jammed in the cradle and he had willingly joined the three foundry men and climbed the ladders that led up to the bell chamber. On the fifth floor they attacked him with staves that they had previously concealed there and he stood little chance as the three of them beat him about the head till he fell senseless to the ground.

"Have we killed him?" asked one.

"So much the better if we have," said the leader. "Beorhtric doesn't like loose ends."

"But, Porthund, killing someone in a church means death and certain damnation," replied the other and with that he fled followed quickly by the third man.

The leader looked for signs of life but couldn't find any, so he left the body where it lay and made his way to the floor below. Then just to make sure, he removed the ladder and continued down to the nave. Turning the key in the tower door for good measure, he left the Cathedral.

* * * * *

After a brief recess the Council reconvened albeit briefly and the king gave his decision that the Ealdormen of Central and Western Wessex should jointly lead an army, raised from within their own provinces and supported by troops from West Mercia to face any new Danish threats. They would also be joined by a group of Viking mercenaries who had settled in the Southwest. Their leader was one Pallig, a high-born Danish carl married to Sweyn's sister Gunnhild whose services Aethelred had bought with gifts of gold, silver and estates. Aelfhelm and the men of the Danelaw would be held in reserve.

Disappointed that a new fleet did not feature in the king's thinking, Wulfnoth was impressed with the way Aethelred had resolved matters without favouring one faction more than another. Aethelweard had not lost face; Aelfric for all his incompetence was the most experienced in the field; the king's new favourites were given a place; and yet the Danish settlers had been found a role. It was a brave plan, but, thought the Sussex thegn, it could also be a recipe for disaster.

The feasting was likely to go on till nightfall and Wulfnoth hoped to excuse himself as soon as he had spoken to Aelfric and the king on Torgrim's behalf. He feared that Aelfric would give him short shrift, but in any case the ealdorman had left immediately the Witan closed. However, as luck would have it, Aethelred did not leave the Great Hall before the food was brought in. Unfortunately, he was deep in conversation with Beorhtric and the City Reeve, but then the latter nodded and both left apparently on the king's orders. For a moment Wulfnoth could hardly restrain himself from following the man and making the Mercian pay for his insult, but the confines of the Royal Palace were hardly the place to settle that particular score and in any case such action would forfeit his chance to petition for his friend. Others were now gathered about the king and Wulfnoth had to wait till the candles had burnt down the best part of two hours before he could approach Aethelred.

"My lord, you have not lost your skill in managing your Councillors," he began diplomatically.

"No, but it is not such fun as it used to be." The old smile was still there. "We face many problems, both from the sea and within our own shores. I'm sorry you did not get your fleet, but ships cost money and the treasury has problems of its own just now. Perhaps in a year or two. We'll see."

"Thank you, my lord."

"You spoke bluntly today in Council?"

"I did, my lord. I know no other way to serve my king."

"We thank you for it," said the king generously, "and one day hope to repay your loyalty."

"There is a small matter, my lord," said Wulfnoth seizing his chance.

The king inclined his head.

"I lodge with Torgrim, the moneyer, tonight and he is the victim of a campaign to discredit him by those who covet his position and wealth. He is much abused for his Danish origins and the favour of the king would restore his standing in the community."

"You go too far, Wulfnoth," Aethelred blazed. "I am reliably informed that the man has abused his licence and undermined the common wealth. He must face the consequences prescribed by law. You will be ill-advised to plead for him or to remain under his roof." And with that the king turned his back on the thegn and the audience was abruptly ended.

For a few moments Wulfnoth was dumbstruck. He had imagined that Torgrim's problems stemmed from a simple case of dog eat dog and would find a sympathetic royal ear. With growing certainty he realised, however, that his friend had fallen into a pit of adders and was in the gravest danger. Without further delay he left the feast and ran.

* * * * *

Some hours earlier Beorhtric and his followers had joined the King's Reeve and city guard as they made their way swiftly down to the moneyer's premises at the corner of Goldsmith's Street and the High Street. There they demanded entrance in the name of the king. Since Eric had not returned from the Cathedral and Torgrim was alone in the house with his daughter he had no option by to unbar the gate and let them in. The reeve ordered him to hand over the keys and the old man was roughly bundled inside the Mint.

"It has been brought to the attention of the king that you have been striking and issuing a debased coinage."

"That is not true, my lord! Bring my accuser here and let him prove his foul accusation."

"There is no need," said Beorhtric. "These coins themselves are sufficient to condemn you." And with that he emptied a bag of pennies onto the table.

"Well," said the reeve, "can you deny they bear the city name and your own mark?

Torgrim examined them carefully and they appeared to be perfect in every respect.

"I cannot deny that they have been struck from my dies and can assure you, Master Reeve, that if they have been made here you will find they are of the correct alloy."

"We shall see, Master Torgrim. We shall see."

Torgrim felt confident that his system of checks would not have permitted debased coins to leave his mint. He always supervised the composition of the alloy and made sure that it was precisely ninety-two and a half percent silver and then the coins were weighed twice before leaving the mint, first in batches of ten and then individually. Any weighing less than twenty-two and a half grains were immediately melted down again. He was sure it was foolproof, but the muscles of his stomach had contracted with apprehension for he knew the consequences of currency fraud for himself and his family. He watched as the reeve placed an official box on the table.

"A simple exercise in weight should be sufficient for the moment," continued the reeve. "As you see I have brought my scales with me for the purpose."

He made a point of demonstrating that the scales were in perfect balance and then placing a small weight in the left hand pan watched as it exerted a downward force. Then taking each of the coins in turn he placed it in the pan on the right. None of them caused the slightest movement of the scales. Next he took a smaller weight out of the box and again placed each coin on the empty pan calling out the weight as each brought the scales into equilibrium. Each weighed exactly twenty-one grains. Torgrim couldn't take his eyes from the process and the colour drained slowly from his face.

At the end of the demonstration the reeve raised his eyebrows questioningly at the moneyer, but Torgrim with his mouth open in horror was speechless.

"Perhaps", suggested Beorhtric, "You would like to use your own scales to check the findings are accurate?"

Seeing a glimmer of hope Torgrim recovered his composure and thanked the Mercian profusely. Then he quickly drew out his own balance and placed it on the table and began to repeat the test, but after weighing the second coin he knew he had been offered false hope as his own scales confirmed those of the reeve's. Utterly defeated he sank to his knees.

"By your own admission these coins were made in your mint. Both the official scales and your own pronounce them debased. Therefore, by the power..." the reeve began.

"With your permission," interrupted Beorhtric silkily. While this man's guilt has clearly been demonstrated the King would not sleep at night if he thought we proceeded to verdict and punishment without the final incontrovertible evidence. Surely we must assay the metal and determine the full extent of this man's crime."

The reeve, while annoyed that his authority had been questioned, had to agree.

Completely bewildered, Torgrim did not know whether the thegn was merely over-scrupulous or a champion of those wrongly accused, but when Beorhtric nodded to two of his men and they began to stir up the embers of the forge he saw the look of amusement on the Mercian's face and knew his fate was sealed.

The formality of melting down four of the coins, separating the metals, letting them cool and weighing the constituent parts took some while it seemed to prove beyond doubt that the accused had been defrauding the treasury of over two grains per penny, making himself a handsome ten percent profit. Even the King's Reeve was astounded by the enormity of the swindle.

The verdict was pronounced and the punishment a foregone conclusion. Torgrim would lose his hand and be thrown out on the streets. Then his only option would be to place his head into the hands of a rich lord in voluntary bondage. But who would want a man with one hand? Those of his household would fare little better consigned to a life of enforced servitude at the behest of the local bishop.

"I am innocent," pleaded Torgrim.

"Then you have the right to clear your name," sneered Beorhtric all pretence of sympathy abandoned. "The iron is in the fire already."

The old man could do nothing, but submit to ordeal and pray, but the Saint had used up his supply of miracles for that day and when the moneyer was forced to grasp the white-hot iron it stuck to his hand and devoured the flesh.

Torgrim screamed.

After the implement had been torn away and thrust back into the fire, Beorhtric roughly examined the seared palm and declared triumphantly, "The hand is forfeit. Do your duty, Master Reeve."

The reeve nodded and Torgrim was dragged over to the table and his mutilated hand was held firmly while an official raised a short axe and brought it smartly down cleaving the wrist bones with a single blow. The burning sensation stopped and the old man felt nothing and watched vacantly as a spurt of arterial blood was ejaculated from his truncated limb. Then the hot iron was applied, the blood vessels sealed and the former moneyer slumped to the floor unconscious.

The reeve and his officials, having performed this last gruesome act demanded by the law, proposed to secure the building, post a guard outside, return to the palace and report back to the King,

Beorhtric waited for him to leave before he and his men returned to the premises where the guard was easily persuaded that it was in his best interest to desert his post. The Mercian and his men then began to search the property and soon discovered Hild hiding in the cellar under the main living room. As a witness to their clandestine activity she presented Beorhtric with a problem. At first he threatened her that if she breathed a word about their return her father would be strangled where he lay, but then decided that it would be safer if she were to disappear altogether. Leaving two of his men to protect his investment, he took her to the West Gate and arranged for the city gaoler to dispose of her.

* * * * *

It was sometime before Eric regained consciousness and then he lay for a while, trying to piece together what had happened to him, but he could remember nothing since the first blow from behind had done most of the damage. His head felt like a wine skin about to burst and there was dried blood in the woollen yarn of his tunic. Eventually, he got to his knees and then stood leaning against the wall still nonplussed. It was only when he had recovered sufficiently to attempt a descent that he realised the ladder had been removed. Obviously he had been duped and deliberately trapped in the tower and the only way out was upward. Reaching the bell chamber he could just see out over the city, but he was unable to attract attention and he knew that his voice, which sounded more like a donkey's than a human's, would fare no better. Gradually it dawned on him that his incarceration had no purpose unless it was to prevent him from returning to the mint and, therefore, it followed that it was not he who was in danger but Torgrim and Hild. Frantic with fear for them he looked about in desperation for a means of escape. There was nothing in the chamber except the bells.

* * * * *

Meanwhile Cerdic had spent some hours in Foundry Lane waiting for the farm equipment to be made and when the finished articles finally met with his approval he made his way across the New Minster grounds, hoping to be in time to collect Wulfnoth's shoes. The bells of the Cathedral were ringing erratically and he was surprised to see a crowd of women outside the building staring up at the tower where a piece of material was flapping from one of the windholes. As he watched the material detached itself from the tower and dropped to the ground a few yards ahead of him. It was a thick woollen tunic.

"Some madman in the tower," shouted a monk who had appeared out of nowhere and dragged Cerdic towards a side door. "You must help me. He might be violent."

Cerdic had no wish to get involved, but the monk was frail and clearly would stand little chance against a madman, so he left the equipment on the ground, picked up the tunic and followed the monk into the Cathedral. They were puzzled when they found the tower door locked but the key turned easily and Cerdic reluctantly led the way up the ladders. They replaced the one propped against the wall on floor four and were about to ascend when a pair of large feet followed by bare buttocks and a naked man made their way down to meet them.

"Mah Herhic, Mahher an Miss Hild," the apparition cried and was already half way down the next ladder before Cerdic recognised Eric and went in hot pursuit.

At the door of the church Eric was confronted with the hysterical screams of women who were convinced that some rampant hairy satyr was about to ravish them. He checked and Cerdic was able to catch up and thrust the woollen tunic over his head. Seconds later, decency restored, the two were running through Great

Minster Street and up the High Street arriving just in time to see Wulfnoth emerging from Goldsmith Street.

All three reached the stockade at the same time and were challenged at the gate by the two Mercians. However, Beorhtric's thugs were no match for two heavily armed men and a wild giant screaming in some alien tongue. They were swiftly overcome, gagged and bound hand and foot. At first everything looked normal, but then Wulfnoth's eyes were drawn to a blackened object above the mint door. On closer inspection it turned out to be a severed hand.

They found Torgrim curled up in a corner clasping his right arm, moaning softly and calling for his daughter. Gently they lifted him on to a bench where he could lean back against the wall and Cerdic fetched an earthenware bowl and filled it with cold water from the cistern so that he could dangle his burning stump in it and gain relief. While Wulfnoth listened to the old man's account of his ordeal Eric went out and returned minutes later with the news that Hild was to be sold in the slave market the following day.

It didn't take Wulfnoth long to realise that any attempt to assist Torgrim and rescue Hild would put them all outside the law. He called the others in and explained the gravity of the situation to them.

"If," he concluded, "we are caught breaking the law Aethelred would pronounce us "nithing" and then anyone could kill us and claim a reward for our corpses. I cannot order you to risk your lives now that those two Mercians can identify us."

At this Eric shook his head and cackled "Na. Na." Then seeing their puzzlement stretched out his hands and made flicking movements with his wrists. "An, ih

I hatch hat fat Hercian Horhund who ahhacked me in her hower, I'll ho her hame for him!"

Cerdic went out into the yard and returned to confirm that the necks of their prisoners had been snapped like dried twigs. Although Wulfnoth did not condone cold-blooded murder, he could not blame Eric for taking revenge and the act certainly solved a major problem.

"You have certainly increased our chances of success, Eric," he acknowledged, "but we must act quickly. We must get Torgrim to a place of safety before morning and then Cerdic, who is the only one not known to the authorities, will attend the slave market posing as a wealthy ceorl, bid for Hild and then join us later. The first problem is where to hide."

"Er Eher Uds," cried Eric pointing to the northeast and making an up and over sign with his hand. Neither Wulfnoth nor Cerdic could fathom what he meant, but Torgrim, whose spirits had been lifted by the possibility of rescuing his daughter, translated for them, "The Leper Woods. He means the Leper Woods. No one would look for us there. Only the monks visit those poor wretches."

Wulfnoth shivered, but had to admit that it offered their best chance of concealment. Meantime he would go and seek out Siferth who with Aelfhelm and his brother Wulfric were lodged in that part of the palace set-aside for important visitors.

"They may be able to offer you and your daughter greater safely in the Danelaw and in any case I need to borrow money for more horses and enough to ensure that Cerdic can outbid anyone and rescue Hild. She is beautiful and will command a high price."

Now it was Torgrim turn to laugh, "There will be no need for that, Lord Wulfnoth. I have riches hidden in a dozen places. Those fools would take days to find them." Suddenly the light was back in his eyes and he led them throughout the premises till they had gathered enough gold, silver and precious gems to satisfy the crew of a longship. Wulfnoth had never seen such wealth.

The sounds of pounding on an oak door initially sent alarm bells ringing, but when they went to investigate they discovered it was the horses at the rear of the building. The two Compton horses had taken their cue from Torgrim's old mare who was complaining that she had not been fed. Now all three were kicking at the stable doors. That partly solved the problem of transport since the cob was equally at home being ridden or strapped between the shafts of the moneyer's covered cart, but once on the road north they would still need to purchase a horse for Hild.

Wulfnoth left for the Palace while Cerdic and Eric spent the next two hours burying the two corpses and loading the cart. On his return they finalized their plans and taking it in turns to keep watch slept fitfully until just before dawn. Then, leaving a broken strong box and a few trinkets discarded in the yard, to suggest that the house had been ransacked and that the two Mercians had made a hurried get away, Wulfnoth, dressed in an old smock belonging to Torgrim, drove the covered cart down the High Street towards the East Gate. Minutes later Cerdic slid the bar down to secure the stockade from the inside, shinned over the wall and dropped down beside the two horses that Eric had left tied outside. Mounting one he led the other in the direction of the West Gate naively assuming that the rescue of the old man's daughter would present no problems.

Among the Living Dead

While the Church had always deemed leprosy to be a divine punishment for moral depravity, few people in Anglo-Saxon Britain had come into contact with those sad, rotting, living corpses, with their inflamed lesions, but for the few who had it was a devastating experience. At a time when the concepts of infection and contagion were unknown, it was fear of moral contamination, family shame and revulsion at gross physical deformity that was enough to convince relatives of the leper that concealment was the only course open to them.

Isolated cases were simply hidden from view, confined to dark corners and only permitted to enjoy fresh air after dark when safe from prying eyes. Such confined spaces and close contact led to a spread of the disease. Instinct must have informed the subconscious that physical contamination played some part in this and then those found to bear the signs of disfigurement were driven from their homes and villages.

Of course some weren't lepers at all, but simply the victims of misdiagnosis suffering from other skin complaints brought on by lack of sanitation, personal hygiene or simply poor diet, but few had the skills to make the distinction, so it was easier and much safer to shun them altogether. For these there was a glimmer of hope, but they didn't know it and it would be snuffed out when close and prolonged physical contact with a genuine leper allowed the disease to transfer.

Lepers or not, these pariahs were often forced to live out their lives foraging in the wild as best they could. Only the more fortunate had loving relatives who regularly left parcels of food at prearranged spots close to the cart tracks. For the rest they lived on whatever they could catch or scratch up from the soil.

In the latter half of the ninth century a profound change took place in Alfred's kingdom. Faced with renewed Viking threats a defensive system of forts was built across the land and gradually new communities grew up in their shadows. Unable to sustain themselves and in their desire to be close to human habitation the ulcerous outcasts were drawn towards these towns and set up makeshift shelters in nearby forests to glean what crumbs they could. Those who could conceal their infirmity would mix with crowds on market days and scavenge among the stalls or beg for alms in the streets. Those who could not shunned wholesome society but were occasionally seen on the outskirts of towns dragging their wasted limbs into the seclusion of the undergrowth.

As trade expanded traffic increased. Producers, merchants and customers continually thronged the roads and more people came face to face with lepers. Descriptions of these encounters bred a new horror of the living dead. The city gates were increasingly shut against them and fear grew.

Christianity saw the disease as the punishment for sins, but ironically it was sin that began to furnish some relief, for it was the citizens of towns such as Winchester who sought to negotiate their own redemption from lives of continuous greed and debauchery by endowing the monasteries so that the servants of God might provided succour to ease the suffering of His most forsaken creatures.

Food, unfortunately, merely prolonged their agony; ointments and lotions gave only temporary relief; and, while prayers encouraged endurance and offered the prospect of peace in an after-life, many still venerated fake relics or clung to the old belief that only ancient pagan incantations offered the hope of a cure in the present.

There were small lazar colonies outside most large towns and Winchester was no exception. They were tolerated as long as the inmates remained invisible behind high wattle fences at least a mile beyond the walls and preferably separated from the wholesome population by fast-flowing rivers. Even on the narrow country cart tracks lepers were expected to shuffle into the invisibility of the undergrowth if they heard or saw other travellers approaching. Driven thus from human society they could be whipped if they used the main thoroughfares of England. Often they were stoned if they approached the city gates.

* * * * *

At first light half a dozen carts were lined up as the gate-keeper pulled the great east doors apart and seconds later the convoy trundled over St Swithun's Bridge to go their separate ways. Wulfnoth turned south on the road for Hantone and the cob immediately broke into her customary trot only to be checked and forced to walk slowly while busy merchants forged ahead in their eagerness to reach the port and take ship without delay.

When their dust cloud had disappeared Eric stuck his head out of the cart and pointed to a track that led left round the bottom of St Giles Hill and Wulfnoth turned the mare in that direction. Half an hour later they had circumnavigated the hill, emerged on the northern side and joined the Beggar's Walk leading to the dense woodland where the lepers found sanctuary.

Beggar's Walk had once been a busy road through the woodland between Eston and Winchester, but as the colony of lepers grew most travellers made a detour to avoid the slightest chance of contamination and consequently the undergrowth at both sides of the road had gradually encroached until there remained only a narrow track where in some parts people were forced to walk in single file. Driving a cart was a risky business since you could not tell where verges hid ruts or boulders.

Wulfnoth's fear that they would be overtaken gradually began to subside as they travelled further from the city. Although he knew that aiding a convicted criminal in direct opposition to the King's wishes could have dire consequences, his concern was not for himself but for his companions who could expect short shrift once Beorhtric's men had possession of Torgrim's treasure. The murder of a thegn would take some explanation, but there again he conjectured they could hardly leave him alive to testify to the extent of Torgrim's wealth. Beorhtric would be forced to hand it over to the King. Inside he knew that if the worst came to the worst he could fend for himself; his encounters with the Danes had taught him that fear evaporated when sword and axe were ploughing the land.

His reverie was interrupted when they reached an area of sparse woodland picked clean of dead and fallen branches at the far side of which stretched a wattle fence. As he checked the horse he became aware of a couple of bent figures pulling a sledge on which they had piled brushwood collected from deeper in the forest. Their progress was painfully slow and he watched as they paused and seemed to struggle for breath before taking up the ropes again to haul their precious cargo closer to the gate.

Despite himself he felt apprehensive. Of course he had occasionally glimpsed these sad creatures before but he had never come into close contact and never dreamed of entering their isolated sanctuaries. War and death he knew well, but "the great disease" as it was being called was an insidious opponent he had yet to confront.

Eric had been alerted by the change of pace and stuck his head out of the covered rear of the wagon. "Ahh, Mah Wuffnah, eher's encohuh. Hafe nah," he beamed as if delighted to have reached this godforsaken place. Then jumping down he took the horse's head and led her through the gate.

Not knowing what to expect Wulfnoth fingered his seax as he might have done when about to enter enemy territory and was relieved when no monsters appeared to challenge their arrival. In front of him were half a dozen thatched wooden constructions clustered peacefully around one larger building. It could have any one of a number of well-kept hamlets like those he and Cerdic had passed through on the road from Compton to Winchester. There, however, the comparison failed since at each of those hamlets the villagers left their houses to see who was passing through and when they realised that the strangers meant them no harm even the children would come out and greet them. Here their arrival elicited no such response: the street emptied; doors were shut: and all signs of life extinguished. Wulfnoth noticed that there was no familiar smell of wood smoke and indeed no smoke rose from any fire despite the sharp cold. He might have been forgiven for thinking the place deserted. Even the two who had been foraging for wood had miraculously disappeared.

Eric, however, seemed undaunted and led the cart up to the largest building and thumped on the door with his great fist shouting, "Magdah, Magdah."

"Magda is his sister," explained Torgrim who had silently slipped onto the seat beside Wulfnoth.

"His sister! What is she doing here?"

"It's her home."

"You mean?"

"Her husband contracted the disease, but the symptoms did not appear until after they were married. When his disfigurement became obvious he was ordered to leave the city. She refused to desert him and they came out here together.

"A courageous woman! She must have loved him."

"Indeed. She cared for him until the sickness devoured him."

"Then why does she stay?"

"At first it was to help the others. When she came they lived in hovels. She set about improving the conditions; helped them to build and organise. All this is down to her. She gave them back their dignity."

The door opened and a slight figure stepped out and greeted Eric who promptly embraced her and swung her round, but she pushed herself free and withdrew.

"Eric adores her and begged her to leave, but then the nodules developed. Unfortunately, she has a particularly virulent form of the disease. She fears for him and tries to keep him at a distance, although they say she's in remission now."

"And is she?" asked Wulfnoth.

"Hard to say," said Torgrim shaking his head. "The monks say so, but who can tell? Lesions dry up only to break out again."

When Eric returned he took them to a small empty hut where they could rest unseen and drove the cart out of sight of the gate. It was clean and they ate some of the food they had brought with them.

As soon as they had finished Magda came and sat on a large stone a few yards from the door. She was dressed in a faded reddish-brown ankle-length tunic, while over her head she wore a cowl with a cloth of the same coarse material covering her nose and mouth. Wulfnoth sat on the doorstep facing her and felt himself in the presence of a powerful spirit. Surprisingly, he realised that his apprehension had evaporated. He could hear her laboured breathing, but he was not prepared for the hoarse nasal voice that emanated from the hidden lips.

"You must forgive us for not greeting you when you arrived. We live here by simple rules. We are forbidden to share the pleasure of your company. Our breath is said to be pernicious. And our touch can bring death as surely as your sword."

He realised that she spoke in short sentences to conserve energy.

"Your brother shows no fear."

"My brother is an impetuous fool. Affection clouds his judgement. He believes himself immune."

"Did you not think so once, lady?"

"No. Never."

"You were in love."

"It's true I loved my husband, but I chose my path. I knew the risk."

"And is there no cure?"

"If you could see my face you would not ask. For some the only hope is death. Each day I pray that God will summon me."

"Forgive my stupidity, lady. I did not understand."

"There is nothing to forgive. But enough of me," she rasped. "My brother has told me of your flight and that Torgrim is in great pain from the dreadful mutilation he has suffered." She paused and he heard her desperate intake of breath. "We have a lay brother visit us each month and he leaves salves and ointments should any of our people injure themselves. He is due tomorrow. I will show Eric which to use in the meantime."

"You are most kind. We will not encroach upon your hospitality longer than necessary. We do not wish to endanger your community."

"You may stay here for two nights. By then those that pursue you will hopefully have cast their net wider. To stay any longer would be unwise. Now I am tired and must rest."

With that she struggled to her feet and allowed her brother to follow her on the understanding that he kept his distance.

Wulfnoth's natural instincts had been to press on northward without stopping to take full advantage of the head start their early departure had afforded. He knew, however, that Beorhtric's men would travel light and easily overtake a heavily laden cart pulled by an old mare. On the advice of Aelfhelm's brother, therefore, he had decided to go west and then take the Ryknield Way, the old packman route north and meet up with the northern lords at Cyningesburh where Wulfric owned an estate. It made sense to avoid the obvious route and Aelfhelm and the northern lords would not be implicated in the escape. It was a longer route than that favoured by Aelfhelm and the thegns of the Five Boroughs but, since they were not due to leave Winchester for two weeks, time was not a priority. They could afford to lie low at the leper colony. Few people would chance entering its gates and he hoped the risk would throw their pursuers off the scent.

The following day Brother Thaddeus appeared covered in bruises. He had been questioned by a troop of ruffians who had no respect for his tonsure and habit. Unable to shed light on the whereabouts of the mintmaster's cart he had been beaten unmercifully and he was very frightened. Nevertheless he dressed Torgrim's wound and spent another hour or two tending to the sores of the inhabitants before setting off nervously for the Minster.

Wulfnoth, who had never found idleness palatable, spent the day fretting. He felt that he was imprisoned in an alien world where the guards were ghostly figures whose presence was felt but not seen. No one came near their hut and only rarely did he catch a glimpse of the rust-brown garb as the other inmates shambled about to attend to the essential tasks of life. Torgrim appeared to have shrunk and was curled up against the wall twitching fitfully and only Eric seemed oblivious to care as he lay on his back slumbering like a baby.

They brought Brother Thaddeus' body back at dusk. Two lepers setting the night traps thought they had heard screams coming from Beggars' Walk and when they made their way back home they had stumbled across the corpse. Recognizing the victim they had put him on their sledge and dragged him back to the compound. Once inside they made straight for the long building where Magda and the other single women lived and banged frantically on the door.

Wulfnoth had been sitting on the large stone outside the guest hut watching the last red streaks of day disappearing above the trees to the west. After a day living among the shadows the sudden commotion immediately put him on the alert and he went over to see what had caused it. The lepers shrank back at his approach, but Magda was kneeling beside the body of the dead monk searching for any signs that could indicate the cause of the young man's demise. The gaping wound on the back of his head seemed the obvious candidate, but she was perplexed by marks on his forearms and wrists. As she examined first one then the other Wulfnoth noticed with surprise that her hands were smooth and unblemished. He joined her on the ground and a brief look at both of the dead man's limbs left him with no doubt what could have caused the abrasions.

"Ropes," he explained simply.

"So it was no accident. You mean he was tied up and then killed."

"It certainly looks like it," the thegn confirmed, but his voice sounded vague and he seemed more preoccupied with the other end of the body. He felt the material of the black habit and then smelt it, before looking closely at the feet. They were covered in blisters.

"This poor wretch has been hung up by his wrists over a fire, or else a torch has been held under the soles of his feet."

"Sweet Jesus," came the hollow rattle beneath the face cloth, "to treat a monk in that fashion is sacrilegious."

"Some men do this for pleasure."

Magda climbed to her feet. "Carry him to the deathroom," she said and without thinking placed her hand on Wulfnoth's arm and drew him to one side. "When a tortured man has told all he knows his life is not worth a crust of famine bread. If, however, he refused to talk they will have killed him for spite." For once her voice was as steady as the eyes that met his above the veil.

"I know," said Wulfnoth. "We must go at once. The net closes in."

"They will watch the gate and place men on every road. You will stand no chance."

"We must try. Eric and I will give a good account of ourselves."

"Then we must increase the odds in your favour."

Her confidence and determination impressed him.

"And how do we do that?"

"There is a small gate at the rear and there are paths known only to those who dwell here." She paused. "If you still run into trouble there is one disguise may render you invisible. Go now and hitch up your mare."

Wulfnoth took no urging to prepare for the journey and roused Eric to fetch the mare while he made sure that Torgrim was ready to travel. Minutes later he heard the familiar gravelly voice behind him.

"Blacken your hands and foreheads with charcoal. Then put these on," she said. "I will show you how to wear the face cloth," and she thrust three sets of neatly folder garments into his arms. "They are not new but they have been washed," she added and in the moonlight he felt sure there was a wicked gleam in her eyes.

"Barely shivering at the thought of wearing a dead leper's clothing, Wulfnoth thanked her and soon all three were dressed in russet and trying to get used to the facecloths which seemed to be drawn into their mouths every time they tried to speak.

"I haik her rheins," said Eric and climbed onto the seat while the thegn helped Torgrim into the back of the cart.

Magda led them to a narrow rear section of the fence, which could be loosened and turned back on itself. He heard Magda and her brother speak briefly and they were through. Looking back he realised with regret that he could no longer see her and had not thanked her for her kindness.

The Cattle Market

Cerdic left the horses with the gate-keeper and sought out the gaoler, an unpleasant fellow who, after refusing Cerdic's offer to pay for Hild's release, derived pleasure in informing him that the girl would remain in the cage until she was taken to the slave market and sold to the highest bidder.

Slavery did not always carry a stigma since no one but the king was truly free. All other men were bound in some measure to those who ranked higher in the social scale. Some, however, especially in high summer when food was scarce entered willingly into formal bondage with a local thegn to protect themselves and their families from starvation. Their lives changed very little except that they worked solely for their lord. It was a formal arrangement and many were released after one or two years of service or on the death of their lord. Others less fortunate, society's outcasts and misfits, who had no friendly lord to serve, would stand alongside the criminals and their families put up for sale in the slave market. If no one bid for them they would be snapped up cheaply by those who dealt in human flesh and shipped abroad to be sold on into lives of degradation and misery.

There was a sparse crowd already in the market-square when Cerdic arrived so he was able to make his way through and find a spot to one side where he could remain fairly inconspicuous, but had a good view of the proceedings.

After about twenty minutes the gaoler escorted a line of a dozen or so sad figures into a large animal pen and they were joined by three rather sheepish individuals from the crowd. They were a motley collection, mostly filthy and half-starved, but two stood out from the rest. One was a powerfully built man with a shock of dark hair and a truculent manner whose arms were bound behind his back; the other was a young woman with high cheekbones and dark piercing eyes that seemed to dare anyone in the crowd to hold her glance for more than a second. She also appeared to be shepherding Hild whose terrified features sought comfort in the ground beneath her feet as she pulled the long grey cloak tightly about her.

The gaoler called for each in turn to be made to stand on a raised platform where the crowd could inspect the goods on sale. He started with the least prepossessing individual, clearly exaggerating his worth only to accept a mere fraction of a silver penny for the husk of a man who might with luck last a few months digging ditches in some foreign land. In like manner he sold all but the last three of his charges at knock down prices to a shifty-looking pair of merchants one of whom quickly slipped a fetter over the wrist of each purchase, while the other tapping his whip against his thigh waited to settle the account.

"Now, Gentlemen we come to three slaves of exceptional quality who will command a high price," announced the gaoler. "The first is a male who would make a fine body servant. Or if its years of heavy work you're looking for, feel those muscles."

Someone had the temerity to do just that and the dark-haired young man swung round angrily and knocked him back into the onlookers. There was a gasp from the crowd and two of the reeve's men ran forward and beat the slave to his knees.

"Just like a young stallion. He'll need to be broken, but once trained he'll prove an outstanding investment. Now who'll bid thirty silver pennies for this fine specimen?"

Two prosperous gentlemen showed initial interest: a shrewd-looking merchant with lined face and narrowing eyes; and a shorter, pot-bellied fellow who was standing beside no other person but Beorhtric. For a moment Cerdic thought he might be recognised, but then remembered that the Mercian had only seen him once at Compton and he was hardly likely to recall a mere stable hand. Eventually the taller of the two purchased the young man for twenty-two pence.

"The next lot, Gentlemen," he heard the official shout, "is this handsome whore who was caught stealing a silver broach from a sleeping customer despite the fact that he had already paid generously for her services. This one must be worth at least twenty silver pennies. Just look at that body, Gentlemen!"

There was a murmur of approval.

"Buy this one and you get a whole lifetime of pleasure for just one down payment." Then, warming to his task, he added, "and when she no longer pleases you can rent her out to your friends."

"Can we try the goods first?" asked a brazen young man, but the woman flashed her black eyes on him and made the sign of the goat so that he shrank back into the anonymity of the laughing crowd.

"Will you start the bidding, sir?" called the gaoler to the taller man, but he shook his head and showed no interest at all. Then he looked round for another bidder, but most were intimidated by her defiant stance and the power of her eyes.

"Two silver pennies," offered the brazen young man.

"Three," a companion joined in.

"Four and we'll share her between us," proposed another.

The woman stood her ground, snarled and tossed her head in the air. The crowd could not take their eyes off her and the gaoler was at loss how to proceed. No one seemed willing to bid seriously for this wild cat.

"Thirty silver pennies," shouted the pot-bellied man and the crowd fell silent.

The woman looked up and smiled. There were no further bids and she was led away to a covered cart.

"Finally," called the gaoler, "we come to a choice young piece of flesh."

Hild was roughly pushed out of the pen and on to the platform.

"Don't damage the goods, boys," he chided winking confidentially. "This one is a virgin, fresh out of puberty."

The crowd were all attention.

"Smile, Girl," he hissed as he forced her chin up with his short staff of office. "Now who'll start the bidding for this prize piece of merchandise?"

"Twenty silver pennies," called Cerdic, but his throat was dry and appeared to be drowned out by a chorus of shouts from the crowd.

"Show us a bit more flesh."

"Lift up her tunic."

"Let's see her thighs"

"And the rest."

Obligingly, the official pulled open the cloak and lifted the front of her tunic with the tip of his staff. There was an exaggerated intake of breath from the crowd and tears streamed down Hild's face.

"Twenty silver pennies," shouted Cerdic.

All eyes turned in his direction and time seemed to be suspended for three or four seconds.

Then a firm voice from the other side called, "Twenty-two." And as he scanned the faces Cerdic could see that the fat merchant and Beorhtric were watching him.

Trying not to appear too eager Cerdic cleared his throat, paused and, looking directly at the official, bid "Twenty-three."

Out of the corner of his eye he could see Beorhtric whispering to the merchant and then turning away. For a moment he felt relieved.

"Come now," cajoled the official, fondling her right breast with his large hand "Surely you'd like to be the first to put something really stiff under her skirt and bring a smile to that face?"

"Twenty-five!" The merchant was putting on the pressure.

Again Cerdic held back a moment and then nodded at the gaoler who said, "Twenty-seven with the man in the leather tunic."

"Thirty silver pennies," responded the merchant.

"Thirty-two," called Cerdic.

"Don't push your luck, my friend," a voice hissed in his ear. "The girl's not for the likes of you."

"Thirty-four," came his opponent's bid.

Determined not to be intimidated Cerdic heard himself say "Thirty-six silver pieces" before the cudgel came down and the light went out.

* * * * *

Hild was led away to the merchant's cart and bundled quickly inside where she found herself stumbling over the outstretched legs of someone sitting at right angles to the opening. Strong hands lifted her up and instinctively she fought to get free. Then an arm was wrapped firmly round her shoulders and a voice whispered, "Shush, child, there's no use struggling against fate unless you know that you can win."

She could feel another's skin against her cheek, but a spasm of fear gripped her muscles and she no longer had the power to resist. She could smell her captor, but then she realised it was the smell of another woman and the voice began to hum gently in her ear. Relief and exhaustion suddenly seemed to join forces with the rocking movement of the cart and, before they had rumbled over St. Swithun's Bridge, Hild was fast asleep.

The Leper's Ugly Face

Eric was a native of Winchester so Wulfnoth was content to let him drive the cart through the woodland while he remained in the back with Torgrim and explained how after they were several miles north of Winchester they would head west to pick up the Ryknield Way and cross Watling Street at a spot well away from London before entering the safety of the Danelaw where they would be under the protection of Ealdorman Aelfhelm. At the same time Cerdic and Hild were to ride to Bosham and take ship for the Humber.

"It will take us deep into Mercia I'm afraid, but by steering clear of the more obvious routes we are less likely to run into trouble." He sounded considerably more confident than he felt for he did not underestimate the determination and vindictiveness of Beorhtric.

"Use whatever money you need, Lord Wulfnoth, but bring her safely back to me."

"Of course, old friend."

"Mah Herdic hood mhan! Hetsh Hild hafe an hound," cackled Eric as he climbed into the back of the wagon and took off his face cloth. "Hunnin ha Eshon hoon. Hus keeh huiweh how." And he put a blackened finger up to his lips.

"No we mustn't wake the villagers," agreed Wulfnoth and then realising that the mare had not stopped he went forward to check her.

As he stepped over the seat and pushed his head under the awning he was surprised to see another man crouching over the reins and would have struck him and sent him tumbling to the ground had he not recognised the sharp intake of breath.

There was not much room on the seat and when he took his place on it he could feel her strong thigh against his as she braced herself to alter the direction of the wagon. This woman never ceased to amaze him. Apparently she was in the latter stages of a relentless all-consuming disease and yet she could call on great mental and physical strength.

"Keep your distance from me. Breathe on the other side of the wagon," the masked voice warned him hoarsely. As he eased himself to the left, she continued, "There's an old track leads over the hills. It bypasses Easton, but Ordie will be different."

"The Benedictine monks own Ordie. We should be safe there."

"It's where we must cross the river. Unless your enemies are fools they will know that."

She was right of course. He should have thought of that himself. Beorhtric would have posted men at all the river crossings. He liked intelligence in a woman and Magda's mind was sharp as a metseax. As the moon found a patch of clear sky and they topped the rise he watched her skilfully directing the mare, which, under her light hands, seemed to take on a new lease of life once they began to drop down to the meadows. Magda was happy to let her have her head and they completed the last three hundred yards at a canter arriving at the river bank about a mile downwind of the crossing. Here apparently without exerting any pressure at all she gently brought the creature to halt before leaning back against one of the posts of the awning.

"I haven't enjoyed myself so much in years," she exclaimed. For a moment the voice was as clear as a bell. Then the effort seemed to catch up with her and she struggled to get her breath. "Now," she panted, "comes.....the tricky..... bit," and once again a roughness appeared to clothe each word as she spoke.

"Take the wagon under those trees and wait for me here," said Wulfnoth. "I will go ahead and see if the crossing is guarded."

"It is beyond the bend in the river. Take care. The path's overgrown in places, but you will see the Ordie Mill on the other bank before you reach it. And if you run into trouble remember you are a leper. The disguise has its benefits."

"I'll return as soon as I can. Eric!"

A bleary-eyed black misshapen face peered through the gap in awning.

"Eric, look after Torgrim and your sister. I won't be long."

Eric grinned, "Ha, Mah Wuffnah."

"Get going," whispered Magda. "We must reach the woods outside Miceldever before morning."

Wulfnoth nodded and left the wagon and his three fellow lepers without another word.

It didn't take him long, however, to realise that Magda had been right about the path. When the moon shone he could see the river and the path stretching ahead of him as clearly as if it were day, but the minute she slipped behind the clouds all was merged into blackness and he was stumbling about at the mercy of every bramble and briar that sought to scratch his face, claw his clothes or trip him up. His progress was erratic and he stumbled into the water on more than one occasion before he saw the walls of the mill looming above him on the far bank.

Dropping down into a ditch he covered the last hundred yards more cautiously until he reached the edge of the road. There he waited for the moon to make her disappearing act before peering over the raised bank. For a few moments he saw nothing and was beginning to assume that the crossing was unmanned, when a horseman appeared from behind the mill and called out angrily.

"Get on your feet you lazy dogs. Lord Beorhtric will have you gelded if his quarry slips past while you're asleep."

"We were only sheltering from the wind," a high-pitched voice bleated.

"Drunk on the monks' ale, no doubt,"

"They gave us some to keep out the cold." The truculent tone, suggested that the second guard was a seasoned soldier and considerably older than his companion.

"Stole some, more like when they were at compline. You'll need all your wits about you if the Thegn of Compton is with them."

"Only a fool would travel this road by night."

"He's no fool I assure you."

"How do we recognise him?" The younger voice sounded nervous.

"You can't mistake his mop of black hair even in the moon light! Strike first and ask questions afterwards."

"Are you not staying to give us support?"

"No I must report to Lord Beorhtric on the Roman Street, but I'll be back so keep awake."

The black outline of the horse and rider turned and Wulfnoth watched as he disappeared from sight.

"Good riddance," said the older man when the sound of the hooves had died away, "Stay here and keep watch. I'll go and see if I can find more ale and something to eat," and he made his way towards the buildings behind the mill.

Wulfnoth lost little time in retracing his steps along the river path and rejoining the others. He explained the situation to Magda and they agreed that their best chance was to make a bold move and bluff their way across the bridge as soon as possible. The wagon would not make the river path, but Magda was confident that she could find a way through the woods to the road.

"The trees will muffle the sound of the wheels until the last moment," she said.

"And we can use the cowls to wrap around the mare's feet when we reach the road."

"Then you had better not sit with me but travel in the back. If they know of your involvement they will recognise you immediately and be on their guard."

"Alright! Eric and I will remain hidden, but if anything goes wrong we'll be ready to surprise them."

Although the moon gave little help in the wood Magda seemed to have an uncanny sense of direction and after fifteen minutes weaving her way through the trees she stopped the wagon a few yards from the edge of the road so that Eric and Wulfnoth could tie the cowls to the mare's feet using the wininga that bound their own leggings. Once they were safely back on board Magda clicked her tongue and flicked the rein gently on the mare's back. Gradually she eased the wagon on to the road. To the occupants each creak of the wheels seemed to split the silence like a battle horn, but they prayed that the sound wouldn't travel far in the wind. Miraculously they reached the bridge without raising the alarm and began to cross.

The vibration disturbed the sleeping man on the far side and by the time they reached the middle he was on his feet shouting and waving his arms wildly.

The moon had shaken herself free of the clouds and Magda could see that he was barely more than a boy. She was tempted to whip the mare into a canter and ride him down, but she hadn't the heart and besides they had agreed to brazen it out. Slackening her pace she called out "Lepers. Unclean. We are lepers. We can only travel by night. Let us pass and no harm will come to you."

The boy seemed to hesitate and step back as if afraid, but another figure emerged from the other side and took hold of the rein.

"A party of lepers is it? A likely story! You've a fine head of hair and soft hands for a leper. Take off your mask and let's see who you really are."

"As you wish," said Magda simply and untied the string that held the cloth.

The man, who had stepped close to the wagon, opened his mouth, but had no time to cry out as Wulfnoth dispatched him with a single blow.

The boy on the other side screamed, picked up a large flat stone and flung it wildly towards the wagon. It struck Magda on the forehead knocking her back into the wagon seconds before Eric had grappled him to the ground.

Wulfnoth, having first satisfied himself that both guards were dead, checked the nearby buildings, before returning to the wagon. Seeing that Eric and Torgrim were treating Magda, he hoisted the two corpses over the tailboard and untied the cowls from the mare's feet before climbing up on the driving seat. Escape rested on removing all sign of their having crossed the river at Ordie and getting as far north as possible before morning and, since Magda had mentioned the forest outside Miceldever, Wulfnoth determined to push on and give her time to recover.

He knew the Roman Street well and needed to follow a parallel course. With the stars now visible he was able to navigate and the tracks were relatively easy to follow in the moonlight.

After about three miles he entered woodland and stopping the cart he went round to the rear. "Eric, help me find a place to hide these two where they won't be discovered for a couple of days."

But it was Torgrim who pushed the bodies over the tailboard and joined him. "Magda is unconscious," he said by way of explanation, "Eric will not let anyone touch his sister."

Using three hands they dragged the corpses into the undergrowth and as fortune would have it found a patch of boggy ground where they left them half submerged under a pile of brushwood before returning to the wagon.

With Torgrim safely back on board Wulfnoth climbed back onto the driving board and putting his head through the awning whispered, "Can I do anything, Eric?"

"Na, Mah Wuffnah. Ehric look afer her."

He had never associated Eric with tenderness, and as the wagon rejoined the track he was surprised to hear the bellowsman crooning softly to his sister as one might to a baby. Smiling to himself he urged the mare into a smart trot and headed north along the Wayfarer's Walk, which ran parallel to the Roman Street and would eventually lead to the dense woodland of Miceldever. By first light he could see the long barrow and the tumuli silhouetted against the sky to his right just as Magda had described them. Cold and suffering from cramp Wulfnoth felt a great sense of relief as seconds later they entered the shelter of the woods.

In places the trees and bushes were so overgrown that the thegn almost despaired of reaching the mounds but eventually he found himself in a small clearing beside one of them. Exhausted, he slipped to the ground unhitched the mare and tethered her to a tree.

Going back to the wagon he listened for a moment and could still hear Eric's voice, but it was quieter now like the last lingering notes of a lullaby sung by a mother to her child who has finally dropped off to sleep. Not wishing to disturb them he gathered leaves and dry grasses and lit a fire, which he fed with fallen branches. Once he was satisfied that it had taken he left the clearing in search of more wood to maintain a blaze that would keep them warm throughout the day.

When he returned Torgrim was rummaging in one of his boxes and pulled out a rich blue cloak, which he took behind the wagon and laid on the ground near the fire. Wulfnoth followed him, his arms full of timber and busied himself stacking it. Minutes later Eric appeared carrying Magda in his arms. She was no longer wearing her coarse leper's garment but a simple white tunic and

Eric placed her gently on the blue cloak, pulling the hood closely round her face.

"She's dead, Mah Wuffnah." Eric was sobbing quietly.

The thegn knelt down beside him and took one of Magda's hands in his. It was cold, but smooth and delicate with long fingers and he bent forward and touched it with his lips.

"Your sister was a remarkable woman," he said. "May I see her face?"

"She'll noh mine, now, Mah Wuffnah."

Wulfnoth carefully folded back the hood and looked at the ravaged face. The shape had retained its youthful elegance but the nasal spine had all but disappeared leaving a coppery-blue cavity and the mouth seemed strangely awry. However, it was the eyes that held his attention; they had remained open, but instead of the usual glazed expression of death they were still bright, peaceful and full of hope.

"She was beauiful, Mah Wuffnah,"

"God has called her, Eric, as she said he would. She'll be beautiful again."

"I hink so," said Eric and began to rearrange her hair.

Wulfnoth remembered another burial and wept.

Across The Wine Dark Sea

When Cerdic came to he found he had been tipped unceremoniously over the wall that surrounded the cattle-market and lay in an overgrown but dry ditch. Apart from a thick head, he appeared to have suffered no other injuries and more to the point neither his purse nor his weapons had been taken. Clearly he had not been recognised and the attack had been simply to prevent his bidding for the girl. The thought of her instantly cleared his head. He could still hear the sound of bidding and quickly pulled himself up to peer over the wall, but the auction in human flesh had been superseded by a sale of sheep. Clambering up onto the top of the wall he saw a dozen black-faced ewes being knocked down to the man who had bought the male slave, but there was no sign of the fat merchant who had been bidding for Hild. Hesitating just long enough to double check the crowd, Cerdic jumped down and made his way through the press of bodies until he reached the new owner of the ewes.

"Sir," he shouted above the noise of the auction, "can you tell me where your companion has gone?"

The man ignored him and Cerdic pulled at his tunic and repeated the question.

"Not now, friend. Can't you see I'm busy," said the man angrily, not taking his eyes off the faces of the other bidders.

He tried once more, but the man pushed him away and two of his servants stood purposefully in front of Cerdic, so that he couldn't interfere with their master while he assessed the quality of each lot, studied the interest among his competitors and gauged when to made his bid.

With no other avenue open to him, Cerdic made no further attempt to distract the sheep merchant and resigned himself to a lesson in the art of commerce and a long wait.

After what seemed another hour or more the man with the lined face and shrewd eyes had completed his purchases and nodding to his servants he turned to leave the crowd.

"May I speak with you, sir?" asked Cerdic politely.

"Ah, the young man who nearly lost me a valuable purchase!"

"My apologies for that, sir. I had not then appreciated the subtleties of an auction, but today I watched a master at work."

The eyes narrowed for a moment as they had frequently when the tall man had observed his fellow bidders, but then relaxed as if he read nothing but genuine admiration in Cerdic's face. "It is I who should apologise to you, young man, for putting business before civility. Now how can I serve you?"

"I asked of your companion, who I fear may have bought the young girl sold earlier."

"He is no companion of mine, I assure you. It was coincidence we stood together. Ah I remember now it was you who bid for the girl, but then dropped out. Did you not have enough money to save your lover from his foul clutches?"

"I could have bought her, though she is not my lover, but the daughter of an unfortunate friend, sir. However, I was struck down from behind and when I woke they had begun the sheep auction and she had gone."

"It is indeed a misfortune, sir, for she was bought by Jacob the whoremonger who comes here two or three times a year to buy women to work in his brothels or to sell on abroad at a profit to others in his trade."

Cerdic was horrified at the thought. "Where does he stay this Jacob for I must find him? I can afford to pay twice or three times what he paid for her. Where is his lodging?"

"He'll be well on his way to Hantone by now. From there he will probably take ship and sail for Rouen on the afternoon tide."

"Then I must follow him and bring her back. My master would not forgive me if I failed him. I thank you, sir, for your kindness."

"Take care, young man. Jacob is not a pleasant character. He thinks only of pleasure and money. Do not trust him to deal honestly with you."

With the warning still ringing in his ears, Cerdic left the merchant and hurried to the Westgate to retrieve the two horses from the gate-keeper and rode quickly to the Palace where he told Siferth and Ealdorman Aelfhelm what had transpired that morning and what he planned to do. They willingly took the spare horse and promised to send word to Wulfnoth. Five minutes later Cerdic had cantered across St. Swithun's Bridge and taken the road for Hantone.

When he reached the mouth of the Itchen he found that the merchant's ship had indeed caught the tide and was disappearing down the broad channel. Frustrated he made his way along the jetty where the other trading vessels were moored only to discover that none was due to sail for Rouen until the following week. In desperation he sought out the Manor of Berthun and was relieved to discover that the old thegn not only recognised him, but seemed genuinely pleased to see him.

"The man who smoked out the Danes and fought so bravely at Portchester is always welcome in my house," he began and would dearly have enjoyed an evening re-fighting the battle over a jug or two of mead, but, realising his visitor was distraught, he listen patiently as Cerdic explained his predicament carefully omitting Torgrim's occupation and the accusation made against him.

When he had finished Berthun unhesitatingly offered a solution. "Your master, Lord Wulfnoth, graciously divided the Danish warships between us and one lies in the harbour. You are welcome to use it and I'll willingly supply a crew."

Cerdic could not believe his good fortune and thanking the thegn for his offer resolved to leave at once.

"I fear, you have missed the evening tide and it will be dark within an hour," said Berthun putting his hand on the young man's shoulder. Rest here tonight and I'll give orders for the vessel to be ready to sail at high water an hour before dawn."

"But Jacob will be half way to Rouen by then."

"Your merchant may have a head start, but he will hug the shore in the dark and if the moon is hidden he will probably seek safe anchorage off the Isle of Wight before attempting to cross to Normandy. Besides, the warship is the faster craft and her captain is a brave fellow who will give you every assistance in your quest."

Cerdic had to be content and after Berthun had left to make the necessary arrangements he fell into a fitful sleep in which, despite every effort of his own crew, the merchant's ship remained tantalizingly out of reach until, in mid channel, it disappeared in a bank of fog and his own vessel began to ship water as the weather closed in. In blind panic he began to bale and finding himself inexplicably alone he was consumed with the fear that be had failed in his duty to his master and that Hild would be irrevocably lost beyond the searoads.

After the restless night in which his subconscious mind had been tormented by the spectre of failure, Cerdic seemed trapped in a state of cataleptic paralysis. Desperately he willed his extremities to function in an attempt to fling himself onto his right side, break the coma and wake up, but his body remained stubbornly rigid.

He was still calling out incoherently when Berthun shook him and broke the spell.

"Five o'clock. It'll be slack water soon."

For a moment he felt leaden, but then blessed relief when he realised that he was fully conscious and there was still a chance to rescue Hild.

"Unfortunately," continued Berthun, "it has been a clear night with a full moon and Jacob may well have crossed the channel."

"If so she will be lost, surely."

"Not necessarily. He will have to travel up the River Seine to reach Rouen.

"But he will be a day ahead of me."

"He will have to pass the port of Jumieges where the monks control the river traffic."

"How will that help?"

"It's rumoured that the monks buy slaves. Some say to free them. Others, less charitable, that if the slaves refuse to take the habit they use them to work on their vast estates. Either way they may have dealings with Jacob or know of his whereabouts."

"I hope you are right, Lord Berthun, but would they bother with a young female slave?"

"Monks are men under the habit," the thegn smiled sardonically.

Cerdic was shocked and would have questioned the older man further had they not been interrupted by the arrival of a seaman.

"You must go now," said Berthun.

"Thank you, my lord. My master shall hear of your kindness to me."

"He would do no less himself. Now get to the harbour. The warship is ready to sail."

Cerdic didn't wait for a second invitation and was soon hurrying down to the quay after the shipman.

Fifteen minutes later he was bracing himself on the aft deck of the sleek vessel under oar and running before a brisk wind as it prepared to take full advantage of the ebbing tide. It had been a bitterly cold but clear night and the empty estuary stretched out before him. Wrapping his cloak tightly over his leather tunic he peered at the horizon hoping to detect the first signs of day. With luck, he thought, they might still overhaul the merchantman in the channel, before they reached the coast of Normandy.

Few if any of the fishing community of Portchester had ventured beyond sight of land and Cerdic was no exception. The beaches of the Isle of Wight had seemed far enough for anyone in his youth, but since becoming one of the Compton household guards he had visited Winchester and had been entrusted by Wulfnoth to rescue Hild. He was determined not to fail the thegn and if it meant risking the open sea and a foreign land so be it. The idea did not daunt him and the prospect of adventure he found surprisingly inviting.

As they entered the Solent the whole body of water under the keel seemed to shake off its torpor, flex its muscles and resolve to go on the march. Placing his feet further apart to gain his sealegs, Cerdic could feel the swell taking charge of the warship and gaining strength minute by minute. The captain ordered the crew to ship oars and conserve their energy taking full advantage of the wind and tide. Soon they were sliding past the familiar landmarks of Cerdic's youth and for the first time he realised what it must have been like in the middle of a vast Viking battle fleet.

In the late morning sunlight they had swept round the point of the Island of Wight and were sailing under the red cliffs of the royal estate at Evreland, but after another half hour hugging the coast the captain set a course slightly west of south.

"Surely if we move further away from the shore we will not spot the trader," complained Cerdic.

"With last night's moon and these conditions Jacob will not linger on English soil. We are best heading straight for the coast of Normandy and with this wind in our favour we should reach the mouth of the Seine well before tomorrow night."

Cerdic had to acknowledge the sense in the argument. Despite Berthun's earlier warning, he had still harboured the hope that they would catch the merchant in English waters, but the fine weather and the miles of empty sea finally convinced him that the captain was right and he resigned himself to a long voyage across the inhospitable waves to a land he had heard of but never seen.

"Have you been there before?" he asked curious as to what lay ahead of him.

"Where?"

"To Normandy."

"Half-a-dozen times but only to the fortress of Harfleur and some of the other Norman ports."

"So you know nothing of Normandy itself?"

"No, but Lord Berthun and some of the other traders have told me much about Rouen."

"Have you never sailed up the river?"

No, but one town is much like another and a river is a river. Don't worry we'll track down your quarry."

Cerdic was comforted by the other's optimism, and determined to glean as much information as possible. "How far up the river is Rouen?

"That I'm not sure, but they say about fifty miles. Apparently the river twists and turns half a dozen times before arriving at the city."

"Then we have a chance to catch Jacob before he reaches his destination?"

"A good chance. Your merchant doesn't know that we are following him and may have goods to sell at various places on his way up river."

"Let's hope so."

"Once the crew are rested there's nothing to stop us from pressing on up stream."

Cerdic warmed to the captain who seemed as enthusiastic in the chase as himself.

That night as the ship cut smoothly through the water he curled up on the aft deck and fell fast asleep, a skill he had acquired from an early age when accompanying his father on fishing trips. When he woke the following morning the wind had freshened and the warship was ploughing the searoads with the sail straining and the mast and riglines creaking ominously.

"Are we in trouble?" he asked apprehensively.

"No trouble at all," laughed the captain. "Have you never fished in rough waters?"

"Not in weather like this. The harbour keeps us supplied when there's a winter storm."

"This is no storm, but the wind is getting stronger and it's increasingly difficult to maintain a precise course."

"Will we miss the coast of Normandy?" Cerdic was alarmed that that his mission would fail."

"Don't worry. We'll reach the coast safely, but we may have to search for the river."

Cerdic had to be content. He marvelled that many of the seamen continued sleeping, unperturbed by the strange motion of the boat and he huddled against the oarwale and gazed across the empty sea.

Several hours later he spotted a feint smudge on the horizon that he took at first to be stray cloud, but gradually as it gained in definition he realised that it was his first sight of the Norman coast. Soon on the port side he could see spectacular white cliffs standing boldly in the afternoon sunshine.

"Etretat," said the captain grinning, bringing the warship closer into the wind. We may have to row, but we'll reach Honfleur within the hour.

As the warship fought its way along the coast it had aroused the attention of watchers on the shore and word of their imminent arrival soon reached the ancient ports of Harfleur and Honfleur so that as they entered the broad funnel-shaped estuary three stout Norman ships moved to intercept.

"Reception committee," murmured the captain, "making sure that we're not hostile." and he ordered the red and white striped sail to be lowered and as the oars engaged the water he pulled on the steeroar so that it lay athwart forcing the vessel to swing to starboard. Minutes later they drew alongside the quay under the tower of Honfleur on the southern bank.

Cerdic followed the captain on shore and into the guardroom at the base of the tower where formalities in a strange language seemed to take forever. Understanding only the occasional word, Cerdic had to read what he could from the eyes and gestures of the Norman officials and hoped that the captain who had presented his own documents was faring better. Eventually there were wry smiles and they were given permission to return to their vessel and proceed.

"Well?" asked Cerdic when they were back on board. "Has the merchant Jacob arrived and if so how far ahead is he?"

"A number of trading vessels passed through much earlier today, but they couldn't say whether he was among them. Then there are three recently arrived and tied up in the harbour. Apparently they have opted to wait until tomorrow's high tide before venturing up river."

"Did he say if Jacob was among them?"

"He'd only just come on duty so he didn't know."

"Did he say anything else about them?"

"No, once they had accepted my documents they seemed more interested in warning me of the sandbars and something to do with the tide. I speak only a little of the language. They kept mentioning "Le Mascaret". Perhaps it is a place on the river. I imagine the channel there is narrow at low tide where the sandbars exposed. Once the tide has turned we shan't come to much harm if we keep our eyes open."

"As long as we waste as little time as possible after I've checked out the new arrivals."

"We'll wait for you here. The crew must take a break and eat. If you don't find him then perhaps we can take advantage of what remains of this tide and reach the next port upstream before the river is in spate."

It made sense and Cerdic felt confident that if the merchant's trader were not to be found in the harbour they had every chance of either overtake him on the river or failing that reaching Rouen before he had time to escape. After all they had Jacob bottled up; there was no way his trader could leave without passing them.

In the late afternoon sunlight he hurried past the tower and made his way down the road that led to the harbour. There he could see the dark outline of three large ships against the western sky. Each was secured to the quay by ropes and in each case the crew had unstepped the mast so that the wind wouldn't rock the vessels and disturb their sleep. When he got closer he could see bodies curled up against the thwarts, but all seemed to be bearded seamen. As he peered down into the first boat he was challenged and realised that at least one member of the crew was on watch.

For a moment he was at a loss what to say, but then took a chance and whispered, "Jacob?"

"Jacob? There's no Jacob on this ship, my friend."

Much relieved to find a fellow countryman he soon discovered that the vessel was a trader carrying English alabaster from London bound for Rouen where it would pick up a cargo of wine for the return trip. His new companion was also able to assure him that the other two vessels were Norman and had arrived from Fecamp that day and were due to return the following morning. Disappointed he returned to the ship and after a brief word with the captain they set off again to take advantage of what remained of the tide and daylight.

Neither of them had seen such a wide river before and as long as they set a prudent course midstream it seemed that little harm could come to them. Soon the towers of Harfleur and Honfleur were dropped away into the distance behind them to be swallowed up by the setting sun. At this rate thought Cerdic they would surely catch up with the merchant's vessel the following day. By dusk they had safely reached a small staging port on the second bend of the river and ran the boat up onto the beach where they could light a fire, eat and sleep for a few hours.

"If the moon is as clear as last night we can chance rowing up river against the current before sunrise and if we run aground there are enough of us to drag us off any Norman sandbank."

An hour before dawn the tide was still ebbing but strong to near gale force winds were tearing up the estuary so that it was becoming increasingly uncomfortable on the exposed beach. The crew were restless and the captain decided to risk relaunching the warship in the hope that they could reach a more sheltered haven further in land. For a few minutes they beat themselves round the arms and shoulders to improve their circulation and bring some warmth back into their stiff limbs before taking up their positions on either side of the vessel. Expertly they ran her forward peeling off in pairs to sit on the oarwale, swing their wet ankles inboard and take their places on the thwarts. Despite the unpleasant conditions it was a smooth operation and when Cerdic and the captain stepped onto the raised stern deck the boat was immediately underway.

With the reflection of the moon on the water visibility was generally good, but as a precaution a man was posted in the prow to warn of unforeseen dangers.

The strength and unpredictability of the prevailing winds precluded the use of the sail, but the high stern and the line of shields slotted into the sub frame of the oarwale not only afforded protection to the rowers, but effectively harnessed some of the power of nature.

However, it took all the concentration and strength of the Captain to read and react to the volatile squalls to ensure that the vessel maintained a fairly steady course.

Fortunately, it was still a clear night and such clouds as ventured from the sea were thin and translucent, racing like ghostly messengers of some ancient angry pagan god. In the moonlight Cerdic had the opportunity to take in their surroundings. At this point the river was still three or four times broader than the Itchen and dark banks stretched on either side. The seamen quickly settled into a rhythm and despite the ebbing tide their journey up stream seemed remarkably swift.

"We're making good progress," he shouted.

"You wait! When the tide turns we'll be flying."

"When will that be?"

"By rights in an hour or so, but it's a broad river-mouth with a great belly to empty so we shall have to wait and see."

Waiting was one thing that Cerdic found difficult and he offered to give the captain a break from steering while there was still a great reach of water around them, but the other shook his head. "You rest now and save your strength. We may need it later."

Resigned once again to inactivity, Cerdic gathered his cloak about him, sat back against the sternpost and shut his eyes. Despite his having slept earlier, the motion of the boat was enough to have him catnapping. For the best part of an hour he drifted in and out of sleep while the warship progressed steadily up river into the heart of Normandy.

Just before dawn one of the rowers caught an underwater obstruction and the shaft, wrenched out of his grasp, rose sharply, striking him viciously in the face and flinging him unceremoniously into the man behind him. In the confusion that followed the ship buried its bow deep into a half exposed island of mud. The impact threw the semiconscious Cerdic forward and his knees and head hit the deck simultaneously. By the time he was on his feet the remainder of crew had swung into action. Under the captain's instructions two men had leaped over the bow and were wallowing up to their knees in treacherous sand exerting what pressure they could while others used their oars in a desperate attempt to free the vessel before the strong winds turned her over. Instinctively Cerdic's eyes sought the weakest point and grabbing three shields threw them onto the bank. Then, heedless of his own safety, he stepped onto the top of the oarwale and jumped. The water came up to his waist, but the riverbed at that point was relatively firm and he managed to make his way forward and join the two seamen near the bow. With the shields affording them a firm foothold and Cerdic's extra strength, the sand suddenly gave a violent belch and sucked on fresh air as the warship slid back into the channel.

Back on board he was surprised to discover that the channel had narrowed ominously and that glistening banks of mud now rose on either side of the vessel. There was still a deep channel wide enough to allow their long blades to plough a furrow, but two of the crew had shipped their oars and while one acted as look out in the bow the other was helping the captain maintain a steady course in the relatively confined space.

However, as the sky gradually lightened, they were able to see that the channel ahead remained relatively wide and its marges were clearly defined by the previous year's bulrushes.

Leaving the steeroar to the seaman, the captain straightened his aching back and looked relieved. Once he had regained the use of his cramped muscles he smiled at Cerdic. "It seems the Norman was right," he acknowledged grudgingly. "This river is treacherous. We're indebted to your quick thinking back there."

"A reflex action I assure you."

"Don't underestimate yourself. Using the shields was a stroke of genius."

"I lost you three valuable shields I'm afraid."

"A small price to pay. Lord Berthun would not have been pleased if I had lost him his ship."

"I trust the river has no other surprises for us."

"I shouldn't think so if we keep our wits about us. Rivers are always deceptive: broad ones are shallow, but narrow ones are usually deep. And after all, large traders sail up to Rouen nearly every day."

"But we can't use sails in this wind?"

"Not yet. Maybe later when the visibility improves."

For the next twenty minutes or so they continued to make progress, but as the river narrowed they made less and less headway and the men at the oars were tiring fast.

First light found the warship approaching a great bend in the river and Cerdic's spirits rose in the expectation that they would soon find more sheltered water that would allow them to raise sail and give the crew a respite from their gruelling task of battling against the ever-strengthening tide.

The captain brought the vessel as close as he dared to the left bank where experience told him the water would be less resistant, but he was mindful that it would also be dangerously shallow and they could still face the risk of running aground again on the muddy deposits and finding themselves stranded. Gradually, however, they edged forward against the flow of the river.

As they entered the next reach under the lee shore the sound of the gale force winds faded away and suddenly from somewhere ahead, beyond where the river twisted back southward again, they could hear the bell of Fontenelle calling the monks to tierce, the third office of the day. To the exhausted rowers it rang like a harbinger of peace and order and at the command of the captain half the crew gratefully shipped oars and manned the halyard and sheets.

Seconds after being hauled up the tall pine mast, the square sail filled and the warship began to live again, its cool keel, oak-strength and curved prow, the ultimate tribute to generations of adze wielding craftsmen from the north. Avoiding the deep channel where the tide still ran headlong towards the sea she sliced through water that was barely ruffled by a cat's paw.

To Cerdic she seemed invincible.

Le Mascaret

It was the vernal equinox and far out west, beyond the sea roads the Atlantic scend was being drawn from the depths of the ocean by the influence of a rare and powerful alignment of the sun, earth and full moon and urged to begin again its twice-daily assault on Europe. But that morning other elemental forces were abroad riding the waves, lashing the surface of the water and driving the sea relentlessly onward. When it reached the rise of the continental shelf it was forced to slow down and the vast body of water that thronged in its wake exerted such pressure that gradually a lead wave formed and imperceptibly it grew in height.

Goaded on by freak storm force winds this tidal wave bore down on the English Channel like some giant sea-monster.

Ever seeking the least resistance it rushed headlong into the Seine sweeping all before it. Within minutes the bore had filled the wide mouth of the funnel-shaped estuary and was careering towards the shallowing narrow neck between the towers of Honfleur and Harfleur. On a normal day the spring tide would reach the foot of the Harfleur tower and as a precaution the steps up into the fortress were a good four feet in height. But this was no normal day and no normal tide. Perhaps there had been some unusual upheaval of the ocean floor; or it may simply have been a freak combination of low pressure, an abundance of fresh water brought down stream by two days of torrential rain in the Vexin and unremitting gale force winds that resulted in the surge wave being squeezed to such an extent that the water had risen three metres in a matter of seconds. The wall of water swept through the lookout's windhole on the seaward side of the tower and would have passed out through the open door carrying all before it had not the rising sea instantly encircled the tower and dramatically cut off its escape. The occupants had no other course but to flee up the interior steps and seek the safety of the uppermost chambers.

The three vessels in the harbour were torn from their moorings and one simply rolled over and sank while the others were lifted bodily onto the quay where they lay stranded like the beached sea-creatures of the sagas described by strangers invited to share the warmth of the mead-hall hearth.

Upstream worse was to happen.

* * * * *

As the Viking warship approached St. Wandrille's the river narrowed significantly and the captain leant on the steeroar and edged the vessel back towards the deeper water of the channel which hugged the inside of the bend. Again they had to fight the ebbing tide and once again he had to station a man at the prow to fend off the increasing amounts of detritus that were being swept down stream. However, with the sail full the ship gradually made headway.

"Like wading through root soup," said Cerdic. "Surely the tide must turn soon."

"You'd think so. There must have been a great storm upstream to have torn this lot loose but tidal rivers make good housewives; they always clear their banks in springtime to make way for new growth. Can't be long now though. Once the water's in our favour we'll be flying after your merchant and by nightfall......"

The Captain's sentence hung in the air cut off by a warning shout followed almost instantaneously by a sickening jolt that threw everyone on board off balance.

A half-submerged limb wrenched from one of the ancient willow trees that lined the riverbanks had been swept unnoticed into their path and, after the initial impact, had wrapped itself tenaciously round the bow dragging the warship broadside to the current.

With the sails dipping ominously close to the surface of the water the crew fought desperately to disentangle the vessel from the unwanted embrace of the tree, while Cerdic, who had been flung backwards by the collision, found himself clinging perilously to the rearing oarwale. Scrambling to regain his feet, he realised that they were being transported down stream. For a moment as the vessel glided in tune with the swell Cerdic was aware of an unnatural calm but as he watched they were swept back round the inside of the horseshoe bend dangerously close to the rocky outcrops of the bank and instinct made him scan the surface of the water for further obstacles.

At first he thought it was a trick of the light for it seemed that the river was rising before his eyes and that they were being sucked towards a great wall of water. On the right it was crashing along with a terrific head as if it would hurl itself clean out of the riverbed spewing its crystal shards over the banks. Struggling between fascination and fear, Cerdic could only stare in disbelief like some vague spectator of the apocalypse as he was hurled into oblivion.

Seconds later the warship was flung high into the air cartwheeling against the rocks so that in a matter of seconds nothing remained save a jumble of splintered timbers and broken bodies caught up in the writhing tail of Le Mascaret.

PART TWO

The Stews of Bruges

"There are very few towns in Lombardy or Frankland or Gaul in which there is not a courtesan or harlot of English stock"

St. Boniface of Crediton

En Route for Flanders

Jacob had not kept close to the shore. After a lifetime of trade he knew these waters well and taking advantage of a clear night ordered his steersman to seek the deepest part of the estuary and to hold that course. Within four hours he had not only left the Hantone channel, but had swept boldly beyond the eastern tip of the Isle of Wight. By daybreak he was negotiating the headland at Selsey and only then when the tide no longer assisted him did he seek the calmer waters of the Sussex coastline. He planned to make landfall near Dover by nightfall before venturing across the channel at its narrowest point and making his way up the coast of Flanders.

Hild was, mercifully, fast asleep on a couple of old fleeces unaware that she had been carried on board the merchant's trading vessel and was sailing inexorably towards Bruges. Beside her lay the raven-haired woman who had been sold into slavery moments before her and was drifting in and out of consciousness.

Alena had been younger than Hild when famine swept the land. It had reduced her own family from small-time weavers of cloth to such abject poverty that her father and mother had sold their home-made loom and then literally starved themselves to death in order for the children to survive, but it had been a futile gesture since her brother and younger sister had died soon after them.

Unwilling to die, she had left her village and begged for food at nearly every door in Winchester. Most had turned her away; some had enjoyed watching her fight over scraps with the mangy curs that roamed the streets; a few had given her stale black bread. Only Torgrim had brought her a bowl of hot cereal stew flavoured with meat juices from his own table. It was meal she would never forget. But pride had prevented her from calling again at the gate of the mint. By June even the rich were feeling the pinch as their grain stocks dwindled and they were reduced to eating famine bread made from broad beans ground up with the coarsest cereals usually reserved for cattle.

Unable to find honest work Alena had lived on beechnuts, roots and wild grasses for over a month before she turned to prostitution and found she had an aptitude for making men desire her and for satisfying even the most insatiable appetites. As she mastered the skills of her profession she was able to demand high fees from a richer clientele especially among the cloth-makers of Staple Street. Two years later she had finally agreed to work exclusively for Theodoric, the King's treasurer, but following a night of deliriously exhilarating sexual passion he had reneged on their agreement and refused to pay her. The silver broach was no more than her due, but he had denounced her to the King's Reeve as a petty thief. That was how she found herself her in the slave market.

Realising that Winchester was no longer safe nor profitable, a rich merchant from Flanders offered the prospect of a new life and a new chance to seek her fortune. Although she had been bought as a slave she was not prepared, however, to remain a high-class prostitute filling a whoremaster's purse. For the present she must bide her time, and when the opportunity arose use her wits to turn events to her advantage. She swore an oath that she would eventually become respectable.

In Hild she saw her innocent self. Despite his intention to sell the girl in some Eastern market, no doubt the old goat wouldn't be able to resist poking her himself and then she would face several years bearing the weight of his wealthier clients until her looks faded and she would be discarded on the streets of Bruges forced to tout for customers among the dregs of the town for a crust of famine bread. The fact that she was Torgrim's daughter made Alena even more determined. Somehow she would find a way to protect Hild from such a life.

Jacob looked down at the woman and wondered why he had spent so much money on a wild cat. She was an investment of course and if he could handle her he knew that her naked sensuality would attract the rich burghers of Bruges and reap a substantial return on his investment. But he too had been excited by her beauty and wildness and thought perhaps to tame her for his own pleasure. His pleasure such as it was! He'd been a young stallion in his youth and when his wife had been alive he had enjoyed a vigorous physical relationship with her, and yet still found time and energy for regular exercise among the young prostitutes. Strangely, however, when his wife had died he began to experience erection problems. Frequently his member had become engorged on entering a willing piece of flesh only to wilt well before either could achieve an orgasm. Gradually for fear of ridicule he withdrew from the nightly tryst. Yet this one, he thought might, conceivably, restore his lost manhood!

She read the hunger in his eyes and smiled, "My new master is pensive and perhaps a little sad to be so far from home," her tone innocently poised between concern and playfulness.

"Perhaps," he said absently and took the hand she held up to him

Shaking her loose hair in the breeze she stood beside him. The crew were eating rye bread spread with dripping and apples bought in Winchester washed down with brackish water from a barrel in the well of the vessel, but clearly he hadn't eaten so she went to fetch him some. One of the seamen felt under her tunic, but she snarled at him and raked his cheek with her long fingernails. When he cried out and clasped his bleeding face she laughed and, tossing her head contemptuously, stepped back to Jacob with the food. As she bowed in mock deference to him he marvelled at her cool self-assurance and twinkling eyes. Lest she overplay her hand she dropped to her knees and sat on her heels letting her body rest lightly against his leg as he sat eating on the oarwale.

"Mind your manners," he growled at the seaman. "This woman is my property and I'll gouge out the eyes of anyone who forgets it."

"So far so good," she thought.

After a fearful night in the Westgate cell and her humiliating exposure in the slave market Hild had slept for over twenty hours, but it had not been the refreshing balm her body craved, more the fitful, headlong flight of a terrified and feverish mind. Fleeting glimpses of

Cerdic had offered the hope of rescue only to be dashed by the triumphant features of Beorhtric and the Flemish merchant, which in turn dissolved into the leering faces of the crowd as they pressed round her to grope and strip her clothes away.

When she woke and found herself at sea in an open boat surrounded by coarse Flemish seamen the full horror of her predicament finally dawned. In desperation she took a last look at their grinning faces and grasping one of the riglines pulled herself up onto the oarwale. For a moment she swayed with the motion of the boat but, before she could throw herself on the mercy of the sea, rough hands dragged her back. Fortunately her dishevelled appearance and a sharp warning from Jacob saved her from molestation and she crawled away among bales of woollen cloth. Alena, who had watched the whole incident, was quickly at her side and cradled the sobbing child in her arms.

As the day wore on the wind dropped and the tides were no longer in their favour so the seamen had to row to maintain progress. Dusk found them well short of Dover, but they put in to a sheltered bay for the night and beached the heavy craft. As the tide was falling the boat would soon be clear of the water, and they would easily be able to relaunch it on the next high tide.

Jacob ordered two fires to be built on different sides of the boat, one for himself and one for the men. After a meal of salt fish and stale black bread washed down with copious quantities of cervoise, the five weary crew men stretched out around the smouldering embers of the their fire and one by one fell asleep.

It was a clear night and Jacob watched the lanterns of ten thousand stars light the passage of the naked moon as she threaded her way through a few thin clouds, like some eastern princess swirling and twisting her lithe nubile body among the transparent veils of her dancing slave girls. He hadn't witnessed such erotic entertainments himself of course, but they had been described to him in vivid detail by the merchants from Baghdad whom he had met in the great market of Pavia. That's where he would sell Hild if she indeed proved to be a virgin. In the East they paid good money for quality merchandise and a flaxen-haired beauty from the far side of the world always commanded a high price. She was already curled up asleep beside Alena so he went to check on the seamen before collecting the sheep fleeces to make his own bed.

When he had gone Alena slipped off her tunic and made her way down to the edge of the sea where she waded into the icy water before bobbing down and washing a month's accumulation of dirt and sweat from her skin. Despite the cold she felt delightfully clean although she knew the sensation would last only briefly since the next hour would demand all her energy and skill to establish her indispensability to her repulsive new master.

Returning to the fire Jacob discovered her discarded tunic and experienced a moment's panic when he realised that she was missing. Looking round, however, he immediately spotted her silhouetted against the moonlit sea. Relief turned to anger and he thought to drag her back to the fire and punish her, but as he strode down towards the water, she half turned and he became aware of her firm breasts and retrousse nipples glistening in the moonlight. Desire banished all other emotions. He would take her there and then on

124

the sand and would have done so had Alena not turned to face him and walking backwards into the water beckoned him to join her. Unable to see her face he found himself at a disadvantage. Nevertheless pulling off his tunic he followed her. As he waded deeper she allowed him to catch up with her, yet she still remained tantalizingly out of reach. Her breasts seemed to float on the water in front of him and he lunged forward towards them. At that point the beach shelved sharply and as he stumbled and fell the cold water took his breath away. When he surfaced Alena was behind him pulling him back towards the shore, where he dissolved into a fit of coughing. Seconds later as he lay in the shallow water trying to regain his breath he was aware that she was washing him and her strong hands were everywhere.

"Come," she said and led him up past the dying embers to the stretch of hard sand where he had thrown the fleeces. Despite his excitement he was still shivering and as he lay on the fleece she gently massaged life into his limbs and then into his member with a mixture of fondling and provocative kisses. When he was sufficiently firm she rolled over onto her back and pulled him on top of her guiding him deep into the warmth of her body. Then pretending to bite him on the neck and shoulder she began moving her thighs rhythmically one after the other until she drew him inexorably towards an orgasm the like of which he had never previously experienced.

Overwhelmed by the way she had restored his virility he panted his gratitude and promised that she would never have to work again. She would be his and want for nothing. In a matter of minutes she had become mistress and he was reduced to the role of thrall. However, it wasn't long before he fell on his back and began to snore loudly.

Free at last from the weight of his grunting body Alena rolled over and crawled away to vomit in the sand. Then she returned to the sea and spent an hour trying to cleanse herself and to wash away the sweat, smell and memory of her obese lover. Only then could she lie down beside Hild and seek the sanctuary of sleep.

The following morning when they had all but lost sight of land Alena still struggled with the urge to shudder every time he touched her. Not that he attempted to fondle her, but he took every opportunity of maintaining physical contact in the confined space of the raised aft deck. He had solicitously helped her into the boat, repeatedly put his hand round her shoulders as he explained their course and deliberately leant across her whenever he had to adjust the sheets. Then he sent the steersman forward and took control of the steeroar himself suggesting that she come and help him. She could hardly complain of his familiarity since she had deliberately embarked on a course to seduce him and flashing her eyes knowingly she slipped between his arms, leant back against his chest and put her hands bravely on the great spar. Fortunately, she did not have to put up with this close proximity for long, since Jacob soon found the task of maintaining a straight course beyond both his skill and his strength and summoned his steersman to resume his duties.

"I must keep an eye on your precious cargo," confided Alena disguising her relief.

"A taste of the whip will wipe that sullen look off her face when we reach Bruges."

"There'll be no need for that," said Alena quickly. "Unsightly marks may reduce her value. Leave her to me. I'll talk some sense into her."

"It seems my thirty silver pennies were well spent," laughed Jacob and, leaving the two women huddled together in the well of the boat, he made his way forward and stood in the bow with the wind sweeping over his bald head as he stared out across the sea to catch the first sight of the flat coast of Flanders in the euphoria of his rediscovered virility.

Behind the Bleak Facade

Since the sail partially obscured the steersman's vision and the other seamen were bent over their oars it was Jacob who first spotted the towers of the collegiate church of St. Donatian that along with the fortress of Count Baldwin dominated the small town of Bruges which had evolved some centuries earlier out of the wetlands of the coastal plain.

Although some six miles inland it was to all intents and purposes an island since it was surrounded on all sides by deep moats controlled by sluices that maintained the water at sufficient depth to offer safe mooring to all manner of vessels. However, landfall at Bruges meant negotiating the salt marshes that lay between the sea and the town. This was a vast area of shallow lagoons created by the gentle influx of the sea and broken only by sand bars where time had allowed vegetation to gain sufficient a foothold. The navigable channels were known only to the local seamen who relied on a combination of instinct and their position in relation to the churches and the Burg. The pot-bellied merchant always felt impatient at this stage in the voyage and while the crew coaxed the ship skilfully through the intricate waterways he thought of the prospect of a rich meat stew washed down with copious pitchers of Rhenish wine. Then he would take Alena to his bed and feel young again in her erotic embrace. As he looked at her strong sensuous sleeping body under her simple tunic and he felt himself respond in anticipation.

Bruges stood on the east bank the River Rei and when Count Arnulf enlarged the fortress he built a stone retaining wall around it and the adjacent polders. By altering and deepening the ancient water channels he transformed a carucate of low-lying land into a habitable island, dominated by the Burg and providing a suitable site for his new foundation - the Chapter and Collegiate Church of St. Donatian.

Although the dwellings of the other prosperous merchants were huddled beneath the count's castle walls, Jacob, because of the peculiar nature of his activities, did not live in the main settlement but on the opposite bank of the river. There behind a forbidding façade overlooking the water he owned a large sprawling building that served both as his home and the centre of his business. On the ground floor was a large hall where he stored and sold his merchandise and behind that were a number of small rooms for the entertainment of his less salubrious clients. Above were his own rooms. In one he ate and planned his various enterprises, while leading off on either side were two bedrooms: the larger of which boasted a huge bed that would not have been out of place in an Eastern palace; the other was simply furnished with a sack mattress stuffed with wool and a pile of fleeces.

He traded in all manner of goods depending on the economic climate and imported English cloth, furs, weapons, ornaments and even hunting dogs for the rich burghers, but his most lucrative commodity was invariably human flesh: eunuchs, slaves, young boys, virgins, whores, whatever his customers demanded, or he could sell on in the markets of the continent. His clients, not wishing to be observed indulging in their favourite pastimes, were more than happy to sneak across the water after dark or to walk briskly over the Breidelstraat Bridge to the market and then slip unseen into the anonymity of the back street that led down to his brothel.

It was early evening before the ship was finally tied up against the jetty of the Steegherei and, while the crew set about landing her cargo, Alena had time to warn Hild to say nothing, but to leave her to try to turn the situation to their advantage. Having satisfied himself that his goods were being unloaded and stored safely Jacob hurried Hild and Alena inside and sent word for his steward.

Before the man arrived, however, Alena seized her chance and drew the merchant to one side. "The girl is calmer now," she said, "but needs to be treated with care."

"A few days starving in a damp cellar will bring her to her senses. Most of my whores have learnt quickly that way.

"But this one is special and cost you a high price."

"That fool, Beorhtric, bore half the cost," boasted Jacob. "He was so concerned that she disappeared without trace."

"Then perhaps she is no ordinary cottar's child," suggested Alena.

"But Beorhtric said she was a nobody."

"Why then was he so eager to pack her off across the sea?"

The question hadn't crossed Jacob's mind. He had never been one for lateral thinking. To him turning a simple profit was all that mattered.

"Perhaps," suggested Alena, "she comes from a wealthy family who may pay handsomely for her safe return.

Presented with the possibility of increasing his profit, his eyes narrowed and she had his full attention.

"If you treat her badly and her father turns out to be someone rich and powerful he may seek revenge," warned Alena. "Powerful men make dangerous enemies."

"True," he acknowledged cautiously. He could not fault the logic of her argument.

"And if for some reason he will not ransom her, we can still groom her to please some rich lord from the East, who will pay even more for a woman of quality. Either way she is a rich silver mine if we handle her properly.

"But she must be taught to do as she's told."

"Of course, but we must not break her spirit. Remember no one can be completely satisfied by a dull woman," she said innocently.

Jacob knew that of course. One night on an English beach with this woman had convinced him that his sexual problems must have been the fault of a string of uninspiring partners since his wife had died.

"And no one will pay as much for damaged goods," she went on.

"No. No. I see that."

"Leave her to me and I guarantee you'll make ten times more than you expected on your investment."

Jacob felt almost in awe of this woman whose body had rejuvenated him and who seemed to have such a shrewd head in matters of business.

"Let her share a room with me where I can discover her real identity and convince her that her future lies in your hands. If her father is not wealthy enough, then I will train her in the ways to please a husband and you will sell her for a fortune in the market at Pavia."

"You must make sure she is a virgin. The price depends on it!"

"Of course! Of course! But you must give me a key so that I can lock her in when you want me to come to your bed. I cannot be responsible for her welfare otherwise."

He marvelled at how she seemed to think of everything and he willing agreed to the arrangement. "You had better use my wife's old room. It's convenient and well away from the servants and the clients."

Her gamble had paid off.

Starvation and bitter experience had taught her that most men were motivated by a desire to accumulate wealth or an appetite for erotic pleasure. Jacob was driven by both in equal measure and any enterprise that promised financial reward invariably heightened his sense of arousal. His eyes bulged, his breathing became shallower and his voice thickened. Wrapping his bear-like arms around her he lifted her off the floor and swung her round in his excitement and would probably have taken her there and then on the floor had it not been for the entrance of the steward who lurched unsteadily as he entered the room carrying a pitcher of wine.

You've taken your time, snapped Jacob, furious at the interruption. "Where have you been?"

"I was in the cellars," began the man trying to hide the pitcher behind his back.

"Stealing my wine," snarled Jacob striking him viciously in the face with a clenched fist.

132

The pitcher flew out of his hands and shattered on impact with the floor spilling wine in all directions while the man staggered and fell to his knees blood welling through his fingers as he clutched at his face.

"Well?" demanded the merchant with undisguised menace.

"I was looking for an empty room to lock the new whores in," the steward gasped searching desperately to excuse himself. Instead he received a brutal but surprisingly well-aimed kick to his lowered head that sent him crashing against the wall.

"Fool, these are not common harlots. They are to be treated with respect. They are under my protection. Princes from the East would pay a fortune to have them dance before their guests."

There is nothing like fear and pain to sober a drunken servant and the steward stopped trying to justify himself and cringed hoping to ward off further blows with his arms, but to no avail since Jacob still had the stamina to drag his victim across the floor by his hair and to stamp repeatedly on his face until he stopped screaming.

Alena had frozen the moment Jacob had begun his frenzied attack. Despite his size his instant aggression was chillingly awesome when he lost his temper. Suddenly the realisation that he could snap her neck with one hand made the future seem far less secure.

"Now get up and bring us some supper," Jacob shouted at the prostrate figure, but the man didn't move, so he rolled the lifeless body over with his foot and the steward's head lolled back awkwardly, his eyes staring emptily out of the bloody face.

Getting no response, the merchant collapsed into a chair, his violent energy spent as quickly as it had been summoned. With the immediate danger averted Alena's instinct for self-preservation took over and she forced herself to go to him and began to massage his heaving shoulders.

"You've killed him," she whispered softly.

"Serves the old fool right. Pity though; he was a passably good cook, the best I've had since my wife died and I haven't eaten properly for two days.

"I can cook," said Alena without thinking.

"You can?" said Jacob and he closed his eyes as her warm hands and gentle fingers induced a feeling of well-being and a desire to sleep.

Once his breathing had become deep and regular she left him and kneeling beside the body of the steward she untied the bunch of keys that hung from his belt and stole from the room. Her first thought was to find Hild who had fled as soon as the brutal attack began, but she was nowhere to be seen. When she reached the lower floor she eventually found her hiding in a great tub among sacks of grain stored under the ladder that led down from the living area. Placing a finger over her lips she beckoned to the girl who crept out and joined her. On the boat she had only had opportunity to comfort her and win her trust and even now there was hardly time to explain their plight and how she had hoped to turn the situation to their advantage. Trying each door in turn they discovered two food stores and a large room with a hearth where meals could be prepared.

"Can you cook?" asked Alena hopefully.

"Of course," her young companion replied. "I have had to prepare food for my father for the past seven years since my mother died."

"Thank goodness for that! My cooking is limited," admitted Alena, but we must cook Jacob a meal that will put him in a good mood."

At the mention of his name Hild began to tremble.

"Don't worry. You don't have to see him."

"Can't we just run away?"

"If only we could, but where would we go? He is a powerful man and this is his country. Trust me. We must humour him until we can plan our escape properly. Tonight, however," she said rattling the bunch of keys, "we shall sleep safely behind a locked door."

Leaving Hild to sort out the food Alena lit a torch from the fire and climbed down another ladder where she found a semi subterranean world of corridors and cellars. Unlike the rest of the house the walls here were made of roughly dressed stone, built to withstand the river, but damp and unwholesome to the touch. The second door she tried was locked but yielded to one of the keys. Inside she discovered a number of sealed jars of various sizes. Trying each lid in turn she found two where the seals had been broken. The larger one contained a thin lymphatic wine, but the smaller gave off a heady smell so she filled a pitcher and was about to make her way back to the kitchen when she heard muffled noises from further down the passage.

Putting the pitcher down beside the ladder she crept cautiously down to the far end of the corridor where she found a metal grill behind which were three young woman were sprawled on straw-filled sacks snoring loudly. Beside them lay a small boy of eight or nine. Seeing her fellow human beings incarcerated to serve men's pleasure enraged Alena, but she knew that any attempt to release these unfortunate creatures would destroy her chances of escape. For the present they must remain caged and continue to be abused by Jacob and his customers. She crept back along the passage.

Meanwhile Hild had uncovered a bowl of fresh mutton that she had cut into cubes and was busy sealing the meat in the pot suspended over the fire. As Alena entered she removed the sizzling pieces and added half a dozen chopped onions to the spitting fat. Leeks, carrots and turnips followed. When they had absorbed most of the fat she threw in two handfuls of barley grains and, much to Alena's surprise, added half a pitcher of wine before returning the meat to the pot.

"That was the best wine," said Alena.

"So much the better. You said it must be a meal to remember," replied Hild as she ground up black pepper corns and rubbed various herbs from bunches that hung from the beams between her hands. Once these were duly added she said simply, "Now we wait."

Jacob had slept for an hour before Alena brought him the refilled pitcher of wine. He watched her as she poured some into a gilt drinking-cup. Then without taking his eyes off her he emptied the vessel, smacked his lips and put it back on the table to be replenished.

"Better help me get rid of this carrion," he said nodding towards the steward.

Alena had no wish to touch the corpse, but swallowed hard and did as she was bid. Jacob took the legs under his left arm leaving her to get her arms under his shoulders and carry most of the weight. Then between them they carried the body over to the windhole. While the whoremaster released the shutter with his free hand and was busy looking to see that no one was watching,

Alena felt the ribcage move and realised that the steward was still breathing. As she began to open her mouth Jacob shouted, "Now!" and when she did not respond he shifted his grip, took the man in his bear-like arms and tipped him over the sill. The splash helped to focus her mind and she bit her lip hard to prevent herself from betraying her shock.

"The river will dispose of the body downstream. No one will think he died here," Jacob said callously.

"No I suppose not," she agreed slowly struggling with the realisation that she had just helped to send an injured man to certain death.

"Now you said you could cook," she heard him say, oblivious of her distress.

"Your meal is sizzling in the pot.

"Good." Then for a moment he looked suspicious. "Where is the girl?"

"She's been helping me, but she is safe now, locked away in the closet." Alena dropped to her knees beside the chair and put her hands on his forearm, her dark eyes wide and conspiratorial. "Don't worry. Leave her to me. She thinks I am her friend. Trust me and I will discover all we need to know about her. Then I can begin to prepare her to make your fortune.

Getting up she handed him the drinking cup. "Now, my lord, your supper is ready. Finish your wine and I'll bring it to you directly."

Back in the kitchen she found Hild had transferred the meat and vegetables into three wooden bowls and was busy mixing flour into the remaining liquid to thicken. Gradually it took on a rich brown quality and the girl smiled as she poured some of the sauce over the largest of the three bowls.

Even by Jacob's standards he had consumed a mountain of food and emptied his third pitcher of wine. He had not dined like that for years and he felt replete. Pushing back the chair he staggered over to the windhole, took off his breeches and pissed into the river. Then discarding his tunic he made his way unsteadily towards the vast bed that took up half of the room and was large enough for three people to sleep in without touching. He would rest for a few minutes. As he lay back he belched with satisfaction and felt like one of the Eastern rulers the merchants at Pavia had described so vividly. He imagined himself being ritually washed by dark-eyed girls in great tubs of water – he'd bought one of those back, but had never got round to using it -- and having his skin oiled before being dressed for a great banquet. Of course he could never bring himself to swallow the eyes of a sheep. Revolting practice! And he was sure their stringy meat would not have tasted as rich as his had been. What a find Alena had turned out to be. She could satisfy the Emperor himself.

He wondered whether she could dance like the girls of Baghdad. Perhaps she would later. He would drink some more wine and then she would weave her way round the room wrapped in thin silks until he was ready to take her in his arms. He closed his eyes for a moment and imagined the pleasure of pumping his seed into his Eastern princess.

Hild and Alena had enjoyed their first real meal for three days, but neither drank any wine. Then they both crept upstairs to explore the closet previously occupied by the former wife of the whoremonger. It was quite a reasonably sized room and there were two cupboards full of clothes. Clearly Jacob did not expect his wife to disgrace him when he rubbed shoulders with the rich burgher class of Bruges. The clothes spoke of a life that was completely foreign to Hild whose father had never sought to parade his wealth, but it reminded Alena of the house on St George's Street where the King's Treasurer had promised her the world and then cast her aside.

Tired as she was she knew there was still much to be done before she could turn the key in that lock and seek the relief of sleep. First she had to put Hild clearly in the picture and make her aware that their apparent new-found privacy was not guaranteed to last. Sitting beside her on the bed she began by describing her earlier conversation with Jacob. She tried to sound confident, but having witnessed the sadistic treatment of the steward she had to admit that her hold over the merchant was precarious.

"A few days earlier and my father would have been rich enough to ransom me many times over," said Hild ruefully, "but now he is either dead or destitute."

"I fear you may be right. Your father was one of the few men who shared his food with the starving masses during the famine. I will always remember his kindness, but no one will lift a finger to help him if he has fallen foul of the men at court. When Jacob discovers the truth we must be ready to convince our fat friend that you are resigned to the idea of marriage and will learn how to be a good wife."

"Is there no other hope?"

"There is always hope. We must continue to buy ourselves time and use it to devise a means of escape. But now, I'm afraid, I must go and pleasure our master."

Hild was horrified at the thought, "But how can you bear to sleep with him?"

"Because if I don't, we'll both be locked in a damp cellar and starved until we agree to open our legs to two or three of his customers every night," said Alena simply. Suddenly the perilous nature of their situation became brutally clear to Hild and she put her arms round her companion's neck and wept. Tears brought some relief and when Alena left the room Hild was determined to sit up and wait for her return.

Jacob still had a hard on when Alena's voice called him back to semi consciousness from the lurid erotic dream he had been enjoying, but since she had figured prominently in his fantasy her naked appearance only heightened his desire to have her again. Despite the amount of alcohol he had consumed, he mounted her successfully and, farting like a stallion, came thrusting rapidly to a climax.

"That was good," she murmured humouring him. "You certainly know how to satisfy a woman." However, her feigned appreciation was wasted on her delighted lover who was already fast asleep smiling at the roof beams. Leaving the fetid atmosphere of the room, she made her way down to the river to flush herself clean, but she still felt soiled when she reached the closet and climbed into the bed. Hild, who was still anxiously waiting for her return, took one look at her face and rocked her gently into oblivion.

Jumieges

Founded by Phibert in 654 the Abbey of Jumieges was situated in a jug-shaped tract of land defined by a succession of graceful curves in the River Seine a few miles west of Rouen. The once vast royal estate had been in the gift of Bathilde the former slave girl who, having caught the eye of King Clovis II, became his queen. Not forgetting her origins she charged the monks to use the wealth generated by the estate to purchase slaves and bring them back to a life of freedom and dignity at Jumieges.

The Abbey was to enjoy a long but turbulent history. Sacked and torched by Ragnar Shaggy Breeches and successive Viking raiders in the ninth century, it began to prosper briefly under Guillaume Longue Epee who had the monk's chapel of St Pierre moved some distance from the unpredictable river and rebuilt on higher ground. After his assassination in 942 the vestiges of the ancient cruciform church of Notra Dame were pulled down and the reclaimed stone dispersed to other sites more favoured by King Louis IV of France. Only St. Pierre and the stout towers situated at each end of the great nave of Notra Dame remained. Nevertheless in the second half of the tenth century Jumieges' fortunes began to revive and by the end of the millennium it had regained some of its former wealth and prestige.

Forestry, commerce, the illumination of manuscripts and above all control over the traffic and fishing rights of the Lower Seine enabled the Abbey to begin the process of reconstruction. To those travelling upstream at the end of the century the white stones of the chapel, the ancient towers and an assortment of monastic outbuildings still gave a sense of order and tranquillity amid the trees.

At each new and full moon spring tides swept up the river bringing with them the abundant riches of the sea and the monks, evoking the exploits of Peter and his brother fishermen on the sea of Galilee, reserved the right to first pick of God's bounty. Shad, pike, carp, salmon and all manner of small fish had the mesh of the nets glistening and bulging with life as they hauled them aboard the Abbey's fleet of fishing vessels. Frequently sturgeon would appear on the refectory table. Occasionally cetaceans and other sea creatures were harpooned and their flesh kept the larder well stocked with meat while their fat ensured a plentiful supply of oil for the lamps that would lift the monastic spirits during the long night office in the iron depths of winter.

It was the monks of Jumieges who were the first to launch their boats after the disastrous visitation of Le Mascaret in 998.

Most of its fury had been spent on the settlements of Villequier and Caudebec where it had breached the banks and flooded the land, but the bore had retained sufficient strength to career majestically past the Abbey dragging in its wake a train of debris that would travel towards Rouen for a further three hours.

Those who had witnessed its devastating power in the Lower Seine believed that it was just one more portent of the millennium and the end of the world. The arrival of the hairy comet, the destruction of Rome, an outbreak of heresy in Sardinia, the conflagration that had gutted the church of Mont-St-Michel and now, nearer home, the invasion of Normandy by the sea convinced a sinful world that the Day of Judgement was indeed at hand.

The monks, who were not above using such events to encourage repentance in others, were themselves more phlegmatic. Having chosen the Rule of St Benedict, they saw no reason to change the pattern of their lives and once the danger had passed their vessels took to the water, but this time they were indeed fishers of men. Scanning the water and scouring the banks they soon came upon the battered remains of the victims of Le Mascaret and brought them back to the Abbey for Christian burial. Among the corpses was the body of Cerdic, who, weighed down by his axe and sword, had clung desperately for some time to a piece of driftwood only to become hopelessly entangled in the branches of a fallen tree uprooted by the excessive water.

In the open space beneath the former church towers the monks of Jumieges laid out the bodies of the dead. On the left they placed those they recognised; on the right strangers. If the latter were not claimed they would be interred in the Abbey grounds. Cerdic might well have been buried with the rest of the crew of the Viking ship had not the manhandling of his dislocated shoulder brought a faint grunt of pain from his lips as he was being wrapped in a makeshift shroud.

Minutes later he found himself lying on a hard stone bench.

"Restez."

The voice came from a tall elderly figure who carried barely enough flesh to keep body and soul together. Confronted by the protruding cheekbones, sunken eye-sockets and sallow skin Cerdic might have been forgiven for imagining that he had passed beyond life and lay in some transitional place waiting for this cadaverous creature to decide his eternal fate.

"Soyez tranquille!"

Cerdic looked blank and then tried to prop himself up, but fell back and grimaced with pain, "My God, that hurt!" he admitted when the pain had subsided.

The old monk smiled, "Ah! You are from England. Now lie still while I look at this arm of yours."

Although grateful to hear his native tongue, Cerdic was sweating and he felt apprehensive. Nevertheless he lay back and let himself be examined.

"You are lucky to be alive, my friend. Many were not so fortunate and lie waiting for burial. You would have been among them, but for this injury."

"Surely some other members of the crew survived!" cried Cerdic turning quickly and wincing with pain again."

"If you don't lie still you may do further damage to that shoulder. So far you are the only stranger we have found alive. We have spent much of the day pulling bodies from the river and I'm afraid by their clothes a number appear to be foreign seamen."

Cerdic lay back again and shut his eyes in despair. Once again he had failed in his quest to save Hild, but not only that; his quest had cost the lives of Berthun's men and the loss of a valuable ship. By comparison his own injury seemed a just punishment for his incompetence. He could feel the old man carefully exploring his elbow and forearm, then each of his fingers; the large rough hands had a sure and gentle touch and Cerdic felt reassured and safe in them. Suddenly they closed round his wrist in a vice-like grip and he felt the sole of a foot pressed hard into his armpit. The pain and the crack were almost simultaneous and he screamed in panic and leapt to his feet.

The monk stood back and smiled. "Well?" he asked.

Cerdic was nonplussed. His head throbbed but he realised that he could feel no pain when he move his arm. The shoulder joint was back in place. He lifted it gingerly at first and then flexing his fingers a number of times he rotated his shoulder backwards and forwards and then grinned, rubbing his shoulder, "You have an unusual healing touch for a thegn of God."

The old man chuckled, "I have learned some useful skills in ministering to the sick. We are not spared the sufferings and injuries of life because we have withdrawn from the world. Farming the land and building fine churches can be dangerous work. Now tell me your name, stranger from across the seas."

"I am Cerdic. I serve Wulfnoth of Compton."

"Well Cerdic of Compton, I am Father Martin, until recently cellarer of the Abbey of Jumieges, now just a simple monk. Do you feel up to examining the bodies outside? If you can identify any of them we shall be able to give them a proper Christian burial."

Cerdic felt unsteady on his feet but followed the old man out to where the shrouded figures lay with their meagre belongings piled neatly at their feet. One by one the faces were uncovered and despite their disfigurements he managed to recognise several of the crew of the Viking ship. The last body was that of the captain whose skill and friendship he had come to value in their brief acquaintance.

Father Martin wrote down each name that Cerdic could recall and simply put "English Seaman" down when a face was recognised but the name unknown. After the grim task had been completed and the flies had gathered once again on the white shrouds Cerdic was violently sick and they returned in silence to the infirmary.

To allow the young man time to recover Father Martin simply said, "Tonight they will be in paradise, my son," and busied himself rearranging the jars of ointment and bunches of herbs on the infirmary shelves. After a while, anxious to dispel his young visitor's gloom, he sought to turn the conversation to the subject of the living, "But what of you, my friend? You are a long way from home. What brings you to Normandy?

"I am seeking a merchant, Jacob of Bruges. Do you know if he has passed the Abbey on his way to Rouen?

Before the monk replied Cerdic felt suddenly flushed and desperately in need of fresh air, but his legs refused to function and he had to sit back on the stone bench.

"Take your time, my son. It is probably a reaction to what you have been through."

"I'll be alright in a minute," panted Cerdic as he felt the spasm subside.

"So you are a friend of Jacob of Bruges are you?" asked the old man, slowly.

"No, but I wish to buy a girl that he has on his boat."

Father Martin's face had hardened, "I think I should take you to Father Abbot. He will wish to question you further. You had better come with me."

With that the old man took him firmly by the arm, hustled him out of the infirmary and led him in silence towards the monastic chapel.

It seemed pitch black inside after the bright sunshine, but as he peered in through the doorway his eyes could make out a number of figures kneeling before a carved wooden crucifix.

"Wait here," whispered the monk, who took a couple of steps forward and coughed gently to announce his presence.

The figure at the prie-dieu did not move for a few minutes but then turned slightly and inclined his head.

Father Martin went forward knelt beside him and spoke in hushed tones that did not carry.

Cerdic waited. Despite the fresh air he still felt uncomfortably hot and momentarily rested his forehead against the cool masonry of the great arch of the entrance. Eventually the kneeling figures rose and walked towards the door.

The two monks could not have seemed different. While Father Martin was tall, spare and slightly stooped his companion appeared shorter, stockier and scarcely more than thirty, powerfully built with a firm set jaw, sparkling grey eyes and a ready smile.

"So you are the young man we nearly buried alive. It seems, young Lazarus, God is not ready for you just yet."

"Mercifully, it would appear so, Father."

"I am sorry that so far not one of your friends has been found alive. But be comforted; we shall give them the last rites of the Church and their remains will find peace on this island where we will pray regularly for their souls."

"Thank you."

"Will you take charge of their possessions and see they are returned to their families?"

"I will, Father, when I return, but once they are buried I must continue my quest."

"Ah yes, Father Martin mentioned something of that. It seems you are acquainted with Jacob of Bruges and seek to do business with him."

"Hardly acquainted, Father. I have never spoken with the gentleman, but it's true I wish to purchase a young girl he bought in the market at Winchester."

"We do not countenance the sale of human flesh." A sudden edge crept into the Abbot's voice. "If that's your trade, you are not welcome here."

"You misunderstand me, Father. I do not seek a slave. The girl in question is the daughter of my master's friend and I seek to buy her so that I may restore her to her family."

The Abbot's face relaxed. "You must forgive us, Cerdic. For centuries we have opposed that dreadful trade of trafficking in human flesh. When Father Martin was cellarer here we used to buy back slaves from men like Jacob, but then he realised he could save himself time and trouble and make even more money simply by increasing his stock of slaves and selling them all to us. It soon became clear that he was merely using us and attempting to turn us into trading partners. The law used to protect him, but since Richard succeeded to the dukedom we have had the right to stamp out the trade on the river and Jacob dare not pass our ports for fear we confiscate his ships."

"Then I have been misinformed and I have not only lost a good ship and its crew but I have failed my master and his friend. By now the fat merchant has escaped and could be anywhere."

"I think it likely he will have made straight for Bruges. With the Seine closed to him and much of Northern France in turmoil he is unlikely to risk a cargo overland."

"Then she is surely lost for there is no way that I can travel through a foreign country and find my way to Bruges. I shall have to return to England and admit my failure."

"Not necessarily, my son. Father Martin is retired now and wishes to end his days in the Abbey of Haspres. I cannot spare another monk to go with him until next year. However, if you are prepared to accompany him, then he could be your guide.

"Thank you, Father, but he is old and I fear our journey will be too slow to save the girl."

"Do not despair, my son and don't be misled by appearances. Father Martin's sparse figure is made of iron. He can walk upwards of twenty miles a day, but we have horses and our former cellarer will ride home in style for he carries treasures for our brothers in Cambrai, precious manuscripts, composed or copied and illuminated in our scriptorum. You will protect him on the road and he will show you the most direct route. If you set out at first light you will be in Bruges in little more than a week."

Exhausted though he was, a feint flicker of hope lifted Cerdic's spirits, yet he hardly dare entertain it lest it prove illusory.

"Then, Father Abbot, if there is still a chance of rescuing her, I must take it. My master would expect no less. However, before we go I must send word to him.

Unfortunately, I have no skill in letters and need someone to write for me."

"Of course, my son. Father Martin, take our young friend to the scriptorum and see that one of the monks writes to his dictation. But where should we send this letter?"

Cerdic explained the circumstances of Wulfnoth's quarrel with the king and how he had set off for the Danelaw to find sanctuary for the injured Torgrim, so it was decided to send the letter via Siferth at the Nunnaminster in the hope that it would eventually reach the thegn.

That evening after the captain and crew of the Viking ship had been buried, Cerdic told Father Martin how he had come into Wulfnoth's service before he collapsed into a fitful sleep onto a straw-filled sack in the corner of the infirmary.

The following morning he was delirious, his body shaking uncontrollably with the ague. It was to be many days before he was fit to travel.

The Danelaw

They buried her in a shallow grave at the edge of the mound just as the last rays of the sun lingered on its summit. In pagan times it would have drawn her spirit into the afterlife and so it seemed fitting that such a moment should signal Magda's journey to paradise.

Torgrim respected her. Eric adored her. And Wulfnoth had felt her strength from the moment she had sat down on the stone outside the visitors' hut when they first arrived at the leper colony. In a male-dominated world her quiet authority had marked her out as a natural leader; she was clear-sighted and decisive and had been willing to risk her own life to help others. In the end she had died assisting their escape. Wulfnoth could think of no man he respected more and no woman save one whose loss had meant more to him.

Eric gathered the russet coarse clothes that had marked Magda out as a leper and threw them on to the dying embers where they shrank in the heat, blackened and burst into flame. Moments later the charred particles were born upwards and carried away on the wind.

"She'll be hutiful again now, Mah Wuffnah, yust like you said!" whispered Eric as he took one last look at his sister's grave. He turned away and, while the others put everything back into the wagon, he busied himself harnessing the mare between the shafts of the cart. He couldn't bear to look back again.

Wulfnoth, however, did not take his eyes from the stark mound of freshly turned earth until they finally left the clearing. Then climbing up he sat beside Eric. It promised to be another clear night and he wanted to cross the Roman Street before the moon was up.

It took best part of a week to travel cross-country, but eventually they reached the Ryknield Way and turned north. Although little used since Roman times it ran straight and true and would carry them deep into the Danelaw. However, they still wore their leper's clothes lest they encounter men from Mercia and were prepared to pull off the road at the slightest hint of danger. Several days later they crossed Watling Street and entered the relative safety of a region that had enjoyed a degree of autonomy since the days of King Edgar. At last they could discard their disguise and travel openly in daylight. A week later they passed the white stone minster church of St Peter at Cyningesburh and at the manor of Wulfric they learnt that Wulfric, his brother, Ealdorman Aelfhelm, and influential thegns of the Five Boroughs were expected any day on their journey to York, where they would hold council with the leading thegns of Northumbria.

With such a party imminent Wulfric's reeve, who had been warned to expect the Sussex thegn, could not offer them accommodation at Cyningesburh but arrangements were made for them to stay at Barnburh an old settlement that Wulfric had recently acquired after the death of the local thegn. It had been one of the early Saxon strongholds that had been erected just below the limestone ridge to command views of Dearne Valley.

Most of the empty buildings had fallen into disrepair, but one end of the low squat fort was tolerably habitable. It was a simple structure, small but secure and dry. Wulfric's reeve assured them they were welcome to use it for as long as they wished and promised that word would be sent to them as soon as Aelfhelm and his master arrived.

Thus it was that Wulfnoth, Torgrim and Eric first came to the village that occupied the high ground above the River Dearne. The village itself was clustered round a stone Saxon Cross where the early Celtic missionaries were said to have preached and where the priest of Cyningesburh came once every few months to say mass and shrive the sinners. It was a sleepy backwater and an ideal place for Torgrim to recuperate and wait for news of his daughter. Eric was in his element making the place habitable, clearing the stream that brought fresh water from Thunder Hole where it gushed out of the ground, tidying the yard and gathering piles of wood for the winter. He also dug a secret hiding place for Torgrim's treasure beneath the floor of the back room that was used to house livestock in the winter. He would sleep there himself and was more than happy to share it with the old mare.

Wulfnoth helped with the work but was clearly anxious to return to Compton and spent much of his time staring across the valley and watching the road for any sign of activity.

One afternoon a feint smudge of dust cloud below the church on the distant escarpment caught his eye. It hovered for several minutes over the causeway that ran through Strafford Sands and slowly seemed to grow in volume as it crawled along that part of the Roman Street that led up to High Melton where it was momentarily hidden from view by a small copse. Then it boiled into life once more in the open space by the Hangman Stone where it billowed out before suddenly evaporating into clear air to reveal a pair of horses pausing for breath before making their way down Ludwell Hill.

"At last!" murmured Wulfnoth and called for Torgrim and Eric to join him. Soon they lost sight of the horsemen as they dropped into the gully of St. Helen's Spring, but then head, torso and horses re-emerged. Moments later a stranger cantered into the yard leading a spare horse.

"I'm looking for Wulfnoth of Compton."

"You have found him."

"My master, Wulfric, has arrived with the northern Lords and invites you to join them before they set off for York."

"Is Siferth of the Five Boroughs with them?"

"He had not arrived when I left, but was expected."

Torgrim could not contain himself, "Is there a maid in the party?"

The messenger seemed surprised at the old man's interruption and looked at Wulfnoth unsure whether to answer a serving man in front of the thegn.

"This is Torgrim, a man of standing and my friend. You may answer him."

"Sir," said the embarrassed messenger, "there are a number of young ladies in the party."

"Is there one called Hild among them?"

"I do not know their names, sir. I only know that my master has sent me to fetch Lord Wulfnoth."

"Old friend, if she is among Ealdorman Aelfhelm's party I will bring her to you. If she is not I will not rest till we have restored her to you."

Torgrim had to be content and watched as Wulfnoth mounted the spare horse and the two riders rode away down Barnburh hill.

Half an hour later Wulfnoth was ushered into Cyningesburh Manor and the presence of one of the richest men in England. Wulfric Spott had the same powerful physique as his brother Aelfhelm, but there the resemblance ended. He was considerably older than the ealdorman and his shock of white hair; his gentle, honest and thoughtful eyes; and the permanent hint of a smile seemed to suggest that he was not one of the obvious movers and shakers of the age, not one who sought political advancement. Yet it would be a superficial assumption to imagine that he was someone who did not take life as seriously as other men and did not help to shape it. He had a genuine concern for the well-being of the kingdom, an intellect second to none and a sensitivity that reached out to the highest and lowest in the land. His altruism was acknowledged by all and his advice frequently sought and highly valued by both church and crown.

"Ah! Wulfnoth of Compton, you are welcome to my house. I trust that the Manor of Barnburh was not too dilapidated to serve your needs."

"Those on the run should not expect luxury. The manor is sound and Eric is already turning it into a home. You will not lose by your generosity to strangers. Torgrim is not a poor man, nor one to remain idle for long. When his daughter is found he will recover his drive and will look to start his business once more."

"But with only one hand he cannot hope to work again surely!"

"He had a skill second to none. He will train others. It all depends on the safe return of Hild."

"That may not be as easy a task as you had hoped," said a voice behind him.

Aelfhelm, who had entered the room a few moments before, greeted Wulfnoth warmly. "You are welcome in the Danelaw, but I have little news to comfort you."

"Thank you, my lord, but what of Hild?"

The Ealdorman explained how Cerdic, had been prevented from bidding for the girl and gone to Normandy in pursuit of the merchant who had bought her.

"Then I must go to Normandy at once."

"Normandy is large country. She could be anywhere. You would not know where to look."

"But at least I must try."

"It is over a month since we saw Cerdic. He may be back in England by now. In any case Siferth and Morcar promised to remain in Winchester a further fortnight and then bring word of any developments. At least wait for them."

"But they will be another two weeks."

"Not so," the Ealdorman assured him, "They're a mad pair and will sleep only when necessary and ride all day and most of the night if the moon gives enough light. They were confident they would catch up with us here at my brother's before we set off for York."

"Give them another day or so and if they are not here," said Wulfric, "I will have a boat and men ready for you in the Humber that will take you to Normandy."

Wulfnoth could see the sense in waiting a couple of days and a boat from the Humber would save him well over a week travelling by land.

However, he did not have to wait two days. Siferth and Morcar rode into Cyningesburh the following morning. But, unfortunately, the news that they brought was to fill the thegn with greater dismay. Cerdic had not returned to England, but a Norman monk had delivered a letter addressed to Wulfnoth. He broke the Abbot's seal and unfolded the parchment with a sense of foreboding, and then found to his frustration that the letter had been written in Latin, a language that he recognised from the court diplomas he had witnessed, but one that he was quite unable to decipher.

He handed it to Aelfhelm, "I can make neither head nor tail of this. Can you, my Lord?"

Aelfhelm shook his head, "Like you I am no scholar but my brother is." And he placed the document in front of Wulfric.

The old man peered at it frowning and then began to nod his head in understanding. After a while he looked up at Wulfnoth.

"I'm afraid this letter may confirm your worst fears. It is in two parts: one clearly dictated by your servant and the other from the Abbot of Jumieges. Let me read it to you: 'My lord I have failed you utterly. Having been prevented from bidding for Hild at the market, I discovered that she had been bought by a whoremonger from Bruges called Jacob. I followed what I thought was their trail to Rouen, but find that he no longer uses this route and will almost certainly have headed directly for his native city. Tomorrow I go in pursuit, but fear

I may be too late. Your servant, Cerdic.' Then, the Abbot has added a note saying that the following morning Cerdic was stricken with a virulent fever and that far from setting out for Bruges the 'seaman's soul is thought to be embarking on its final journey.'"

"God rest his soul," said Wulfnoth sadly. "I asked too much of him and sent him to his death. He did not fail me. But it is I who has failed my friend Torgrim. I promised to bring back his daughter and now it seems it was no more than a false boast. It'll break the old man's heart, but I must go and tell him."

"You have done your best, said Aelfhelm."

"My best was not good enough."

The old man had been silent for some time, but then showed why he had been a valued advisor to the Witan since the time of King Edgar. He would listen, assess a situation and then recommend logical and decisive action. His voice was quiet but commanded attention. "Wulfnoth, The king apparently does not require your services at present and you have done your business here. My offer of a ship still stands. Go at once! Your friend Torgrim can stay at Barnburh as long as he wishes. We will acquaint him with the situation. He will understand. If you bring his daughter back imagine his joy! But if your quest is unsuccessful, then time and the knowledge that you risked the searoads for him will temper his despair."

The prospect of action immediately raised the thegn's spirits, "It's a long shot for a selfbow, but at least I shall have tried everything," he said with obvious relief.

"We could of course both go to Bruges," said Siferth quietly.

"We? You have done enough already and your place is here. Besides, you have a meeting with the Northern

Lords in York. I'll go to Bruges and make one more effort to find the girl though I fear the trail will be cold by now."

"It will be colder still if you do not go at once," replied his friend.

"True," answered Wulfnoth and turning to his host he said, "I am once more indebted to you, sir. If there is the slightest chance of finding her and bringing her back home then I must take it."

The old man smiled. "Bruges is only three days away with a fair wind. You could leave on the night tide. My men will see you as far as Barton on the Humber and my captain will have the vessel ready. Tomorrow night, young Wulfnoth, you'll sleep under the stars on the searoads."

The Whorehouse

The restorative effect of ten hours uninterrupted sleep was remarkable and first light found Alena at the windhole looking across at the town. Initially she had hoped to steal a sufficient sum to buy passage on a boat and escape back to England where they could set themselves up in either London or York, but the smallness of the settlement and its distance from the sea made the prospect of discovery and recapture far more likely. Without outside help the plan was doomed from the start. For all his crudity and the unsavouriness of his profession, Jacob was a man of means and money talked. She had no desire to face his fury when they were caught and dragged back. Somehow she had to make herself indispensable, but that would take time and Hild had preciously little of that.

The sound of clamouring voices and the rattle of ironwork emanating from below interrupted her thinking. Making her way down to the cellars she realised it came from cage containing the prostitutes who were complaining about not being fed.

When the light of the torch illuminated the end of the passage, the shouting ceased. Alena hesitated.

Sensing that the footsteps had stopped coming towards them the tenor of the voices changed and took on a wheedling character, "Come on, Jan. We're starving. You wouldn't want us to starve, would you?"

"How can we perform well if you don't feed us?"

"Jacob's friends don't like skinny women."

When Alena appeared at the other side of the grill there was stunned silence for a moment, but the tallest of the women quickly recovered.

"Where's that lazy bastard, Jan? Why hasn't he brought us any food this morning?

"The steward took an unexpected swim in the river last night," said Alena watching the woman's reactions. "I doubt he'll be serving breakfast again."

"The bastard's dead then?"

Alena raised an eyebrow noncommittally.

"So who are you?" demanded one of her companions, a mousy-haired creature, who shook her head in an effort to control her astigmatism as she spoke.

"I'm his replacement," said Alena simply.

"Garn! You're one of his new whores. He'll take a whip to you if he finds you've escaped."

"Jacob wouldn't trust a woman," the third, a small foreign-looking girl with long straight dark hair and sallow skin, said cautiously. "How did you get out there?"

Determined to appear distant Alena ignored the question and letting her hand drop to her belt played the steward's bunch of keys through her fingers.

For a moment the women stared at her in amazement and then at each other their mouths open, but no words coming out. Then their eyes met as if a new understanding was beginning to dawn.

Mousy-hair dropped to her knees and clutching at the hem of Alena's tunic cried, "Thank God! That bastard, Jan used to starve us and beat us black and blue. Jacob didn't know half of what was going on. We'll cause no trouble. You'll see, as long as we're treated properly."

At that moment the girl made a lunge through the grille for the keys, an action that caught Alena off balance and she found herself pulled forcefully against the bars of the cage. Although the old leather resisted the first two jerks, it finally snapped and the bunch of keys was torn from her belt. Thrown backwards Alena ended up sprawling on the floor while her adversary held her prize aloft in triumph.

In the struggle the torch had fallen from Alena's hand and landed among some straw in the corridor setting the dry stalks crackling into life. Instinctively she snatched it up and stamped on the smouldering embers, before turning to face her attackers.

The third prostitute had lost no time in attempting to unlock the cell door, but the tall woman impatient at her companion's lack of success grabbed the bunch, pushed her aside and began frantically trying each key in turn.

Alena realised that if they forced their way out of the cell before she could win them over to her plans they would disappear in the myriad of back alleys that ran behind the waterfront leaving her to take the blame for their escape. Of course they were certain to be caught eventually, but it would be no consolation to her when she found herself sharing their vermin-infested prison. There was no time to be squeamish. She had to act decisively.

The woman screamed when the burning torch was thrust into her face and as she tried to protect herself the bunch of keys fell from her hands onto the straw. Alena retrieved it before any of the women could stop her and they were left to vent their frustration by shaking the bars of the cage.

"Stand back or I'll set light to the straw and you'll burn to death in this rathole," Alena shouted above the din and when she made to carry out the threat the three women retreated and falling on their knees dissolved into tears.

"Jacob's sleeping off a hangover but the row you make is likely to wake him and he'll be in a foul mood if he has to deal with you himself."

They looked wary. Experience had taught them that the appearance of Jacob was the last thing they wanted so they stood sheepishly as they watched their new gaoler making herself comfortable sitting with her back resting against the corridor wall.

"Jan usually treated us better when Jacob was away," ventured the tall woman hopefully changing the subject. "Sometimes we'd get two meals a day and leftovers from his own table."

"He was a good cook, but he was drunk last night and we had no supper," snivelled the mouse.

"Well Jan's dead and floating down the river," said Alena as coldly as she could.

"How d' you know?"

"Because I watched Jacob kick him to death and then helped him dispose of the body." She paused and the mouse twitched uncontrollably while the other two women looked at Alena with a new degree of respect.

"And if you cross me again I'll see that you join him," added Alena hoping that her eyes conveyed the right measure of anger and brutality.

"We'll be no trouble. Honest," bleated the mouse. "We're so hungry we don't know what we're doing half the time, do we, Judith?" She turned to her tall companion for corroboration.

"I don't know whether to feed you or tell Jacob that you attempted to escape."

In the torchlight the whites of the women's eyes confirmed their dread of the whoremonger.

"Don't tell Jacob we tried to escape. Ogive and I both carry the scars from the last time he caught us," whispered Judith.

"Alright," said Alena, "but listen carefully to what I say. You may think Jacob is cruel, but if you cross me you'll wish Jacob was here to protect you."

Suitably chastened Ogive, Judith and the girl listened and were surprised when Alena asked, "Do you really want to escape from this rathole?"

When they all nodded sheepishly she continued, "First you must carry on as if nothing has happened and perform for his customers as if you enjoyed your work. If you do as you're told, I'll see this cell is cleaned out and that you're well fed. Then if all goes well you'll be free within two months and you can forget that this place ever existed."

For a moment the three women struggled to grasp the significance of what she was saying and then, when it finally dawned on them that their years of abuse might soon be over, their pinched faces seemed to light up with the reawakening of hope.

"Remember," said Alena, putting the cold edge back in her voice "you do exactly as I tell you and don't breathe a word of our plan to anyone else, or all our corpses may end up in the river."

When she had sworn them to secrecy, Alena smiling for the first time rose to her feet and said simply, "Now for breakfast!"

If the remains of the previous night's stew, cheese, an apple and some of the new seasons chestnuts weren't enough to convince Judith and Ogive, that the wheel of fate had finally past its nadir, then the liberal jug of cervoise certainly made them glow with a new optimism. They were still afraid of Alena, but for the time being she had won their confidence since she offered them their best chance of survival.

As she turned to leave them, the girl took her food to the back of the cell and called in a gentle voice, "Walram."

Alena had totally forgotten the boy whom she had seen in the cell the previous evening and watched as Judith propped the boy up while the girl fed him small pieces from the bowl of stew. He seemed only half aware of what was going on.

"Is he alright?" she asked.

"As well as can be expected when you're cooped up in this pigsty all day and forced to suck cock while being buggered each evening to satisfy the perverted desires of Jacob's sodomite clients," Judith retorted angrily.

Alena knew that such practices went on even in England, but she had never encountered one of its victims before. It could be her own brother who had died of starvation sitting there on the straw. She had chosen her profession but this poor wretch had been sold as a slave and forced to suffer nightly abuse to fill the purse of a whoremonger.

"He looks so dreadfully pale and lifeless," she whispered.

"He's ill," snapped Ogive, "because the fear of bad dreams makes him struggle to stay awake at night and then when he does fall asleep lack of food makes it difficult for him to wake up. If he's lucky he'll be dead before Easter."

It was Jacob who deserved to die, thought Alena. Even the Church, whose prelates winked at fornication, could not stomach unnatural acts. Prostitution may be a necessary evil: the other would always be anathema.

"I'll get you all out of here as soon as I can," promised Alena and leaving the torch in the metal loop on the wall she stumbled back down the corridor and up the ladder stopping only when she reached the windhole and could feel the fresh air on her face.

* * * * *

Jacob slept late and when he finally woke he was surprised to find newly-baked bread on his table. The smell was irresistible and he broke his fast with distinct relish so it was some time before he realised that the house was unnaturally silent. On his return from trips abroad to markets such as Winchester or Pavia there was usually a stream of customers knocking at the door eager to buy cloth or other foreign goods and he would have to supervise the sales to make sure that Jan didn't swindle him by selling too cheaply or stealing a tranche of the profits by clipping some of the coins and slipping the shavings into his own purse. Then he remembered that Jan was at the bottom of the river. Perhaps he had slept through the knocking, but then why weren't the whores screaming for food and where were Alena and the girl? He went into his wife's old room but found it empty. He began to panic, ran down the stairs and burst into the hall where he kept his stock and made his sales.

He was taken aback when he found Hild seated at a stool and bent over the table compiling a list. Beside her stood Alena, the short leather whip that Jan used tucked into her belt.

"I thought...." he began.

"The master had come to count the takings, Hild. Show him the list so that he can see he has made a good profit."

Without daring to look up Hild held out the parchment and opened the box, which was three quarters full of silver coins.

Torn between curiosity and profit Jacob hesitated but greed won and he soon totted up the morning's receipts. He had to have the list explained to him, and then in order to satisfy himself he double-checked by counting all the stock that was left. The profit exceeded his expectations. He was forced to admit that he could not have bettered their return.

Alena explained that both she and Hild were used to dealing with customers and as Hild was able to read and write she could record each transaction as well as drive a hard bargain. Neither would stand any nonsense from the merchants and artisans. When it came to the richer clients she herself had a special talent to charm them into parting with their money.

Jacob chuckled and swept the coins back into the box. "That you have," he acknowledged. "You're good you are and honest not like that thieving servant of mine. Pity he had to die. He was a good whoremaster and had a way of keeping them docile." Suddenly he looked wary. "The whores! I haven't heard the whores this morning and they always scream and shout unless Jan chastises them. The bitches must have escaped!" And he turned to go and search the cellars.

"You've no worries on their account," said Alena drawing herself up and deliberately standing in front of him. "I can manage your whores. They've been fed and watered and will be ready for exercise when your friends arrive this evening. It's surprising what this can do in a woman's hand," and she caressed the whip at her belt before letting her hand rest lightly against his tunic, "Besides you don't have to pay me," she said playfully as she felt him stir. "Slave, whoremaster and mistress all rolled into one. As good as having a wife!"

Jacob marvelled at his good fortune: the woman had revitalised his sex drive, cooked like the count's own chef, dealt with his customers and all at little or no expense to himself.

"Better," he said, wishing he could have exercised his rediscovered manhood there and then on the wooden floorboards, but realised that he would have to forgo that pleasure until after his meeting with the Burgrave and leading merchants of the town. "I have business all day, but will return for supper. After that I will show you how much you please me. Can you manage here until this evening?"

"There is only salt meat in the store, my lord, but if you will let me go to the market, I can buy fresh fish and vegetables. Even a great man needs such food to maintain his strength and sharpen his appetite."

"Take what you need. Keep an eye on the girl though and lock her in her room while I am gone."

As they walked to the door Alena whispered, "She won't escape from me I promise you, but I must begin her training in case her father does not ransom her and we have to sell her in the market at Pavia."

* * * * *

As soon as Jacob left for his meeting in the Burg, Alena and Hild slipped out of the loathsome house and hurried along the jetty to the market place where they found the bulk of the traders still squatting on the ground beside neat piles of spinach; rows of leeks and endive; and elaborate pyramids of onions, apples and pears. Torgrim had taught Hild to be a shrewd buyer and she steered Alena towards the less fashionable pitches where the goods were piled in untidy heaps. Rooting about in these, feeling and smelling each article in turn she soon amassed a selection of sound fruit and vegetables haggling continuously to get the best price.

Carrying their purchases in a small sack they crossed over the Breidelstraat Bridge, made their way past St. Donatian's Church and down the narrow alley under the fortress walls to the fish quay where a string of vessels were unloading the night's catch of herring and a great assortment of other fish unfortunate enough to have been trapped in the nets.

Back in Winchester most people were used to freshwater fish caught in millponds or in the River Itchen while herring were invariably the white variety preserved in the great tubs of salt, so Alena suggested that they watch which types the local women bought before venturing to make their choice. Hild, however, had another reason for waiting.

Having often accompanied her father when he travelled to Hantone to purchase precious stones she would pass the time wandering along the sea shore where the fishermen of the Solent were busy dividing their haul of fish by species, size and quality into baskets. Whiting and plaice were always held in great esteem and commanded the highest prices, while at the other end of the line shellfish such as oysters, cockles and periwinkles served the poor. In between lay a myriad of glistening marine life. Towards late afternoon when her father rejoined her she would snap up fish at a bargain price and always managed to include some unfamiliar variety to delight him at supper.

As they were strangers they knew the Bruges fishmongers would try to charge them high prices so the delay proved to be an excellent strategy, for as soon as the crowd had thinned the sellers were anxious to be shot of the last of their catch and return home to sleep after their strenuous night's work. Choosing her time carefully Hild approached a tired looking fisherman and after inquiring the price for a couple of large fish, shook her head sadly and offered only half the amount. When this was refused she smiled sweetly at him and proposed that she would pay the full price on condition that he threw in all his other remaining fish. Seeing little prospect of further customers, he reluctantly agreed.

Alena could scarcely contain her admiration for her young companion and as soon as the deal had been done and the fish put safely in another sack she hurried Hild from the quay and back into the alley where both women collapsed in laughter. It was the first time in four days that either of them had been able to forget the bleak future that threatened to engulf them. Fresh air and freedom, albeit temporary, had offered them a glimmer of hope, like a shaft of frail sunlight signals the prospect of a passageway opening up through purple banks of slate-dark clouds. But minutes later, however, the two women were hurrying back across the bridge towards the gloomy façade of their prisonhouse.

Once inside they released Walram from the cellar and he sat silently by the kitchen fire watching Hild prepare a fish and vegetable stew, while Alena arranged for the prostitutes to clean out their cell and fill their mattresses with fresh straw. She took care to make the three women sit at the back of the cell whenever she had to open the door, but promised them that if they accepted her plan she would endeavour to arrange for them to enjoy the freedom of the house whenever Jacob was out. Listening quietly over their bowls full of hot stew they willingly swore to play their part.

When the whoremonger later reappeared the house had returned to normal. Walram was once again incarcerated in the clean cellar with the three women, Hild, who had prepared a fresh pot of the rich fish stew for Jacob, was safe in the locked bedroom and Alena dressed in one of his wife's tunics ready to serve her master. The rich fish stew seasoned with pepper and herbs proved to be a favourite with the merchant and he vowed he had never tasted better but it served merely as an entrée before the delights of the bedroom. By nightfall Jacob, well content with his own performance, lay with his arm around Alena.

"Your customers will arrive soon and I must go make sure that the whores are eager to satisfy them," she murmured.

"I suppose so," replied Jacob reluctantly, "but you will return soon."

"Of course," she began. Then struck her forehead with the base of her palm, "but we have one problem."

"What is that, my love? Surely there is no problem you cannot solve."

"No, but if you are not careful you'll no longer be able to satisfy your more debauched customers."

"What do you mean by that?"

"The boy whore has the flux and is like to die of it. In any case in the state he's in an untimely accident or merely the smell will put them off."

"Are you sure?" asked Jacob, a touch of annoyance creeping into his voice.

"Of course I'm sure."

"Damn the child. We might as well dispose of him as soon as it gets dark. No good feeding the brat if he's going to die. There was a time when it wouldn't have matter. The streets were full of starving urchins who wouldn't have been missed. Now I'll have to wait and buy a replacement in the market at Pavia before Christmas.

For a moment Alena thought she had over reached herself and that Jacob would throttle the boy at once.

"I can cure him," she said quickly. "Given rest and a concoction of sliced bramble root, everlasting, mugwort, and ewe's milk and he should recover in a fortnight."

"I hope you're right."

"Leave him to me. I haven't let you down yet, have I?"

"No," he acknowledged.

"That should buy the boy time," thought Alena and quickly changed the subject. "Have you sent word to England to see if the girl's father will raise the ransom?"

"No," he admitted.

"Then we must do so at once. The market at Pavia is only three months away and we must know where we stand if the virgin is to command a high price."

"Such a tantalising and erotic bed fellow yet such a shrewd business woman," thought Jacob.

"However, did I manage without you?"

"Then you will see to it today?" she asked innocently.

"I will have to find a scribe who won't ask awkward questions."

"But, my lord, can you not read and write?"

"I never had the time to learn, "he answered sheepishly.

"Then it's lucky that I can."

"Good. Good! I'll tell you what to write."

"No. Better still. The girl can write it. I know she has the skill and I can tell her what you wish to say and how the business is to be transacted. Seeing her hand will tear the old man's heartstrings and we can demand a higher sum."

Jacob could hardly hide his admiration. She was a gold mine and would make him rich beyond his wildest dreams.

"You think of everything," he said, "but make sure there is no mention of me or where she is being held. Tell him to give the money to the captain of the ship we send.

* * * * *

Later, having spent an hour composing the letter, Alena watched as Hild wrote the words in a bold hand on a sheet of parchment in the hope that it would not only buy them time, but be the means of their rescue. Then Hild read it back to her.

"Father,
  I am in the hands of a powerful slave merchant
   Who'll <u>Be Ruthless Unless Given Enough Silver.</u>
  <u>Just pay 300 silver pennies to his Agent the Captain</u>
   <u>Of the Blackbird</u> within one month,
    if you wish to see me alive again.
                                                Hild"

Since Hild had no idea what had happened to Torgrim or indeed if he were still alive they decided to send the letter care of Lord Wulfnoth of Compton. She felt sure that he of all her father's friends would know what to do.

When Alena, who had learnt the note by heart, read it to Jacob later, he frowned. "I do not have a vessel called the Blackbird."

"It is the English for le merle noir. Anyone who sees the carved bird on the ship's stem post will recognise it instantly."

"Clever…. clever." Jacob was impressed, sealed the letter and sent for the Captain of *Le Merle Noir*.

During the next few days life in the whorehouse drifted into an uneasy pattern of business as usual interspersed with stolen periods of freedom and laughter whenever Jacob was out. The prostitutes were well fed and performed their duties with greater skill and animation in the knowledge that they were part of a conspiracy, while Alena and Hild strove to make themselves indispensable finding release in their daily visits to the markets and exploration the town.

The Hounds of Satan

Not surprisingly, however, the regular appearance of the two foreign women did not go unnoticed. Word spread like water after torrential rain, flooding the market place, spilling through the side streets, cascading into the gutters and gushing down the Breidelstraat where it burst onto the concourse of the Burg, forever seeking cracks and crevices that would enable it to trickle down to the lowest levels of the town.

Nudges were exchanged between stallholders, eyebrows were raised among customers, servants whispered to servants and stewards confided in their masters. Meanwhile the merchants and artisans who frequented Jacob's saleroom could talk of little else but the two women who managed his new consignment of merchandise. Hild, so it was rumoured, was a rich heiress who could read and write and was travelling to Italy to be married to a great prince. But it was her companion about whom tongues indulged themselves most passionately. Alena's physical attributes were enhanced at every turn of this great river of gossip so that by the time it reached the lecherous circle of the rich and powerful she had become an object of intrigue, attraction and desire.

Curiosity drew the young male members of this socially elite flock stalking and grazing the banks of the

River Rei eager to confirm the reports. Satisfied that rumour had not been exaggerated, all but the wethers and bedridden rams then spent their evenings boasting their determination to be the first to tup the raven-haired Anglo-Saxon with the wild eyes.

Among the more imposing dwellings that clustered beside the ancient fortress lay the house of Wenemar who controlled the manufacture and supply of weapons to both the court and the garrison and he was entertaining a group of seasoned hell-raisers. Galbert, the castellan and governor of the fort, a sallow-faced, raw-boned man whose sharp eyes habitually narrowed over his prominent cheek bones, sat in the place of honour to the right of his host, whilst Gervaise, the burgrave, a heavily-built man, who ran the civil affairs of Bruges, sat on his left. Opposite at the foot of the table was Erembald, a young man barely twenty, the only openly acknowledged bastard of the count and, consequently, a man of great wealth and influence whose charming smile belied his innate ruthless self-indulgence. Wenemar himself was a product of a society that occasionally opened its arms to a low-born man of exceptional qualities. In his case the combination of an apprenticeship with a Frankish blacksmith in Cologne, a natural feel for balance and beauty and the determination to out-perform his rivals had left him at the blade edge of an industry that was sought after throughout the courts of Europe.

This elite group called themselves the Knights of St. Hubert, but there was nothing holy in their association, nothing remotely connected to the saintliness of the eighth century Bishop of Liege. They honoured rather the wild young nobleman of his youth, the avid hunter of the Ardennes who bred the powerful and dignified pack hounds of the chase for the French court.

To others they were the Hounds of Satan. Alas the talent that was gathered in that room had the dubious reputation of being the most debauched in Flanders.

Because of his peculiar talents Jacob had been made an honorary member of this group and would normally have been present, but he had recently been conspicuously absent from their gathering and it was he who was the topic of their conversation.

Galbert wiped his mouth with a scrap of bread and threw it to one of the great long-eared hunting dogs they prized so.

"How comes it Jacob has shunned our company since his return from England? You see him everyday, Gervaise, at your tedious council meetings of the burghers. What's his excuse?"

"He claims that Jan his whoremaster has run off and that he must manage his affairs himself, but my servant tells a different story. He says his cousin, Jan, was beaten senseless by our friend and then flung in the Rei. When he struck the cold water he regained sufficient consciousness to struggle to the surface and keep himself afloat while the current carried him as far as the Breidelstraat Bridge where he managed to crawl out and stagger to his cousin's. For some days he couldn't speak, but has recently recovered his tongue, although his life still hangs by a thread. If he dies they plan to accuse Jacob of murder under the count's new laws."

"He'll need his friends then or suffer the consequences. If nothing else my father is a stickler for the law."

"It was at the request of my "tedious" council, as you call it, Galbert, to tackle civil unrest that the count resolved to outlaw murder in the town, so Jacob may find himself hard pressed to prove his innocence."

"That may be true, but business commitments are surely an excuse. My spies tell me it is two women who run his business now?"

"Your spies are almost certainly right," said Wenemar. "My steward mentioned some such thing when he returned from buying new fleeces for the winter."

"You old men are out of touch," mocked their young companion. "The women are the talk of Bruges. One is quiet as a mouse, but the other something quite extraordinary."

"Have you seen them, Erembald?"

"Seen them, Gervaise? I've breathed the air they breathe and plan to sample their goods before long."

"Jacob is usually generous enough to let us have first serving of his new whores on this oak table of mine."

"Apparently they're not whores, Wenemar. Jan's beating was because he made that mistake. My servant says that Jacob was apoplectic when his cousin used the word."

"Then perhaps he aims to keep them to himself." Galbert's eyes were reduced to menacing slits.

"The word among the burghers is that the quiet one is betrothed and destined for a royal marriage."

"Then why is she lodged with Master Jacob the whoremonger and not with the count?" snorted the castellan, his eyes snapping open with indignation."

"Jacob is many things and his trading empire takes him to the Courts of both the east and west. If her journey is secret he provides an ideal means of travel and his seamen and muleteers are renowned for being the best in Flanders."

"A likely story and I suppose the other is her chaperone?"

"Yes, Galbert, but chaperones are usually old crones. This one is different, however. She has the spirit of a gipsy and the body to taunt and exercise a man to death, especially one who's past his prime."

"I can still plough a long straight furrow with the best."

"If she is so exceptional it's small wonder then he begrudges us the pleasure of their company," grumbled the swordsmith. "My weapon is sorely out of practice."

"But by letting them walk the streets each day he flaunts his possessions under our noses." For a moment Erembald looked petulant, but then the smile returned. "Let us send word to him that we deplore his lack of charity and want a share in his good fortune."

"Capital idea," said Gervaise thumping the table, "He can hardly refuse."

"Brotherhood demands he keeps no secrets from us," added Wenemar indignantly.

"Tell him we would have the women visit us here or we will feel he does not value our friendship." Apart from enjoying the prospect of scoring over the merchant, Erembald, who was the only one to have seen Alena, was driven by a sadistic desire to feel her struggling underneath him like a wildcat before he finally forced her to succumb to the excitement of orgasm.

Wenemar called one of his servants, but it was the castellan who spelt out the message he was to deliver to their absent colleague.

When the man had left Galbert simply said, "He'll understand what we mean."

* * * * *

Life in the whorehouse had improved for all concerned during that week. Although Hild wrote everything down meticulously Jacob scarcely gave it a glance, assured by the sight of the moneybox and the knowledge that the takings always exceeded his expectations. The house was quiet and his straight customers to a man congratulated him on the renewed enthusiasm of his whores. Meanwhile his own sexual drive had improved significantly and although he only performed successfully once each night Alena satisfied him completely. For the moment he was at peace as he sat with Alena over a final pitcher of wine before retiring.

"I hope the affairs of the town have not made my lover too tired to satisfy the hunger of the one who manages his affairs at home."

"And how do I do that?" he asked feigning innocence.

"A husband would know what to do."

"A husband indeed! Is not the role of mistress enough for you?"

Alena had no chance to reply for at that moment Hild knocked on the door and announced the arrival of a messenger.

Jacob would have refused to see him, but Wenemar's servant had followed her silently up the stairs and stepped insolently into the room.

"My master and his friends, the Knights of St. Hubert, sent me to ask after your health, sir. They have missed your company and trust that you will soon be well enough to join them. They invite also the two ladies who stay with you and ask me to say that you lack generosity if you do not introduce them to your friends. Lastly they instructed me to warn you that the death of your servant Jan is likely to cause problems and they assume you will be grateful for their support."

Jacob listened in silence, his jaw tightening and his face paling with every word. He nodded to the man. "Tell them." He paused. "I'll see them soon."

The messenger bowed and left.

When the man had gone the whoremonger was visibly shaken.

The words hadn't worried Alena, but the atmosphere sent a shudder running through the muscles of her shoulders and as it passed she found herself shivering with cold.

"Did I miss something?" she whispered.

"Damn them! They know about Jan and expect me to hand you both over to them."

"Hand us over?"

"Yes."

"Who are these knights?"

"Their victims call them the Hounds of Satan, but they are four of the most powerful men in Bruges."

"But why do they want us?"

"So that they can treat you to a great banquet and then take it in turns to rape you on the great dining table in Wenemar's." It amuses them to give young women a night to remember and then exact payment."

Alena had heard of such things happening.

"Then we shall refuse to go."

"They could hold my life in their hands, so I may be forced to give you up."

"Do they do think they have the right to take their pleasure with any woman in Bruges?"

"Usually it's the unmarried ones or those who husbands can be bought. Otherwise the Church would have the courage to denounce them. If only you were my wife!"

Alena was horrified, but saw her chance

"Tell him I am."

"It would do no good. This is not the North of England where men have wives according to the Danish custom. Here it is not recognised which is why that bastard Erembald will always be illegitimate whatever he claims. The Church will not recognise any marriage that she hasn't blessed."

"Then ask your friend the provost to give us a blessing. After all he is a client. Tell him you wish to marry me at Mass on Sunday and if he refuses well you can let it be known where he spends his Monday nights."

Jacob was wide-eyed. In his wildest dreams he would not have thought of blackmailing the most powerful cleric in Bruges. The outrageousness of the scheme amused him.

Spymaster

Eadric of Shrewsbury had learned from an early age that power was the key to wealth. Born in a time of vicious political struggle, he finally made his bones in the lawless society of Mercia that followed the death of Ealdorman Aelfhere in 983. His ruthlessness and disregard for the older nobility soon came to attention of the young king who, having suffered throughout his minority under the rivalry of the powerful appointees of his predecessors, now sought a new breed of men who would be loyal to him alone.

Thus the Shropshire thegn embarked on a career that would eventually see him rise to great wealth and power as the principle enforcer of the kingdom.

That was to be in the future. At present he was Aethelred's chief spy and, as such, had eyes and ears at every port, so when *Le Merle Noir* made landfall at Dover word soon reached him that she planned to put into Bosham before returning to Flanders. It seemed an unnecessary stop, unless she carried a message for Wulfnoth, the wretched Thegn of Compton who harboured his small fleet of warships there. He had marked him down as a troublemaker during the Council meeting and he knew that his brother Beorhtric detested the man from Sussex. In any case private letters from abroad had the stench of treason about them, so it was in his interest as well as that of the king to intercept them.

Consequently his men were watching when *Le Merle Noir* was pulled up on to the beach at Bosham and waited until the captain left the boat and made his way up the path towards the church. There they waylaid him and demanded his business on shore.

Assuming they were local officials, the captain of *Le Merle Noir* openly admitted that he carried a letter from his master to Lord Wulfnoth of Compton and had been told to return in a fortnight for a reply.

The spies explained that Wulfnoth was away from his estate, but promised to see that the letter was delivered without delay and the captain was happy to return to his vessel and sail home with his cargo.

The following day the letter was handed to Eadric at the palace. He scanned the contents pensively before handing it to Beorhtric

"It seems, brother, the wretched Thegn of Compton has friends abroad who write to him in code. Can you make head or tail of this?"

Beorhtric read it through and then stiffened when he saw the name Hild.

"Damn Jacob. He was supposed to dispose of the girl."

"What girl?

"Old Torgrim's daughter. He was supposed to have dumped her in the stews of some foreign city. The letter is a ransom note from her."

"Let me see that letter again." Eadric studied more closely. "This is no simple ransom note. It is a plea to be rescued and tells the recipient who holds her and precisely where she is to be found.

I don't see how?

The clue is in the second sentence. "The ship was *Le Merle Noir*, but she writes the English name "Blackbird". Once you see that your mind is alerted and you notice the underlining and capital letters. 'Be Ruthless Unless Given Enough Silver" is Bruges and in the second sentence your friend Jacob leaps out of the water like a river salmon.

"Cunning little whore!"

"You seem to have failed miserably in your little scheme," said Eadric scornfully. "The moneyer has escaped justice and the vast wealth that you promised me has disappeared along with him. The king will not reissue the licence until the matter is resolved. His friendship with Wulfnoth goes back a long way and the fact that the thegn spoke up for Torgrim has given him pause for thought."

"I'm sure that cowhand Wulfnoth had something to do with his escape, but I lost all trace of him beyond Ordie and I know he has not returned to Compton."

"My spies confirm that he's not been seen in Sussex since the meeting of the Witan, which would suggest that he and his friend have found sanctuary in the Danelaw. And now, brother, the daughter comes back to haunt you."

"But your men have intercepted her letter."

"True, but there may be more."

"I should have drowned the bitch myself in the River Itchen!"

"Perhaps. Perhaps not."

"But if Wulfnoth learns of her plight, he has powerful friends who will champion her cause against me."

"If you can prove he was implicated in Torgrim's escape then perhaps some profit will eventually come out of it."

"How so?"

"If the king is satisfied of the moneyer's guilt and Wulfnoth's complicity in his escape then the thegn must be outlawed for aiding a nithing and we can rid the Council of an irritation."

"Yes, but meantime I must send someone to Flanders and have the girl killed, before she can implicate me."

"That would be foolish. Go to Flanders by all means, but wring the truth out of her. Find out where her father could have hidden his treasure and find me some real evidence to link Wulfnoth to the old man's escape. When you have done that you can kill her or simply cut out her tongue and chop off her hands if you prefer. But, whatever you do, steer clear of the count; he'll show little mercy to those who flout his laws."

"Let's hope I can find her before she sends more letters."

"Fortunately we have friends in Bruges who are less squeamish than the count. Go to the house of Wenemar, the swordsmith, who lives near the fort. He will help you find this girl if she is in the city. When you return, come straight to me. Don't attempt anything stupid on your own."

Eadric dismissed his brother with a flick of his hand and returned to his work.

Across France with Father Martin

Cerdic's fever broke after several days and despite having been at the very threshold of the abyss the grim reaper failed to gather him into his barn. Once the crisis had passed his body began the slow process of self-healing and he fell into a deep unconscious sleep. Father Martin could do little for him but maintain the fire, moisten his patient's lips and wait.

Then one night shortly before Matins when the rest of the community was wearily making its way to chapel, the monk, who was placing another log on the infirmary fire and counting his good fortune in being released from attendance at the night office, heard a profound murmur of contentment as the foreign seaman yawned, stretched and re-entered the world of the quick.

"So you have decided to come back to us, my son. God be praised!"

"Cerdic blinked, "I was not aware I had been away, but I feel that I have been trampled by a wild boar. And I know I could eat one."

"You will have to make do with the contents of this pot-au-feu and think yourself lucky you are in the infirmary. The other monks won't smell flesh until Sunday, but the Rule of St Benedict allows for the sick to have meat to build up their strength."

"But I am not sick," declared Cerdic and sprang up to prove it, but only proved just how unsteady he was on his feet having lain supine for the best part of a week.

Father Martin's sinewy arm shot out and supported the young man and the monk insisted that he sit on the stone bed for several minutes before attempting to rise again. "You have been delirious for several days, my son, and we were convinced your soul was heading for paradise. Father Abbot set me to watch over you and the whole community has been praying for your recovery. It seems God is not ready for you yet. When the fever broke Father Abbot insisted that I kept a pot of stew over the fire to nourish you as soon as you woke up."

Taking a wooden vessel from the board that held the various utensils required in the infirmary he ladled out a steaming bowl of rich stew from the pot and placed it in the hands of the young man. Cerdic fell upon it with relish; hunger having driven all other thoughts from his mind.

"Take your time, young Cerdic," cautioned the monk smiling. "You have your whole life ahead of you." And he reluctantly filled the bowl again.

Cerdic dipped his hunk of black bread into the bowl and then looked up into the monk's wistful face. "Are you not going to share a bowl with me?"

Father Martin grinned. "Father Abbot said I could wipe out the pot when you had finished. He holds it a great sin to waste God's bounty."

"Have some of mine, Father. There can be little left." And he held out the bowl to the priest.

"No, my son, There's still plenty in the pot. I made sure of that!" And the grin widened. "Our Lord praised the wise virgins who took enough oil to refill their lamps at the marriage feast. Besides, Father Abbot believes I should build up my strength for the journey we are going to make, so a few pieces of meat are hardly likely to endanger my soul."

The mention of the journey brought everything flooding back and Cerdic was despondent. "How could I have forgotten my duty? Have I really been lying here so long? Will my master ever forgive my incompetence? Is Hild now really lost forever?"

"Questions! Questions! Questions! God has not forsaken you so I doubt if He will forsake a young girl who is obviously so dear to your heart! Trust in God. In a few days you may be fit to travel."

"A few days! I must go at once."

"No," said the monk firmly. "Tonight you shall sleep here in the Abbey. Tomorrow if you are strong enough we shall visit Father Abbot and when he sanctions it, we shall set out for Flanders. Remember, Cerdic, I too have waited to make this journey. When it is light we shall go to the chapel and ask God to bless our enterprise. If it is His will that I will reach Cambrai and that you rescue your sweetheart, then in a few days we shall both feel like two young men starting out on a great adventure.

Cerdic was filled with admiration at the blind faith of the old monk and with shock at his insight. He himself had barely known the girl for a day, before watching her wretched treatment in the market place, and only now did it dawn on him that the monk was right. He had indeed been in love with Hild from the time he had last seen her.

The realisation only served to intensify his wish to set out for Bruges at once, but at that moment a bell rang to summon all to chapel for Mass and Cerdic, determined to show that he had completely recovered, accompanied Father Martin.

Having broken his fast, the monk was unable to receive the Eucharist that morning so he did not join his brothers in the choir, but elected to stand at the back of the chapel, a fact that suited Cerdic, who was able to take the precaution of standing with his back against the west door in order to seek its support should exhaustion suddenly make him feel unwell. During the Abbot's sermon, however, he was particularly grateful to be able to sit on the cold stone bench that ran along the rear wall on either side of the door.

After Mass there was great excitement among the Community at seeing the young seaman whom they had believed to be at death's door so obviously alive and well. When Father Abbot emerged they fell silent and he eyed Cerdic quizzically before smiling.

"So," he said, "God has seen fit to put you on the road to recovery, my son. Now we must get some colour back in those cheeks. You look as pale as that reprobate monk who has been looking after you."

Father Martin cackled in delight.

"I am fully recovered, Father, and must leave for Bruges at once," protested Cerdic, but Father Abbot would hear none of it. He was adamant that they should remain at least two more nights to ensure that both were fully fit to undertake the arduous journey across France.

They would remain in the infirmary and although Father Martin was expected to join his brothers in chapel for the various offices of the day, he was once again excused the night office and instructed to take all his meals with his patient.

"Travellers," said Father Abbot with an air of mischief, "need to be sustained for a journey. It is fortuitous that one of our calves was drowned in Le Mascaret and the brothers of the kitchen have hung the sides for Easter, so I have instructed them to send a generous portion down to you." He winked broadly at Cerdic and then sighed. "I know Father Martin would prefer a life of abstinence, but I rely on you to see that he eats properly from now on. We would not want the Community at Haspres to think we starved our old monks to death in Normandy."

Cerdic was about to protest at the delay, but the abbot raised a hand and continued. "Time in preparation is never wasted. Father Martin tells me that you were in charge of your master's horses so your responsibility will be to select a couple of suitable mounts from the stables. Take your time for they must carry you throughout Normandy, France and Flanders these next two weeks. Make sure they are sound in wind and hoof. Father Martin will be in charge of provisions and clothing. In the meantime Father Prior will organise the manuscripts for Haspres and the other Abbeys of Cambrai. Tomorrow we shall plan your route and I will prepare letters of introduction to various monasteries where you will find hospitality on your way.

Conscious that his own impetuosity had already resulted in disaster, Cerdic resigned himself to the delay and protested no more but took himself off to the stables to look over the horses.

Cerdic and Father Martin eventually rode out of Jumieges both wearing the black habit of St Benedict.

It had been thought prudent to disguise the Englishman for a number of reasons. Although Normandy was by and large peaceful, France was lawless and a pair of monks would offer fewer prospects of rich pickings for the bands of cutthroats and thieves that haunted its highways. In addition the cloak not only hid Cerdic's weapons, which might have suggested an armed escort for a monk carrying rich treasure, but which would also enable him to conceal his limited command of French under the guise of a vow of silence.

Their journey through Normandy was uneventful. Bypassing Rouen they covered over thirty miles to reach the monastery of Neufchatel-en-Bray where Father Martin received a warm welcome, since as Cellarer of Jumieges he had been instrumental in provisioning the new foundation some three decades earlier. This fact and their status as travellers ensured that they were accommodated in the guest-house and, after Cerdic had overseen the stabling of the horses, they dined well, enjoying particularly the soft cream cheese for which the abbey was famous and a whole jug of wine between the two of them.

On their second day they entered France crossing the Bresle at Aumale where they spent the night in the hay store of a deserted dwelling taking it in turns to keep watch lest they be taken by surprise, but apart from the howling of wolves they remain undisturbed. The third evening found them outside the Cathedral at Amiens where once again the abbot's letter opened the door to hospitality.

Two days later they reached Haspres without mishap and were relieved to deliver the sacred texts into the safe keeping of the Abbey. Father Martin's had reached his monastic home, but it was to be another two days before arrangements were made for two young monks to accompany Cerdic on the final leg of his journey.

Until Death Us Do Part

As the year 1000 approached the whole of Christianity cringed with apprehension, convinced that the apocalypse revealed by St John was indeed about to happen. In recent years comets had stalked the night skies; the City of Rome had been razed to the ground; and now news had reached Bruges that the sacred Church of St Michael the Archangel off the coast of Brittany had been totally consumed by fire. Even the hardest of hearts began to fear that the end of the world would occur sometime before the millennium.

The threat of impending doom ensured that the collegiate church of St Donatian was full to capacity on the Third Sunday after Easter. The count, surrounded by military and civic dignitaries, was joined by the families of the men of property, the well-to-do burghers and the artisans, while the common people, unable to find room, thronged the great sixteen-sided ambulatory leaving the streets of the town deserted. Thus it was that Alena's marriage to Jacob was not only blessed by the Church, but witnessed by practically all the citizens of Bruges.

Groom and bride had been reserved places on the left hand side of the sanctuary opposite Baldwin's seat and moments before the Benedictine monks of the chapter filed through the congregation they made a striking entrance. Jacob, resplendent in imperial purple silk smuggled out of Byzantium, nodded respectfully to the count but did not deign to acknowledge the presence of his former associates preferring to fix his eyes on the sanctuary straight ahead of him in what he hoped would be seen as an air of grandeur appropriate in a rich and successful merchant with international connections. Alena in contrast had chosen a simple white tunic for the occasion, tucked her luxurious black hair under a cap and kept her eyes focused on the stone flags of the church.

As the last haunting notes of the introit seemed to linger high above the faithful, the provost, still smarting at having to give in to blackmail, made his way slowly down the aisle determined to get his own back on the bridegroom, who had threatened to expose his regular visits to the brothel.

He had only seen Alena on a couple of occasions before and then only fleetingly as he stole secretly up the back stairs of that godforsaken house. Now as she stood before him and raised her wide, dark eyes from the floor he wondered how such a demure creature could bear to marry that vile procurer of flesh. No doubt the wedding had been arranged, he thought, perhaps she was the sister of some foreign client, the price to be paid for silence. She of course would be completely innocent of the secret use he made of the premises.

Therefore, when it came to his sermon he could not, resist the temptation of dwelling on the epistle of the day repeating the opening words of St Peter. "Refrain from carnal desires which war against the soul" and then drawing a comparison between the Jacob of the

Old Testament symbolizing the Jewish people enslaved by sin and the portly whoremonger whose establishment had been a centre of degradation in the town. "Yet," he marvelled, "with the day of tribulation at hand this Jacob of the Steegherei had been brought back to the Church by his love for a sweet innocent woman and now wished to regularise the state of his relationship through the indissoluble sacrament of Marriage."

Jacob was furious that his squalid little sideline should be so blatantly exposed and he would have risked denouncing the hypocrisy of the cleric had not Alena placed a restraining hand on his arm.

At the end of the ceremony the provost drawing him to one side spoke menacingly through his teeth, "Break your promise to me and I will see to it that you face excommunication. Then the people of this town will tear down your house and destroy you."

Turning to Alena he said simply, "Daughter, if your husband ever gives you cause for grief the Church will always protect you."

Within an hour the bells of St Donatian's were ringing out over the town in celebration and Jacob, who realised he had made a dangerous enemy in the Church, had enough wit to make the best of a bad job. He emerged into the sunlight of the Burg extolling the sanctity of marriage and the virtues of his wife. At least, he conjectured, such a public declaration of his "conversion" served also to raise the profile of his marriage. All of Bruges now acknowledged her as his wife and he encouraged the spread of a rumour that Hild was, not only her cousin, but the heiress of a great fortune in England who would soon marry a rich nobleman from Italy. That, he thought would scotch any lustful intentions of the Hounds of Satan to gang rape either of his women.

As to the Church a large donation to the Cathedral and the promise of more would ensure the favour of the bishop and seal the lips of the provost. For the time being he needed to appear in the full glow of his new respectability.

Much to his customers' dismay the facilities of the whorehouse were suspended. The whores would remain since he still owned them, but they would be given other duties and fed in lieu of wages. Alena and Hild would continue to run his legitimate trade while he ingratiated himself with his fellow merchants by showing an enthusiastic interest in civic matters. This was only to be a temporary arrangement, however, as he had no intention of abandoning his lucrative business in selling flesh. As soon as he could settle his difficulties with his fellow knights he planned to reopen the brothel and toyed with the idea of adding blackmail to his portfolio.

For her own reasons Alena acted the part of a dutiful wife, well aware that her husband's reformation would not last. When Jacob was out the doors were securely locked and when they visited the market Walram and one of the whores always accompanied them.

The only thing that continued to worry her was what the future held for Hild.

Although Jan remained gravely ill he seemed to rally and there was hope that he would recover. Determined to scotch any civil proceedings that might be brought against him, Jacob secretly visited his old whoremaster early one morning and gave him a ruby broach on the understanding that he withdraw all allegations of the assault and let it be known that his injuries were the result of a drunken fall. If Jan then went back on his word, the merchant could always claim that the ring had been stolen from him by the former servant and any beating was merely just punishment for dishonesty. At last he began to feel safe.

Gathering of the Hounds

When Beorhtric arrived at Wenemar's he found that a meeting of the Knights of St. Hubert had been called for that morning. Erembald had already arrived and was seated in the great hall with the swordsmith. Galbert had sent word that the Count required his presence and Gervaise, who had called the meeting, was late as usual.

"This is indeed a surprise, my Mercian friend. What brings you to Bruges? Do you come here on your brother's business or is this a social call?"

"Eadric is indeed interested in ordering another consignment of weapons, but there is a personal matter in which I may need your help."

"That sounds intriguing," Erembald was grinning. "No doubt there'll be some pleasure in it for us."

"The Knights of St. Hubert always like to help their friends," said Wenemar. "What is it that we can do for you?"

"It's rather delicate you see since I nurse a grievance against a member of your club."

For a moment Erembald and Wenemar became guarded and waited for him to continue.

"Oh, no, not Galbert though he has no love for me."

"Galbert is a snob," said Wenemar. He enjoys our sport, but resents anyone whose ancestors have not served the Counts of Flanders for over a hundred years. However, we need him. His membership of the Knights gives us............ respectability."

"No it's not he, not one of your inner circle, a lesser light, more of a hanger on."

They relaxed.

"The whoremonger, Jacob, has something of mine. He was well paid to do a job, but it seems that greed has got the better of him and he plans to sell it to the highest bidder."

At that moment Gervaise was shown in and threw himself into a chair theatrically. "Jan is dead," he announced abruptly, "and his cousin claims that Jacob has finally killed him. Apparently our friend was seen leaving the house shortly before they found the old man lying on the floor. In his hand they found Jacob's ruby broach, which he must have torn from the whoremonger's cloak. It looks as though our false friend is back in our power."

"You are in luck, friend Beorhtric," said Erembald brightly. "It seems we all wish to teach the merchant a lesson."

"What is your grievance against him? I thought he was a useful source of entertainment."

"He's always been good for a fresh supply of choice meat for our table, but he recently returned from England with two beautiful women and refused to share them with us," explained Wenemar.

"When we demanded our rights he married the dark-haired Alena and claims the other one has royal connections and we may not have her!" Erembald could not hide his resentment.

Beorhtric burst out laughing. "You are easily fooled. Alena is a common slut renowned in England for her uncommon skills in the bedroom. You're welcome to her. The other is the daughter of a Danish mintmaster and my property. Her father denied me a share in his business and has escaped me. When I have forced her to divulge her father's whereabouts, you can willingly force her to open her legs as often as you like. She's always been destined for the whorehouse and Jacob was charged to see that she got there. His punishment we can decide together.

Erembald was furious. "A common whore? Just a common whore! The bitch is going to pay for taunting us," he said, somewhat irrationally. He had been infatuated by Alena's looks and convinced that she must come from a respectable family. He knew how to satisfy women and had envisaged taking her with such gentle mastery that her shock at being violated would gradually have turned to wonder and joy at the pleasurable climax she would undoubtedly achieve. Now he wanted her experience to be one of pain and lasting horror. He would shag her witless and leave her battered, bloody and hysterical.

Gervaise was equally incensed but his anger was directed solely against the merchant whom he had introduced into their select group and who had not only treated them shabbily but with contempt. "I vote we deal with that great tub of lard once and for all. He should be arrested for the murder of his servant. I want to see him squirm under torture until he begs our forgiveness and then his fate is entirely in our hands.

Beorhtric did not want to get involved with the courts. It wouldn't help him and could lessen his chances of tracking down Torgrim and the wealth that he had spirited away. Besides he was personally looking forward to beating the whoremonger to death for trying to cheat him. "Surely, gentlemen, this is a matter of honour for you as much as it is for me and honour should be satisfied before we resort to the courts. We should confront him face to face and I need to question the women before you exact your revenge on them."

Wenemar would have cheerfully marched over the Breidelstraat with Beorhtric and enjoyed a sadistic pleasure in using some of his latest instruments of torture, but murder would only risk the count's wrath and put them all outside the law so he cautioned against precipitate action, suggesting that they wait to consult Galbert.

"This is a civil matter not a military one and as burgrave I represent the civil authority in Bruges." Gervaise was jealous of the castellan and his influence with the Count.

"You are right of course, my friend, but Galbert is a founder member of the Knights of St. Hubert too and, as one of us, he also has the right to have a say in this matter."

"Well at least we should send word to Jacob that Jan is dead and that a certain piece of jewellery makes him the obvious suspect. It will make him sweat and he'll be begging for our help before nightfall."

"We hardly want to warn him of our intentions," said Erembald darkly, but the glint in his eye returned as he added, "It would be a shame not to witness all their faces when the truth dawns on them."

"Then we wait for Galbert."

"If you insist, Wenemar. We'll give him till suppertime. After that he forfeits his right to express an opinion and we can act as we think fit." Gervaise had to be satisfied.

Beorhtric felt frustrated. He'd had a long journey and was eager to complete his business and take his revenge, but for his part he had to be content, knowing that as a foreigner he had no rights under Flemish law and he dare not antagonise the only friends he had in Bruges.

A Moment of Crisis

Jacob had spent most of the morning out on the coast beyond the marshes scanning the horizon for the sight of *Le Merle Noir* laden with merchandise and hopefully carrying the ransom that Alena and Hild had assured him would be paid by Torgrim. It was two days after the deadline he had set and he had half made up his mind that if it didn't arrive that day he would cut his losses.

When he returned Alena greeted him with the news from the market place that Jan had suffered a relapse and been found dead.

"Dead?" said Jacob in disbelief, "but he was well enough when I left him this morning."

"You fool. You should have kept well clear of him. If you were seen there, you could be blamed for the old man's death."

Jacob could have kicked himself for his stupidity. Despite his care he might have been seen. If only he had mentioned to someone that the broach was missing. To do so now would sound like a feeble excuse especially if a witness could place him at the scene of the crime. What crime?

He thought desperately then blustered, "The old man was alive when I left. As for the broach they will think I must have dropped it."

"You left your broach?

"I gave it to him to keep his mouth shut. I thought the old fool was going to live. What am I going to do?" and he sat wringing his large hands pathetically.

Putting her arms around him as she would to comfort a distraught child Alena whispered, "Do nothing. Leave everything to me. No one has mentioned murder. You are safe for the moment."

That was true thought Jacob, but for how long. When the broach was recognised, he would surely be questioned and his life would be back in the hands of the Hounds of Satan. Suddenly his mind was made up and he leapt out of the chair, knocking Alena brusquely to the floor.

"I have to go out this afternoon to arrange transport," he told her curtly. "Make sure that Hild is ready to travel. We leave for Pavia tomorrow. There is no sign of a ransom and Byzantine gold will make a powerful bargaining counter with my enemies at home." With that he disappeared slamming the door violently behind him.

His manner and the announcement took Alena totally by surprise. Having secured her own position she had assumed Hild safe too. Even if the letter did not bring rescue she had allowed herself to believe that her hold over the merchant was such that she could convince him of Hild's indispensability and that they would ultimately escape from his clutches. Now the great edifice of her plan was beginning to crumble. She needed time to think.

Retribution

With a considerable struggle Alena and Walram had dragged the great tub into the kitchen and by mid afternoon they were filling it with water heated over the fire. It was an extravagant use of fuel but Alena had once been made to prepare such a vessel for the king's treasurer, Theodoric, who claimed it made him feel like the king.

By the time it was half full Walram was beginning to find the kitchen too warm and wandered over to open the reed shutter that covered the windhole and enjoy the fresh air so he was first to shout a warning that Jacob was making his way along the jetty. Before the whoremonger arrived, however, he was back in the cellar and Alena was ready to give the performance of her life.

Slipping out of her clothes she donned the fine long red tunic that she had found among the belongings of the merchant's former wife who had clearly been a relatively slim creature in her youth. It was a good fit, loose at the bust, but tight enough to accentuate the physical contours of her hips.

Then taking care to lock Hild safely in the bedroom, she returned to the kitchen. There she waited.

* * * * *

Having arranged for two of his wagons to arrive at daybreak Jacob did not want to be seen on the streets and was surprised to find the door barred against him. For a moment he thought that Jan must have slipped out. Then he remembered that Jan was dead and he had left his household in the charge of a woman he had known barely four weeks. An uncomfortable feeling of apprehension came over him and he banged on the oak panels. When this elicited no response he became worried and beads of cold sweat broke out on his forehead. The bitch must have taken the opportunity of his absence to steal his money and escape with her precious little companion into the back alleys of the town or take ship to God knows where? In his panic he began to pound on the door, and it was only when exertion and frustration had brought him to his knees that he finally heard the beam being withdrawn.

"Why, my lord, you are earlier than I expected," Alena said helping him to his feet, "but I trust you will find everything to your satisfaction."

"I thought," he began gasping for breath, but failed to complete his sentence as he was overcome by a fit of coughing.

With difficulty Alena helped him to his feet and across the threshold. "Come, sit by the fire," she said and steered him into the warm kitchen where she knelt at his feet and began to remove his mud-splattered boots.

As he recovered he looked down at her and realised that he could see right down her cleavage. The sight of her heaving breasts drove away his fears and he became aware of the huge tub. Gradually it dawned on him that Alena had been preparing a surprise for him. He tousled her hair and began to luxuriate in his good fortune.

She looked up and smiled. "An Eastern Prince deserves such attention when he returns to his tent," she murmured as she began to undress him.

It should always be like this he thought.

Moments later having tipped the last pot of hot water into the tub she invited him to step into his bath and when he had lowered himself into the water she knelt behind him and began to massage his shoulders.

"Do you really intend to sell Hild into slavery in Pavia, then?" she asked innocently.

"Of course. Your idea of the ransom has failed. I was a fool to listen to you."

Alena said nothing but eased him back gently so that the warm water ran up over his chest and shoulders.

"I trust you have taught her some of your skills. In the East they expect a woman to pleasure a man. It's said they have three or four virgins to bathe them."

"Would you like her to assist us so that you can judge if I have trained her well?"

"I would enjoy that. She's still a virgin I hope. They demand that. Pity though," he chuckled. "I could have fucked her after you. I suppose I can fondle her and she can give me the kiss of life."

"Close your eyes tightly and I'll call her," she whispered letting her lips caress his ear.

He closed his eyes and surrendered himself to pleasure.

"Come in," she cried. "The master requires your assistance with his toilet."

Jacob immediately felt aroused, but the warmth of the water and the caress of Alena's hands induced a feeling of lethargy and he began to drift into oblivion.

He felt other hands on his arms and his legs being lifted upwards so that he was slipping deeper into the water. The grip tightened and he felt himself sliding under the surface. In sudden panic he opened his eyes and the last things he saw were the grinning faces of Judith and Ogive as his head was forced down and water rushed into his open mouth. For almost a minute he thrashed about, but the strong hands held him and eventually all motion ceased.

The Whoremonger of Bruges was dead.

The Protection of the Church

There was little time to celebrate their new freedom and the three women set about removing the evidence of their actions. Women who killed their husbands and servants who killed their masters could expect no mercy. The bath was emptied put back under the ladder and refilled with sacks of grain. Jacob's body was dried and dressed again in the tunic he had been wearing earlier. The corpse was laid back in his chair at the table on which were set the remains of a large meal and two empty jugs of wine. Then they spilt wine on the body and a considerable amount on the table so that it ran over the edge. Finally they smashed one of the platters against a wall and dropped the third wine jug on the floor where it lay in several pieces. With the scene set Alena sent Walram to the St Donatian's with the request that the head of the religious community come at once to the house on the Steegherei.

The provost's first thought was that Jacob had decided to renege on his promise and was going to threaten to expose him after all, unless he paid handsomely to preserve his good name. But then the message would have come from the whoremonger himself, not his wife. Perhaps Alena had learnt the dreadful truth about her husband's clandestine sideline or worse still the evil beast might have abused his new wife. The provost

210

was in a quandary so he armed himself with a dagger concealed beneath his robes and set off to make the journey over the Briedelstraat. Five minutes later he arrived outside the brothel where he was greeted by a distressed Alena who grabbed his arm and quickly ushered him inside.

"Thank God you've come, Father. My brute of a husband flew into a rage at dinnertime and after beating me like a servant he collapsed on the floor. My cousin Hild and I managed to get him into a chair, but he is unconscious and despite all our efforts we cannot revive him."

The provost observed the state of disarray and stepped carefully over the broken shards to examine the reclining figure. Obviously the man had consumed far too much wine and was intoxicated, but then he thought drunks usually sleep fitfully. Jacob's breathing, however, was not even laboured. He put his ear as close as he could to the man's mouth and heard nothing. Then he felt all over the chest and felt nothing. He raised the eyelids with his thumbs and moved the head from side to side, nothing! Clearly all vital signs had ceased.

"I fear, my lady," he said, "he is beyond anyone's help."

Alena gasped and held onto the table for support. "Surely, "she said, "You can do something."

"I'm afraid not, my lady. Your husband is dead."

"Then I am alone in the world."

"Do not distress yourself, lady. If the truth were known you are well rid of him."

"I know he could be cruel, but he was my husband. Now I am a widow and I have to fend for myself. Who will protect me against those who would try to steal my property?"

"But the law will protect your rights."

"Will the law save me from those who people call the Hounds of Satan who have already vowed to have me and my young companion, Hild, satisfy their lust? My husband may have been an evil man, Father, but at least he stood against such debauchery.

For a moment the provost choked. The idea of Jacob as a champion of virtue striving against the sins of the flesh was too preposterous. The Church might sometimes turn a blind eye to prostitution as an understandable evil. However, the provost had indeed heard of the Hounds of Satan. They were a different matter all together. They preyed upon the innocent. Rumours of their feasts abounded in the city, but they were powerful men and few dare accuse them openly.

"If the rumours about them are true the Church will speak out and condemn them," the provost assured her.

"They are true, Father. For myself I care not, but my companion is a child, a young virgin for whom I beg the protection of our Holy Mother, the Church. Who else can protect the innocent?"

"You shall have it, daughter. The Church will not fail you, or your young companion."

"Thank you, Father, but what of my property? Will you speak to the count on my behalf? You are the one man in the city I can trust." The dark frightened eyes appealed to him.

It was not often that a vulnerable woman threw herself on his mercy, especially one with such rare looks and such a fine figure. Instinctively he held her in his arms.

"My child," he said, "you are safe with me. The Church will protect you."

For a few moments she allowed herself to be pressed against his body, so that he could feel her breasts rising and falling against his cassock. Eventually she shyly withdrew from his embrace and letting her eyes widen innocently she declared, "I shall not forget your kindness, my Lord Provost." Before he could answer, however, her eyes clouded again and she added tearfully, "But how can we be sure the count will guarantee my property?"

"I promise I will go and speak with him tonight," the provost heard himself say.

"Go now then, for pity's sake, and while you are gone I will bolt the doors and wait eagerly for your return."

With that she hurried him out of the house and on to the quay.

Count Baldwin who had ruled Flanders since 988 was a man in his late forties with shoulder-length hair and a finely trimmed beard a full five inches in length. He ruled with an iron fist moving from castle to castle, from Ghent to Saint-Omer, from Oudenaarde to Bruges holding court and dispensing Justice. This year the Spring Court was due to begin after the Feast of the Ascension, but he had already spent two weeks in Bruges planning alterations to the defences of the city.

When the dark-haired, grey-eyed visitor arrived from England the count had been sitting over a huge meal discussing these with his gaunt castellan, Galbert, and Baldwin had insisted that the newcomer join them at table.

"You are a rare visitor to Flanders, Wulfnoth of Compton, and most welcome."

"Thank you, my lord."

"I hear," the count continued, "that while the ealdormen are squabbling among themselves you are left to defend Aethelred's kingdom single-handed against the Danes."

His visitor inclined his head and smiled at the compliment.

"Aethelred allows them too much power. I may be a vassal of the King of France and the Holy Roman

Emperor, but in Flanders I hold absolute power and none of my subjects would dare oppose me. Consequently the Danes haven't troubled us for over a hundred years."

"Flanders has been fortunate to have a dynasty of strong rulers."

It was the count's turn to acknowledge the complement.

"That may be true, but my ancestor's line of forts has proved an impregnable barrier on our great flood plains."

"Alas our land is too accessible to invasion, our long coastlines being far more vulnerable than those of Flanders. We must, therefore, build a fleet to defend our shores."

"But the ealdormen do not share your views."

"Alas no, at least not those of the Council who enjoy the king's favour."

"And you, I take it, are currently out of favour?"

"I have indeed incurred his displeasure, but powerful friends in the North protect me."

"I'm glad to hear it," said the count and pouring his guests a glass of wine brought an end to the social niceties. "But you also seek the help of an old friend. Otherwise you would not be here."

"It is not an affair of state, but a personal matter that brings me to Flanders."

"Indeed?"

"A good friend has been wrongly accused of a crime and his daughter sold into slavery," said Wulfnoth and, while he explained the circumstances to Baldwin, Galbert's eyes narrowed.

"You say the merchant Jacob bought her?" asked the castellan.

"My servant witnessed the sale, but it was arranged by one Beorhtric, a thegn from Mercia who with his brother Eadric has wormed his way into the king's favour."

"I've met the man," said Galbert slowly and added, trying to distance himself from trouble, "an upstart who has scant regard for truth and honour."

"That being the case you have my full authority to assist my friend, Lord Wulfnoth, in the rescue of this child."

At that moment there was a commotion outside the room and the captain of the guard entered to announce the arrival of the provost.

Pausing barely long enough to bow to the count, the cleric launched into a graphic account of Jacob's sudden demise, the threats of the Hounds of Satan and Alena's fear that she would now become destitute. Fearing that he had presented the case too passionately, he suddenly affected a pious seriousness.

"You, my lord," he concluded, "witnessed the Church give her blessing to this marriage barely six days since. The Church must seek justice for her now and ensure that her property rights as widow be confirmed."

"You argue eloquently, my lord provost, and you are sure the woman had nothing to do with the death of her husband?"

"Certainly not, my lord. She thought he had merely been taken ill, but I could tell at once, not only that he was dead, but that he had collapsed through over indulgence. He had a reputation for excess and there were clear signs that he had eaten a mountain of food and washed it down with vast quantities of wine."

"Then she shall certainly have my protection and all her rights."

At the mention of the Hounds of Satan the castellan's sallow complexion had turned a shade lighter, but discipline and self-preservation prevented him from betraying his connection with the Knights of St. Hubert.

"But tell me, provost," the count continued, "what do you know of a young woman by the name of Hild?"

"She is the young companion of the Lady Alena and, despite her distress, the mistress begs that she, too, receive your protection."

"She already has it. It seems, Wulfnoth, you are in time. Bring the young lady to me tomorrow so that I can meet her before you return to England. Galbert, accompany Lord Wulfnoth. Take troops with you and place a guard on the house.

"If you will accompany me, sir," the castellan bowed stiffly to Wulfnoth "we will collect a party of men from the garrison."

Baying of the Hounds

The bell of St Donatian's rang clearly over the city reminding people that the Collegiate Chapter was being called to attend Compline in the Cathedral.

"Six o'clock," said Erembald beaming at his colleagues. "Time for pleasure!"

"Galbert has had his chance," said Gervaise, thumping the table. I doubt he'd have the stomach for this business anyway."

"Can we go now, Wenemar?" Beorhtric was impatient and relieved that the castellan had not arrived.

"Yes," agreed the swordsmith. "We followed the rules. He cannot complain."

He gathered his tools and equipment and led the others out of the river door and into the boat that was moored at the little wooden jetty.

Five minutes later they had left the Groenerei and were rowing silently up the Steegherei where a few stokes of the oars brought them directly under the clients' door to the brothel.

"Give me the rope," cried Erembald and leapt agilely out of the boat.

"Quiet now," said Wenemar.

"We'll surprise the old fart," chuckled Gervaise as he clambered onto the quay.

"Not if you cackle like that."

"How do we get in?" asked Beorhtric.

"We'll check the shutters, but most likely we'll have to break the door. Your English axe should make short work of it."

"Remember my business first; your pleasure later."

"Perhaps we can combine the two," said Erembald enthusiastically rubbing his hands.

"Perhaps. Any luck?"

Unable to shift any of the shutters, Wenemar shook his head and then nodded to Beorhtric who drew the long-handled axe from his belt and gave it two swings around his head before planting his feet firmly on the ground in front of the entrance.

Seconds later the wood splintered and a further strike left a hole large enough for Wenemar to reach through, force the beam upwards and release the door.

The four men made straight for the living quarters on the upper floor where they burst into the main hall and discovered Alena and Hild cowering behind a settle.

"Where's that murdering bastard, Jacob?" asked Gervaise.

Alena shook her head and tried to shield her companion who was staring in horror at Beorhtric.

"He thought he could wriggle out of his commitment to us, but Jan was found dead this morning." The burgrave was enjoying his sense of power. "Your husband killed him and we hold his life in our hands."

"You'd better tell us, madam." Erembald smiled. "We have a score to settle with him and we want to see his face when his wife provides the entertainment for the Knights of St. Hubert"

"I see the Dogs of Satan have to hunt in a pack," the eyes flashed defiantly.

"We are no common breed, whore," snarled the young man cuffing her round the face. "We're thoroughbreds, Hounds of the Chase," and he would have struck her again had not Wenemar, given a shout of triumph from the bedroom.

"The coward's skulking in here pretending to be asleep," and with that he grabbed the whoremonger by the ankles and hauled him off the bed.

His three companions circled the body and began to kick the corpse on all sides in an attempt to force some response out of Jacob, but the merchant failed to react.

"The bastard's dead," said Erembald in disgust.

"You've killed him, Wenemar, you fool," complained the burgrave. "Now he'll miss our revenge and escape the law."

Wenemar knelt down and examined their intended victim. The grey complexion, the cold skin and above all the smell confirmed what had already begun to dawn on him and looking up at the others he burst out laughing. "The bastard's dead all right. He's been dead for quite some time."

In the commotion the two women had slipped quietly out, lifted the oak beam and were trying to ease open the main door when a powerful foot struck the timbers and it slammed shut. They were trapped.

Beorhtric picked up the screaming girl and carried her back into the hall, while Erembald attempted to drag the spitting and scratching Alena after him. It took the assistance of Wenemar to subdue her and she was flung unceremoniously onto the floor beside Hild.

"You'll pay for that, you bitch," screamed the young man, blood welling from gouges in his cheeks and he punched her full in the face so that she fell back striking her head on the floorboards.

"Enough," shouted Beorhtric, "You promised me I could question the child first. Then you can have your fun."

Grudgingly Erembald gave way.

Beorhtric pulled Hild to her feet and sat her in Jacob's large chair where she shrank back in terror at the man who had mutilated her father.

"We have unfinished business, child. Your traitorous father escaped with money belonging to me and has gone to ground. You are going to tell me where I might find him."

"Never!"

Relief that her father had escaped gave her courage, but two vicious slaps had her cringing against the back of the seat.

"These Hounds of Satan as the common people call them are my friends and they plan to mount you one by one until you learn that you are a bitch and come willingly when your masters call for you to entertain them. Now where is Torgrim likely to be hiding?"

Hild's eyes were wide with fear, but she shook her head and received another clout from the back of Beorhtric's hand.

"I don't know," she blubbered. "I thought he was dead."

"Liar, you wrote a note to him and sent it to that Sussex thegn, Wulfnoth, who has also conveniently disappeared."

Hild realised that they would not believe her and said no more.

"Leave her alone. Can't you see she doesn't know?" Alena was on her feet trying to shield the frightened girl. "The letter was to buy time."

"A likely story! And who, madam, would believe a whore caught stealing from the king's treasurer?"

"She's not a whore," cried Hild. "Everything she has done has been to protect me."

"Then you must owe her a great debt. Perhaps the Hounds of Satan should have her first while you watch and then perhaps you will answer my question."

Gervaise and Erembald didn't need a second invitation and pinioning Alena to the ground, while Wenemar took out four spiked iron rings and began to hammer them into the floor.

Hild screamed, but could not see what was going on as Beorhtric had pushed the seat back against the wall and was lashing her wrists to the arms of the chair and obscuring her view in the process. When he had secured her she could see that Wenemar had attached ropes to Alena's wrists and ankles and the others were threading them through the rings.

Beorhtric joined them and each took up the strain so that Alena was spread eagled in the centre of the hall.

"Leave her alone," Hild yelled.

"Say nothing," Alena managed to scream through her teeth as she felt the strain on her joints, but the burning pain she had been expecting didn't materialise as the four men secured the taught ropes to the iron rings.

"We may tear her apart later when we have finished with her, but before then you will have told our English friend everything he wants to know," Erembald confided as he passed Hild's chair.

"But I know nothing!" She was sobbing uncontrollably.

"You'll be begging to tell us soon," said Erembald and added in a whisper, "Let's see which dog is first to get the scent of the quarry."

Wenemar was holding four straws and said, "Choose," as he held them out to the others.

Erembald chose first, followed by Gervaise, but Beorhtric refused saying, "Other men's whores are not to my taste. I shall save my energy to bring back some colour to this girl's cheeks if she is still obstinate."

"As you wish," said Wenemar politely and selected the third straw with his teeth before dropping the fourth on the floor.

A comparison quickly determined the running order. Much to Erembald's disappointment Gervaise would lead the pack, he would follow and Wenemar bring up the rear.

While the burgrave struggled to get his tunic off and discard his breeches, Erembald and Wenemar beat the table, roared encouragement and howled like a pack of wolves.

Gervaise walked over to the supine figure and bowed to her. "Madam," he said, "I have the honour of being the first to serve the widow of that evil bastard, Jacob, the notorious whoremonger of Bruges." And leering at her he bent down and ripped the thin red tunic from neck to hem. He noticed that Alena's strong breasts looked curiously flat as her taut body lay exposed beneath him, but the sight of her futile struggles aroused him and he howled as he knelt between her outstretched thighs.

The pack took up the howl as he threw himself forward onto her, brutally forced entry and began to work himself up into a rhythm.

Hild let out a high-pitched scream and the room was suddenly silent, but Gervaise did not notice striving desperately again and again as he lingered on the brink of ejaculation.

Alena had clamped her eyes tightly to shut out what was happening to her so she did not see the knife blade at her throat. She only opened them again when the arterial blood began spurting all over her face.

Erembald and Wenemar, who had been taken totally by surprise, were quickly pinioned and bound by the soldiers.

The castellan dropped his knife and stood up motioning the soldiers to remove the half-decapitated torso of the burgrave. Then going over to the window he opened it and shouted down to the captain of the guards he had posted round the house, "The women are safe. We have caught the culprits. You can return to the fort."

Wulfnoth, impressed by the efficiency of the castellan, put up his sword and making his way over to Hild found that the girl had fainted. Not wishing to wrench her back to reality until order had been restored he began quietly to loosen the cords that bound her arms to the chair.

Meanwhile the two remaining soldiers set about cutting the ropes that held the blood-soaked Alena spread-eagled in such a grotesque manner. When her limp body didn't respond to their attempts to revive her they assumed that she must have died under her dreadful ordeal.

"Leave her and take this carrion downstairs," Galbert ordered and held the door open while they carried away the corpse of Gervaise.

"Say nothing if you want to save your skins," he muttered under his breath to the two remaining Knights of St Hubert. "The women are under the protection of the Count and anyone attempting to harm them could face the rope or worse. With luck and money put into the right hands you might escape with your lives." He could feel their hatred, but both nodded and wisely held their tongues. Then pushing the two of them through the door in front of him he followed the soldiers downstairs.

"I can do that," whispered Hild as the thegn struggled to free her legs. "Help Alena."

Seeing that she was quite composed Wulfnoth nodded, went over to the woman and covered her naked body in his cloak. Then gently supporting her head he was trying to wipe way some of the blood from her mouth when she coughed and opened her eyes looking straight into the his face. For a moment she saw only pity in those eyes but then shock as Beorhtric's axe struck his shoulder.

Moments before the castellan had broken in, second sight had alerted the Mercian to danger and he had stepped unobserved into the bedroom. He would have fled altogether but the bedroom had no window and so he waited listening through a crack in the door.

As soon as the soldiers and the castellan left the room he saw his chance to escape and edged the door open. It appeared that only one man stood in his way. Slipping his axe from his belt he was easing his way into the room to make a dash for the exit when he recognised the Thegn of Compton. In a frenzy of hatred he swung the axe at the dark head and would have split it in two had not a cowled figure crashed into him at the critical moment.

In the melee that followed, Beorhtric leapt for the windhole and disappeared.

When the castellan returned he was shocked to find Alena cradling the injured Wulfnoth in her arms while a Benedictine monk was comforting the girl.

PART THREE

A Woman of Some Importance

"In order for such a woman to act with good judgement she must know the yearly outcome of her estate. She must be knowledgeable enough to protect her interests so that she cannot be deceived. She should know how to manage accounts, attend to them often and oversee her agents' treatment of her tenants and men."

Christine de Pisan (1365 – C.1430)

The Count's Justice

Law and order invariably depended on the presence of the count. Whenever he was in residence the townspeople of Bruges could seek justice through his court, held for several days during his visitation, so the case of the old whorehouse as it became commonly known was heard almost immediately. However, it was faced with a problem, since the burgrave, who would normally have presented the case, was not only dead but had apparently been the principal villain. The task, therefore, fell to the castellan, who, bowing formally to the count, stood for a moment looking around the court with the air of one who had a thorough distaste for the business, but who saw his duty to present a disinterested assessment of the facts so that justice might be done.

Careful to keep his own involvement out of it he laid the blame squarely on the foreign agent Beorhtric and the dead man who had apparently been conducting a vendetta against the merchant Jacob.

"They," he declared, "had planned the whole thing. Erembald and Wenemar, who had also been swindled by the merchant, were foolishly persuaded to join them, believing the intention was merely to frighten Jacob. When the merchant apparently collapsed and died they were petrified believing that they would face execution under the new laws passed by the count.

"Naturally, they wanted to leave, but the burgrave had threatened to lay the whole blame on them if they left before he had taken his revenge on the merchant's widow. They had been hoping to slip away quietly, but the intimidating foreigner Beorhtric had barred their way. However, when the soldiers arrived they had immediately given themselves up without a struggle and, having sung like a couple of raucous godwits in flight, now threw themselves on the mercy of the count.

"The Mercian, it transpires, not only swindles honest men out of their businesses, but also kidnaps young girls and sells them to unscrupulous brothel keepers. Regrettably, in the confusion of the arrest, the foreign mercenary managed to escape justice. The burgrave, however, had been caught violating the woman in a bestial manner and had been summarily put to death. They were the real criminals. One had escaped justice and the other had been justly punished. Wenemar who has served the Count faithfully for many years and due for an honourable retirement and young Erembald were clearly unwilling accomplices. "They", concluded the castellan, "should be treated leniently."

Alena was about to protest, but the castellan held up his hand and continued.

"It is all very well to punish the guilty," he said, "but this court has a duty to the victims.

The woman Alena had only just become the bride of a rich merchant and looked forward to a long and prosperous married life. When her Jacob died suddenly from over indulgence the accused not only abused her husband's body, but attempted to rape the widow and now she faces an uncertain future. Surely in the interests of simple justice this court must ask the count to grant her his protection and give her sole ownership of all her former husband's possessions.

Alena was astounded, but a murmur of approval swept round the court.

"In addition," she heard the castellan continue, "She should receive a wergild not only from the estate of the late burgrave but also from Wenemar and Erembald for although they did not actually take any part in the violation of her they were not brave enough to stand up to the vicious threats of two inhuman creatures. Cowardice surely does not deserve death," he concluded. "Let their punishment be banishment, a hefty fine and a lifetime of shame."

The murmur of approval became a roar.

Convalescence

Wulfnoth was unable to attend the court. Although the axe had missed its mark, the blade had bitten deep into his left shoulder and was a matter of considerable concern. The castellan had insisted the thegn be taken back to the fort to be treated by the garrison physician who had bound the wound tightly to stem the blood and had proscribed that it was not to be disturbed for several days.

Cerdic, having shed his monastic guise, was loathed to leave his master, but Wulfnoth was adamant that after his servant had accompanied Alena and Hild to the court and once judgement had been delivered, he set sail so that Hild might be reunited with her father without delay. Beorhtric's ship had been impounded and the crew imprisoned, but there was no sign of the Mercian so it was imperative that they waste no time in getting Hild to England before Beorhtric's brother, Eadric, had been warned to look out for them. Wulfnoth felt sure that the estate at Compton would still be under surveillance so he ordered them to risk the longer sea voyage back up the east coast straight to the safety of the Danelaw. It would he knew be quicker. He himself would follow once his injury had healed.

Therefore, as soon as the case was over and the pall of deep purple storm clouds that had oppressed the channel for two days finally dispersed, Cerdic escorted Hild to the quay where they boarded the Northumbrian ship. The captain slipped the mooring lines and the sleek vessel was rowed down the narrow waterways towards the sea.

Alena, who now enjoyed the protection of the count, spent much of her time visiting Wulfnoth in the garrison sick quarters. For him these visits were a delightful break from the tedium of the sickbed while she found the thegn's advice invaluable in assessing her new possessions and commitments.

Apart from the whorehouse and *Le Merle Noir* she owned two other ships designed to bring a variety of goods to Bruges from all over Europe. Wulfnoth told her that her position as mistress of such a fleet made her central to a whole trading network not only in Bruges, but throughout Flanders. Fleeces, lengths of cloth, silks, trinkets and hardware bought by the burghers and artisans would eventually make their way in barges down willow-lined rivers to Ghent and the other new towns that were springing up.

She was quick to appreciate the potential offered by the nascent cloth industry, but also realised that the livelihood of dozens of families would rest on the successful trading of her vessels. The dramatic change that was taking place in her life both excited and frightened her and in Wulfnoth she found someone who not only foresaw the difficulties, but who offered solutions and inspired her with the confidence to face whatever challenges the world of commerce might hold.

Both looked forward to her visits and he seemed to be progressing well, but after four days the wound began to burn and the flesh around the shoulder looked puffy and red.

Alena was concerned and sought assurance from the physician, but he declared himself satisfied with his patient's progress.

On the fifth day she was horrified to find the thegn delirious and demanded to see the wound for herself. At first the physician refused but then shrugged his shoulders and unwound the bandages that held the dressing. The smell and one look at the livid state of the wound were enough to convince even him that all was far from well.

"I fear, madam, the wound has done for him."

"It is not the wound that has done for him," she retorted, "but your ministrations. If he remains here he will surely die. Have him taken to my house. There he will stand a chance."

"As you wish." The physician had smelt death before and was relieved that he could wash his hands of this foreigner. "I will inform the castellan that you have taken responsibility for his life," he added, unpleasantly. Then fully conscious of the fact that she was in earshot he turned to his assistants and said, "Take our friend back to the whorehouse and much good may it do him."

"It is not a whorehouse," she blazed, her black eyes boring into him. "It is a respectable property and one in which your patient will recover from this unhealthy place and your lack of skill."

The physician withered under her fury and he stared after her speechless.

Alena lost no time in organising the assistants warning them that if they did not take proper care with their load they would suffer dire consequences.

Once back at the whorehouse Wulfnoth was put to bed and, while Judith and Ogive held him to prevent him thrashing about, Alena took a hot seax and forced open the angry edges of the wound releasing an eruption of grey and yellow puss. Ignoring his screams, she painstakingly squeezed and cleaned out the wound flushing it repeatedly with a mixture of warm water and Rhenish wine. Then she packed it with sweet smelling herbs hoping against hope that they were beneficial and rebound the wound. As soon as the pain from this primitive surgical process ceased exhaustion drew the thegn into a fitful sleep and Alena felt that he could be left to rest.

She herself could not. The words of the physician had stung her too deeply and she was determined to strip the house of all signs of its previous function and expunge its reputation as a brothel. She enlisted the help of Judith, Ogive, the dark girl Rosela and the boy Walram and together they systematically threw out the baggage of the past and began to clean each room in turn.

By nightfall half the house was transformed and she returned to check on her patient for the final time but found him still feverishly tossing about on the bed, calling out on his dead wife and child so she crept in beside him and held him in her arms until both eventually fell into a deep sleep.

The Woolhouse

During the days that followed his arrival at the whorehouse Wulfnoth's condition see-sawed continually as the poison ran through his veins. He could be hot or cold, hungry or nauseous, lucid or confused. Alena knew that she must drain the wound every day until the poison had left his body. Frequently in his tortured sleep he would cry out for Ragnhild. In his more lucid moments he was frustrated that he was not allowed to resume his accustomed active life and then exhausted by the simple effort of climbing out of bed to relieve himself. Physically and emotionally he was in a state of almost permanent tension like the string of a battle selfbow. He was elated in the mornings when Alena first entered his room, but when the time for redressing his injured shoulder approached he became apprehensive and as the metseax was inserted into the wound, he would panic and scream, pounding the bed with his sound fist and cursing the implacability of his guardian angel. She felt for him, but knew that she must resist all feelings of compassion until the work was completed. At all other times he delighted in her company and when the day was done and he finally fell asleep she still slipped into the bed to be near and watch over him during the night. Subconsciously he must have felt her presence for his muscles relaxed instantly and his breathing no longer disturbed the night air.

One morning as his condition improved he woke before her but lay hardly daring to move. Then as she stirred he closed his eyes and feigned sleep so that she could steal from the room and her nightly vigil remain secret. He could still smell her presence and longed for her to return.

When she did, however, it was with the metseax and the fresh herbs and he had to endure the daily torture as the wound was once again eased apart, the dried blood-stained herbs scraped away and the pink flesh of the deep gash exposed. He continued to wince and swear with pain as she rinsed and repacked it. Then a wave of relief swept over him as she replaced the bandage. Throughout the process she bit her lip and tried to remain impassive.

"There," she said at last. "It looks much healthier today."

"I'm sorry," he said. "I've been injured many times in battle and suffered leeches and blood-letting and once a poultice of hot oats and fresh dung was applied, but I have never felt such dreadful pain."

"Think yourself lucky you didn't suffer the fate of King Ella at the hands of Ivar the Boneless," she said smiling now that the thegn's ordeal was over.

"I know and I am grateful for all that you do for me," he said looking straight into her dark eyes.

For a moment she felt embarrassment but could not think why. "I couldn't let you die at the hands of that garrison 'quacksalver', she blurted out and then, looking down at his bandaged shoulder, she quickly changed the subject and added, "You are strong and the flesh builds up in the wound as it gradually knits together." The embarrassment passed. "Besides," she laughed, "I need you to be well to advise me how to manage my affairs."

"Of course," he said relieved in his own way that she did not simply view him as a helpless patient. "The lady owns a fleet of ships. Have you seen them yet?"

"No, my lord, I have not dared to enquire about them."

"But *Le Merle Noir* is back in Bruges, surely."

"Oh yes. The captain has unloaded his cargo. It is in the hall below, but as yet I have not dared to start selling to the merchants until I check if anything is missing."

"Then you must do that at once, but has the Captain paid his respects to the new owner of *Le Merle Noir*?"

"He has called twice but I wouldn't see him."

"But why ever not?"

"Because, he has been boasting that Jacob's widow will prove to be an easy mistress who can be hoodwinked and that he expects to do well if he rolls the right dice."

"Then he's in for a shock when he meets you."

"Perhaps, but I'm not sure what questions to ask him. I know nothing about trade routes and shipping cargoes."

"You must tell him to come this afternoon." The thegn suddenly felt well for the first time in a week. I will tell you what to ask."

"I still have no idea what orders to give him."

"I will sit beside you. Tell him I have ships of my own and that you could not see him before because you wished to consult me on the possibility of expanding your fleet."

"But I'm at a loss as to how I will manage three ships let alone contemplate a fourth."

"You would take it in your stride as you have taken everything in your life. You will show him you are a force to be reckoned with, someone with bold ideas about the future. The thought of a new ship, more profitable cargoes and new markets will act as a carrot and he will want desperately to have a part of that future."

The thegn's faith in her ability boosted her confidence and the possibilities offered by her new status as an independent and wealthy mistress engaged in trade suddenly began to dawn on Alena sending her mind racing.

Walram was sent with a message instructing the captain to report to Mistress Alena in the afternoon giving her ample time to prepare herself and plan her strategy.

Wulfnoth couldn't manage to dress himself, but with Alena's help he was presentable in his old tunic cleansed of blood and darned to hide the rent made by Beorhtric's axe. A cloak hid his injured arm and his belt and sword hung carelessly from the back of Jacob's chair. Alena and Judith searched through the clothes of Jacob's former wife and found two tunics, one a richly woven English cloth with a silky finish and a raised pattern, the other a simple linen one.

When they returned Wulfnoth smiled. "Mistress and servant! You would not look out of place in an English manor house. As mistress you should have the seat," he added and made to rise, but she knew well that he still needed to be supported.

"I shall do well enough on my feet. I have never been one for sitting," she said simply.

When the captain arrived, Judith wearing the linen tunic and cap to hide her flowing hair greeted him at the door.

"The mistress will see you in the upper hall." And turning on her heel she preceded him upstairs.

The captain was taken aback; he had never been beyond the ground floor in Jacob's time and he was surprised how clean and tidy everything seemed. Once at the top of the ladder he was made to wait while Judith knocked on the oak door and then announced his arrival.

"The Captain of *Le Merle Noir*, my lady."

Entering the room he only saw the powerful figure of Wulfnoth seated by the table and, snatching off his Phrygian cap he stood awkwardly in front of the thegn, waiting. Wulfnoth looked back at him in silence.

"Well, Captain, have you come to report to me or to stare at my visitor?" Alena, who had been standing looking out of the window, came forward and stood at the other end of the table.

The captain, unable to hold both in his line of vision, was disconcerted and looked from one to the other.

"Look at me, sir. I am Mistress of *Le Merle Noir*. Lord Wulfnoth is a valued friend from England, who is here merely to advise me on expanding my fleet. Now, captain, was your trip successful?

The captain fumbled for words. "Partly, mistress," he heard himself say. He had come to the whorehouse certain that the grieving widow would be an easy prey to his plans to exploit Jacob's death, but everything was suddenly going wrong. She overawed him and Lord Wulfnoth himself was here in Bruges and where would he stand if the fleet were enlarged?

"Well?" he heard her say.

"Well, mistress," his mouth struggled to keep up with the thoughts that jumbled in his brain, "We've come back with two dozen cattle hides, bought at a good price, woollen blankets, tin, two auroch drinking horns, yes and half a dozen bronze bound buckets, but although I returned to Bosham there was no word from his lordship."

"We know about the letter," said Wulfnoth. "Apparently you put it into the wrong hands."

"But they said that your lordship was away and that they would see that it was delivered." He was on the defensive.

"It is of no consequence now," said Alena coolly, "but if I keep you in my service you will be well advised to take more care in the future."

He began to realise that he had underestimated this woman.

"I demand absolute loyalty from my servants."

He swore that she should have it.

"And I want men of vision."

Now she had lost him.

"If, and when I buy a new ship, it will deal exclusively in the wool trade and it will require a captain who can distinguish between quality and cheap goods. Tell me," she asked. "What is the capacity of each of my ships? For example, how many fleeces can each carry?"

He was surprised by the directness of the questions, but at least he felt on safer ground.

"*Le Merle Noir* could carry three dozen fleeces," he declared confidently "and *Le Geai des Chenes* and *La Pie Bavarde* at least sixty apiece." Then, he added dismissively, "But of course it can only be a seasonable trade since most of the English sheep are slaughtered at the beginning of winter and those that are left for breeding will not be shorn until the summer."

"Any fool knows that," she said tartly, inwardly cursing herself for her own stupidity. "I am thinking of the future. In the winter we will trade in a whole range of implements for spinning and weaving. Did Jacob not trade in those?"

"No, mistress. He said they were cumbersome. In any case he usually wanted us to bring whores to work here in the whorehouse and they can take up a lot of room."

Alena raised her hands like a pair of claws and turned all her fury upon the unfortunate man who, thinking she was going to gouge his eyes out, cowered before her. "Jacob is dead," she shouted, "and, if you dare to call my house a 'whorehouse', I'll have you whipped and thrown into the count's oubliette."

Reduced rapidly to the state of an abject serf, the man looked up at her, stammered an apology and then, when he saw that she was not going to strike him, muttered lamely. "But it has always been called that, mistress. Tell me what should I call it?"

Now it was her turn to be forced to think quickly. "Why," she hesitated and then as if it were the most natural thing in the world she said, "'The Woolhouse'. And don't you forget it!" Then before he had time to recover she snapped, "Now, where are my other two ships?"

"*Le G...G...Geai des Chenes*," he stammered, "will be making its regular trip to Hantone, but *La Pie Bavarde* will be somewhere in the Inland Sea."

"And when can we expect them in Bruges?"

"*Le Geai* should arrive the day after tomorrow, but *La Pie* anytime before the end of the year."

"Return to your ship then, and when the others arrive send their captains to me at once." With that, Alena called for Judith to show the captain out. The interview was over. When he had gone Alena collapsed onto the floor at Wulfnoth's feet convulsed with laughter.

"Did I do well?" she managed to giggle at last.

"You played the part magnificently," he conceded. "I'm glad I am not in your service."

She looked up at him in disappointment, but then when she saw him grinning she flashed her eyes in a coquettish manner and asked innocently, "Would you not serve me, sir?"

When he looked serious she dropped her eyes and said simply, "I'm sorry, my lord. That was insensitive."

"No offence taken," he whispered and put his hand on her shoulder so that she leant back against his knees.

That night when she looked in upon him he was already sound asleep, clearly untroubled by nightmares or fever. She kissed his raven-dark hair and crept silently out of the room.

Barnburh

Cerdic and Hild arrived safely in the Humber and within hours they reached Barnburh where the girl was finally reunited with her father. The old man, who had clung to a blind faith in the promise of the Thegn of Compton, was overjoyed and Eric was beside himself and fussed over the two of them like a mother duck. Cerdic suddenly felt out of place and thought to slip away quietly, but Hild came after him and taking him by the hand led him back to the hearth and he was persuaded to join in the family celebration.

That evening Hild took charge of the cooking pot as if it was the most natural thing in the world. Then when they had all eaten and as they sat round the glowing embers of the fire she gave them an account of her enforced journey to Bruges and, avoiding its more unpleasant aspects, the part played by Alena in her survival. Torgrim wanted to know how she had been rescued, but Hild insisted that they sleep and promised that on the following night Cerdic would tell them of his adventures and the arrival of Lord Wulfnoth.

Then Eric retired to the stable to sleep over his master's treasures and Hild having covered the fire with ash curled up on the floor between Torgrim and Cerdic.

During the days that followed Cerdic and Eric set about restoring part of the adjoining building, replacing the rotten timbers with sound planks and re-thatching the roof. The front part was to serve as a bedroom, while the rear could easily be transformed into a workshop where Eric and Torgrim could set up a forge and teach some of the local village boys how to smelt and cast metal. Since his daughter's return the old man had acquired a new lease of life and unable to do intricate work himself wished to pass on his skill as a jewelsmith.

However, their first task was more mundane, but essential to their survival. Eric had found the frame and wheel of an old plough in the village, but the wheel lacked a rim and the ploughshare and coulter were missing so replacements had to be made. Under Torgrim's supervision Cerdic and Eric sweated in the forge for two days until they had fashioned a strong enough metal hoop and two passable blades. Once the plough had been rebuilt they borrowed a team of oxen from Wulfric and began the painstaking task of cultivating sufficient scrubland to provide the family with winter vegetables.

When the job was completed Cerdic had no further excuse for putting off his return to Compton and knew that his duty lay in helping to manage the estate in his master's absence. Even in the absence of his master he knew that Alfred, as reeve would take charge and that Swithred and Oswy would rally round, but if the Danes invaded the manor his place was to be at their side.

He had become part of the family, but Torgrim and Hild realised that he must leave them to sow the crops that would sustain them later in the year, so they embraced him, wished him well and watched as he rode past the sliced furrows and glistening clods of brown earth to disappear down into the Dearne valley heading south.

Winter in the Woolhouse

Back in Bruges summer was short-lived. Autumn came and went and the temperature plummeted. The land was metal-hard and the waterways froze over. The keen edge of the wind drove those who braved the elements to hug the buildings as they forced their slanting way through the bitter streets. Winter with her icy fingers had even clawed her way into the Woolhouse through every crack in the timber walls.

Inside Alena's servants contrived to keep the invader at bay, covering the floors with fleeces and nailing skins over the crevices wherever they felt her breath. By day, however, they still went about their duties in the cold house with an enthusiasm that was warmed by the knowledge they were no longer mere slaves to serve the pleasure of those who had frequented the flesh-stews of their former master.

Alena had offered hope and they had willingly knelt before her and placed their heads in her hands. She was their mistress now, mistress by choice and none now thought to leave her service. Judith and Ogive, who had known nothing but brutality since birth, felt they had entered paradise; Rosela, with dim memories of a happier childhood, talked vaguely of revisiting Southern Italy at some time in the future; and as for Walram he could only remember a life of street fighting with stray dogs for scraps of food. Alena was the mother he never had and he worshipped her.

At lunch and again at dusk when their tasks were done all four congregated as one family in the kitchen where a pot hung simmering gently over the fire that crackled continuously and they laughed, dreamed and chattered or simply lay back watching the smoke drifting heavenwards out through the hole high up in the thatched roof.

At night they all slept together for companionship and warmth round the glowing embers of the ash-banked hearth.

For much of the day the mistress worked alongside her servants, but always reserved certain hours for her patient convalescing in the upper bedroom where a brazier of live coals gathered from below the high water mark of the distant seashore was sufficient to lift the chill. Here Alena and Wulfnoth spent fruitful time discussing how to get the best use out of her three ships before attempting to expand her fleet and to exploit the growing demand for English cloth.

When her other two ships returned their commanders duly presented themselves before Alena, who had grown in assurance in her new role as ship owner and trader. Neither had a good word to say about Jacob and both unreservedly accepted their new mistress, but it was the captain of *La Pie Bavarde* who made the greater impression.

After giving a full account of his voyage and presenting a detailed and accurate list of his cargo, he recommended that all three vessels be taken out of the water and laid up so that while the weather precluded sailing, their rivets could be checked, any damaged cleats replaced and fresh tarred rope worked into suspect joints between the clinkered planks. He would willingly undertake the work and promised that the whole fleet would be ready to be returned to the water as soon as it was safe to venture back across the searoads.

Wulfnoth took an immediate liking to the man and was relieved that, when the time came for his return to England, Alena would be assured of at least one dependable retainer.

When the captain had gone Alena talked of her early life and described how her father and mother had spun wool and weaved cloth for a living before the famine struck and proposed that as soon as Wulfnoth could travel they would visit other settlements in the marshes to see if there was a market for hand spindles and looms so that she would be able to import good quality fleeces and sell them directly to a web of artisans.

Sometimes they would talk late into the night and then out of affection as if it were the most natural thing in the world they would share the same bed for warmth and comfort, secure in each other's presence, but, sensible to the scars and bruises inflicted by their former lives, they made no further demands upon each other.

By the end of January Wulfnoth's injured shoulder had knit sufficiently for him to resume a fairly normal existence. Snow fell and the weather felt warmer and by the thaw he was able to wield an axe and split logs for the Woolhouse fire. He spent his mornings with the captain of *La Pie Bavarde* supervising work on the ships and his afternoons accompanying Alena in search of new markets, but as much as he enjoyed both activities he knew that it could not last. As a thegn he must be ready to serve his king; as a father he had a son that he wanted to hold in his arms; and as a landowner he had an estate to run and a vast family of servants that depended on his leadership and protection.

Flanders was at that time little troubled by the Danes. The towns were set back from the sea and the approaches, through constantly changing waterways across the marshes, lost any invading force the essential element of surprise. The rest of the land itself was poor and offered little in terms of plunder, besides which the count paid a nominal wergild, so the striped sails were rarely sighted off the Flanders coast.

In England, however, with its wealth and a coastline of river mouths and sandy beaches it was a different story and with spring approaching he was anxious to return to Compton before the Vikings mounted another season of invasions.

At the first signs of a spell of settled weather both he and Alena knew that the time was fast approaching when he must leave.

"When I am gone," he said one morning as they lay in bed together, "will you keep something for me?"

"Of course," she murmured enjoying the smell and warmth of his presence. "What is it?"

"Count Baldwin's account of Beorhtric's criminal activities in Flanders. If he attempts to blacken my name as a traitor it should help to destroy his credibility."

"Then I shall keep it safely locked in a box on the table beside my bed. And if I wake in the night and feel lonely I shall look at it and think of my English lord."

They shared a physical and emotional intimacy and they both realised that parting would be painful, but they would sail separate searoads in the certainty that nothing would sever the bond that had grown between them.

So in the second week of April Wulfnoth left Bruges and returned to England on *Le Merle Noir* accompanied by *Le Geai des Chenes*. When they arrived in Bosham the thegn assigned a warship to each vessel and while *Le Merle* went east heading for Sandwic, *Le Geai* sailed west towards Hantone, both in search of teasels, hand-spindles, weaving looms and batons. They did not expect to find good quality wool at that time of the year, but the thegn had promised to purchase a number of the new season's fleeces as soon as the annual shearing began.

Meanwhile Wulfnoth could focus his attention on home, so mounting one of the two horses he had brought with him he rode hard for Compton spurred on by the desire to see his son Godwin.

He found the boy playing in the yard where a couple of stable lads were busy sweeping out the stalls and Cerdic was checking the evening feed. The latter had heard the approaching horses and was ready to greet his master the moment he cantered through the gate. As soon as he had handed over the two magnificent animals, Wulfnoth held his arms out to his son, but the boy wouldn't look at him and seemed more interested in driving small birds from the manure heap with handfuls of chalk gravel. During the next half hour he tried several times to distract the boy from his cruel sport and persuade him to sit and watch the creatures rather than torment them, but to no avail. Eventually Estrith appeared and insisted that it was well past the boy's mealtime. Reluctantly, he let the boy go and joined Cerdic, who was still fussing over his two new charges, to learn about events in the North. Satisfied that Torgrim and Hild were safe from the Mercians, he then climbed up to a favourite vantage point above the manor and looked out over his estate.

Since the Royal Council of 998 had put its faith in a military rather than a naval solution to the problem of renewed Danish raids and Ealdorman Aelfric had been kept on as one of the joint commanders, Wulfnoth felt no desperate compunction to make a hasty return to the Court. His sword was still at the service of his king, but he also knew that his support for Torgrim might have soured relationship with Aethelred. With luck his part in the moneyer's escape might not come to light since Beorhtric could hardly mention his suspicions without drawing attention to his own role in attempting to dispose of Hild. However, if the worst came to the worst Wulfnoth also had the letter from Count Baldwin implicating the Mercian in murder and the illegal trade in slaves for the purpose of prostitution.

When he returned he found Estrith waiting for him

"Has my son finished his meal yet?"

"He has, my lord."

"Then bring him to me. I want to talk to him."

"The boy is asleep now."

"I would have liked to see him before he went to bed."

"He didn't want to see you."

"But why? It seems he wants to shut me out of his world."

"Are you surprised, my lord?"

"I thought he would have been pleased to see me."

"He hardly knows you."

"He must remember me."

"He has not forgotten you, my lord, but he doesn't trust you."

"But I'm his father. Why doesn't he trust me?"

"He's a child my lord. He is confused and feels insecure. He didn't know his mother and for two months you rejected him. And after the Danes attacked you were so wrapt up in the estate and your precious ships that it was months before you had time to be a real father. Then for over a year you became the centre of his world only to disappear without a word over nine months ago. In the meantime Asa has born a living child of her own and naturally spends more of her time with him. Is it any wonder that Godwin feels insecure? His life is in turmoil and he is afraid that if he becomes fond of something it will disappear. He doesn't trust the world."

The old nurse shook her head sadly and left him.

Later that evening he ate with all his retainers in the hall and listened carefully while each reported everything that had happened since his sudden departure the previous year. Alfred declared himself delighted with the harvest; the grain store, which had been rethatched in the summer, was full to capacity; the land raked; and seed was daily being broadcast. Two of the four sheep had died in the snow, but the swine had thrived as they always did. He also reported that no-one from the Court had visited although a group of strangers had appeared inquiring after the whereabouts of the thegn at the end of May, but they had been thrown off the estate. Periodically they had been spotted at Bosham and in some of the surrounding villages up until Christmas, when they had finally disappeared. Swithred reported that the coastal defences were sound, the beacons dry and each furnished with an ample supply of kindling and logs. Finally, Oswy, who was never satisfied with the state of the fleet, said a new ship was nearing completion and the timber purchased for another to follow. All in all Compton seemed to have flourished in his absence. Clearly he had chosen well and the estate was in good hands. Now, if the Danes allowed, Wulfnoth could devote his time to his neglected son

Secluded among the Downs, season followed season and in the cycle of ploughing, planting, growth and harvest Wulfnoth had always found a sense of fulfilment and serenity, in the knowledge that his own stewardship of the estate was a vital link between past and future.

He was determined that Godwin would inherit his love for the land and so the following morning he brought a large basin of water into the kitchen and placed it on a stool. Then pretending to ignore his son he knelt down beside it and set the two half shells of one of the walnuts he had brought back from Bruges floating on the surface. Into each one he dropped a grain of gravel repeating the process until one or other of the shells was so low in the water that a globule of water rolled over its lip causing the shell to capsize and sink to the bottom of the basin scattering its cargo on the seabed. Retrieving the sunken shell he repeated the process.

Curiosity had drawn Godwin to the stool and he crouched beside his father, fascinated. Apparently absorbed in his task Wulfnoth took no notice of his son and slid his hand down to the bottom of the basin again, pulled out a shell, blew the water out of it and was about to launch it again when he heard a whisper beside him.

"Can I have a go, sir?"

"Of course," the thegn whispered back and pretending to look over his shoulder to make sure that no one else could hear them he handed the dry shell to Godwin.

Soon they started a competition to see who could sink the other's boat and when Wulfnoth's shell lurched to the bottom Godwin was ecstatic. Eventually when they had splashed water all over the floor Estrith drove them both out of the kitchen like naughty children.

In the days that followed the two explored the river that fed the estate watermill; racing sticks under the planks; trying to be first to spot the shy red squirrels scurrying back to their holes in the trees; and if they were very quiet watching the kingfisher's iridescent display as it darted over the water.

When the warmer weather came the thegn delighted in taking his son with him seated on the front of his saddle as he rode into the village or toured the outlying fields. Invariably the blond-haired child was the centre of attention fussed over by the women and greeted with cheery waves of the ceorls and villeins, who all remembered his enchanting Danish mother with affection. The lad revelled in his father's company and began to show a burgeoning love for nature as it came back to life around him.

At the beginning of May they went further afield in the direction of Charlton where they took a detour and walked the horse through woodland watching the shafts of sunlight slanting through the trunks onto great swathes of bluebells and wild garlic interspersed with patches of wood anemone and celandine. Godwin dressed in a bright red tunic was fascinated and ran through trees setting off a kaleidoscope of colour.

In the second week of May, garlands of snow-white may blossom cascaded from the trees above the ragged robin, cow parsley and lady's lace that lined the grassy tracks of the Compton estate. Oak, ash and elderberry had broken into new leaf and the gnarled beech tree with its great armpits and elbows was practically in full sail. Godwin could not help but be aware of the symphony of sounds that emanated from the hedgerows, which were alive with bees searching to fill their sacks with pollen and the next generation of a dozen species of small birds demanding to be fed.

Wulfnoth would willingly have spent the whole year watching his son's wonder and delight as he explored every aspect of this ever-changing world, but he was conscious that the boy was becoming too attached to him so he involved Alfred and his twin boys in these outings whenever he could. The boys were much the same age as Godwin and he was anxious that they should play together as often as possible. Soon the trio began to devise their own amusements and liked nothing better than to be able to play hide and seek and chase each other around the buildings attached to the manor, which allowed him to ride over to Bosham and see for himself the new ships that Oswy said were ready for inspection. Now his fleet numbered eleven vessels. It would have been twelve but he had arranged for one to be sent to Berthun to replace the one that had been lost in Le Mascaret on the Seine. After couple of hours on the water he could find no fault with either ship and congratulated the shipwright on his skill. Then to everyone's delight he ordered a further vessel, one twice the size that could also be used to carry cargo.

"We shall need to hire more seamen then," said Oswy.

"Perhaps," said the thegn, "but surely you and Alfred must have relatives back in Warblington, young men willing to work for me who could be trained in seamanship."

"I have three younger brothers who can find no place on the land. They'll leap at the chance of working for you, my lord."

"Good. As 'Master of my Fleet' the matter is in your hands. I mean to have twenty ships one day, so we will need to cast our net wide. But pick the best and choose your best seamen to train them. Swithred will help with military training. Then we know we'll have sound crews."

Oswy could scarcely contain himself, but knelt before the thegn in acceptance of his new status and responsibility.

Wulfnoth placed his hand on Oswy's head and whispered, "Right, get on with the job, then."

While down on the coast he had looked out across the water and remembered his promise to Alena. Her ships were due at the end of the month, so he must visit the Chichester market to buy enough fleeces after the annual shearing to fill her three boats. At the same time he decided to buy a dozen lambs not simply to replace the two sheep lost in the winter but also to form the basis of a flock to be reared on the Compton estate. Perhaps one day he could supply her with his own fleeces.

He took Alfred and the four estate lads with him on his trip to Chichester. He and Alfred rode while the lads took it in turns to drive the wagon. On the way back two would drive the sheep while the other pair would bring the fleeces on the wagon.

They were so busy loading up the wagon for the return journey that at first nobody noticed a column of black smoke rising from the south. It was only as the wagon turned westward that they recognised the awesome warning that the striped sails of sea-raiders had been sighted off the coast. Leaving the lads to make their own way back to Compton, Wulfnoth and Alfred galloped headlong straight for Bosham where they found that ten warships were already heading towards the harbour. One, however, the fastest, remained on the mud flats half in and half out of the water waiting for the thegn so that he could join the fleet and direct operations. At the sound of the horses the seamen sprang into action completing the launch while he and Alfred hurried on board. Cerdic arrived from Compton at the last moment with an armful of axes and joined them on the boat.

The oars slid effortlessly through the water and the warship surged into life. When they entered the harbour they were on the heels of the fleet and by the time they were halfway across the great stretch of water they were alongside Oswy in the lead vessel. There was little wind and the masts had deliberately not been stepped so they could creep unobserved under the lee of the sandspit that led to the harbour entrance.

One of Oswy's seamen slipped ashore and crawled up the sand to a position where he could observe the approaching Danes and give the signal for attack. The oarsmen lay their blades flat on the water, their muscles relaxed but their ears straining to catch the whispered order that would send their bodies forward to begin again the rhythmic movement that would drive the prows flying like arrows against the intruders.

It was slack water but the sea-raiders would have to adjust their sail sheets as they negotiated the entrance of the harbour. They might even lower their sails as the wind died and Wulfnoth wanted to attack them when their minds were otherwise occupied.

Unlike a military encounter where leaders like Aelfric would have encouraged their troops to set up a chant of "Ut.Ut" in the hopes of frightening an opposing force into giving ground, Wulfnoth demanded total silence from his crews until they physically engaged the enemy vessels. That silence he said would instil uncertainty into the enemy.

"Row!" he and Oswy whispered almost simultaneously to their crews as the signal came from the sandspit. Side by side the two lead vessels shot out from behind the headland and they fell upon either side of the first of the Viking ships as its crew were lowering their oars into the water. Having removed their own shields, they were able to ship their own oars while the vessel's prow shattered those of their opponents. Leaving a couple of seamen to hold the boats together, Wulfnoth and Oswy led their individual crews in an axe attack on the unprepared Danes. The assault lasted a matter of minutes before they returned to their own vessels to look for more prey. In the lull Wulfnoth ordered the wolf banner to be displayed from the sternpost so that the enemy had no doubt whom they faced.

The other ships in the fleet protected by their shield walls fanned out and converged on the largest of the remaining Viking ships successfully ramming three of them amidships leaving their occupants floundering in the half-submerged vessels, a prey to the axe or sword thrust.

Although the Danes had superiority of numbers, surprise coupled with the efficiency and ferocity of the Saxon attack soon made the rest retreat to their base on the Isle of Wight.

For a moment Wulfnoth was tempted to give chase, but discretion persuaded him to break off and the Saxons spent the next half hour disposing of any Danes who remained alive, dragging the bodies on to the sandspit where they could be stripped of clothes and weapons. Two enemy vessels had been sunk, and two others captured.

All in all it was a satisfying victory and two new ships were added to the fleet. Whether it would provoke a punitive attack by the Danes, or whether they would avoid Sussex and look for softer targets in the future remained to be seen.

* * * * *

Several days later Siferth arrived at Compton and Wulfnoth was eager to catch up on news from the North.

"And how are Torgrim and his family?" he asked once his friend had slaked his thirst and they were alone in his private room.

"Torgrim is well and his business thrives. He is an asset in the Danelaw. You know he now employs four apprentices, one of whom shows great talent. In fact I have brought you two pieces of his work so you may judge for yourself." With that he laid two small bundles on the table. "That one is for you but the other is for your man Cerdic who seems to have made quite an impression on mistress Hild."

"He would make her a fine husband. I should be loathed to lose him and Torgrim would hardly consent if she had to leave Barnburh and make her home here at Compton."

"Perhaps, but now she is safe he will surely think of her happiness."

"You may be right. If Cerdic is of like mind I shall not stand in his way wherever they choose to live."

With that he sent for his servant, who had been seeing to the rubbing down of Siferth's horse. "I shall not broach the subject of marriage, but he must have his gift and life will take its course."

"He will not raise it. He is bound to you like a huscarl. Like Alfred, Swithred and Oswy he owes everything to you. He'll live and die in your service."

"I am indeed lucky in my servants."

"You chose well and treat them with respect. He'll never forget the sword you gave him after the attack on Portchester."

"It was no more than he deserved."

Cerdic arrived and Wulfnoth motioned him to pull up a stool and join them. "Lord Siferth says you are my 'huscarl'. It is a term they use for body servants in the Danelaw. Do you think it is appropriate?"

"It is an honour, my lord. My head lies in your hands." Cerdic knelt at his feet.

"So be it!" said Wulfnoth placing his hands on each side of the man's head. "Yet if you ever wish your freedom, you have only to ask."

"Thank you, my lord."

"Sit down. Lord Siferth brings us news of friends in the North."

Cerdic's eyes registered immediate interest.

"Our friends are thriving. Torgrim has sent me a gift." And he began to unwrap one of the bundles. Inside was a gold and garnet cloak broach decorated with a wolf's head and a note, which read. 'A gift that I hope is worthy of the man who rescued my daughter'.

"I have never owned so rich and personal a gem," said Wulfnoth and showed it to the others.

"No more than you deserve," answered Siferth handing it back.

"Now, Cerdic, there is a gift for you which I suspect was made by a lady." Wulfnoth pushed the other bundle across the table.

"But I did nothing, my lord," he protested. However, he eagerly unwound the cloth exposing an exquisite walrus ivory comb carved on each side with intricately interlaced animals and held it in his hands turning it over again and again.

"A novel piece! Five months in the Danelaw and her work is inspired by Viking art," commented the thegn, but Cerdic was not listening.

"I think your huscarl serves two masters," observed his northern friend.

Cerdic, snapping out of his distraction, protested, "No, my lord. I swear to you. I owe loyalty to no other man."

"Perhaps to a woman then," suggested Wulfnoth.

Cerdic could only blush sheepishly. And the two thegns laughed.

"I'm afraid my other news is not so good," said Siferth, when the amusement was over and Cerdic had been allowed to retreat with his present to his beloved horses.

"Oh!"

"The Danes are causing havoc in Kent."

"We watched their wave-stallions sailing east. One of my ships shadowed their fleet until they reached Dover and then they stood off and appeared to be heading for their homeland."

"Would they had been, but they swept into the Medway and lay siege to Rochester. I was in London with the king when word came from the Bishop begging for an army to support the Kentish levy."

"And was one sent?"

"Aelfric advised against it. Since Aethelweard's death he is premier Ealdorman. He claimed it was too risky until Eadric arrived with his Mercian troops. As usual the Court dithered and by the time the army was assembled Rochester had been sacked and the determined men of Kent driven from the field of slaughter. Now the Danes all but rule the whole of the south-east."

"Surely something can be done even now."

"Well the army is growing and Eadric has proposed a fleet of ships to support it."

Wulfnoth clenched his hands in triumph.

"New vessels are being built in London this very minute and ship owners from all over England have been told to offer their services to the new commander."

"At last! I can supply thirteen warships and the finest crews in England. Who is in command of the fleet?

"Ah!" Siferth paused. "Aelfhelm told the Council that only you had the experience and skill to take on the Danes, but he is increasingly sidelined by Aelfric and the Mercian faction and those in their pay who despite envying their rise, still sell them their voices for favours. His suggestion was shouted down."

"So who was chosen?"

Siferth hesitated. "Eadric has persuaded the king to appoint his brother to that position."

"His brother!" Wulfnoth was incredulous. "The man barely knows prow from sternpost! He'll be a disaster. I'll not serve under him."

"He wants your ships, but won't have you personally in his fleet at any price. He told the king you could not be relied upon to follow orders. Aelfric of course backed him up."

"And what did Aethelred say to that?"

"He said you had been successful in the past, but Eadric said they were insignificant victories against inferior forces and Beorhtric reminded him of your support for Torgrim. We tried to rally support. Aethemaer and all the men of Cumbria supported us, but Ealdorman Leofsige of Essex who raised half the forces urged the King to act at once. Beorhtric was there and our arguments meant delay. Ealdorman Aelfhelm and I left in despair."

"Well I can put to sea and snap at the Danish heels. At least they cannot condemn me for that, but I'll not risk my ships under his command. So, tell me, Siferth, where do you go now?"

"I shall return north and wait until I'm summoned."

As soon as Siferth had left, Wulfnoth, Alfred and Cerdic left for Bosham where they were joined by Swithred and Oswy. There they held a council of war during which the thegn explained that although the King had not specifically called them to serve in the fleet they could expect the warships to be commandeered. At first Oswy and Swithred were enthusiastic, but when they heard who was to command the fleet and that Wulfnoth was to be specifically excluded they shared the thegn's misgivings.

"Once you surrender your ships to that creature," said Cerdic, "you will never see them again. He's a grasper like his brother and he bears a grudge against you."

"We could take the ships to Bruges until this affair blows over," suggested Oswy.

"That would put you outside the law and Eadric would have you put to death when you returned."

"But you are our lord. Our loyalty is to you, not to some Mercian, not even to the King," said Swithred.

"Dangerous words. Aethelred might not see it that way. I know that Cerdic and Oswy have placed their heads in my hands, but you and Alfred are still free men. I cannot command your loyalty."

"We are yours to the death as well you know," said Alfred and knelt on the floor in front of Wulfnoth where Swithred joined him.

"It seems you have four huscarls now, my lord," said Cerdic as Wulfnoth accepted their oaths.

"Then I accept the loyalty of you all, but I will not hold you to it against the king for that is where my loyalty lies. Now listen. I have a plan to serve the king and still keep control of our ships."

The following day Wulfnoth's fleet slipped out of Bosham creek and into the channel heading east. Immediately they stretched out in a line abreast each a hundred yards apart. Every so often the two with the typical red-striped sails of the Norsemen would change station so that they took it in turns to sail closest to the shore to keep a watch on the coast for signs of Viking activity while the others kept out of sight. The first signs were at Rye where smoke billowed above the town. Wulfnoth withdrew his fleet southwest keeping the bulk of them out of sight of land but leaving one to watch the mouth of the River Rother. As the sun began to drop down in the evening sky they returned line astern to disguise their numbers and approached the town out of the sun and on the evening tide. Four Viking warships were lying on the beach unguarded, so Wulfnoth withdrew the bulk of his fleet leaving five vessels.

Clearly the Danes, who had met no opposition on the searoads, did not expect attack from that quarter and were busy sacking the town. Swithred took his vessel into shallow water so that Cerdic could lead a party of seamen ashore and, meeting no opposition, they ran all four of the enemy ships into the water where each was tied to the stern of one of their own vessels. The whole operation was carried out in twilight and as dusk finally settled they towed their prizes out to sea unobserved.

* * * * *

Meanwhile, the English fleet was completed and ready to sail down the Thames to relieve Rochester. Beorhtric, however, refused to move until the exact number of the enemy vessels had been established and Aelfric would not commit his land army until Beorhtric had driven the Danish ships out of the Medway. Eventually word came that the Danish fleet blockading the river was substantially smaller than they had first thought and Beorhtric led his fleet out of London. However, by the time they reached Gravesand conflicting reports arrived and he withdrew, by which time the Danes had learnt of the vast boat building that had been undertaken up river and recalled their vessels from around the coast to reinforce their blockade.

Wulfnoth shadowed the Danish warships as they left the southwestern ports and was thus able to reach the Isle of Scape unopposed. There he sent word to Aethelred that he was in a position to harass the enemy from the sea if the ship army would attack from up river. Still Beorhtric hesitated which emboldened the Danish fleet and lost any element of surprise. Wulfnoth's warships engaged in a number of hit and run skirmishes, but eventually as autumn approached the whole Danish fleet was able to sail out of the Thames laden with silver and gold. Even then Wulfnoth's small fleet managed to inflict some damage on the stragglers, but could do nothing to stop the enemy sailing for home.

The Millennium came and went and it seemed that despite the dire warnings of the Book of Revelations Satan had not been unchained to wreak havoc upon the world – at least not upon England for the Vikings did not return that year, but were busy in Normandy.

Beorhtric half convinced the king that it was all down to his preservation of the English fleet whose very existence he claimed 'had struck terror into the hearts of the invaders', but when Wulfnoth sent Aethelred the four warships captured in Rye he did wonder whether a more daring commander might have achieved more.

Nevertheless the king spent much time in that first year with his new favourites in Shropshire. Eadric, always seeking ways to increase his land holding, saw an opportunity in the northwest where he was determined to settle his score with the thegns of Cumbria who had opposed him in Council. On the pretext that they were harbouring Danes he persuaded Aethelred to join him in a punitive campaign. Success brought Aethelred relief and Eadric grants of land that he coveted.

In the autumn, however, news arrived that the Danes had returned to their former winter quarters on the Isle of Wight from which they could not only strike anywhere on the south coast of England as the mood took them, but also attack Normandy to the south.

At a hastily arranged Council Eadric proposed an alliance with Normandy offering to go to Duke Richard's Court in Rouen and negotiate an arrangement that would bind the two rulers to support each other in time of need, but Richard's terms were at first deemed unacceptable to the English people. However, renewed attacks in the following summer; the total humiliation of the fleet and land army; and a crippling demand for a wergild of twenty-four thousand pounds persuaded Eadric and Aethelred that the Witan would no longer oppose Richard's demands.

The Full Council was summoned to attend a meeting in Winchester at Candlemas in 1002 and word came to Compton from Siferth that there were rumours of a momentous change of policy and Aelfhelm, whose star had been waning, was in need of all the support he could muster.

Conscious that his leather tunic had given credence to Beorhtric's attempts to brand him a mere seaman on his last visit to Court, Wulfnoth thought hard about his appearance. Cerdic who was to accompany him again would wear a brand new leather tunic and be armed with the double-edged sword with the inlaid hilt as befitting the huscarl of a powerful thegn. For himself it would be the fine green tunic embroidered with gold thread that Alena had given him when he left Bruges. They would both wear green cloaks and his would be fastened with the gold and garnet wolf broach. He was determined not to embarrass Ealdorman Aelfhelm.

When they eventually cantered into the packed stable yard in front of the Old Palace of Winchester on the two identical liver chestnut horses they caused a number eyebrows to be raised.

"Will you dress all your huscarls in their master's colours or is this one special?" asked Siferth as he steered Wulfnoth through a small doorway that led into a side chamber while Cerdic checked the stables allotted to the horses.

"This one is special and has earned his attire. However, when I stand alongside my northern friends I don't want Beorhtric to scorn Aelfhelm's choice of allies."

He'll not do that. The whole Court knows how you crept into Rye and stole four warships from under the noses of the Danes, while his claim to have preserved the fleet in London for a counter attack begins to ring hollow when they rot in harbour and still dare not take on the enemy. Sending those vessels to Aethelred was a master stroke."

"I thought it wise to show I was not fighting on my own account."

Inside the room he found a gathering of the northern lords. Apart from Aelfhelm and his brother Wulfric, there was Siferth's brother Morcar, Thurbrand from Yorkshire and two younger men whom he did not know. They had all been deep in conversation that stopped abruptly as they entered, but when the ealdorman recognised the new arrivals the group relaxed.

"You are welcome here, Wulfnoth. I think you know everyone except my two sons Wulfheah and Ufegeat. This is Wulfnoth of Sussex and a good friend and we all have need of such friends at this time."

"Anyone who has the interests of England at heart has my support, but tell me, Lord Aelfhelm, what is it about this meeting that gives you cause for concern?"

"Aethelweard was the last of that distinguished old guard of noble advisers who held this country together for a quarter of a century. Since his passing Aelfric and the Mercian upstarts have poisoned Aethelred's mind against the men of the Danelaw, equating us with each new wave of Viking invader. In short they question our loyalty and seek to forge an alliance with Richard of Normandy so that we will be sidelined. Then they will find an excuse to pick us off one by one as they did with the Cumbrians. Aethelmaer, who succeeded his father in Wessex-Beyond-Selwood, is the only ealdorman to support us and he is due to join us before the Council sits."

At that moment the door opened and the ealdorman entered with a young man of eleven or twelve years of age. All the northern lords immediately stood up.

"Ah, Prince Athelstan," said Aelfhelm bowing to the young man, "you honour us with your presence."

"Aethelmaer promised I would find friends here. I see he was not mistaken," said the Prince and he acknowledged each of the northern lords as they bowed in fealty to the heir to the throne. When he came to Wulfnoth he glanced at Aelfhelm hesitating momentarily.

"The Thegn of Compton, my Lord," the old man whispered.

"The only man in England who repeatedly outwits the Danes," Aethelmaer added.

"Ah yes, the Seawolf! My father has spoken of you. Is it true, sir, that you are not only a master of the sea, but that you have twice led your men in the thick of a land battle against the Danes and cut them to shreds?"

"It's true, my lord, I have seen some action."

"They say you left none of them alive."

"War is brutal, my lord. They're few who survive a defeat."

"My Lord Aelfric has survived many!"

"Then he is fortunate, my lord."

"He's a coward and a traitor, so I'm told, yet my father does not dismiss him."

"My lord," said Aelfhelm, "Your father rules a disparate kingdom and if he moves against one faction in time of war he may upset the delicate balance."

"But is he not planning to do just that with this new treaty?"

"Perhaps, my lord. Therefore, we must assure him of our loyalty."

"It should be obvious since my mother the queen was born and bred in the Danelaw. Why does he have to listen to those crows from Shropshire?"

"There's no ealdorman in Mercia, Lord Athelstan. I'm sure he merely uses them as his eyes."

"They frighten me."

"They frighten us all," said Thurbrand grimly.

"True. They are the most unscrupulous men in the kingdom," acknowledged Aethelmaer.

"Eadric's an evil bastard who'd barter his own mother if there was any profit in it," The Yorkshire thegn didn't mince his words. "Beorhtric is merely incompetent, but has a vicious streak. They both loathe you, Wulfnoth."

The Prince looked at Wulfnoth again. "And how have you annoyed these black crows, Master Seawolf?"

"He has ruffled their feathers on more than one occasion," said Aethelmaer with admiration, much to Wulfnoth's surprise.

"They are feathers I would delight in seeing plucked," said the young man turning back to Wulfnoth gleefully. "And will you fight for me when I am king?"

"I swore allegiance to you over the bones of St Swithun the day you were born. My sword is yours whenever you require it."

"Prince Athelstan," said Aelfhelm, "This is a man you can trust with your life."

"I know, Lord Aelfhelm. Otherwise you would not have brought him to me. My Lord of Compton, You will always be welcome in my court. But now I must rejoin my father before I'm missed." And with that the young aetheling jumped up, grinned and disappeared through the door.

"A fine young man. He'll make an excellent king one day," Aelfhelm observed with some pride. "His father was king when he was twelve and for six years used as a counter in a power struggle. Thank God he'll be spared that when he eventually succeeds. Well, my friends, we should take our seats in the Great Hall before the King arrives. Let's prove our loyalty and show him he has no need of Norman help."

Wulfnoth was surprised to see how much Aethelred had changed since he was last at Winchester. Four years before he still looked young and athletic, but now, as he sat flanked by Eadric and Beorhtric, he appeared bloated and seemed almost furtive, his eyes flicking from face to face as if trying to read the thoughts in the minds of each of his councillors. After a few moments he addressed them morosely.

"Once again we have been able to buy off the Norsemen, but we know full well that will not satisfy them indefinitely. Next year or the one following will see the striped sails riding the searoads again. Our shores are long and vulnerable and no man can predict the exact time or place of their attack. Consequently our ship army is unable to engage the enemy before they land and our southern land armies are stretched, so that they frequently face battle at a disadvantage."

"An English fleet stationed in our southern ports under a leader who is not afraid to attack the Danes at sea would ensure the safety of our shores," suggested Aethelmaer. "Surely it is time Wulfnoth of Compton was given command of the ship army!"

"The man denied me ships that would have given me victory in the Medway," Beorhtric burst out furiously. "He is unfit to command."

Wulfnoth was on his feet, but Aelfhelm forestalled him, "He is the only seaman fit to command and if he were given the fleet the men of the Danelaw would send an army to support him."

Aelfric started to protest, but the king ignored the ealdorman and continued, "It is true we could bring in forces from the Danelaw, but as we found in Cumbria many there are sympathetic to their Danish cousins."

"My lord, I must protest." Aelfhelm was shocked at the insinuation. "The men of the northeast are loyal to a man."

"I'm sure you're right, Aelfhelm. We do not doubt they would defend my northern borders if attacked, but would they want to leave their lands undefended to protect those of others in the south against their kin? Surely it would be too much to ask."

Before Aelfhelm could answer Aethelred turned to address the rest of his Council. "I have given this matter considerable thought. The future safely of the realm depends upon an alliance with Richard Duke of Normandy. It will clearly be to our mutual advantage for our joint fleets will make it impossible for the Danes to winter on the Isle of Wight."

He paused and a ripple of questions broke out around the Great Hall.

"Can we trust the Normans to keep their side of the bargain, my lord?" asked Aethelmaer voicing the concern of many.

"You need have no fears on that account. Negotiations are already well advanced and Richard has offered us the hand of his sister Emma as a pledge of his commitment, a gesture that we have graciously accepted."

The implication of the king's words brought a communal gasp of shock followed by a stunned silence, which was eventually broken by the bishop of St Germans.

"My lord, the pagans of the southwest take more than one wife. How can we spread Christianity if the king himself indulges in such practices?"

"Take care, Bishop," snapped Aethelred. "There are wiser heads in the Church who understand the necessity of political marriages."

Ealdorman Aelfhelm now the second most senior member of the Witan rose once again to his feet. Suddenly he looked tired and his voice shook with emotion. "My lord, I must council you against such a move. The queen has served you well and bred a fine clutch of royal sons to secure the succession of your line. A political marriage with Normandy would have strings attached."

"We are not naïve, Aelfhelm," interrupted the king. "We are well able to deal with Norman trickery."

"I would not presume to doubt it, my lord, but Richard would demand that any male offspring born of his sister be acknowledged as your heir."

"Let him demand all he likes. I already have an heir. The matter is settled."

"But, my lord, the matter has not been fully discussed in Council."

"You can discuss all you like. A king has to act. Eadric of Shropshire has negotiated a treaty that will protect the realm for years to come. Richard's sister will arrive in the spring. Our marriage and coronation will take place straight after Easter. The die has already been thrown."

"And what will happen to my mother?" Athelstan cried.

"Your mother has already left the Court and will spend her days in the Abbey of Wilton.

"And what of me, father?"

"Nothing else has changed. You remain at Court as heir to the throne."

With that Aethelred rose and accompanied by Eadric and Beorhtric left the chamber and the council broke up in disarray.

Wulfnoth spoke briefly to Ealdorman Aethelmaer, before Siferth drew him away to the antechamber where they found Athelstan and his younger brother Edmund surrounded by the Northern Lords. Each took an oath to serve the prince and support his claim above all others to the throne of his father when the time came.

Lest they be discovered the meeting was brief and leaving the two princes they all took horse and rode for

Compton where they spent two days discussing how they might remain loyal to king and yet protect the interests of the prince. Apart from Aethelmaer and the Bishop of St.Germans in Western Wessex they realised that none of the other members of the Witan could be trusted to support them. If the treaty collapsed and the marriage was called off or if the marriage failed to produce a male heir then all would be well and their conspiracy need never come to light. Conscious, however, of the threat posed by Eadric and his network of spies it was agreed that Cerdic should act as their go-between.

The royal wedding ceremony duly took place in Winchester followed immediately by a coronation that gave the Norman queen far greater status than that enjoyed by her predecessor. Aethelmaer and Aelfhelm grudgingly attended. They could hardly do anything else, but their body language and coldness to Emma did not enhance their position with either the king or his new queen. Aethelred was annoyed, but convinced that time would reconcile them to his new consort. Emma, who had been made aware of their opposition to the marriage and their support for Athelstan, managed to hide her resentment and smiled radiantly, but Eadric's face, was furious and he determined to take revenge on the two ealdormen at the earliest opportunity.

Wulfnoth had been relieved not to be summoned to Winchester for the royal wedding. He preferred the obscurity of his estate to the division, intrigue and favouritism of Court life.

Although some news filtered across the country, he decided that he would send Cerdic up to York as soon as the harvest was in and there was no longer danger of Danish raids. This became possible in early September and Cerdic set off north wearing a nondescript cloak over his leather tunic. If he were stopped on the road he did not want to draw attention to the fact that he came from Compton. However, he did carry the ivory comb in his purse, a gift for Hild and Wulfnoth's permission to approach Torgrim for the hand of his daughter. Taking the old stone road that led to London he had crossed the Thames in three days and heading north on Irmin Street he was soon in the relative safety of the Danelaw eventually reaching Lindsey where Siferth's brother Morcar was the dominant thegn, there being at present no ealdorman.

Reaching the Dearne he pressed on up the old packman way until he could see the cluster of squat buildings that housed the nuns of St. Helen's and further on the manor where Torgrim and his family had set up home in the old fort above the village of Barnburh.

Smoke rose in a thin columns above the dwellings and he guessed that one of them would be the forge fire still smouldering and could imagine Hild stirring the cooking pot while her father washed the dust and grime from his face and arms before sitting down to eat. He was still picturing the scene when he reached the crossroads at the top of Melton Hill and began the descent to St. Helen's Spring where he slid out of the saddle and let the horse drink. Although he was impatient to reach his destination, he wanted time to rehearse the speech he would make to the old man when he asked for the hand of his daughter. Despite the fact that Wulfnoth had assured him that now Hild was safe Torgrim's only concern would be his daughter's happiness, he was still apprehensive as to how his suit might be received. Torgrim was a rich man while he was merely a huscarl as they were called in the Danelaw. He might want a man of property for his son-in-law. Perhaps the girl could not bring herself to leave the father who had relied on her ever since his wife had died. Perhaps the comb had been nothing more than a simple thank-you gift for bringing her home safely. Perhaps she did not feel anything for him. Perhaps his own desire had clouded his judgement. Perhaps he should press on to York and approach Torgrim on his way back.

He had almost decided to do just that when a voice broke into his despondent reflection.

"I must just soak my feet in cold water or I'll be a mass of blisters before I reach home," the young man said breathlessly as he threw himself down beside Cerdic. "I have run all the way and they burn like the Devil's must on the hot stones of Hell."

"It's been unusually hot today," said Cerdic pleasantly, making more room on the grassy bank for the newcomer. "Have you come far?"

"Only from Wildetorp, a village between here and Sprotburh Falls, where I have been helping stook the sheaves on one of Wulfric's farms. The young man grinned and wiggled his toes and then looked critically at the sole of each foot before plunging them both into the stream again. "Just five minutes. They're fairly hard, but you can never be too careful."

"Do you have far to go?" asked Cerdic.

"Only to the new house at this end of the village, but I can't wait to be home. My wife is expecting a child any day now and everyday when I finish in the fields I wonder if I shall be a father. It's a queer feeling, you know. Well not knowing really. Do you think I will make a good father?"

"I'm sure you will," laughed Cerdic.

"That's a relief. I think so too, but you can't always be sure, can you?"

"No I suppose not."

"I mean the future is another world, isn't it? It's like the weather. We can't control it, but unless we step into it bravely, we'll never know, will we? Well I can't stop here gossiping all day. I must be off."

"I'll come with you." The young man's exuberance had raised Cerdic's spirits and he knew that his own destiny required only the confidence to seek Torgrim's blessing and to ask Hild if she would marry him."

He would have asked if his companion knew how they all were up at the forge, but he found it impossible to get a word in edgeways.

"It's quite a responsibility having a family. I mean an extra mouth to feed and my wife won't be able to work as much as used to, at least not straight away, but people in a village are always ready to lend a hand. We'll manage I'm sure."

He paused for breath and Cerdic started to speak, but was interrupted before he had said two words.

"We shall have to choose names of course. They're very important. If it's a girl I shall choose one from the bible. Sarah's my favourite, but my wife likes Ruth or Orpah. Of course it may be a boy, that's different. My wife is determined to call him Ulf, but all the men in my family are called Elmet. You see my grandfather came from Elmet, so the people called him Elmet. He died just before my father was born so he was called Elmet.....out of respect, I suppose. That's my name too. You see it sort of stuck, so perhaps it will have to be Elmet, if it's a boy; but there again, it will be rather confusing and I would like to think that he will grow up to be a real individual, independent, not just one in a whole string of Elmets."

"Of course," agreed Cerdic.

"By the way what name do you have?"

"Me? Oh I'm Cerdic."

"Cerdic?" Elmet tried out the name once or twice. "Cerdic? Cerdic? Yes I see. It's a very good name. Were you named after your father?"

"No. No. My father was Aescwine, but I was called Cerdic after the first King of Wessex."

"Are you a prince, then?" the young man stopped and stared wide-mouthed.

"Nothing of the sort. All the men in my family were poor fishermen. I suppose my mother just liked the name."

"Oh that's all right then," said Elmet with great relief. "But I still like the name. Yes I like it very much. Would you mind very much if we took your name for our son; that is, if it is a boy?"

"Not at all," said Cerdic amused by his companion's enthusiasm.

"That's very decent of you. Of course I shall have to ask my wife. They can be funny about things like that. Names I mean."

"I suppose they can."

"That's our home," said Elmet when they reached the village, proudly pointing out a new dwelling. "Wulfric said I could build it there, because I'm a good worker." It was little more than a hut with the thatched roof reaching down to the ground on either side with walls of mud-coated plaited wattle to front and rear. It was too small to keep a fire inside so one burned outside. A baby's cries could be heard piercing the air from within and Elmet stood uncertainly rooted to the spot.

"It sounds as though you are a father," said Cerdic. "Well! Are you going to greet your son, Elmet?"

"Yes. Yes, of course," said Elmet breaking the invisible power that had held him fastened to the spot. "But it may not be a boy."

"Boy? Girl? What does it matter, Elmet? You have a child and a lusty one at that," laughed Cerdic.

"You will wait. Won't you? My wife must see the man he is named after. If it is a boy, that is," he added almost apologetically.

With that he was gone and Cerdic, who had walked the horse up the hill, mounted and sat patiently listening to the sounds of excitement emanating from the hut and wondering what his own welcome would be like up at the old fort.

After a while the door opened and Elmet skipped out and danced round the fire. "It's a boy. It's a boy," he shouted and picking up a half burnt log that had rolled to one side he tossed it gleefully into the embers.

A dishevelled woman then appeared carrying a child in her arms, but at that moment the fire cracked into life sending a billow of smoke up into the air and despite the fact that she dived back inside coughing with her bundle, Cerdic had recognised her.

Return to Bruges   September 1002

Although the physical pain caused by the loss of his wife had eventually diminished, Wulfnoth had for the first two years continued to feel that Ragnhild's spirit still inhabited the estate. Often he would go out and looking up at the night sky he would talk to her, sharing his concerns about their son, seeking her advice on this or that development, or simply confiding the secrets of his heart. His brief encounter with the remarkable Magda among the shadows and the passing of her ghost with the last rays of the setting sun had made him realise that spirits belonged to another world. Gradually, even the presence of Ragnhild's spirit had faded into the ether as if she had finally gone back to a home on some distant star.

Only once had she returned when he was burning up with fever in Bruges and then she had remained only until the fever broke and she had left him in the healing arms of Alena.

At first he had felt guilt at his feelings for the woman whose body he had respected, but whose bed and whose embrace he had shared for several months. Since returning to England, however, he had not for one moment forgotten her and after having been separated from her for more than three years he longed to see her again.

They kept in contact via the shipments of equipment and raw materials he supplied for her burgeoning cloth industry. The actual purchase of fleeces he left to Alfred who in his capacity as reeve of the Compton estate always attended the market at Chichester. Over the years the young man had developed an instinct for the timing and pitching his bids in such a way as to discourage competition. Consequently, he was able to make a number of assiduous purchases.

Twice a month during the season *Le Merle Noir* would arrive at Bosham where the fleeces were stockpiled in readiness. Swithred would supervise the loading and prepare a tally stick giving one half to the captain and returning the other to Alfred who kept meticulous accounts for the estate.

Wulfnoth would love to have written long letters to Alena explaining how he felt, but he knew that her reading and writing skills were limited and that someone else would have to read them to her. The thoughts that he wanted to express were far too personal for another's eyes. In any case he didn't trust the captain not to open them on route, so he made do with brief notes. When Godwin was old enough to understand he would make the trip back across the searoads.

Meanwhile sheep breeding at Compton was also proving successful. At least once a year Wulfnoth would accompany Alfred to Chichester market and they would spend the morning talking with sheep farmers and examining the ewes prior to the sale. They were not merely interested in seeking sound breeding stock, but in assessing the quality of the fleece by running their fingers through each animal's coat in search of the finest wool. On one occasion they even took the risk of picking an unproven second tup purely on the quality of its wool. By lunchtime they would normally have selected the animals they believed would enhance their flock and then Wulfnoth would leave the bidding entirely in Alfred's hands.

The second tup proved to be a successful breeder invariably siring twins and even occasional triplets. In three years the flock boasted twenty ewes, eleven of which were old enough to breed. In the fourth year sixteen lambs were reared successfully and by late August they were fatter than ever before. The wethers, and there were, mercifully, few of those, were then butchered for meat to help sustain the growing army of estate workers and seamen during the winter. One male, however, had been kept intact, but would probably not be fertile for another two seasons.

The country was quiet, the Danes had been paid off with a massive wergild and it would be some weeks before word came from the north, so Wulfnoth decided to put a long-cherished plan into action. He sent word to Oswy to have his own large trader ready to sail and selected the original ram, two older ewes and four of the youngsters to make the journey to Flanders. On the first of September with an early morning tide and a fair wind they slipped out of Bosham and by the following evening were tied up against the Woolhouse wharf.

A teenager stood on the quay watching the foreign vessel with its unusual cargo and stepped out to bar the way as Wulfnoth leapt on shore.

"Do you have business here, sir?"

Wulfnoth thought his face strangely familiar but could not place him.

The boy stood his ground. "I asked if you had business here on this wharf."

"Of course, but it is no affair of yours, young man. Stand aside. You are blocking my way."

"It is my duty, sir. This is a private wharf."

"So too is my business which is with the lady who owns the Woolhouse."

"With my mother?"

"I do not believe the lady Alena has children. At least," he corrected himself rather apprehensively, "certainly not gangling young men of your age."

"Well she is not my real mother, but she has always been a mother to me as far as I care to remember."

Suddenly the light began to dawn and Wulfnoth clicked his fingers and pointed two or three times at the youth with growing recognition. "Of course! Of course!" he said, "you must be Walram, but you were scarce more than a child when I last saw you."

The door of the Woolhouse opened behind the young man and a woman with a chatelaine dangling from her waist stepped out to see who was causing the commotion. The sun was setting directly behind the thegn and it was a few seconds before she recognised him. "Lord Wulfnoth!" she screamed and dropped into a curtsy.

"Judith," he said, "Tell this young man who I am."

"Walram, Don't you recognise him. This is Lord Wulfnoth from England and the Mistress's........" She didn't finish the sentence and seemed genuinely embarrassed by her attempt to describe the visitor.

Wulfnoth was embarrassed, not by what she had said, but by her subservience.

"Come Judith, This isn't Baldwin's Court. Where is your mistress?"

"Not here, my lord. She's bought another house in Ghent and frequently spends a day or two over there. We expect her back before Saturday when *La Pie Bavarde* returns."

"I see. Well! I have brought her seven sheep. Perhaps Walram can find grazing for them and a boy who will keep an eye on them so that they don't stray."

"There's common land beyond the market, my lord, and plenty of lads who'll happily sit with them all night to earn the price of a loaf of bread. I'll help the captain get them ashore." And with that Walram climbed down into the vessel.

A small blond boy was sitting among the sheep. "Hi!" he said looking up as Walram stepped into the pen. "Have you come for these poor creatures? They didn't enjoy the sea voyage, you know. They made a real mess down here. They'll be glad to be on dry land again. My father says I've got to wash this area when they've gone."

"He's a hard man, your father," Walram grinned at him.

"Oh no! We threw dice and I lost. If I'd won he would have had to do it."

"I see," said Walram amused as much by the arrangement as with boy's self-assurance. "I'm afraid I'm not used to sheep so will you help us get them on shore."

"Of course. The captain's setting up a block on the quay, just like the one we have at Bosham. Then he'll lower a sling and we have to make sure it rests under the sheep's belly. Then it's his job to pull it up. I wouldn't stand over there if I were you."

"Why?" asked Walram, mystified.

"Well that sheep isn't."

288

"Isn't what?"

"Isn't a sheep."

"Oh! I see."

"He's a ram."

"Ah!"

"He was supposed to be separated from the others by that wattle fence, but he broke out and tried to mount one of the ewes. My father had to tie him up like a hog or we'd have capsized in the channel. Now his feet are loose again he's quite likely to lash out and those hooves can be lethal."

Walram stepped across to the other side of the boat and as soon as the sling came down they began to unload the cargo.

Wulfnoth was disappointed that Alena was not in Bruges, but he promised Godwin that the following day he would take him to see the Burg and the great stone Church of St Donatian. If the count happened to be in residence then they would pay their respects. That night Judith served them hot soup, good quality white bread and a plate of fish that Walram had caught in the Steegherei. They were both tired after spending most of the day on the sea and Godwin nearly fell fast asleep at the table. When Judith came with a second pitcher of wine she gently led him through to the kitchen where the servants slept on sack mattresses stuffed with wool from cheaper fleeces that were unsuitable for the fine material made on the two looms that had pride of place in the main hall of the Woolhouse. It was obviously going to be a warm night and the fire had been allowed to go out, but it was full of comforting smells and Godwin curled up in a corner and slept soundly.

After another glass of Rhenish Wulfnoth could hardly keep his eyes open and by nine o'clock the thought of the large empty comfortable bed in the adjoining room was irresistible.

Stripping off he climbed into it and discovered new linen sheets of the finest quality and hoped that Alena would not mind his using it in her absence. However, he didn't worry about it for long; within minutes he was fast asleep and soon dreaming of flocks of black-faced sheep filling the Woolhouse yard.

Back in England, Queen Emma was determined to exploit her new status. She knew well that Ealdorman Aelfhelm had spoken out against her marriage and remembered his frosty attitude to her at the wedding ceremony. Now that his power over the King appeared to be on the wane she decided that the time had come to settle her score with him.

She was astute enough to realise that she could hardly accuse him of treason and that a pretext had to be found to engineer his downfall. That pretext offered itself through her marriage settlement whereby Aethelred had granted her various estates and parcels of land. One of these included the town of Exeter, which had a high proportion of second and third generation Danish settlers.

Emma had installed Hugh, a Norman knight, as her reeve and he was forever complaining about the unruly behaviour of these Danish enclaves and the arrogance of the mercenary Pallig who had deserted Aethelred but been pardoned in the recent truce. Here was the catalyst that would bring down her enemy.

In order to effect her plan she decided to enlist the help of Eadric and his brother, Beorhtric.

While she saw through Eadric for the duplicitous creature he was, she recognised that he was a rising star and sought to use him for her own ends. He had after all helped to negotiate the treaty with Normandy, professed to be anti-Dane and there was no love lost between him and Aelfhelm.

One morning when Aethelred was out hunting she and Hugh sought him out in his quarters above the gatehouse. This room had the double luxury of allowing him to observe anyone who approached the palace while enabling his spies the advantage of entering and leaving with the minimum of attention. As usual his brother, Beorhtric, was with him when the queen entered.

"Madam you do me great honour. How can I be of service to you?"

"I am a new comer to this land and I need a man I can trust."

"Surely, madam, you have many loyal servants among your Norman attendants," said Eadric cautiously.

Of course but that's the point. They are Norman and many of your people do not trust them. I need someone who can advise me on English matters and defend me against those who slander me.

"Then you have come to the right place madam," said Beorhtric. "My brother is the king's right hand and controls the Witan. He will be only too willing to advise you and deal with any enemies you have."

Eadric who was not ready to commit himself was angered by the interruption, but strove to regain the initiative.

"True I have a certain influence, madam, but I am merely one of Aethelred's loyal servants. I do not have real power. I am not an ealdorman."

"One day you will be," said Emma. "Mercia has no natural leader."

"Aelfhelm advocates Siferth of the Five Boroughs to fill that vacancy."

"Aelfhelm is out of favour and I mean to see he stays there. I'm sure my husband is waiting for the right moment to appoint a more loyal subject to the post."

Eadric smiled, appreciating the carrot, but also the measured way the queen proffered it.

"The royal wife of the king is kind to think so."

"The royal wife of the king would be a strong advocate for those who support her."

"Thank you, madam. A loyal subject should support his king and his queen, so what is it that you wish my advice on?

"There is unrest in my town of Exeter. The Danish settlers will not accept the authority of my reeve, Count Hugh. They have the audacity to call him a foreigner. They say the taxes he imposes are grossly unfair and produce a string of excuses for non-payment. Yet those taxes are mine by right."

"True, madam. You should lay the matter before the king, your husband."

"They claim they have the ear of Ealdorman Aelfhelm and that the people of the Danelaw will support their cause against me."

"That's treasonable talk, madam. You did well to bring the matter to my attention. I cannot think that the old man would be stupid enough to risk tearing the country apart. He is more likely to counsel the king to caution."

"Then I will be denied my taxes."

"Not if we can get to the king first and sow suspicion in his mind. We must make him think that Exeter is but one of a number of towns where Danish settlers are plotting treason. With careful planning we can deal with each pocket of resistance at the same time before Aelfhelm is aware of what is going on. Then we can turn our attention to the Danelaw.

"I see I was not mistaken in seeking your advice."

The count's favour; the fact that she was the owner of three ships; and the strength of her personality had given Alena the power to transform the old brothel into the hub of a thriving cloth-making industry.

The small rooms at the rear of the building where Jacob had entertained his customers and where they had paid to ride the flesh on flea-ridden straw-filled mattresses had been thoroughly purged of the last vestiges of that dreadful trade. The bare rooms had been lime-washed several times and bunches of herbs hung to sweeten the air. It was here that the new sacks of wool were brought and the contents sorted into coarse, medium and fine grades, any damaged pieces being discarded and burnt. Then it was taken out and washed in a lixiviation of vegetable ash. When it had dried in the sun it was beaten and combed to remove the tangles.

At this point it was brought into the main hall, which had been converted into a spinning and weaving factory. At one end women could sit with distaffs and hand spindles producing the thread and at the other were the two imported weaving looms. These had an assortment of weights hanging on either end to hold the warp while women had the laborious job of passing the weft baton over and under the individual threads. It was here that a continuous piece of cloth gradually emerged mothlike to begin a new existence, a wonder that had never ceased to fascinate Alena since the time when as a child she had watched her father work before famine had torn their family apart.

But the process did not stop here. The woven cloth was taken outside again to two large open sheds which Alena had had built against the walls. In one it was soaked and trampled underfoot in wooden troughs to prevent future shrinkage and thickened with clay before being hooked onto tenters to be dried and stretched into shape.

In the second shed a solution of wood ash, woad, madder or some other vegetable root was prepared in great hot tubs where the cloth could be repeatedly plunged under the surface by means of long poles to produce the vibrant blues, reds, yellows and greens that made Alena's cloth so striking.

However, to compete with the best imports and untie the pursestrings of the richest citizens of Bruges her finest cloth needed an almost silk-like texture. To acquire such a finish the nap had to be raised and shorn several times, a job she entrusted only to Ogive and Rosela and which took place upstairs in the room formerly used by Jacob's long deceased wife. When she was satisfied, the cloth was folded and pressed under wooden boards ready to go on sale.

A number of families relied on Alena for their livelihood. The men could serve on her ships, but she would only allow women inside the Woolhouse. The older ones undertook the heavier tasks of preparation, washing, fulling and dyeing and generally worked at the back and in the sheds. Young girls, however, were trained in the skills of spinning and weaving and Alena insisted that they learnt both so that she could rotate her staff not only to prevent boredom, but also to ensure that the process need not be disrupted by absence. If they were really skilful they could assist Ogive and Rosela upstairs in the hope that eventually one or two of them could take over the job of finishing the cloth, if Rosela ever did return to Italy or Ogive's eyesight deteriorated.

Outside the Woolhouse Alena still supplied her web of artisans with raw materials and purchased cloth from them. Now that she had bought a very small timber-structured house with wattle and daub panels overlooking the River Leie she could sell her cloth to the people of Ghent as well as Bruges. On the first day of each month she would ride over with Ogive, open up the house and sell her wares. Usually when the days were shortening they would stay over night sleeping in the little room above the shop.

That day, however, business had been brisk and she had sold out earlier than expected so she and Ogive decided to return to the Woolhouse riding the twenty miles or so cross-country, making the best of the late afternoon sunshine.

As the shadows were lengthening it crossed her mind that two women alone presented an easy target and if one of the horses should fall lame they were at the mercy of any brigands roaming the land. She shuddered at the thought recalling her violent treatment at the hands of the Hounds of Satan and resolved to take on a male servant who could accompany her in future. Walram was still too young and the abuse that he had received at the hands of Jacob's customers had left scars.

Being brought up by three women had given them a chance to heal, but he needed to mix with people of his own sex and a slightly older man that he could trust would be good for him.

She realised that she too had shunned male company since that fateful day four years before. Caring for Wulfnoth and the security of his presence during the night had initially given her a lifeline, but after his return to England she had let no other man into her life. Her dealings with court officials and with the church were conducted with strict formality and while each captain reported to her on his return she always contrived to receive them at her place of business among the looms in the main hall.

Of those who had sought to rape her she saw nothing. The castellan rarely set foot outside the Burg. Wenemar and Erembald remained banished, but occasionally they had appeared in her nightmares, their wolfish grins leering at her as she struggled to free herself from imagined restraints. So it was with some relief that they crossed the Dijver and trotted through the deserted streets till they reached the small courtyard where they rubbed the horses down before feeding them and making their way into the Woolhouse.

Tiptoeing into the kitchen they stepped over the sleeping figures and dipped two bowls into the cauldron of soup that remained hanging above the embers of the fire. It was still hot. Then they whispered their goodnights and Alena tiptoed out again and made her way up the stairs to her private rooms.

It was a warm night and she opened the shutter and as she drank the soup she looked out of the windhole across the river Rei at the formidable fort.

It was a view that filled her with emotional uncertainty. Four years in this foreign land had seen her rise from slavery and degradation to a position of prosperity and grudging respect. Rich burghers and their wives who relied on her for quality cloth would acknowledge her in the street, but as the wife of the former whoremonger and as a rape victim she was socially unacceptable. She provided work for a dozen families and those who worked in the Woolhouse looked upon her with awe and accepted her without question as their mistress, but there was no one in whom she could confide, no one she could call a friend. Only Wulfnoth and Hild had ever come close, but they were far away in England and her lack of literary skills precluded any correspondence other than the lists and pricing of goods that she exchanged with the former. She had received a number of letters from Hild, but, unable to make head or tail of the sentences, she had locked them away in the box in her bedroom. Beyond the walls of the Woolhouse the world thought her cold and aloof, but inside herself waking or sleeping she still lived in fear and was desperately lonely.

Apart from replacing the ladder with a proper staircase, the only other alteration she had made to her private rooms was to have a new windhole put in the bedroom. She couldn't bear a stuffy atmosphere and apart from in the depth of winter she would always sleep with the shutter wide open. Having finished her soup she made her way into the darkened room felt her way round the bed and opened the shutter. It was only when she turned back to the bed that she saw the dark hair on the bolster. For a moment she froze in panic, but then noticed the green tunic and sword that lay across the stool. Satisfying herself that it was indeed the Thegn of Compton, she relaxed, slipped off her clothes and crept in between the linen sheets.

Wulfnoth slept on and her initial delight in finding him in her bed was tempered with a tinge of disappointment. Sighing she kissed him on the shoulder, whispered "Goodnight" and resigned herself to sleep.

The touch of her lips disrupted the pattern of his sleep and he rolled over coming to rest when he came into contact with her body, his right thigh resting on hers and his right arm across her breasts.

"Alena," he murmured still half asleep.

"My lord," she replied softly.

"Is it really you?" he asked consciousness breaking through the blanket of sleep.

"No one else I assure you," she protested, slipping her arms around his neck pulling their naked bodies together tightly as if she sought to bury herself inside his embrace.

They kissed passionately and she could feel his body respond to hers.

"Make love to me, Wulfnoth," she whispered with a sense of urgency in her voice.

* * * * *

For the first time in her life she had enjoyed the fulfilment of honest love.

She had sobbed with relief, caught her breath with excitement and cried out, "Ay.....Yay..... Yay..Yay ..Yay... Yay...Yay" with her first experience of genuine orgasmic pleasure before drifting into a deep refreshing sleep.

Alena felt no desire to get out of bed the following morning when the feisty chorus of house sparrows woke her with their incessant chatter outside the windhole. With the sun playing on their naked bodies all she wanted to do was to relax beside her lover, smell his presence and listen to his regular breathing.

Then she remembered the golden-haired child fast asleep downstairs. His presence in the kitchen had surprised her, but then she had shrugged her shoulders and presumed that Judith had taken pity on some poor homeless wretch. Now the truth dawned on her. It had to be Wulfnoth's son, Godwin.

Climbing out of bed, she made her way down to the stream that fed into the river and dropped unobserved into a gravel-bottomed pool. Under her loose flowing tunic the freedom of the clear water matched with her carefree mood. Bracing herself with her forearms, she let the rest of her body drift lazily under the surface and watched as the first flashes of sunlight chased away the last vestiges of the night. Turning over onto her knees she drew the tunic up over her head and wrung it out. Then she stood up slipped it back over her head and returned to the Woolhouse.

The women stirred as she raked out the ashes and put a couple of split logs on the fire.

"We will all need a good breakfast today. Rosela. Send Walram out for extra milk: Lord Wulfnoth's son will be thirsty when he wakes.

"I can't, mistress. Walram spent the night looking after the sheep."

"The sheep?"

"Yes, mistress. His lordship arrived with seven sheep."

"But what am I supposed to do with seven sheep?"

"He said you could grow your own wool, mistress."

"Did he indeed! Well, perhaps one of you would fetch the milk."

"Of course, mistress."

"Judith, Bring the boy upstairs when he wakes. I'm sure his father will wish to see him."

"Yes, madam."

With that she carried a pitcher of water up stairs and joined Wulfnoth who was stirring.

"Some people can sleep in bed all day," she said.

"Only when it holds memories of the arms of a beautiful woman."

"Or of a shepherdess perhaps?" she said tossing her head in feigned pique.

He laughed and she couldn't keep a straight face, so she threw herself on top of him, but then looked at him seriously. "Will you teach me to read, Wulfnoth?"

"Of course, but why?"

"So that you can write to me when you are back in England."

"But....."

"You know you will go back and I could not bear the loneliness again."

"You could come with me."

"And what would happen to those who depend on me here?"

"Surely someone could run the business for you."

"There is no one. Walram is too young and in any case he needs someone of his own sex that he can trust. I need a man I can trust when you are not here. Find me someone, Wulfnoth."

"When I have to leave I will send you one of my huscarls and I will write lots of letters so you must learn to read or you won't know how much I miss you. We must start today. I will write you a letter and you shall learn to read from it."

Alena brightened up and then suddenly leapt off the bed and fetched a box from the table. "But I already have three letters from Hild. You can use those to teach me?"

"Has no one ever read them for you?"

Alena shook her head. "No," she said. "They are private and outside these walls there is no one here I can trust."

Wulfnoth made no comment, but took them from her and unfolding the parchment read each one to her

The first was full of Hild's gratitude for the woman who had protected her from a life of misery; the second described their new life in the Danelaw and begged Alena to visit them so that her father could thank her for the life of his daughter; and the third was about Cerdic the young man who had taken her home for whom she was making a comb. Each finished with the same sentence, 'Write to me.'

While Wulfnoth read them Alena sat hugging her knees and tears welled from the corners of her eyes and ran down her cheeks.

"I can not write. I cannot tell her how much I miss her. How much I want to see her again."

"You shall," said Wulfnoth drawing her beside him and putting his arm around her. "Look, "he said. "Each letter begins with a greeting. 'My Dearest Alena.' Today we shall practise the letters so that you can reply, 'My Dearest Hild.' It is quite simple.

She kissed him and wanted desperately to make love to him again. Then she remembered.

"Godwin will be awake. I have told Judith to bring him up. You must get dressed."

When Godwin and Judith arrived with the breakfast they were seated at the table and Alena was writing the word 'Dearest' with her finger in the surface.

"Ah!" said Wulfnoth. "Godwin, come and meet the lady who saved my life and nursed me back to health when I was in Bruges four years ago."

"Madam, My father has spoken often about you and you are indeed as beautiful as he said."

Alena squeezed Wulfnoth's hand and then held out both to his son. "You are welcome, Godwin. Your father is my dearest friend, but he is generous. I did no more for him than he for me. I owe him my life too and all I have. Come and join us for breakfast."

Although Wulfnoth did not hide the fact that the volatile political situation in England might demand his instant return, the three spent the next few weeks together. They called on the count and were graciously received, they visited Ghent and they wandered happily through the streets of Bruges. Both Godwin and Alena spent an hour each day learning their letters, and by the end of September they were both quite proficient. They were beginning to feel like a family and Alena would always visit the kitchen at dusk and kiss Godwin goodnight. Then she would go back up stairs and by the light of a rush candle she would write him a chalk message on a piece of slate and leave it beside him.

Then and only then would she climb into the great bed and spend the rest of the night in Wulfnoth's arms.

Godwin began to wake up early each morning to decipher the secret message left by his bed. When he had worked it out, he would run up to the bedroom and squeeze in between their naked bodies and triumphantly read out the words. He had accepted their relationship as the most natural thing in the world. Then he would sit at the table in the living room and write his reply, so that it was ready by the time they had dressed and Judith brought the breakfast.

One morning in the beginning of October Wulfnoth went out on his own and wandered through the market stalls until he found one that sold parchment. He bought three large sheets, a number of smaller ones and a vessel of ink. Returning home he cut a couple of goose quills and gave them to Alena.

"It is time you replied to Hild," he said.

Her eyes lit up as she felt the strange material. "It's just like the ones she sent to me."

"Yes and now you must write to her."

"But what shall I say?"

"Tell her everything that has happened since she left. How you are the most important cloth-maker of Flanders. How your ships trade with a half a dozen countries and how much you miss her."

"Can I tell her how much I love you?"

"And how much I love you. You can tell her anything you like, but you must make all your letters small or you won't have enough parchment."

PART FOUR

The Royal Succession

"When the royal wife of old king Aethelred was
pregnant in her womb

All the men of the country took an oath

That if a man-child should come forth as
the fruit of her labour

They would await upon him as their lord and king

Who would rule over the whole race of the English."

Vitae Edwardis (C11th)

Cyningesburh

After the humiliation of seeing Hild with Elmet's son in her arms all Cerdic's hopes had tasted like ashes in his mouth and being unable to speak without choking he had fled from the village and ridden blindly until he had found himself deep in Melton Wood with a lame horse. His misery turned to self-reproach and he cursed himself for causing the unfortunate animal to suffer. With no other option he turned back to seek help at Wulfric's manor. This was fortuitous, however, since Aelfhelm and the Lords of the Five Boroughs were all there. Wulfric Spott was too ill to travel, but they needed his advice and his manor was conveniently situated for all concerned.

There had been rumours of the queen's pregnancy, but they had come to naught. Nevertheless they fuelled fear in the Danelaw that the day must soon come when they proved to be true. Then the alliance with Normandy would take on a more sinister prospect and the balance of power would shift significantly. An Anglo-Norman monarch might resent the degree of autonomy enjoyed by the North since the days of King Edgar and attempt to impose the culture and laws of the rest of England on the men of the Danelaw.

Consequently, the Northern Lords needed to sound out what support they could expect from the rest of the country, if they resolved that the Danelaw openly declare its unwavering commitment to Athelstan's cause against all others present or future. Above all they needed to know where Aethelmaer, Ealdorman of the Western Provinces, stood. He had always been close to the prince and had spoken against the Norman alliance, but to contact him required either a long sea voyage or sending messengers through land controlled by Eadric.

Cerdic's arrival gave them another alternative. If word could be sent to Wulfnoth he might be willing to travel to the Western Provinces without drawing attention to what might be construed by the king as a conspiracy against the queen and any new royal progeny.

The following morning Aelfhelm arranged for Cerdic to choose a replacement from Wulfric's stable and he gratefully began the return journey to Compton to acquaint Wulfnoth with the resolve of the Northern Lords and their request.

Although he stopped each night to feed, water and rest his new mount, he had little interest in food himself and slept fitfully so that when he eventually reached Compton he was utterly exhausted. He had lost weight and looked desperately ill. Despite his protestations Estrith insisted that he that he went to bed and that someone else be sent to carry his message to Wulfnoth.

* * * * *

Thus it was Swithred and Oswy who arrived in Bruges with the news of the latest unrest in England.

Alena and Wulfnoth both knew the time would come when duty would demand the thegn's return, but both also knew that only the separation of death would be final.

"Of course you must go," said Alena at once, "but promise me you will write to me as often as possible."

I promise and I will come back, but I must ask a favour of you too. England is not a healthy place at present. I fear there may be civil war. Will you keep Godwin here until it is safe for him to return?

"Of course," she said simply.

"Thank you. It will be a relief to know he is safe with you. I shall leave Swithred here to protect you both for the time being. When Cerdic recovers I will send him to you to take his place. You know him and he will need something to occupy his mind and help him to overcome his disappointment at the loss of Hild.

"He will be most welcome here."

"Swithred can then return on the ship that brings Cerdic and take word to Aelfhelm that I am engaged in his business. Meanwhile Oswy will accompany me to the Western Provinces. Once I have discovered where Aethelmaer stands we shall return to Bosham and I will write to you.

"I shall miss you," Alena said sadly. Then she added more brightly "When Swithred leaves he can carry my letter for Hild and congratulate her on her marriage, but I will not tell Cerdic that I am writing to her."

"Perhaps you are wise."

To avoid being summoned to Winchester Aethelmaer had claimed Danish incursions and serious unrest in the Western Provinces necessitated that he personally supervise the reconstruction of many strongholds beyond the Tamar. Effectively as far as the rest of England was concerned he could be anywhere in that wild pagan country, so Wulfnoth made landfall at the Cathedral of St Germans where he sought out the bishop, whose attempt to remonstrate with the king had marked him out as a man who would not only be sympathetic to the cause of Prince Athelstan, but likely to know of the Ealdorman's whereabouts.

Thus it proved and after sharing the hospitality of the Bishop's table, Wulfnoth put to sea again and headed westward again hugging the Cornish coast until he reached a second River.

The Fowey being a tidal river was navigable for several miles, the flow of water enabling crews to ship oars and enjoy the rare beauty of its long reaches, broad bends and tranquil creeks where grey heron stalk their prey, snipe probed deep into the mud and kingfishers with their vibrant electric blue plumage darted through the light and shade of the tree-lined banks.

Centuries before a local ruler had fortified a high rocky outcrop some two and a half miles up stream, but it had fallen into disrepair and in any case it was too far inland to prevent the Vikings from sneaking into the river and mounting a surprise attack that would open up an easy route into the heart of the peninsula.

Aethelmaer had chosen to build his new defensive position at the mouth of the river just a few hundred yards inside the narrow entrance of the natural harbour. In essence it was a fortified residence on a grand scale. Covering some five acres it was surrounded by a deep ditch and stout stockade of seven-foot high timber posts. The five-bayed great hall was over eighty feet long and provided living quarters for his retainers, while smaller detached buildings lay on either side. One was of wood and housed the kitchen while the other was an imposing two-storied construction of stone that served as the private room and bedchamber of the ealdorman. It was a fitting residence for a man descended from a line of West Saxon Kings and offered protection from the sea as well as the last stage in an escape route should danger come from in land.

Two men on watch high above the river mouth watched as Wulfnoth steered the warship towards the rocky entrance and word of his arrival quickly reach Aethelmaer. A single vessel with a small crew presented little danger, but a dozen heavily armed retainers lined the shore when Wulfnoth landed and he was immediately escorted through the burh-gate and across to the stone house where Aethelmaer stood waiting.

His eyes looked troubled at first, but then lightened up. "And what has prompted the Thegn of Compton to seek me out?"

"I come from Aelfhelm of Northumbria and the Lords of the Five Towns, my lord."

"They are valued friends who watch the world as I do, but the Wolf who savages the Vikings is welcome on his own account. Come let us eat after your voyage. Then you can tell me all your news."

Wulfnoth was impressed with the unusual two-storied stone residence and Aethelmaer explained how he had seen such a building in Rouen.

"I too have seen stone used in private houses. In fact I came directly from Flanders where I have spent the last three months living in a two storied house with a stone gable, but the rest was made of timber planks."

"I thought you said you brought word from Aelfhelm and the men of the Danelaw."

Over bowls of beef stew Wulfnoth explained how Swithred had arrived in Bruges with news that the North proposed to support the Aetheling Athelstan in defiance of any future demand that King Aethelred might make that the Witan gives its allegiance to progeny born of his new queen, Emma.

The ealdorman said nothing while a servant took away the stew and large baskets of apples, pears and walnuts appeared on the table. Then Aethelmaer commented dryly. "Fruit, nuts and modern building methods are the only things I can stomach from Normandy."

"Then you too would risk offending the king on this issue?" asked Wulfnoth seizing his chance.

"Most certainly. That is why I am building a defensive position that will sustain attack from both the sea and land. Fortunately Eadric's spies do not venture this far west, but as you saw we still take precautions when strange vessels appear in our harbour."

"Then may I take word to Lord Aelfhelm of your resolution in this matter?"

"Of course you may. I come from a line of Anglo Saxon Kings and would not see a Norman sit on our throne.

"Your royal lineage is well known, my lord."

"You, too, belong to the bloodline of kings."

"Not I, my lord. My parents came from simple stock.

"That is what you were meant to believe." The ealdorman walked over and stood in front of the windhole where Wulfnoth found it difficult to see his face. "Have you never wondered how simple people should own the estate at Compton?"

"My father was a faithful servant and received the estate after years of loyal service."

"True, but only partly true. Your father, as you call him, was a brave thegn who served my father Ealdorman Aethelweard well. He was his body servant and probably his closest friend."

"I had no idea, my lord."

"Nor should you. Your father was sworn to secrecy."

Wulfnoth was intrigued and waited for Aethelmaer to explain.

"When I was a young man I fell in love with my cousin Cwenburh," said the ealdorman wistfully. Then his voice took on a harsher tone. "Unfortunately the scholar monk Alfric, the one who is now archbishop, denounced the marriage as a breach of the laws of blood and Aethelweard, my father, had me sent away."

He turned and stared out over the river. "I had no idea that Cwenburh was pregnant. I was banished to Rouen for nearly two years." He paused and when he continued his voice was sad. "When the child was born my father took him from his mother and arranged for her to be sent her to the Nunnaminster in Winchester where she was shut away from the sunlight and died of grief."

For a moment his voice choked and he could not continue.

"What happened to the child?" Wulfnoth asked apprehensively.

"The child?" asked Aethelmaer vaguely, wrenched back to the present. "The child, my son, was given to a loyal retainer who was charged with his upbringing and given an estate in Sussex on the understanding that he would keep the child's origin a secret." Then turning back into the room he said, "You must realise, Wulfnoth, that I knew nothing of this other than that my beloved Cwenburg had died in a nunnery. It was only after several years, when my father confessed what he had done, that I learned the truth. That was when I came to Compton and took you on a visit to Winchester. You are descended from a line of West Saxon Kings. Your blood is as good as Aethelred's. Better perhaps, since it stems from an older branch of the Cerdics."

Wulfnoth felt an emptiness within, shattering the illusions of a happy childhood that despite having ending in bloody violence had given his life a sense of simple order. Not all the ghosts of Aethelmaer's shocking disclosure could hope to breathe new life into the dreadful void.

He left the room and his biological father without a word and wandering down to the harbour entrance he stared out to sea and sought solace in thoughts of the gentle couple that had raised him, the blond sea-raider's daughter who had born him a son before returning to the restless currents and the dark-haired woman who gave him such sensuous tranquillity. They were his life now and would always remain so.

After an hour he felt more composed, but realised that he needed time to come to terms with his past. Therefore, he decided to send Oswy to the Danelaw by sea, with assurances of Aethelmaer's support for Prince Athelstan, while he took the coastal path and began the long journey back home to Compton alone.

The avaricious Eadric had set his sights on the vacant ealdormanry of Mercia well before Queen Emma had hinted that she might support his candidature in return for his assistance in dealing with her estate problems and in toppling Aelfhelm. Her support of course would be most welcome.

She had been astute enough to realise that an indirect attack on the Danish settlers of Exeter could be the catalyst that might destroy Danish influence throughout the kingdom. He had seen the need to widen the issue and find a compelling pretext to force the king to take precipitous action.

The opportunity to set the plan into action arose several days after the feast of All Saints when Eadric was invited to join the king and queen at supper. He was deliberately a few minutes late giving Emma ample opportunity to raise the matter of her reeve's difficulty in collecting taxes in Exeter.

As he entered the hall he heard the queen saying, "Even though the harvest was good this year they still claim they cannot afford to pay."

"Then Hugh must insist," the king said simply.

"When he does they say they have been warned not to pay good English money to a Norman queen."

"Warned by whom?" demanded Aethelred angrily.

"By their old leaders I suppose."

"Their old leaders? I'll wager Pallig, is behind this."

"Pallig, my lord. Who might he be?" the queen asked innocently.

"A treacherous Dane to whom I gave money and land in return for his help against the sea raiders. Ah, Eadric!" He broke off seeing the Shropshire thegn for the first time and motioned him to join them. "Sit down. Sit down. The queen has uncovered a serious problem with the Danish settlers in Exeter."

"My lord?

The King explained and waited expectantly, but Eadric was strangely silent.

"Well? Do you not think the matter serious?" asked the King indignantly.

Shaking his head as if he had been preoccupied with another matter, Eadric gave what he hoped sounded like a measured reply. "It is extremely serious, my lord. It is not only an affront to the queen, but a direct attack on your authority."

"Exactly! So I shall order Aethelmaer to surround the town and bring the culprits to me."

"Ah! You cannot do that, my lord."

"Cannot? I am the king!" shouted Aethelred. Then when he saw Eadric's thoughtful face, he looked puzzled and added "Why ever not?"

"Well for one reason Aethelmaer is apparently dealing with unrest among the Celts of Cornwall. He could be anywhere in that wild peninsula."

"Then Aelfric of Wessex must deal with the matter. Even he should be able to sort out a few rebels."

"An example must be made, my lord, but first I must recommend caution."

"Caution!"

"Yes, my lord."

"If you know something of this matter...."

"There have been rumours, my lord. My spies bring reports of unrest. This might be part of a wider problem."

"Unrest. What do you mean? The ceorls are always complaining that they cannot afford to pay taxes."

"The Danish settlers are different, my lord. They sprout like weeds among the wheat and choke the native people of your kingdom. I was late tonight because I was waiting for information from Oxford. I did not wish to raise the matter until I was certain."

"Certain of what?"

"It appears that the Danish settlers in a number of towns........"

"There," Aethelred said turning to the queen, "I told you Pallig was behind this."

"My lord, the Danish settlers see the Norman Alliance as a threat to the privileged position that your father, King Edgar, allowed the Anglo-Danish people. If Exeter were simply an isolated case I would recommend that we act at once and hang the ringleaders, but if there is widespread unrest we must prepare accordingly."

"Well is there?"

"Disturbances have already been confirmed in Oxford as well as Exeter, but there may well be others. There is one rumour there of a plot against your life. Give me five days and we will discover the extent of this rebellion and take appropriate action."

"We must call the Witan!" exclaimed Aethelred with growing alarm.

"No my lord, the Council leaks like a badly calked ship. Everything must be prepared without their knowledge. You must keep the advantage of surprise."

"Can it be done without raising suspicion?"

"We shall even surprise the ealdormen with the decisiveness of your bold action."

"Then you have my permission to proceed."

"Who will deal with the traitors of Exeter?" the queen asked.

"My brother Beorhtric, my lady," said Eadric. He has a special skill in such matters."

"What of Oxford? And what if you find further threats against me?" demanded Aethelred.

"With your authority, my lord, I can gather men secretly from Shropshire who will strike every town at the same time and rid you of this vermin, but I shall take care of Oxford myself. By the feast of St Brice all your enemies will be crushed."

The Feast of St Brice   November 13th 1002

Wulfnoth sidestepped the mutilated body of a heavily
built middle-aged blond man whose naked belly
had been ripped open so viciously that his intestines lay
glistening in the central gutter, but could not avoid the
river of blood that ran between the houses of the Danish
quarter. Behind him people froze at the sight and were
trampled by other fleeing inhabitants who screamed in
terror as they sort to escape the apparently indiscriminate
slaughter meted out by the hands of the howling mob that
smashed its way through the narrow passages leading to
the market place. With his dark hair no stranger could
mistake him for a Dane or imagine that his family
heralded from across the eastern searoads. Nevertheless,
he had taken the precaution of unsheathing his sword and
brandished it in front of him to deter anyone from
attacking him. He looked fierce enough for a sea pirate
and those who had lingered to gather up their valuables
before venturing out of their dwellings cowered against
the walls holding their pathetic bundles in front of them
like shields so that he had to force his way past them to
reach the safety of the open square. Eventually those who
had avoided the blood-soaked seaxes burst into the
sunshine, where thankfully they found order of a sort.

A group of heavily armed strangers stood at the
entrance and stopped each individual as they emerged

from the dark alleys and instructed them to stand before a table where they were examined by a local official, made to identify themselves and to give the name of the street where they lived. If they came from the Danish Quarter or their names or accents betrayed their Danish origins they were directed into a line guarded by two ranks of fearsome ruffians that led towards that part of the market place usually reserved for the meat sellers. If they were not Danish they were bundled screaming back into the warren of side streets.

For a moment Wulfnoth thought that they were going to manhandle him, but when they saw his weapon drawn they kept at a safe distance and merely made to bar his way into the square.

"Identify, yourself!" shouted the man at the table who seemed to be acting under some duress.

"I am the king's thegn. How dare you block my way! Tell these mercenaries to stand aside or I'll cut my way through."

"I'm sorry, sir." said the man, suddenly chastened, "but we can't be too careful. We act on the king's orders. A thegn from Shropshire brought them last night. He arrived with a troop of Mercians and mercenaries, wild men from beyond King Offa's great boundary ridge. He's not a man to cross, sir, if you know what I mean. It's more than my life's worth to let anyone apart from the foreigners into the market square. Only people from the Danish Quarter can remain here. The others must return to their homes"

"Well I am no foreigner."

"I realise that, sir."

"Nevertheless, you'd better let me pass."

"If you insist, sir, but I must ask you to speak with the King's Messenger."

"And where do I find this King's Messenger of yours?"

"On the other side of the square, sir. You can't miss him; he's mean as a midden rat with great long arms," said the man who was struggling to regain his composure. "You'll find him supervising the business end of the queue," he added, but he avoided all eye contact.

Wulfnoth sheathed his sword, turned on his heel and went in search of the King's Messenger. He had been vaguely conscious of the shouting that emanated from the far side of the square, but it was only as he walked along the queue towards the crowd in the distance did he began to feel uneasy. Then, when he turned the corner and entered the covered section, the full horror became clear. The semblance of order that he had witnessed on entering the market square had been a sick charade designed to lull the unsuspecting Danes into a state of false hope and compliance so that the methodical and systematic extermination of an underclass of society could take place.

The queue had been stopped twenty or so paces from the entrance and then at regular intervals half-a dozen were allowed to go forward. Once they turned the corner they were grabbed by a group of fearsome savages. A handful of grain was forced into their mouths and they were dragged forward unable to scream. Their possessions were then ripped from them before they were flung facedown on one of two butcher's tables where they were systematically executed by the single stroke of an axe.

Wulfnoth first reaction was to intervene and stop the wanton bloodshed. He knocked the axeman to one side and demanded to speak to the King's Messenger.

"Ah the Thegn of Crompton," said a familiar voice behind him "Hold him and remove his weapons."

"A thegn from Shropshire! I might have guessed it was you Beorhtric or that foul brother of yours."

"Have a care, thegn. You are interfering with the king's business."

"The king would not countenance such vicious savagery against his own people."

"I am the King's Messenger and carry the direct commands of King Aethelred and he held up a parchment that had lain on the table. Perhaps the Thegn of Compton recognises the king's seal."

Wulfnoth could not deny it. Despite his relatively minor position on the King's Council he had witnessed a number of state documents seeing his name written down dutifully after the king had signed them and had watched the great seal being applied. There was no doubt this was Aethelred's seal and the king's characteristic signature was unmistakable.

"So you see, Councillor. To attempt to interrupt our legitimate business would be an act of treason."

Wulfnoth felt impotent. If he still had his sword he might have killed one or two but as it was he was powerless.

"No such orders were discussed in Council." He spoke defiantly.

"How would you know? You attend so rarely and your friends from the Danelaw find excuses to absent themselves. Besides the king is not bound by the Council."

"But these people are honest citizens.

"Honest citizens! People who refuse to pay the king's taxes, who dishonour the queen and plot against the life of our king! King Aethelred has sworn to make an example of them."

"But that will divide the country and bring down the wrath of Swegen Forkbeard."

"Little good will that do him and his sea-wolves. Now we have an alliance with Normandy, they will not dare to attack our shores ever again"

"That's wishful thinking."

"Only if you and your friends from the Danelaw are in league with the king's enemies. You are a traitor. When the king hears of your actions today you will be declared 'nithing' and your precious estate at Compton will be confiscated."

"The king knows where my loyalties lie. I'll not be lectured by his messenger."

Wulfnoth stood his ground, but realised that he was perilously close to the quicksands.

The stand off was fortunately broken by the arrival of two Mercians who brought news that important hostages had been discovered.

Beorhtric was visibly delighted and with a final word of warning he invited Wulfnoth to accompany him.

They left the market square and escorted by a group of Beorhtric's henchmen arrived at the ancient wooden church of St. Pedrog where they found fifty or so Danish settlers who had sought sanctuary in the building. At one end a man and three women had been segregated from the others and stood defiantly facing the soldiers.

"Ah, so we have found the ringleaders at last. Strip them."

"But what have they done?" demanded Wulfnoth.

"They have plotted to murder the king and intend to invite Swegen of Denmark to replace him. All such vermin have to be exterminated."

Most of the naked group seem to have shed their dignity along with their clothes except for the tall blond woman in her late twenties. She stood and outfaced her accusers with her head held high. Wulfnoth noted her clean strong limbs, the luxurious quality of her golden shoulder-length hair and that her breasts still retained the firmness of youth, but what impressed him most was her chin and the look of defiance in her eyes as she spoke.

"I am Gunnhild, the sister of Swegen, and I am a hostage under the protection of King Aethelred. You have no right to abuse me and my people."

"You're a dirty Danish whore," sneered the King's Messenger. "and we'll abuse you in any way we please. You, soldier, show her what an English weapon is like."

"She's under the protection of the king, you fool. She must not be touched," shouted Wulfnoth horrified at what they proposed.

"Bind that Dane-lover's wrists and secure him. If he speaks again, kill him," snarled the King's Messenger. Now, soldier, fuck the bitch."

The soldier could hardly believe his luck and while his comrades pinned Gunnhild on her back in front of the altar he forced her legs apart and lifted his tunic. It was impossible to struggle and Gunnhild made no sound, but fixed her eyes on the oak beams of the roof expressionlessly.

As the man's buttocks strove with accelerated jerks to reach his first orgasm in a month Beorhtric seemed elated and the other soldiers cheered their comrade's efforts. Wulfnoth shut his eyes unable to watch.

Once the man had achieved his climax, Beorhtric quickly lost interest and spoke briefly to another soldier who nodded and left the church.

Then he turned back to the man who now stood grinning but red-faced after his exertions. "Now get that ring off her finger. The king will be pleased to accept it when I make my report."

Gunnhild held out her hand indifferently and the soldier struggled to remove it

"I can't shift it, sir. It's too tight or else the knuckle has swollen,"

"Then cut it off,"

"How, sir?"

"With an axe, you fool, but don't damage the ring," said Beorhtric callously.

Despite being seasoned in battle blood, Wulfnoth retched bile as he watched the axe sever the fingers of her left hand.

"That is how we deal with both English and Danish whores," Beorhtric sneered. "I'm surprised our East Saxon thegn hasn't the stomach for it."

"Only the impotent derive sexual pleasure by watching other men abuse women," Wulfnoth said with contempt.

White with rage Beorhtric kneed the helpless thegn viciously in the crotch and, snatching a staff from one of the guards, repeatedly struck him about the face and head until he slumped forward semi-conscious.

"Get him out of here," snarled Beorhtric and Wulfnoth was bundled unceremoniously out of the church while a stream of soldiers carrying faggots walked in.

He was vaguely conscious of the rest of the queue being herded into the building and the great oak doors being slammed shut, but stared with horror and disbelief as the smoke pouring through the windholes.

Seconds later and the screaming began.

"Well, Eadric, have you rooted out those foreign weeds that choke the kingdom and seek to kill me?" Aethelred, who seemed relaxed after a successful day in the saddle, was warming himself by the great kitchen fire watching the glistening carcass of a wild boar being turned slowly by a small boy who perched precariously on a stool.

"My spies confirmed that the unrest was more widespread than we had imagined, my lord. Conspirators were identified in a number of towns. However, I am pleased to report that we have rounded up the ringleaders in Oxford and a number of smaller towns and they have been summarily dealt with."

"And what of my town of Exeter?" The queen was slightly put out that Eadric had not reported to her first and was eager to hear of her own possessions.

"Madam, my brother Beorhtric dealt with that matter. I hear that all went smoothly, but have not yet received his personal report. Otherwise you should have known at once, my lady."

"The queen is jealous for her estates, Eadric. She thinks more of them than the safety of her husband."

"Not so, my lord, but a job half done and the weeds will thrive again."

A door opened and Beorhtric was admitted to the royal presence.

"Ah! Your brother appears at last. Well, Beorhtric, can you set the queen's mind at rest? Have you had as much success as your brother Eadric in dealing with these rebels?"

"I trust so, my lord. My lady, the rebels have been punished and the town is yours again."

"If that is so you shall be rewarded by a grateful queen," declared Emma. "So Count Hugh can return and begin to collect my taxes without any interference."

"He can, my lady."

"You have done well. Hasn't he, my lord?"

The king nodded graciously, "It would certainly seem that he has."

Beorhtric was eager to impress the king with his efficiency. "Exeter has been purged of all your enemies, my lord."

"And how can you be so sure of that, my Mercian friend?"

"There is not a man, woman or child of Danish descent left alive within the town."

Aethelred paled. "The women and children too?"

The words were simple enough, but Beorhtric failed to catch the note of apprehension in the voice.

"Yes, my lord. The stench of their burning flesh could be smelt for miles around."

"And the Lady Gunnhild?"

The king's voice was distinctly hoarse, but Beorhtric pressed on. "She did not escape, my lord, but like her treacherous husband she and her child fed the flames and within days their screams will reach the Danelaw and serve as a warning to all the traitors who oppose their rightful king."

For a moment the king said nothing.

"Here is her ring, my lord.

Aethelred knocked the proffered gift out of his hand and sent it spinning across the stone floor.

"You fool. She was under my protection and as such a valuable hostage against the return of Swegen's longships."

Eadric had read the signs long before his brother, but had been powerless to stop Beorhtric's enthusiastic account of events. Now he needed to show statesmanship. "My brother is over zealous, my lord, but his rash actions may yet be turned to your advantage.

"How so?"

"You will have appeared decisive and ruthless in stamping out rebellion. Other Danish settlers in your kingdom who plot against your life will now think twice, before conspiring again you." He seemed to be thinking on his feet.

"And what of my people in the Danelaw?"

"Aelfhelm will shilly-shally as he always does, not daring to risk open rebellion, but always remain lukewarm in his allegiance."

"He may oppose my wishes, but his advice has often proved sound."

"He opposed your treaty with my brother and spoke out against our marriage. Was that sound advice then?" Emma burst out spitefully.

"True, but he was concerned for my son Athelstan and his purpose was to protect the succession."

"And what of your promise to my brother and to me? Will not a son of our union have as much if not more right to succeed his father?"

"Yes, madam, when you have born me a son! Meanwhile Athelstan remains my heir and I must put up with Aelfhelm's opposition in the Witan."

"Then you need a new leader in Mercia, my lord, an ealdormen of equal status who will act as a deterrent to that mad old man." The queen had not intended to promote Eadric's cause so soon.

"Perhaps, madam, but the time is not yet right. We may need his support if Swegen decides to seek revenge. Do you not agree, Eadric?"

"I'm sure you are right, my lord. His weakness for caution and his allegiance to Athelstan serves your purpose for the time being, but once a new prince is born to the queen he will prove troublesome."

"We understand each other, Eadric.

The Shropshire thegn knew that, although he had to be patient for a little longer, the seed had been sown. Bowing to the royal couple, he led his sibling from the chamber.

Outside Beorhtric stomped petulantly beside his elder brother indignantly trying to justify his sadistic attempts at root and branch extermination.

"You told me to spare no-one. I thought the king would relish the annihilation of Danish vermin."

"Yes, he does, but, while it is vital that he shows himself to be powerful and decisive, to slaughter an important female hostage in so barbaric a fashion, without Swegen having broken the truce, casts a slur on his honour."

"Then you hold me responsible for your losing face. If I have upset your plans........."

"No, brother, all went according to plan although I feared for a moment that I had overreached myself. In fact things couldn't be better."

"How do you make that out?"

"The king will be blamed for your actions and the fragile unity of England will be undermined.

333

The nobility and the powerful bishops will take sides and Aethelred will be isolated and come more and more to rely on his loyal retainers. We were not born into one of the powerful families. We have been useful to him, but he had no intention of making me an ealdorman. However, now the queen has put the idea into his mind he will see the advantages and once Aelfhelm's usefulness is at an end our time will come. At the moment our future is dependent on the queen and her ability to produce a son."

"And will she continue to support us?"

"The queen is less squeamish than our king and she was delighted with your thoroughness in dealing with her little problem in Exeter."

"I am relieved that someone was delighted with my efforts."

"Oh I am delighted too, brother. I can always rely on your thoroughness."

"Then you should be pleased to know that I have finally dealt with that upstart Sussex thegn, Wulfnoth. He tried to interfere, but I had him disarmed and arrested. By now his body should be at the bottom of the sea."

Eadric's eyes narrowed. "I hope you are right." He said. "He is a dangerous fellow and an old friend of the king. You would be wise not to mention that you had anything to do with his disappearance."

Correspondence

Alena woke early and spent a couple of hours writing her first letter. She was becoming quite proficient and was eager to show off her newly developed skill. It was addressed to Wulfnoth saying how much she missed him; how much she loved him; how she longed for him to hold her in his arms. She said that now she was a letter writer she would write to Hild and tell her all about the handsome man that she loved. Then she promised to look after Godwin and teach him everything she knew about the making and selling of quality cloth. Finally she wrote, "Come soon" and finished with an elaborate if rather shaky letter "A". She folded the parchment carefully, applied the wolf's head seal ring that Wulfnoth had left behind and put it safely in the box where she kept Count Baldwin's report on Beorhtric's criminal activity and her letters from Hild.

The following morning she wrote to Hild. She began by saying how she had longed to answer her friend's letters, but had only recently learned how to write. She told her of her success in the wool trade and how Wulfnoth had helped her and how she had found love.

She expressed a wish to see her friend again, but understood that a rift between the king and the men of the North and East had caused unrest in England. Since Cerdic's recent return from Cyningesburh he had been too ill to travel, she said, so Wulfnoth had undertaken to carry a message from Ealdorman Aelfhelm to Ealdorman Aethelmaer, but if matters worsened she herself could send a ship to the Humber River to bring Hild and her family safely to Bruges. Finally, she congratulated her friend on her marriage and the birth of her son. At the end of this letter she wrote her full name.

As she was about to put this letter into the box she had an idea. One of her ships had arrived the night before and was moored on the Steegherei by the Breidelstraat Bridge. Instead of waiting for Cerdic to arrive she could send Swithred in *Le Merle Noir* at once. She wanted her letters to arrive as soon as possible and at the same time Swithred could deliver Wulfnoth's message to the ealdorman without delay. *Le Merle* would sail for Bosham and then up to the Humber. It was the obvious course of action.

But Swithred would not be convinced. He was Wulfnoth's huscarl and as such the thegn's orders had to be followed to the letter. It was his duty to wait until Cerdic arrived from Compton.

"There is no knowing when Cerdic will recover," she argued. "Remember Osmund died of a fever. If he doesn't recover you could be stuck here for weeks and my Lord Wulfnoth's message to the northern lords may arrive too late."

"It did not seem that important," began Swithred. "He only promised to visit Ealdorman Aethelmaer to sound him out in matters concerning the Aetheling."

"But if the message is delayed Ealdorman Aelfhelm will think that Wulfnoth has not received his request and he will have to send someone else."

"Perhaps so, my lady"

She tried another tack. "Words sometimes contain hidden meanings of great importance. We don't know just how vital Lord Wulfnoth's message is."

"That's true, but with respect," Swithred was adamant, "I have to protect you and young Godwin."

"We don't need your protection here. The count has guaranteed my safety. I am a woman of standing, respected by the burghers. Bruges is my town." And she wanted to add, "And I am in love," but she sensed that she was getting nowhere and pushed the matter no further. If Swithred would not go, he could not stop her making other arrangements.

That evening she approached Walram who readily agreed to carry the letters for her. Then she summoned the captain of *Le Merle Noir* and told him to leave immediately for Bosham and thence to sail up the east coast to the River Humber where he should wait for Walram before returning to Bruges."

"But the cargo has not been loaded yet," the captain complained. There were always ways for a captain to make money when he carried a cargo.

"The cargo can wait until you return," said Alena quickly, irritated that the man should question her instructions.

"If the weather deteriorates when we return we shall have to lay the vessel up for the winter and then the cargo won't be delivered until next spring."

"That is my business," Alena snapped. "The cargo can wait. Walram carries letters for me," she added importantly.

"As you wish, madam." The captain was disappointed, but his curiosity had been aroused.

He had had no idea that his mistress was literate. Perhaps the voyage could after all be turned to his advantage.

The next morning *Le Merle Noir* slipped her lines and made for the open sea.

* * * * * *

For all his willingness Walram feared he might not be a good sailor so he readily accepted the captain's advice to drink copious amounts of cervoise during the channel crossing. By the time the coast of England was in sight he was drunk and sought refuge on the raised aft deck where he fell into a heavy sleep.

It was easy then for the captain to lift the letters from the boy's belt and to read the names on the outside, but he was afraid to break the seal, not that it would have done him much good for he could not read. However, he knew of someone who could and who might pay him handsomely for the opportunity to do so.

En route for Bosham *Le Merle Noir* made an unscheduled stop at Dover where the captain went ashore and sought out the building used by Eadric's spies to keep watch on the comings and goings of the various trading vessels that used the port. He had long since been recruited by Eadric who had an eye for the malcontents of society and recognised the value of seafarers especially those who had previously been waylaid carrying letters.

It took several hours for the letters to be faithfully copied and for the seals to be reattached so that the untrained eye would see nothing untoward to suggest they had been opened.

Consequently it was nearly dawn when the captain returned to his ship just in time to see Walram being violently sick over the side. Unable to replace the letters in the boy's belt, he waited thinking how best to turn the situation to his advantage.

Eventually the vomiting stopped and the boy sat back against the oarwale his face drained of all colour. "I have failed my mistress. I wish I was dead," he sobbed miserably.

"Steady, yourself, young man," said the captain quietly as a plan began to form in his head. "Things may not be as bad as you think."

"She will never forgive me. She trusted me and I have failed her. What am I going to do?"

"Look," said the captain reassuringly. "Mistress Alena need never know that you endangered her ship in your drunken state last night."

Walram's mouth fell open. He had thought the loss of her letters bad enough. Now the spectre of causing the loss of one of her ships rendered him speechless with horror.

"No one has been hurt," the captain went on conspiratorially. "The crew will say nothing and I, well........well, I understand how a young man reacts when at the mercy of the sea for the first time. I shall not mention anything in my report."

Walram was drowning in guilt, yet realised the captain was offering him a lifeline. "You are kind, sir, and I am grateful to you, but I have also lost the letters which she had entrusted to my care."

"The letters! Oh goodness me no. When you knocked me from the steeroar and lurched about the boat we feared that you would end up overboard so we took your letters for safe -keeping. See, here they are safe and sound with their seals unbroken. You can deliver them safely and our mistress none the wiser."

Walram could not thank the captain enough swearing that he would be in the man's debt for the rest of his life and he resolved never to touch cervoise again.

Later that day much relieved and chastened he stepped onto the shore at Bosham where he found Oswy had just returned from the Western Provinces and dutifully handed over the letter addressed to Wulfnoth.

The following morning *Le Merle Noir* sailed back up the channel before heading north up the east coast.

It took them four days to reach the Humber River and find someone in the service of Ealdorman Aelfhelm who could be trusted to provide them with horses and show them the way to the Village of Barnburh, a journey that was going to take a further two to three days. Determined to ingratiate himself further with the Mercians by discovering the exact whereabouts of the moneyer and his family, the captain had offered to accompany the young man across country. Blissfully unaware of the man's ulterior motive, Walram was delighted and the two rode out together reaching their destination towards the middle of November.

When they arrived they found only Torgrim, Eric and a couple of apprentices working at the forge in the old fort. The old man told them that Hild had gone with two of the smiths to the market at Nottingham and was not expected back for a week. They were welcome to stay and wait for her return.

Walram was keen to accept the old man's hospitality, but the captain, who had discovered all that he needed, explained that they really must return to their ship without delay or they would not get back to Bruges before winter set in. Reluctantly, the young man felt obliged to return with the captain, so he gave Alena's letter to Torgrim and an hour later they were back on the road.

When they had gone Torgrim turned the letter over in his hand and smiled when he recognised the impression of the wolf's head in the wax seal. He remembered the pleasure he had had in making the seal ring for his friend and wondered if he had written the letter for Alena. Then his keen eye spotted a hairline crack in the seal and signs that fresh wax had been applied to rejoin the two halves. He assumed that the writer had wished to add another sentence or two, but was puzzled that the thegn had not simply replaced all the wax and applied the seal again. He couldn't rid himself of the idea that the letter had been opened and read by someone other than the sender. It irked him, but he could do nothing until his daughter's return.

That was not for another four days and Hild, who was too impatient to listen to her father's concerns about broken seals, simple tore it open and stared at the strange hand and then at the signature. She was overjoyed to have news from Bruges at last. She read avidly. Alena was alive and well and her business prospered. She was in love with her father's friend, Lord Wulfnoth. How Hild longed to see her again and half thought to make the long sea voyage south to Flanders, but winter was approaching and her father always suffered severe pain in his mutilated arm in the cold weather. It would be difficult to leave him. Besides the young smiths in the various smelting shops spawned by the original forge relied on her to oversee the production and selling of a whole range of metalwork. There were ploughshares, coulters, goads, iron shoes for the wooden spades; sundry tools and nails; fish hooks and awls; tenterhooks, picks, borers and needles; keys and locks; knives and spoons; as well as all manner of jewellery from buckles to broaches and pendants to be made and sold. Only she seemed to be able to predict what quantities of each would be required in a given season and only she could set prices that would ensure that their stalls would sell out by the end of a market day or at the fairs held in the great towns on feast days. She could not leave until she had trained someone to take her place.

She read on, her hand trembling at learning of Cerdic's illness, but then stared completely nonplussed by Alena's congratulations on her wedding.

It was not until several hours later that she remembered Elmet's decision to name his son Cerdic after a chance meeting with a stranger. Had the young man who brought her home from her ordeal in Bruges returned unexpectedly and left with the impression that she was married? She would ask Elmet to describe his stranger and must write immediately to Alena to clear up the misunderstanding and to find out if Cerdic had recovered from his illness. Next year, if her father's health improved she would ask if she could visit the friends who had rescued her.

Dead to the World

Fortunately the man responsible for securing his bonds had been more interested in watching his friend's violation of Gunnhild than in making sure the rope was tight enough to prevent movement. Had he done so Wulfnoth's fingers and wrists would have been numb with cramp and useless. However, he had immediately realised that he could work one loop over his fingers to maintain circulation, and by concealing the slack inches in his left hand he had still appeared to be firmly bound.

His attempts, however, to remonstrate against the massacre of the Danes in the blazing church had resulted in a number of skull-cracking blows from Beorhtric and his brain had sought refuge in total insensibility.

Now as he found himself lying under a pile of old clothes in the back of a deep-sided wagon some distance from the town, he gradually recovered from his comatose state and after several minutes felt strong enough to address the matter of escape. At first he thought he was alone, but then heard the voices of two men arguing beside an open fire several feet away feet away.

"I don't see why we have to wait until dark; the man is dead and this part of the river is deserted."

"Then you obviously don't know Beorhtric. If he finds out that we haven't followed orders we'll be the ones lying at the bottom of the river. Make yourself useful and find a couple of boulders to weigh him down. We want the tide to drag him out slowly."

Despite the battering that he had taken it didn't take Wulfnoth long to free himself from his bonds and peer over the side of the wagon. The remaining man was sitting on the ground with his back to him. Carrying the rope he climbed over the far side of the wagon and covered the distance before the man had a chance to be aware of his presence. It was simplicity itself to slip the noose over his head and force him to the ground gasping for air.

When the first man returned struggling with his large stone he complained bitterly that his companion was still sitting beside the fire with his Phrygian cap over his ears. As he lowered his burden beside him he barely felt the seax sliding up under his ribcage and coughed with surprise when it penetrated his heart.

The following morning two extra naked bodies were floating in the estuary and it was assumed that they were Danish settlers who had been caught trying to escape from the Mercians and their savage allies.

Walking upstream Wulfnoth found a place where he could wash away the sense of shame at what he had witnessed done in Aethelred's name. If the king had indeed sanctioned the ethnic cleansing of Anglo-Saxon England then he had violated the code of honour and forfeited the fealty of his people. This coming so soon after the alliance with Normandy and the king's marriage to Emma spelt a widening of the rift between Aethelred and the Danelaw. When Swegen came to avenge the death of his sister, as come Wulfnoth knew he must, it could provoke civil war throughout England. The only hope now lay in the Prince Athelstan.

For the present Wulfnoth decided that he would remain "dead".

Not wishing to draw attention to himself he discarded his own clothes and, donning those of one of the Mercians, drove the cart along the coast road. He was in no hurry to return home and a villein going about his lawful business was unlikely to draw the attention of Eadric's spies.

Gradually a plan formed in his mind. He would slip unnoticed into the estate at Compton draw up a will and summon his huscarls. Then he would return to Bruges and lie low. His disappearance would not at first seem strange and then later it would be assumed that he had been lost at sea. Of course Beorhtric and his brother would know differently, but they could hardly admit to having murdered him. The will, he hoped, would ensure Godwin's inheritance. With the situation in England so volatile he could not risk sending word to his friends in the Danelaw, so he resolved that on Oswy's return from there he would send him back to Fowey to ask Aethelmaer to protect the interests of his grandson.

Three days later, with only Estrith and the resident huscarls privy to their lord's intentions, Cerdic took command of *The Black Wolf*, the latest and sleekest vessel in the Bosham fleet and headed out to sea. At the last minute a hooded figure had joined the crew and only when they were clear of land did he slip the hood back and shake loose his black hair.

Back in Bruges Alena was adamant that both Wulfnoth and Cerdic continue to recuperate throughout the winter. The injuries to the thegn's face had almost healed, but he had been left with unsightly scars, while Cerdic remained unnaturally withdrawn.

By December the boats were laid up for the winter. The weather turned bitterly cold, but life in the Woolhouse was warm and comfortable.

Violent storms on the north east coast had delayed *Le Merle Noir's* return and then winter had set in so the captain had been compelled to lay the vessel up in the upper reaches of the Humber. When they eventually headed south the following year they caught sight of Swegen's wave-stallions approaching the channel. Despite his wish to call in at Dover to send word of Torgrim's whereabouts to Eadric the captain was forced to take the longer sea route and head directly for Bruges.

Two days later Walram stepped onto the jetty of the Steegherei.

They had almost given him up for lost and were relieved at his safe return. Alena who was anxious to hear news of Hild felt disappointed that Walram had not seen her. Wulfnoth was pleased that Torgrim had prospered.

He showed no surprise that Swegen had returned to avenge his sister's death and for the first time in his life he felt that the Dane had some justification for his actions. He advised Alena to suspend her trade with England for the rest of the season.

His own position was further complicated by his attempt to prevent the original massacre and by now he had probably been declared "nithing", a state that would result in the confiscation of his estate at Compton. For the present he dare not set foot on English soil, but *The Black Wolf* made regular crossings by night when the stars guided the steering oar and his huscarls had orders to evacuate the household at the first sign of danger.

Swegen's Revenge   Exeter Spring 1003

The black ships with their striped sails had swept past Bosham and struck Exeter.

Blockading the estuary the Danes besieged the town, but the people made stout defence and with the road to the north-east still open had every prospect of holding out until Ealdorman Aelfric could bring his forces to their aid.

However, Count Hugh, the Queen's Reeve, was determined to prove that he and his garrison of Norman knights were well capable of dealing with an ill-disciplined rabble. Opening the gates they rode out on horseback expecting the sea raiders to flee back to their boats

Instead the Vikings fell away on either side in good order allowing the horsemen to penetrate deep into their centre and then regrouped cutting off their retreat.

Finding himself hemmed in on all sides Hugh could not manoeuvre his troop effectively and fearing that that his men would be dragged one by one from their mounts and slaughtered demanded to speak to their leader. He was bundled unceremoniously through lines of shield beaters and found himself kneeling before a tall man with a forked beard. With the prospect of imminent death facing him Hugh proposed a ransom of £1000, food for the Danish army and the hospitality of the town in return for his own safely and that of his men...

An hour later the gates of Exeter were thrown open, the citizens slaughtered and Hugh himself was hacked to death in the market square. Then the town was looted and put to the torch. Finally the walls from east to west were systematically reduced to rubble.

Swegen's revenge had begun.

When news of what had happened reached Winchester Aethelred ordered Aelfric to commit the great army that had been gathered to protect the realm. The opposing forces met a few miles from Sarum, but when the enemy was in sight the ealdorman fell to his old tricks again inducing a bout of vomiting and retired from the field leaving his army in disarray. Swegen swept the English aside, burnt down the settlement at Wilton and sacked Sarum before returning to his ships laden with treasure.

Several months later, however, two letters arrived one addressed to Wulfnoth and another to Alena who was overjoyed when she recognised Hild's handwriting and eagerly read its contents. Her friend was safe and well and promised to visit as soon as she had trained someone to run the business for them. She was certainly not married and feared that a terrible misunderstanding had taken place. Had Cerdic been the stranger whom Elmet described? Had he really been so close to her? She longed to see him again and sent a broach for his cloak. Her father had grown more cautious of late seeing danger at every bend in the road. He had even imagined that Alena's letter had been opened on route swearing that the seal had been tampered with. He was getting old of course but if he remained in good health she would bring him with her as soon as the searoads were safe for travel.

Wulfnoth and Godwin were out so she ran down into the yard and found Cerdic and Walram and read the letter to them. Cerdic was overcome when she gave him the broach and excusing himself he left the yard and walked along the riverbank in the direction of the Breidelstratt Bridge. Walram looked pale and when Alena asked him if he was unwell he immediately confessed to his drunkenness on the voyage and the temporary loss of Alena's letters. She was angry at first but at the sight of his tear-stained face she remembered his youth, put her arms round him and forgave him. The fact that the captain of *Le Merle Noir* had said nothing about the incident worried Alena but it was not until later that she could discuss the matter with Wulfnoth and when the thegn suggested that the boy be put in the care of Arnulf, the captain of *La Pie Bavarde*, she readily agreed.

His own letter was from Aethelmaer with news that the ealdorman was back in favour at court where he discovered that Aethelred was furious with Beorhtric for exceeding his orders in Exeter and that Wulfnoth was free to return. Indeed, it was imperative that he did so. Swegen's recent sacking of the city had only deepened the rift between the king and the Danish settlers and his voice could be added to those who urged compromise.

It would be a wrench. His exile in Bruges had proved most fruitful. Alena had born him a son in 1003 and was pregnant again. With a young family she was no longer able to give her full attention to the business of the Woolhouse and while at first it was easy to channel her instructions through Wulfnoth the situation satisfied neither of them. He could not leave her until other arrangements were put in place.

That, evening after the children were in bed, she called the household together in the upstairs room and invited Arnulf the Captain of *La Pie Bavarde* to join them.

Hence forth, she told them she wanted each of them to take on greater responsibility. The house was to be enlarged considerably to accommodate her growing family and Judith was to be in charge of running it.

Rosela would oversee the manufacture and sale of cloth in Bruges. Ogive would move to Ghent and manage the shop there. Arnulf would be responsible for all her ships and overseas trade. Walram would be assigned to him to learn seamanship and see the world. When he returned he too would take on more responsibility.

She expected to be consulted, but they would be responsible for the day to day running of the business. In return they would have a share in the profits.

Arnulf accepted his new role with enthusiasm; Walram with delight; but the women, fearful of their own ability, expressed apprehension. Alena's eyes flashed momentarily. "Look what we have achieved," she stormed and then more gently, "I came from nothing, but together we have built up an enterprise that is the envy of every burgher in Flanders. Without your help and support none of this would have happened. I would not ask you to do anything unless I believed you had the ability to do it."

Reassured, each placed her head in Alena's hands, Arnulf bowed and Walram flung his arms round her neck and kissed her.

"They still worship you," said Wulfnoth, snuggling back down into the warm sheets later that night, "and I know why."

* * * * *

With matters settled in the Woolhouse the thegn could concentrate on England. Although he had the utmost trust in his huscarls, his presence at Compton, however fleeting, was essential to give a sense of identity to those who lived and worked on the estate and to keep the wolves of Court at bay. He also needed to demonstrate his support for Athelstan whilst building bridges with the king. Despite his absence during Swegen's devastation of Wessex he wanted to show that he was prepared to defend the kingdom at all cost. Then there was the matter of the captain of *Le Merle Noir*. Cerdic would go with him of course and if he found that Torgrim and Hild were in any danger, his huscarl could be sent north to protect them.

Thus it was that he and Cerdic boarded *Le Merle Noir* and set sail down the coast of Flanders before crossing the channel at its narrowest point. During the course of the journey they arranged for the captain to overhear them discussing a plan to bring about the downfall of Eadric and his brother. The wind was favourable and the sixteen oarsmen bent to their task so they made excellent progress. However, after a few hours an unpleasant drizzle had set in and the two passengers made themselves as comfortable as possible among the casks of wine that made up the bulk of the ship's cargo. When eventually they sighted land the captain woke them explaining that two of the riglines appeared to be badly frayed near the masthead and rather than risk losing the mast he intended to put in at Dover to buy replacements. Wulfnoth nodded consent and complemented him on his wisdom. Then wrapping his cloak about his shoulders the thegn settled down in the well of the ship and closed his eyes.

Immediately they reached port the captain left the ship with his leather hood pulled tightly round his head and shoulders against the weather. Wulfnoth and Cerdic followed at a discrete distance observing him glancing round furtively before hurrying past the rope-maker's yard towards one of the harbour buildings. Keeping to the shadows they watched him enter and crept up to the windhole where standing close to the wall to avoid the eavesdrip they could overhear sufficient of the conversation to confirm their suspicions.

When the door reopened the hilt of a seax rendered the captain unconscious while the sharp point of another swiftly dispatched the occupant. Trussed and gagged, the captain was carried back to *Le Merle Noir*, where it didn't take much persuasion for the craven creature to admit that he had been a paid informant of Eadric for several years and had been trying to pass on the conversation he had overheard and also directions on how to find Torgrim.

At first light the trading vessel slipped out of Dover and, pausing only to dispose of the body of the late captain, was unloading its cargo at Bosham before sunset.

* * * * *

Autumn came to an abrupt end that year and the icy talons of winter took a relentless grip on the dead earth. Snow covered the land so that many distinguishing features were obliterated and travel was all but impossible. Trees grew lichen-like hoar beards an inch thick. Those foolish enough to venture from familiar paths frequently fell foul of snowdrifts, which provided a larder for ravenous wolves or preserved the victims' bodies perfectly in icy tombs. Wulfnoth and Cerdic were holed up in Compton for weeks. The manor needed every hand and the thegn worked alongside his retainers and slaves to bring the sheep off the Downs and drive the pigs into the yard. Most of them were slaughtered and the carcasses salted down. Snow had to be repeatedly cleared to afford some grazing for the remainder, but their diet would have to be supplemented from the meagre store of summer turnips and pulses. The winter ground on. Across the whole country low temperatures, short days and long nights saw men and beasts sharing food, warmth and shelter. At least no one came to confiscate the estate.

The searoads were slate grey and mountainous. No one was foolhardy enough to risk his life on even the coolest keel and boats were dragged many yards above the tidemarks of earlier winter storms. Only the bodies of dead sea-monsters littered the sands.

It was not, therefore, until early May that Wulfnoth and Cerdic left Bosham in two fully manned warships and sailed eastward up the channel before striking north. On the afternoon of the third day they had just beached the vessels on the sand about a mile north of the River Yare, when a smudge was seen developing on the horizon. In the late sunlight this gradually resolved into a hundred pieces and each bore the unmistaken striped sail of one of Swegen's wave stallions. The Danes had returned.

Clearly two vessels stood no chance against this huge fleet and Wulfnoth ordered Cerdic to relaunch *The Black Wolf* immediately and sail north to rescue Torgrim and Hild.

Conscious, however, that he had been absent when Swegen's army had destroyed Exeter and ravaged Wilton and Sarum, he himself determined to stay and help defend the kingdom. The second vessel was carried into a forest and hidden by the crew while he borrowed a horse and rode inland to warn Ulfkytel of Norwich of the danger and to offer his services. In the event with no standing army it proved impossible to defend the town and the East Anglians were forced to sue for peace.

However, under cover of the truce and while Ulfkytel was occupied in raising the agreed danegeld, Swegen and his raiding army stole up from their ships again and lay siege to Thetford which they eventually sacked and then in the space of one night reduced to ashes.

Stung by the treachery Ulfkytel and Wulfnoth gathered what troops they could and gave battle. For best part of an hour they stood shoulder to shoulder cutting a bloodpath in the shield wall. This time it was the Danes who were unprepared. Although many of the East Anglian thegns were killed, far greater numbers of the blood-soaked corpses of the invaders were left staining the battleground, never again to dance over the searoads.

Swegen and the remnants of his army fled empty-handed with barely enough men to man their longships.

Returning to his vessel Wulfnoth shadowed the Danes for several hours before returning to Bosham and his estate.

In Anglo-Saxon England royal succession had traditionally depended on the approval of the Witan. It was imperative that the king was of strong character and where possible of proven military ability and the Witan would generally give its approval to the eldest aetheling if he were mature enough and a suitable candidate. If he were not, it might offer the crown to the most capable member of the royal family, although unscrupulous ealdormen had often favoured a long minority that would prolong their own hold on power, but that was a risky strategy that might trigger an invasion by a foreign candidate.

However, when a king put away his wife and took a second or a third, his wives invariably would jealously fight for the rights of their own offspring and some would not even shy from arranging the murder of rival claimants.

Aethelred's first marriage to Aelfgifu, the daughter of Ealdorman Thored of Northumbria, had been extremely fruitful. In a decade she had born him nine living offspring including three healthy sons, but almost continual pregnancy had taken its toll and by the end of the century she had begun to lose her looks.

Aethelred, encouraged by Eadric's description of Emma's youth and attractiveness, had found it easy to appreciate the political and other benefits of a new marriage. He had known Richard's price, but had thought that once Emma was in England and safely married some pretext would eventually arise which would enable him to repudiate his promise.

With the arrival of Emma, however, all that had changed. She was indeed stunning; full of vitality; young and tall like a sapling breaking into Easter leaf. Her dark chestnut hair shone in the sunshine and was only eclipsed by the mischievous glint of light in the flecked pale blue eyes that gave the lie to her innocent smile. A wiser man might have read them as a warning, but Aethelred's soul had been instantly lost to this vibrant temptress.

Handling the young flesh of his new bride had brought a long-forgotten thrill to Aethelred which in the nights that followed she had exploited time and again shamelessly teasing him during their foreplay until he could deny her nothing. Whenever they made love he would find himself swearing that she alone ruled his heart; that he would deal with anyone who offended her; and that, if God granted them the blessing of children, he would find a way to ensure that their progeny would take precedence over his other offspring.

That, however, was only one of Aethelred's problems. Midway through the fourth year of the new millennium he was beginning to have serious doubts about the wisdom of his policy of relying on Aelfric and Eadric to the exclusion of other members of the Witan.

The purging of the Danish settlers on the feast of St. Brice had not only further alienated Aelfhelm and the men of the Danelaw, but it had unleashed the wrath of Swegen's revenge exposing Aelfric's innate cowardice and calling in question the value of the treaty negotiated by Eadric with Richard of Normandy.

Had Emma produced an heir things might have been different. Twice she had announced that she was pregnant and twice she had suffered a miscarriage within the first three months, so that Aethelred now began to doubt whether their union would ever be blessed with children. Her primitive sexuality still excited him and there was nothing he would refuse her, but if she did not produce an heir, Richard of Normandy would hardly risk coming to the support of his brother-in-law. News of the recent destruction of Norwich and Thetford and the prospect of Swegen renewing his attacks the following year convinced him that he would have to swallow his pride and attempt to unite the disparate elements of his kingdom. Perceiving no alternative he ordered the recall of the Witan.

Soon after Martinmas word was sent out to the ealdormen and chief thegns that the king wished to hold a great council at Christmas to determine the future of the realm. With Athelstan coming of age and no sign of an Anglo-Norman prince it presaged a return to the old order and those who had clashed spears with the Aetheling received the summons with relief and anticipation, reflecting the joyous expectation of the Church as she entered the season of Advent. Wulfnoth decided the time was right for his reappearance at court.

As the various lords and leading thegns made their preparations to travel to Winchester they were not to know that Emma had chosen the First Sunday of the Ecclesiastical Year to announce that she had been pregnant for over three months and that this time she was certain that she would not only go full term, but that she was carrying a male child.

Aethelred was overjoyed but decided that the news be kept secret for a further four weeks until such time as they could be sure that she would not miscarry. Soon her condition became obvious and under protest she withdrew to the bedchamber.

Most of the Members of the Council arrived on the twenty-third of December and much of the mundane business of government was dealt with. Along with the others Wulfnoth was called upon to witness some of the state papers. The king seemed far more relaxed than the last time they had met and once the diplomas had been signed he expressed his delight to see his old friend. Perhaps it was fortuitous that Aethelred had his arm around Wulfnoth's shoulders when the Shropshire thegns arrived. Incredulity drained the colour from Beorhtric's face, but Eadric seemed more amused than surprised, inclining his head very slightly to the Thegn of Compton before addressing the king.

* * * * *

When the Witan gathered on Christmas Eve, however, the feeling of euphoria was abruptly shattered by the announcement of the queen's condition and the edict that all freemen within the land must take a solemn oath that "if a man child should come forth as the fruit of her labour, they would await in him their lord and king who would rule over the whole race of the English."

Morcar was on his feet before Aelfhelm could stop him. "Surely, my lord," he began, "you jest."

When the king failed to answer he attempted to justify his outburst. "I mean with the prospect of further Viking raids no man in his right mind would pledge allegiance to an infant, let alone the promise of a woman's belly!"

Conscious of anger welling in the king's face, Aelfhelm struggled to retrieve the situation. "My lord, forgive my young friend. His only concerned is the safety of the realm."

"Do you still attempt to thwart my wishes?" bellowed the king beside himself.

The silence that followed was eventually broken by Beorhtric who shouted across the chamber, "If you defy your king in this you had best leave the council. You are no longer welcome here."

In the confusion that followed Wulfnoth and Aethelmaer slipped quietly away and no one attempted to stop Aelfhelm and the men of the Danelaw from storming angrily out of the palace. They alone refused to take the oath.

The rest of the Council were subsequently cowed by the presence of Eadric and Beorhtric supported by a number of their relatives who had secretly been admitted to the gathering to quell any further dissent.

When Emma was due to give birth it should have been a time of great rejoicing, but it coincided with a period when famine stalked the land and few were immune to his griping hands. The villeins, bordars and cottars agonised over how much grain to save for the next season and when to harvest the last of their crops. The town's people of Winchester fared even worse, suffering great deprivation once most of the smoked-cured meat and salt fish had been eaten. The serfs faced starvation and a lingering death. Outside the gates of the palace violent crowds gathered howling for food so Aethelred decided to move to his fortified manor at Islip and it was there that the new royal prince was born in early June in 1005.

Across the whole of England even those in the great houses found themselves more concerned with husbanding their own lands than indulging in court intrigue. Nevertheless resentment grew and with it support for the eldest son of the former Queen Aelfgifu. With Aethelmaer disappearing back into the wilds of the Western Provinces, many began to look to the Danelaw and Northumbria for leadership.

Nothing that went on in the realm could elude for long the eyes and ears of Eadric's network of spies and soon he was in a position to establish a list of dissident wealthy thegns who, despite the edict of Aethelred, continued to promote the cause of Athelstan. They were spread across the country, but the most important of them were Wulfgeat, who had served the king loyally since 990, Siferth and Morcar of the Five Boroughs and Thurbrand the Hold. Individually they posed no great threat to the kingdom, but it was clear from the continual stream of messengers that travelled between Eastern Mercia and York that behind them stood Ealdorman Aelfhelm.

He was a horse of a different colour one who not only commanded loyalty throughout the Danelaw, but the respect of many throughout the whole kingdom. He had also proved to be a stumbling block in Eadric's own ambition to become Ealdorman of West Mercia and if it could be proved that he still defied the king then he was ripe for culling.

Wulfnoth could wait. On the one hand he was a boyhood companion of the King, had gained a reputation for success in a number of encounters against the Danes and had given valuable assistance to the East Anglians in the defence of Thetford. He appeared to be a born survivor. Such a man could prove useful. On the other there was Alena's letter and the fact that he had tried to interfere with the ethnic cleansing at Exeter. Then there was the secret meeting that had been held at Compton. His abrupt exit from the Council confirmed that his sympathies still lay with Athelstan and the people of the Danelaw. Such information as he had could remain in its pigeonhole and the watch on the Compton estate might reveal further evidence of treason. On reflection, therefore, Eadric decided that as Wulfnoth remained well down the pecking order he could be dealt with at a later date. Even the matter of Torgrim's gold-hoard would have to wait a little longer.

Famine had driven Swegen from his winter quarters on the Isle of Wight and his ships had been shadowed returning to Denmark. That should have given cause to rejoice, but empty bellies continued to breed discontent among the people who openly blamed the king for their suffering.

Aethelred, already annoyed that he was unable to parade his new son and heir, Edward, before the rapturous gaze of the citizens of Winchester, was furious, therefore, when Eadric, presented evidence that many of the Witan had reneged on their oaths and openly declared their support for Athelstan. His first thought was to have his eldest son flung into a dungeon, but the young man had left court and his whereabouts were unknown. Frustrated, he determined to vent his spleen on those elements within the kingdom that conspired to thwart his choice of Edward as his heir. However, not wishing to widen the rift that had opened between him and his people, he chose Eadric to be his instrument giving the Mercian a completely free hand in dealing with his enemies.

The Mercian's first act was to produce a list of trumped up charges against Wulfgeat, suborning witnesses to accuse him of "unjust judgements and arrogant deeds". The thegn was duly tried; he was declared "nithing"; his extensive estates were forfeited; and he was banished. The king who found himself the main beneficiary seemed duly pleased.

Eadric, who was well aware of his master's vacillating nature, proposed that his next target should be Morcar whose flagrant defiance of the king's edict had led to the collapse of the Christmas Witan. Again the king had nodded his assent.

While Eadric was sifting through reports in search of further evidence of treason to strengthen his case against Siferth's younger brother, the queen entered the little room above the gatehouse.

"Well?" she demanded as Eadric rose with a sheaf of parchments in his hand.

"Madam?"

"How long must we spend hunting the cubs while the old wolf hides himself away in York?"

"Madam?" said Eadric again feigning innocence.

"Aelfhelm. He is the pack-leader. Cut off his head and the others will soon come to heel. Morcar is a young puppy and can be strangled at any time. Kill the old man and you show everyone the price to be paid for disloyalty."

"Madam, preparing a case against Ealdorman Aelfhelm will take time. He has great support in the Danelaw and is much respected in the Witan."

"Preparing a case. You and your spies and legal niceties! Can you not murder the old man and have done with it?"

"My lady, it is not quite as easy as that."

You have the king's authority. What more do you need? Besides, his death would create a vast administrative hole in the kingdom with the other northern lords tainted by association it will be easy for me to persuade Aethelred that he has no other choice but to appoint you as Ealdorman over all Mercia with the task of subduing the whole of the Danelaw."

The simplicity of it appealed to Eadric and he determined on a bold strategy to deliver the ealdorman into their hands.

Winter lingered late again the following year and
few seeds germinated. Grass seemed sparse as
hair in leprosy and the cattle that had survived the
annual cull grew thin on their meagre rations. Many fell
prey to hungry wolves while others to the knives of the
desperate people. Men and beasts starved together. The
whole land remained hard and unforgiving.

For several years, however, Alfred had established a
rigorous routine on the Compton estate that might have
served as a model for the Julius Work Calendar:
ploughing and planting, sowing and reaping, preserving
and storing, rationing and feasting so that the manor
was always well-stocked. He also prevailed on the
captain of *La Pie Bavarde* to send barrels of nuts and
dried fruit from the ports of the great Inland Sea.
Swithred and Oswy played their part too taking turn
and turn about to cast nets into the great harbour of
Chichester and provided a regular supply of fish. Estrith,
for all her years, still ran the household and nourishing
meals were provided with monastic precision to all who
lived and worked on the estate, so that even when the
gripe of famine was felt across the rest of the kingdom,
life at Compton remained tolerably comfortable.

In May *The Black Wolf* returned to Bosham. Cerdic,
who had had strict instructions to take Torgrim and his

family directly to Bruges, reported their safe arrival. He was also accompanied by the ten-year-old Godwin as Wulfnoth felt it was time for the boy to learn the responsibilities of running an estate.

The following day, however, a messenger from York brought news of a rumour sweeping the country that the Mercian faction had at last fallen out of favour at Court and that they had been sent packing. This was apparently confirmed when Eadric and Beorhtric were seen in Chester in the company of Welsh tribesmen and men from Cumbria who had risen against Aethelred five years before. Given the division that already existed between Aethelred and the people of the Danelaw and the rift over the succession, Aelfhelm thought it prudent to call a meeting of all those sympathetic to the aetheling.

Wulfnoth felt it was his duty to attend and proposed to take Godwin with him.

On the feast of the Birth of John the Baptist eleven people sat around the table in the main hall of Aelfhelm's fortified manor: the Ealdorman himself, Aethelmaer, the Ealdorman of the Western Provinces, Ulfkytel of EastAnglia, Uhtred of Bamburgh, Thurbrand the Hold, Siferth, Morcar, Wulfnoth, Godwin and two young men, Prince Athelstan who was slight and pale, and his younger brother Edmund a fine muscular sixteen-year-old youth; the spitting image of his father.

Conscious that such a gathering could be construed as treason Ealdorman Aethelmaer was attempting to clarify their position. "It is true that we have all sworn to uphold the right of Prince Athelstan to succeed his father when the time comes, but we are loyal subjects and as members of the Witan we hold a sacred duty to England. If there were to be a rebellion in the northwest we must be ready to offer unconditional support to Aethelred. Otherwise when Swegen sees how divided we are he may be tempted to seek the throne for himself."

All eyes next turned to Aelfhelm.

"What you say it true," he began, "but these divisions are of the king's own making. Although there is suspicion of the people of the Danelaw they remain loyal to their king. They would not seek a Danish overlord."

"Not unless we're forced to bend the knee to Prince Edward," warned Morcar darkly.

"We'll have no Norman-spawned infant forced upon us," added Thurbrand.

"That is not the question here," interrupted Edmund, "My brother is already a man and the Witan, no longer under threat from Shrewsbury, will acknowledge him as heir. If my father dies all England will rally to his cause."

"That is without doubt, my lord," continued Aelfhelm. "Many members of the Witan who were intimidated at Winchester have since secretly offered their support to Prince Athelstan, but in the meantime we have to face possible rebellion as well as the near certainty that Swegen's warships will return.

"The king himself should lead us," said Thurbrand. "If he has rejected the poison that comes from Shrewsbury and will not press us to anoint a scarce wet-nursed infant, we could raise a standing army large enough to defeat any rebellion and any Danish invasion. Then once Athelstan and Edmund have distinguished themselves in battle he and his people will appreciate the sense in what we say. "

"But the aetheling has been ill and is not sufficiently strong to stand in the shield wall," protested Siferth.

"I will fight for him if my father will let me fight at his side," declared Edmund.

"The king does not relish the field," commented Aethelmaer dryly.

"Then I will fight alone for England."

Aelfhelm smiled at the determination of the young man. "Let's hope it doesn't come to that, my lord," Then looking round the table he asked, "Are we all agreed that as long as Aethelred still lives and breathes we honour him as our king?"

When the others nodded their support he continued, "Then the king must take the field. There is no one else at present to unite the country. We of the Danelaw will write to him, expressing our just demands, but assuring him of our loyalty and offering him our full support against his enemies."

"In that we are agreed," said Aethelmaer visibly relieved.

Later that evening Aelfhelm drafted the following letter which all witnessed.

"To Aethelred, King of all England, Greetings.
The people of the Danelaw, clash spears with their Royal Master in duty and friendship. They will stand in the shield wall and fight to the death to defend him.
Forgive our reluctance to anoint your son Edward. If, God forbid, death were to rob us of your wise hand on the oar that steers the ship of state, the succession of an infant king would encourage Swegen to seize his

chance and mount a full scale invasion to devour
the whole kingdom. Not one of your royal sons
would succeed you.
We would further beseech you to reject the thegns
of Shrewsbury who seek only to feather their own
nests. They are no friends to the Cerdics, whom the
men of the Danelaw honour as their true kings."

Several weeks later a reply bearing the royal seal arrived
in York. It was from the king commending Aelfhelm for
his loyalty and proposing a meeting at the royal manor
of Cookham just south of the River Thames.

Cookham   Autumn 1006

O n a cold bright day towards the end of September Aelfhelm, accompanied by his two sons Wulfheah and Ufegeat, left the Danelaw and rode into the great forest of Windsor to confirm the support of the people of the Danelaw. He had already noticed that the leaves on the trees on either side of the hedgerows had begun to turn and there were hints of gold and splashes of fiery red amidst the subtle verdant tones. It always surprised him that the season seemed more advanced in the South. Soon under the canopy of oaks, ash and elm the shades of green lost their distinct character and merged into a darker backcloth. The cheerful sprays of hawthorn berries and the red hips of dog roses gave way to sinister ropes of poisonous bryony and among the autumnal detritus of the forest floor fungal spores produced their often-deadly fruit. It was the season when witches walked abroad seeking the lurid death cap, spotted scarlet and destroying angel to prepare their evil potions. Aelfhelm shivered. Perhaps it was witchcraft that had poisoned the king's mind, a spell cast by some vile hag that Eadric had unearthed in Mercia, but now, thank God, that noxious upstart had overreached himself and the scales had fallen from Aethelred's eyes.

He disliked the wood. He preferred the moorlands of the North where he could fly his hawks. Unlike

Aethelred, he found no pleasure in crashing about in the undergrowth hunting wild boar.

His reflections were interrupted by the voice of his youngest son, Ufegeat, "We're hungry, father. Can we not stop and eat?"

"Not yet, Ufegeat. Be patient a little longer. Soon we will feast at the king's table and I promise you your eyes will stand out on stalks at the sight of it."

"Do they eat better than us then, father?"

"Kings always eat well, Son, but they say that, since his Norman marriage, Norman cooks hold sway in royal palaces. You will see rare dishes and strange fruit."

"Then let us hurry. I want to feast my eyes and my stomach."

By mid afternoon they had crossed the Thames and arrived at the manor of Cookham, an ancient hunting lodge deep in the forest that Aethelred had had turned into a royal residence. There, they were challenged by a sentry whose back-shaven hairstyle proclaimed that he was a Norman. Mildly surprised, but not unduly worried, the Ealdorman dismounted. Perhaps the king feared that the treason had spread to his own guards and was taking no chances. The Northumbrian mounted escort was directed to the stables, while Aelfhelm, and his two sons were ushered directly into the main hall where they were politely requested to wait.

On the table lay a bowl of apples, pears and plums, but Aelfhelm forbad them to touch the fruit until the king appeared. In the minutes that followed the two young men became impatient and began to explore the room.

"What's this, father?" asked Ulfgeat picking up a heavily armed piece from a board game set out at one end of the table beside what was obviously the king's chair.

"Put it down, my son. It is part of rare gift sent by Richard, Duke of Normandy on the betrothal of his daughter, Queen Emma."

"But they are such strange creatures."

"It is the Norman version of an ancient pagan wargame. The one in your hand is a Norman knight; on his left in the corner stands the massive castle of Falaise, though it was once a charioteer; and on the other side the bishop replaces the elephant, a fabulous beast supposedly favoured by the Arabs. The Church did not approve of the original game, so the change is designed to placate the Pope."

"What are the small pieces in front?"

"They have always been foot soldiers and the tallest piece at the back wearing a crown is the king."

"What about this little one next to the king," asked Wulfheah, who had been drawn to the table.

"That should be the counsellor, a member of the Witan, but since Emma was crowned beside Aethelred it has become known as the queen."

Wulfheah had barely enough time to put the piece down on the table before another Norman servant arrived.

"My lord," he said bowing very formally, "there is wine and food prepared to refresh you after your long journey."

"Where is the king, Norman? Bring me to him for I must speak with him directly."

"The queen, my lord, has given express instructions that you are to be served refreshment the moment you arrive."

"The queen? I have not come to see the queen," replied Aelfhelm testily. "Sir, where is the king? It is the king, not the queen, that I have come to see."

"But he is not expected till nightfall, my lord."

"His letter spoke of urgency."

"No one knew when you would come, my lord. The king has ridden to Windsor to muster more troops. We were told to have food ready in case you arrived before him. Will you not sit and eat, my lord."

Realising that the man was only doing his duty, Aelfhelm felt a pang of conscience that he had lost his temper.

"Can we not eat something, father?" asked Wulfheah. "We're starving."

"If it is the king's wish, then we shall eat," said Aelfhelm and took a place at the table where he was eagerly joined by two very relieved young men.

Almost immediately, a succession of Norman servants served strong red wine and brought a variety of hot and cold dishes to the board. There were capons with crab-apple verjuice; tansied omelettes flavoured with tart perennial herbs and spices that would have made the long journey from Pavia; a variety of honeyed biscuit; and sweet pain perdu.

Once they had overcome their amazement, Wulfheah and Ufegeat waited only for a surreptitious nod from their indulgent father before falling ravenously on the food. Aelfhelm remained silent and ate frugally.

"This is better than stewed oats or dried cod with onions and cabbage, father," said Ulfgeat gnawing the meat from a chicken bone, "but the wine is not to my taste. Give me northern ale any day."

"You don't know when you're well off," laughed Wulfheah. "King's and queens don't drink beer."

They had both turned their attention to the biscuits when a party of horsemen was heard outside. Aelfhelm told them to finish what they were eating and be ready to meet their liege lord. He himself was beginning to rise from his stool when the door burst open and gang of ruffians rushed into the hall taking them completely by surprise. The old man was pinioned against a wall while the two younger men were quickly trussed up on the floor among the scattered chess pieces like game birds ready for the spit.

"By what right do you assault us?" Aelfhelm demanded defiantly when he had recovered his breath. "I am the Ealdorman of Northumbria and a leading member of the Witan. If you have any sense at all you will release me at once."

"We know well who you are," a cold voice penetrated the general din. Behind the crowd stood the stocky figure of Porthund, the hangman of Shrewsbury, with a savage looking bloodstained mastiff straining at the leash. Slowly he made his way through the throng pausing casually to pick up the chess queen and place it carefully in its place on the game board.

"Wretch, you have overreached yourself this time," said Aelfhelm. "The king has returned with fresh troops and my bodyguard is within earshot."

"Your bodyguard," Porthund spat on the floor, "has made its last stand and the king is still in Winchester. They were our horses you heard. We have been hunting and my mastiff has already brought a vicious old she wolf to the ground and now he will witness the dispatch of another."

"Hang him from the central beam of the building," ordered a familiar voice from the shadows in the doorway.

Realising that he had been totally duped, Aelfhelm's knees buckled and those restraining him let him sag to the floor.

"Stay!" Porthund spoke sharply to the mastiff and the dog immediately dropped to the ground, but remained alert watching its master's every move. Then the hangman of Shrewsbury slipped a noose around the old man's neck and tossed the other end over a massive oak roof timber.

Wulfheah and Ulfgeat, who had been gagged at the outset, could only roll their eyes in horror as the Mercian pulling on the rope, dragged their father first to his knees and then to his feet until he was dancing from one foot to the other. Instinctively, the old man grasped the rope in an effort to prevent the noose from tightening around his windpipe, but seconds later his feet were off the ground and his legs left jerking convulsively in the air. His face turned first red then puce as he struggled frantically to breathe and the ruckle of his strangled choking, broken only by intermittent gulps for air, seemed to last interminably.

"Get it over with," ordered the voice from the doorway when the old man's gasps showed no signs of coming to an end. "Then I can return to Winchester to inform my brother of the death of a notorious traitor. The unexpected news will undoubtedly please the king and it will quickly bring to heel all others who oppose his will."

Securing the rope, Porthund picked up the figure of the queen from the table and forced the piece deep into Aelfhelm's throat clamping his hand firmly over his mouth for good measure.

After one final spasm blood poured from the old man's nose and his arms fell limply at his sides. The ealdorman was dead.

Expecting to follow their father's fate, Wulfheah and Ulfgeat instead found themselves lifted onto stools with their backs against the table.

Porthund looked down on them. "Unfortunately, it has been decided to spare your lives," he said, "but then you must do something for us in return."

Fear was replaced by incomprehension on the faces of the two prisoners.

Porthund went on in a matter of fact voice, "You have to understand that your father was a constant thorn in the king's side, opposing him in the Council and refusing to take an oath of allegiance to his chosen heir. Not satisfied with that he stirred up treason in the Danelaw and, therefore, deserved to die. Let his death be an end and serve as a warning to all others that the king will no longer tolerate disloyalty."

Unable to speak they could only try to express their hatred though their eyes. The Shrewsbury hangman, however, took their fixed stares as a sign of resignation.

"You will take the king's message back to the people of the Northumbria and the Five Boroughs," he continued. "If they throw themselves on the mercy of their rightful sovereign, he will forgive them and you will be rewarded. If they persist in treason he will hunt them down ruthlessly and you with them."

Porthund smiled and then nodded to another Mercian to remove the gags.

Ulfgeat spat in the Mercian's face.

"That was not wise," said Porthund wiping away the spittle.

"Murderer, we shall avenge our father's death," shouted Wulfheah defiantly, "We shall raise the Danelaw and lead an army against all those who poison the king's mind."

"We shall see you hanged like the dog you are," added Ulfgeat.

"I doubt that," said Porthund angrily. "Replace their gags.

"It seems," said the voice in the doorway, "we shall have to make our message even more clear. Blind them both. Then have them released into the Danelaw."

"It will be my pleasure," said Porthund as Beorhtric slipped out of the room.

The horrified young men thrashed about wildly unable to protest or defend themselves in the face of imminent mutilation. Each ones head in turn was forced back onto the table and held rigid so that Porthund could set to work.

Forcing his index finger deep into each eye socket in turn he succeeded in severing the eye muscles so that he could scoop out the eyeball and tear it free from the optic nerve.

Sensing the sadistic enjoyment of its master the mastiff stood drooling in anticipation.

It was not disappointed for after each mutilation the Mercian tossed the jellylike sphere into the air and the dog caught and swallowed it in one movement.

PART FIVE

Aethelred's Ship Army

"The way was open

for a determined man of obscure origins

to establish himself as the king's indispensable
right arm."

Origin Unknown

Renewed Danish attacks throughout central Southern England and another ignominious flight of the English forces at Kennet, saw the King accompanied by his court cross the Thames to the relative safety of Mercia. Thus it was that that the Christmas Council that year was held in Shrewsbury.

Of the old guard only Aelfric and Aethelmaer attended. Aelfric, whose moods swung between self-doubt and the conviction that no blame could possibly be attached to him personally, found the courage to appear, but then as premier ealdorman his absence after his recent defeat might have provoked accusations of treason. Aethelmaer, who was related to the king and whose fortress at Fowey had successfully prevented Danish incursions into Wessex beyond Selwood, left the West Country with a degree of reluctance and with a strong retinue of Cornishmen.

The leading thegns of Northumbria South of the Tees, those of York, those of Holderness and most of those from the Five Boroughs were neither summoned nor inclined to appear. After the murder of Aelfhelm and the blinding of his sons discretion had taught those loyal to Aethelstan to keep a low profile within the relative safety of the Danelaw and wait for better days. Only Ulfkytel of Norwich whose reputation had been enhanced by his resistance to Swegen in 1004 and Uhtred of Bamburgh, who annihilated the Scottish army at Durham in 1006, felt confident enough to attend.

The only other thegn to achieve distinction in defence of the kingdom was Wulfnoth, but he could not be found.

After Aethelred had opened the proceedings, Eadric welcomed them to Shrewsbury and spent several minutes attempting to explain away the problems that had beset England throughout 1006. The root cause, he said, was that following the famine of the previous year Swegen had established a foothold on English territory from which he could attack anywhere on the south coast whenever he chose. No longer did he have to risk a two-day journey over the searoads. At the same time the unexplained and unfortunate murder of Ealdorman Aelfhelm had, he claimed, not only robbed England of a wise and valued member of the Witan, but also provoked a lawless power struggle in the Danelaw that now endangered the very unity of the kingdom. As a consequence Wessex and Mercia had been faced with the impossible task of taking on the brunt of the invasion alone. Unfortunately, illness had prevented him from being able to support Aefric. Assuming the guise of an elder statesman, he declared that there was no point in attempting to apportion blame and that it was time to draw a line under the past and plan for the future.

The king nodded, "So which of my ealdormen will raise me another army to drive the Danish pirates from the South of England once and for all?" When no one replied he turned to the premier ealdorman. "Can you, Aelfric?"

Aelfric, who moments before had felt relief that his military skill had not been called into question, was immediately on the defensive. "My lord, the people of Wessex have continually born the brunt of Swegen's attacks. Last year the fyrd was on campaign throughout harvest time and the crops rotted again in the fields. Many more families will die of starvation this winter. Few will be fit enough to take their place in the shieldwall."

The king grimaced and turned to Aethelmaer. "Cousin?"

"Wessex Beyond Selwood is vastly under populated, my lord. We can barely raise enough men to secure the ragged coastline of your west country. Is not this a time to call upon Richard of Normandy to honour his pledge and send a fleet to drive the Danes from their winter base?"

"Normandy it seems has problems of its own and Richard sends word that he is unable to help until he has subdued the Bretons."

"Typical of a Norman! He has secured England's crown for his own family by virtue of his sister's marriage, but declines to come to the aid of the Cerdics."

Aethelred clenched his teeth and ignored the implied criticism. "That leaves only my thegns. What of you Ulfkytel and the men of East Anglia?"

"It's true, my lord, with the help of the Thegn of Compton we defeated Swegen and drove him back to his homelands these two years since, but at great loss. One third of your East Anglian thegns were killed and many are still not replaced. However, if it is your wish I shall march what men I have to Wessex and make one last stand against the invader."

"And if you fail?"

"We fail and England falls."

The starkness of the situation was beginning to dawn on Aethelred.

"My lord," said Eadric sagely, "Your ealdormen, few as they are, have spent their lives defending your kingdom. They have repeatedly served you with distinction in the field. Surely it is time for them to lay aside their weapons. It would be unfair to expect Aelfric or Aethelmaer to raise and lead another army against Swegen, when there are younger men not of the same rank perhaps, but men like Uhtred who has already proved himself in destroying King Malcolm's forces in the north."

Uhtred clearly expected to succeed his father Waltheof as Ealdorman of Northumbria Beyond the Tees, but, as Eadric knew well, he also had designs on uniting the whole of Northumbria and leading an army south to defend Wessex would be a risky way to achieve his aims. He was quickly on his feet, "My lord, my sword is always at your command, but if you leave your northern borders unprotected King Malcolm will raise yet another Scottish army and seek again to expand his territory at your expense. You cannot fight a war on two fronts."

Eadric looked weary and sighed almost imperceptibly. "Uhtred is right, my lord. He is your strength in the north and deserves to succeed to his father's title. Ulfkytel is brave and can hold the east, Aethelmaer the south-west. Wessex needs time to rebuild its strength. You need to appoint men of strength to rebuild the different regions of your land. Take Mercia for example. It is the heart of England and yet for far too long it has lacked the direction of an ealdorman and played little part in defending your kingdom. It would also act as a counter that would curb the unrest in the Danelaw and restore the power of the Cerdics."

Emma smiled and placed her hand on the king's arm.

Aethelred's mood appeared to lighten, but did not commit himself.

However, while Eadric's deliberately measured words seemed to offer a way forward, others present viewed the thegn as a potential rival and saw them as a thinly disguised bid for power.

"I would be more than willing, my lord, to deal with the Yorkist rebels," declared Uhtred quickly, "and make the whole of Northumbria a shield against attack from sea or land."

"I'm sure you would, Uhtred, but Ulfkytel might make a similar claim," suggested Eadric.

"Not so." Ulfkytel turned to the king. "My lord," there are still good men in York and Lindsey who given the chance will serve you well and bring that region back within the fold. I am content to rebuild the land of the East Angles and hold it against all your enemies within or without."

Aethelred acknowledged the offer. "Then it seems we must redraw the map of England and rebuild the regions in order to defend my kingdom."

"And what of the starving people of Wessex? Do you all expect Swegen to sit idly by on the Isle of Wight while we accomplish this rebuilding?" asked Aelfric. "His Danes will pour back into the south as soon at the spring weather arrives."

"I did not suggest it would be an easy task," said Eadric, "so once again we must buy ourselves a period of time."

"Another danegeld you mean?"

"Yes and this time one that will keep him in such luxury that he will not need to leave his native land for at least two years.

"And then do what? Argue among ourselves until his treasure chest is empty again and he comes back for more?" Aelfric sounded despondent.

"No!" exclaimed Eadric. "To regroup and set each region a task to build a fleet so large that we can defend our own shores and make him seek easier spoils elsewhere."

"But that will mean raising even more money!"

"The alternative is to bend the knee to Swegen. The Cerdics will be no more and we shall all face the axe."

"And who will lead this battle fleet of yours?"

"That will be for the king to decide, but my brother Beorhtric is the only one with recent experience of commanding the king's fleet."

"And last time he refused to commit his ships and come to my assistance," said Aelfric bitterly. "And in the end the king's fleet rotted in the mud of London."

Eadric was furious and momentarily allowed his cultivated pose of statesman to slip. "Who do you suggest then? Your friend, the Sussex thegn, perhaps?"

"He may not respect authority, but at least he could do no worse than Beorhtric!" retorted Aelfric bluntly.

"He is the only man with daring enough to pull it off," observed Ulfkytel trying to defuse the situation. "I'll provide twenty ships built in East Anglia, but only if Wulfnoth is to have command."

"We have been here before only to reject the one man who has a chance to succeed," commented Aethelmaer dryly.

"I'll build another twenty in the north if Wulfnoth is to have command," said Uhtred.

Eadric bit his lip in an attempt to conceal his fury that his carefully thought-out plan was coming unstuck, but the king seemed amused.

"It is agreed," he said, "but where is Wulfnoth?"

"My spies tell me he is in Bruges, my lord," Eadric reluctantly admitted.

"Then bring me word as soon as he returns."

"Yes, my lord, but for the present it is essential that no word of your intention to build a grand fleet should pass beyond these walls. Time enough to summon the Thegn of Compton when the Danes are gone."

Before the Council closed it was agreed that a huge danegeld would have to be raised and that once the Danes had left Aelfric should concentrate on ensuring that the Wessex thegns and villeins apply themselves solely to the securing a good harvest. Ulfkytel should draw up a list of suitable candidates to swell the ranks of the East Anglian thegns and Uhtred would be confirmed as his father's heir and the future Ealdorman of Northumbria Beyond the Tees. The king for his part would consider re-establishing the former region of Mercia and Eadric would prepare plans for the funding of the grand fleet.

Finally to seal their agreement Aethelred proposed that before the Christmas gathering ended Eadric, Ulfkytel and Uhtred should be bound closer to the throne by marrying his three daughters: Edith, Wulfhild and Aelfgifu. A new order in England had begun.

When news reached Compton that the Danes had finally withdrawn from the English mainland, unstepped their masts and drawn their sea stallions high up the sandy beaches of the Isle of Wight, beyond the reach of even the worst of winter storms, Wulfnoth breathed a sigh of relief and felt that he could safely leave the estate in the capable hands of Alfred. In the final week of Advent, accompanied by Godwin and Cerdic, he boarded *The Black Wolf* and set sail across a flint sea for the coast of Flanders to celebrate Christmas with the rest of his family in Bruges.

Their arrival at the Woolhouse caught everyone by surprise. As soon as the door opened Wulfnoth and Godwin shot passed the stunned Judith and raced up the staircase eager to be the first to greet the woman who had become the mistress of one and the mother of the other.

Alena heard the commotion on the stairs and instinctively pushed the two young toddlers into the bed chamber placing herself firmly in front of the door to face whatever danger was about to break in upon her. She was still less than thirty and unlike many of her age had retained the looks and poise that had excited the desire of the young men at the Winchester slave market nearly a decade before. The rich swirling dark hair and flashing eyes defied anyone who threatened to endanger the lives of her children and as the two men burst through the door and fell into the room she had the metseax ready to plunge into the first one who rose to his feet.

When she realised that the intruders, both on all fours, were laughing partly with exhaustion and partly at the look on her face, she struck them both several times, not with the metseax, which had fallen from her hand, but with two richly embroidered cushions. Seconds later Alena found herself wrapped in the intense embrace of a dark-haired man and the hugs of his younger blond companion. When she finally managed to extricate herself from their clutches and catch her breath she managed to shout, "Aelwig and Aethelflaed come out and meet your father and brother."

Gradually the door opened and a boy and girl gazed sheepishly at the two strangers.

Meanwhile Judith and Rosela had set to and prepared an extra room uncovering the windholes, lighting fires, filling sacks with fresh straw and making sure there were sufficient woollen covers to keep out the cold when the temperature dropped at night.

By four o'clock dusk was settling over the rivers and the citizens of Bruges were leaving their daytime occupations to seek the warmth of their fireside hearths. Torgrim, Hild and Eric were due back from the workshop the old man had set up beside the market square and Cerdic had gone out to meet them.

Unable to contain his desire to see the man to whom he owed so much, the former moneyer, with the ever-faithful Eric at his side, hurried back past the Breidelstraat Bridge to the Woolhouse, leaving Hild and

Cerdic to make sure that the forge fire had been put out before locking up the premises and returning home. He was so overjoyed to see Wulfnoth that at first he was unable to speak and simply clasped the thegn to him with his good arm, tears streaming down his cheeks, but eventually mastering his emotions he poured out his profuse thanks to the man who had rescued his daughter.

"My friend," said Wulfnoth, "there is really no need. It is a duty to fight injustice anywhere, but when the victim is an old and valued friend it is a joy that brings its own reward."

"Not only did you save a wretched old man from destitution, but restored to him the one reason he had for living."

"Then I am doubly blessed."

"We are both blessed, my lord," said Torgrim.

"Maher Wuffnah hood mhan," said Eric as he helped Torgrim to a stool beside Wulfnoth's chair. Then he shuffled off and left the two together.

"Eric seems quiet tonight."

"Poor Eric! He still blames himself for everything."

"How so?"

"He says that if he hadn't let Porthund and the other two Mercian foundry workers jump him in the cathedral tower Hild would not have been taken from us."

"Porthund? I had not realised he knew his attackers."

"Oh Yes. He knew all their names and I pity them if he ever meets them again.

"I see!"said Wulfnoth thoughtfully. "I'll speak with him and try to set his mind at rest."

"I hope you have more success than I have had," said Torgrim, shaking his head. "He should not blame himself."

"No indeed. I'll speak with him........ And how is your daughter, my friend?"

"Thrives, sir. Thrives. Now that she sees Mistress Alena every day and since that misunderstanding with Cerdic was resolved the light shines even more strongly in her eyes. She is content, my lord."

"Only content, Torgrim?" asked Alena mischievously.

"She is in love, Mistress Alena."

At the moment Hild appeared through the upper room door pulling a reluctant Cerdic after her.

"You both claim to be blessed," said Alena. "I think, my lord, your huscarl wishes to ask you both for a blessing."

"Mine is already given."

"As is mine," said Torgrim, "but I shall miss her when she leaves for Compton."

Cerdic and Hild knelt before Wulfnoth and Torgrim.

"Well, you good for nothing slave, what have you to say for yourself?" Wulfnoth began.

"My lord," began Cerdic shaken by the rough tone of his master's voice, but when he looked up he saw that the thegn was desperately trying to stifle a laugh.

"Well! Are you so much in love that you have lost your tongue?"

"Stop teasing him, Wulfnoth."

"I would like leave to marry, my lord."

I told you years ago you had only to ask and you would be free of any obligation to me. You have my blessing."

"And mine too," said Torgrim lifting his daughter to her feet and embracing her.

However, Cerdic remained kneeling. "Sir, I have no means of my own and no desire to leave your service and yet it might still be dangerous for Hild to live at Compton."

"Hild will have wealth enough for you both," said Torgrim, "and, although I cannot bear the thought that she will be parted from me, you can go and live anywhere in the world you choose."

"But I cannot live on my wife's dowry. I must seek to earn the means to provide for her."

Alena and Wulfnoth exchanged glances.

"So be it," said the thegn. "If the lady Alena will accept you as her huscarl, you have my blessing twice over."

They knelt before Alena and placed their heads in her hands. "On one condition that if at any time my lord is in danger and has need of your good right arm you will not hesitate to fight at his side."

"Agreed, my lady," said Cerdic and kissed the palms of her hands.

"I have one further favour to ask of my former huscarl, but that can wait," said Wulfnoth.

The marriage was consummated that same night and then the entire household prepared to celebrate Christmas.

* * * * * *

Eric's tendency to compensate for the loss of half of his tongue by heavily aspirating those consonants that required the tip of that fleshy muscular organ to provide the subtler distinctions of sound still made it difficult for the others to understand him, but, when Wulfnoth and Cerdic questioned him about the events leading up to their flight from Winchester, Torgrim was on hand to translate.

It transpired that the bellowsman had an excellent memory and could not only remember the names of his three assailants in the bell-tower of the New Minster, but could describe them in detail.

"Porhun", their leader, was apparently Porthund, a thickset creature from Shrewsbury, who had sought to ingratiate himself with the organ master, but who treated all others with contempt.

"Chrohha" was one Creoda from Chester with a hangdog expression and a distinct nervous tick.

"Mahoh" was Madog, a thin gangling red-haired fellow from beyond the Marches who had two fingers missing from his left hand.

"Whun hhay hey'll fheel heese hans awound heir hecsh, Mah Wuffnah!" declared Eric making squeezing motions with his great hands. "Whun hhay!"

"Yes, Eric, one day," said Torgrim gently.

"With your description, Eric, if they are still in Winchester, we'll find them," Wulfnoth added and turning to Cerdic he said, "Will you do me one last service?"

"Willingly, my lord, with Mistress Alena's permission."

"You both know you already have it," said Alena. "But why do you not go yourself, my love?"

"My presence in Winchester asking questions would alert Eadric. Cerdic must carry a letter to Ealdorman Aethelmaer. Now he is back in favour he spends much time in Winchester. He is also discrete. If anyone can run these creatures to earth, he can. And, Torgrim, give me a list of any of your workers who might have been bribed to produce debased coins from your dies. We'll leave no stone unturned to prove your innocence, my friend!"

"Of course," said Torgrim. "I had to employ some casual labour when two of my apprentices left after receiving beatings from Mercian gangs. Hild can write down their names for me."

"Do you wish me to wait until Ealdorman Athelmaer has the information, my lord?"

"No, Cerdic. Your place is here with your mistress and with your new wife. She will not thank me for separating you for anything more than a few days."

"*Le Geai des Chenes* makes regular journeys to Hantune," said Alena, brightly "If Lord Aethelmaer uncovers any evidence he can send it through her captain in a letter addressed to me."

"Can you be sure of your captain?" asked Wulfnoth cautiously. "We cannot endanger Lord Aethelmaer."

"Oh Yes!" Alena seemed amused. "He learned his lesson years ago. Walram is now captain of *Le Geai des Chenes* and I'd trust him with my life."

A Visit from the Princes   February 1008

The first few months of 1007 had been spent in negotiating the truce with the Danes, and finding the £30,000 danegeld demanded by Swegen. Such a large sum could not be raised in coin alone, so elaborate arrangements had been made to supply provisions and for the sale of estates to prominent Danes who wished to remain in England and agreed to offer their allegiance to Aethelred. However, the bulk of the tribute money had to be collected through taxation a process which took well into the summer.

Only when Swegen and the longships had finally disappeared from English waters could the fyrd be stood down and the people address the soil of Wessex turning their hands to the plough and broadcasting the seed that would eventually bring an end to two years of famine.

Although Compton had emerged from the raids comparatively unscathed Wulfnoth, Godwin and Alfred had set about improving the productivity of the estate, clearing scrubland, extending the acreage of meadow and restocking. The thegn's own contribution to the danegeld had been assessed at 60 shillings and Wulfnoth had felt the need to increase output and replenish his purse.

Aethelred had decided that the building of his ship army must begin early in the following year once the icy grip of winter had been broken. As soon as conditions improved he took the unusual step of sending Athelstan and his brother Edmund to Compton to inform Wulfnoth that he needed the thegn's help to plan the composition of a grand fleet and that his experience and skill would be required in London on the feast of St. Matthias in the second week of Lent.

When the two princes arrived Wulfnoth greeted them in the main hall.

"I'm honoured that the future king of England should visit Compton."

"My father would not have it so. Now that Edward is declared aetheling he sees me fit merely to deliver his messages."

"Surely the choice of king does not lie solely within his gift. After a king dies the Witan chooses his successor."

"Treasonable words, sir, but in any case my father has altered the composition of the Council to suit his purposes."

"So I hear, my lord, but the full Witan has the habit of confounding the wishes of kings for the good of England. I hope you know you have many friends there who will speak for you when the time comes."

"I do, sir, and am grateful for it."

"Tell me, my lord, is your father serious about this ship army and my part in it?"

"You have heard about it then?"

"Ealdorman Aethelmaer tries to keep me informed of affairs of state, my lord."

"It is true, Lord Wulfnoth. This time my father means to have a fleet and is convinced that only you can bring him success upon the waves. He speaks of no one but you to lead his sea stallions."

"Then I will serve him as I always have."

"Then the messenger has done his duty and I must report to my father without delay," said the prince with a touch of bitterness,

"Can we not see your ships while we are here?" asked Edmund who had remained unusually silent since their arrival. "They say the harbour at Bosham is one place the Danes dare not visit."

"With pleasure, my lord," said Wulfnoth.

"I too would like to see *The Black Wolf*, but my father insisted that I return at once and, since Eadric has placed a spy among my bodyguard, I have little choice in the matter. However, Edmund is my eyes and ears. He is not so restrained. His body servant is utterly loyal and in any case he can always claim the need to visit his estate at Sandwic."

Athelstan left Compton at first light and half an hour later Wulfnoth, Godwin and Edmund and the prince's servant rode south towards Bosham.

It was mid February and had been bitterly cold at night, but there was little wind, the sky was clear and the sun felt unseasonably warm on their faces as they cantered past the wooden church and drew up at the manor where Oswy and a couple of seamen took charge of the horses. A dozen or so dismasted vessels were laid up for the winter, upside down on stout oak horses, but two lay on the sand above the high water mark ready to be run into the sea at the first sign of danger. These were *The Black Wolf* and *The Godgifu*, sister ships and the pride of Wulfnoth's little fleet. After a word from Wulfnoth a dozen seamen ran the former into the water and seconds later she was ready to put to sea.

Edmund was amazed at the discipline of the crew who bent their backs rhythmically as one and drove *The Black Wolf*, swiftly down the estuary.

"She is flying," he said with admiration. "What a pity there is so little wind."

"There will be plenty when we reach the great harbour of Chichester," Wulfnoth assured him.

They spent the next two hours first tacking to counter an on-shore breeze and then finally running back to Bosham before the wind. By the end of the day when they had returned to Compton, Edmund was ready to ask another question.

Over a meal of mutton stew he lamented the fact that his father had forbidden all contact with the people of the Danelaw. Only Aethelmaer was permitted to negotiate directly with leaders of York, Lindsey and the Five Boroughs and his reports had to be made to the king alone. Eadric had closed all the roads from Mercia, Uhtred had secured the River Tees and Ulfkytel had been ordered to seal the southern border. Consequently Athelstan had no way of keeping in touch with his supporters. "My father," Edmund concluded, "would not think it amiss if I spent time on my estates in Kent. If you would be willing to lend me a vessel and crew I can sail to the Wash and act as my brother's go-between?"

The question took Wulfnoth by surprise. The young man had impressed him. While Athelstan appeared to have a frail constitution, Edmund was physically strong and mature beyond his years. He kept his emotions in check and when he spoke it was with the conviction of a man who had assessed all his options and knew his own mind.

"The sea can be a dangerous place in winter and in any case such a venture would be difficult to undertake in secret. Eadric has spies everywhere and if it became known it would alienate your father."

"I am aware of the risks and realise that it would also place you in an impossible position if the facts became known. Yet for my brother and the good of England I must make contact with our friends from the Five Boroughs."

"So be it," said Wulfnoth. "Godwin will arrange for *The Godgifu* to set sail tomorrow and, if you are willing, he will sail with you. It will be good experience for the boy and a chance to acertain the attitude of the people of the Danelaw after the murder of Aelfhelm."

Although Winchester was regarded as the capital of England, London with its ancient fortress built by King Alfred was on rare occasions used as an alternative royal residence and for the moment Aethelred had no wish to return to Wessex. It was, therefore, with a mixture of nervousness and excitement that Wulfnoth arrived at the palace.

He was still the king's thegn. His whole life had been spent fighting the Danes in the service of the king and now Aethelred was at last prepared to build a grand fleet which would enable him to sweep those predators from the sea once and for all.

His euphoria, however, suffered a major set back when he found Aethelred and Eadric poring over a long roll of parchment while Beorhtric sat idly rolling a pair of dice by the windhole.

Wulfnoth was convinced that the two Mercians had been behind the murder of Aelfhelm and had a nagging feeling that the king had condoned it. Otherwise why would he have chosen to celebrate the Christmas before last in Shrewsbury? He couldn't prove anything of course having heard nothing for several months from those in the Danelaw who had aligned themselves with Prince Athelstan. Eadric's continual presence at the king's right side made him feel distinctly uneasy.

"Ah at last," the king's eyes lit up, "You and I have work to do, my old friend. You know Eadric, and his brother of course. He has been a great help in this venture, but it is your skill and daring that will bring it to success."

The Mercian smiled and inclined his head, but there was no warmth in the greeting.

Beorhtric on the other hand looked positively venomous.

"Wulfnoth's spectacular success against the Swegen's longships is well known," Eadric acknowledged diplomatically. "His input will be most valuable."

However, Beorhtric could not resist adding spitefully, "I am surprised he did not pick off any of the Danish stragglers in his recent encounter. They would have served to swell the numbers of our present fleet."

"That might have hindered Swegen's departure and risked what few warships we have for little gain. The stragglers as you call them were the most cumbersome and least seaworthy of vessels."

"You see, Eadric, we have chosen well!" exclaimed Aethelred, thumping the table. "Wulfnoth understands the sort of vessel we need to defend my realm. With his expertise and daring next year my grand fleet will send Swegen and his pirates wandering the seabeds in search of treasure." For once at least the king seemed to have regained his old enthusiasm for adventure.

"It would seem so, my lord," conceded Eadric, "but we may require a variety of craft."

"Perhaps," agreed Wulfnoth. Much as he loathed the Mercian he felt that a degree of tact was called for especially as the king had seemed genuinely elated by his own arrival. "How advanced are your plans, my lord?"

"This is to be a national effort, Wulfnoth," he began authoritatively. "We need at least 120 warships and everyone must play his part, but I am relying particularly on you and the men of the coast to help build and sail my fleet. Uhtred, who is to be Ealdorman of all Northumbria, has already promised twenty vessels will be built in the north. Ulfkytel, another twenty in East Anglia. You already have a similar number in Bosham. The rest will be built in London. Mercia will be responsible for supplying the bulk of the timber and, once all the designs have been approved, you and ....." Wulfnoth caught a slight hesitation in the king's voice and an almost imperceptible drop in tone, "....Beorhtric.... will build me a further sixty warships there. Now what do you think of my plan?"

Wulfnoth recoiled at the prospect of working with Beorhtric, but could see no way of avoiding it. "Who is to design these warships?" he asked desperately trying to play for time.

"Of course you will be responsible for design," said Aethelred and added quickly, "and you will be in overall command of the fleet when we are at sea. Now what sort of ships do we need?"

Seeing no avenue of escape Wulfnoth resigned himself to the inevitable. "I have brought a design that will suit our purpose," and with that he unrolled a parchment and laid it out on the table.

The detailed sketch with its list of numbers and measurements clearly surprised them and it was several minutes before Aethelred broke the uncomfortable silence, "They are considerably smaller than I had imagined and rather .... unattractive."

"My lord, to win a seabattle we must concentrate on smaller well-braced vessels, designed to skim nimbly over the water and make quick inroads into the enemy fleet rather than larger ships built simply to impress everyone."

"But they are like fishing boats!" scoffed Beorhtric. "Can you imagine Swegen Forkbeard and his pirates crossing the great seas in such flimsy craft?"

Ignoring the man, Wulfnoth addressed the issue. "When the heathen raiding parties first came they frequently used ships with less than a dozen pair of oars. Swegen's great longships are designed to transport vast armies across the oceans. His battles are fought on land where men can stand firm and wield the axe, not on the unpredictable crests of the sea. The greater the length of a vessel the slower it is to answer the steersman. The warships that I will build you will have the same lines, the same flexibility, but mine being shorter, will turn much faster in the heat of battle. As your commander I will direct the fleet from one such warship."

"And how will the common sailors and fyrdsmen recognise their leader if his warship is indistinguishable from a hundred others?" asked Eadric.

"Because my warship will be ahead of theirs," snapped Wulfnoth. "My sail will be black and the wolf standard will fly from my stern-post. My lord," he turned again to the king, "if all your ships were built to my design and manned by trained seamen I promise you I'll cause such havoc in Swegen's fleet that he will be unable to mount an invasion on English soil."

"It seems," said Beorhtric, "we have only to provide the materials and the Thegn of Compton will destroy the Danes single-handed. I still say we need to match the

Viking longships and even then," he added importantly, "the king and all his commanders must have much larger vessels to demonstrate their authority." He returned to his dice.

Wulfnoth knew that he was in danger of antagonising two powerful enemies, but stood his ground. "That will be for the king to decide!"

The statement was clearly meant as a snub, but was irrefutable and Beorhtric angrily flung the dice into the windhole.

Another silence ensued.

"If I am to build this fleet, my lord, I shall still require vast quantities of oak and ash as well as the season's new growth of osiers. It is the quality of the wood as well as the skill of the shipbuilder that determines the spirit of a warship."

"Naturally," said Aethelred without committing himself "and Mercia will provide the bulk of the materials.

"At present we are engaged in the task of compiling a list of thegns who hold in excess of ten hides of land," explained Eadric. "The king has decreed that every substantial land owner must contribute sufficient material for at least one warship."

"The king has also decreed," added Beorhtric savagely, "that those holding over 300 hides will be responsible for providing material for larger vessels with sixty oars and they will have to equip them with sufficient helmets and mailcoats."

"That need not worry you, Wulfnoth," added Eadric quickly. "You concentrate on the warships you are commissioned to build."

"Unfortunately, however, that will include my brother," said Beorhtric with a degree of feigned resignation.

Eadric was furious. "Your presence here is becoming tiresome, Beorhtric. Be good enough to return to Mercia. With the King's permission," he bowed in deference to Aethelred.

Beorhtric might have stood his ground and argued, but a curt nod from Aethelred signalled that he was dismissed. Flicking out one of his long arms, he swept up his dice and left.

Wulfnoth raised his eyebrows.

The king looked uncomfortable. "I have appointed Eadric an ealdorman," he explained, "He and his brother will have plenty to do gathering material throughout the whole of Mercia."

Wulfnoth nearly choked. "But Mercia is landlocked," he heard himself say.

"True, but it has good timber and it must play a full part in this enterprise. In any case I have decided that some larger vessels must be constructed. We must have a balanced fleet."

"It is essential that the king and the leading members of the Witan must be protected at all costs," added the ealdorman.

The thegn tried one last time to make them see sense, "It is smaller sleeker sixty-foot warships that will cause havoc among the enemy and win you this war."

You build me thirty of your harriers on the Thames at the east end of London below Alfred's fortress and Beorhtric can build thirty larger vessels on the banks west of the river Fleet."

Wulfnoth knew that further argument was useless. At least he would be spared working closely with Beorhtric.

"Naturally," confided Aethelred, "if you are successful in destroying all the Danish ships you will be rewarded with land and, with Aelfric failing, I may soon need a new ealdorman in Wessex. Then we will be in a position to rebuild the rest of the country."

Wulfnoth felt that he was being sucked into a world of political intrigue and while the king still personally held his allegiance, he no longer trusted him. In any case he was conscious that he was also pledged to the cause of Prince Athelstan and he had no wish to be part of this new dispensation.

A Secret Mission to
the Danelaw   Spring 1008

When Edmund and Godwin set sail in *The Godgifu*, Wulfnoth insisted that Swithred who had grown up in the sea-water swamps of the Wash should captain the vessel especially since Godwin was only twelve and Edmund for all his eighteen years had little experience of the sea.

After two days they had passed the mouth of the Thames and left the land of the East Saxons where they crossed the treacherous waters of the Wash without mishap and entered the mouth of the River Welland which meandered through a great swampy marsh abounding in fish and wild fowl before reaching the village of Crowland—a few hovels gathered around the Abbey of St Guthlac, built on a small island of high ground—where they spent the night. From there the countryside was less marshy and it eventually passed into the cultivated lands of Siferth at Stamford.

On his return to Compton Godwin was bursting to describe the full extent of their secret mission to Stamford keen to report to his father that the people of the Danelaw had reaffirmed that they held the King as their sovereign lord as long as he was not implicated in the death of Ealdorman Aelfhelm. Siferth, he said, had dropped onto one knee before Edmund in the Hall of

Lawmen and pledged the homage of the entire nobility of the Five Boroughs not only to the King, but also to Edmund's brother, Prince Aethelstan as the future king of England. The only mishap had occurred on their final approach to Stamford when one of Siferth's villeins had loosed an arrow from his selfbow and struck Edmund's body servant a fatal blow in the throat. Siferth had had the man dismissed and banished from the Danelaw and in recompense he had offered his son Sigewith to act as body servant to the prince.

Two days after Corpus Christi, Wulfnoth, Godwin, Oswy and his most experienced shipwright passed through the southern tower of the low wooden bridge that linked Southwic with London. Reining in his horse the thegn paused to survey the opposite bank of the river and the ancient walls of the fortress.

"Will you stay in the fortress while the work is undertaken?" Godwin's question sounded a note of caution.

"No," replied Wulfnoth. "Alphege, the Archbishop of Canterbury, has offered me a small manor on this side of the river so that I can see the whole fleet gradually take shape on the far bank. I shall cross the bridge each morning to work along side the men and living over here means that I will not have to share a roof with the Ealdorman of Mercia and his vicious brother."

"A wise precaution, father," commented Godwin dryly. "Everyone in the Danelaw believes they were responsible for the death of Lord Aelfhelm."

"I'm sure they're right," said the thegn. "Let's hope no one else was involved."

"Shall we build the ships, over there, where those boats are?" asked Oswy, pointing to the Bridgegate at the far side of the bridge.

"No. The fishermen will still be needed to provide fish not only for the town, but to feed those of us working on the grand fleet. We shall build them down stream of the bridge as far as the fortress and beyond where there is that inlet. The fortress will then protect our work."

"Right," said Oswy, following the thegn's directions. "The river is tidal so we shall have to work above the high water mark, but the timber can be brought in to the east of the fortress and dragged up or down stream as required."

Wulfnoth nodded. "I have suggested that Beorhtric has it brought round the town by wagon."

"Can we trust him to supply sufficient quantities of sound wood?" asked Oswy.

"No, which is why I have asked Ulfkytel to arrange additional supplies from East Anglia."

"You take no chances, Father."

"I cannot afford to. Now let us take a closer look at the other bank." And with that they walked their horses over the bridge to examine the foreshore before remounting and making their way round the wall. Half an hour later Wulfnoth passed through the Bridgegate and into the fortress to present his plans to the king.

* * * * *

Work eventually began by midsummer.

To the east of the town lay a flat area of sparse vegetation. Any tree that might have prevented the uninterrupted view from the fortress had been felled and what bushes there were had been kept trimmed, so that between the gate and the river several acres of low scrubland had lain undisturbed since the time of Aethelred's father. Cattle grazed there cropping the grass and could drink at will from the sheltered inlet. It would make an ideal spot for processing the rough tree trunks.

The first of these were due before Lammas, but although vast quantities had been accumulated on the west of the River Fleet nothing reached the east of the town. When Wulfnoth complained Beorhtric blamed the weather, the condition of the roads and the lack of suitable wagons. Fortunately by the beginning of September Ulfkytel came to the rescue when teams of oxen arrived, pulling wagons each bearing either a mighty oak or ash felled in the Danelaw.

Within hours men from the town were swarming like ants among the stricken giants with their antler-bone tools stripping the bark while the women carried off the unexpected largesse to fuel their cooking fires. Others trimmed the bare trunks after which the men from Bosham, under the watchful eye of the master shipwright, began driving in wedges to split the heartwood lengthways into timbers that would form the backbone of each warship. Then deftly wielding the adze these skilled craftsmen began to shape the keel, stem and stern posts, while others addressed the ash to form the strakes and oarwale. Others still worked on the masts, cross pieces and oars.

As soon as sufficient raw materials had been prepared construction could begin in earnest. Down on the riverbank above the high tide mark Oswy had chosen four level sites for the work. There the keels were laid, the stem and stern posts fitted and the ribs married into them. Then one by one the strakes were added, each overlapping the other to the sound of hammering as copper nails were driven home. In addition, thick ropes of osiers, held in place by cleats, lashed them securely to the ribs. Meanwhile fires were lit to heat the tar that would help seal all the joints. Experience had shown that such a construction would increase the elasticity of the warship enabling it to withstand even the roughest seas. Once Wulfnoth and the master shipwright were satisfied, the masts could be stepped and the fine woollen sails unfurled.

Gradually the fleet took shape and twenty vessels were completed before winter set in. The rest would have to wait until the following year. In May 1009 all thirty warships were ready to sail down river and make their way along the coast to gather at Sandwic.

"You promised that my brother should have joint command of your fleet."

"But that was before Ulfkytel and Uhtred urged that I appoint Wulfnoth in overall command on account of his experience and victories at sea."

"But he has never led more than a dozen ships against the enemy. Surely the responsibility of your great ship army is far too much for such a minor thegn from Sussex. He will not command respect. My brother on the other hand is a natural leader. When he gives orders, men obey."

"I know of Beorhtric's powers of persuasion, but so far he has failed to produce his thirty ships. They are not ready, while Wulfnoth's ride at anchor off Sandwic with those supplied by Uhtred and Ulfkytel."

"My brother's vessels are much larger than the others, designed to strike fear into the enemy and to give greater protection to you and those who command them. Such ships take time to build, but they are nearly complete, my lord, and you and I will be sailing down the Thames with Beorhtric within ten days."

"Perhaps, but my mind is made up. Wulfnoth shall have sole command. I trust his seamanship."

"But is he loyal, my lord?"

"He is an old friend and I trust him implicitly."

"My informers tell me differently."

Aethelred frowned, but his natural insecurity prevented him from dismissing the slightest hint of treachery.

"There is a long list of accusations against Lord Wulfnoth, but it is alleged that his latest act of disloyalty involves your son, Prince Edmund."

"How so?"

"He has encouraged the prince to conduct secret negotiations with the people of the Danelaw, expressly against your wishes."

"My son has done what?"

"He has been in Stamford with Siferth."

"But that is treasonable."

"My brother has a witness who will swear to it."

"Bring him to me and then send for my son. We'll tax him with it and if he denies it confront him with your brother's witness."

Aethelred spent the next hour with the bowman Siferth had ordered to be dismissed.

* * * * *

Eadric had deliberately arranged for Edmund to arrive at the royal chamber when both king and queen were present. He knew that Emma would be a natural ally in the web of intrigue he had begun to spin.

"Eadric tells me you are in league with my enemies." Aethelred believed at getting straight to the point when dealing with his sons.

For a moment Edmund's face fell, but then he quickly recovered his composure and stared back at his father waiting for Aethelred to reveal what precisely he knew.

"You have plotted with the traitors who live in the Danelaw to depose me and place your brother, Athelstan, on my throne."

"That is a base lie, my lord. The leaders of the Five Boroughs honour you as their king."

"Did not Siferth kneel to you and say that he would serve your brother as king?"

"Only on your death; or..." he hesitated, "... if it was found that you had ordered the death of Ealdorman Aelfhelm."

"Aelfhelm had to die," the Queen stormed. "He was a traitor. He opposed the king's right to choose my son, Edward, as his successor."

Aethelred stared at the queen, but said nothing.

"You do not deny it then, father?"

"I do not have to deny or admit anything to you. You are a child and know nothing of affairs of state."

"I am eighteen, sir, six years older than you were when you took the throne."

"You will never succeed to my crown. Nor will your brother. If you oppose my will you are a traitor like Aelfhelm and your friends within the Danelaw."

"And all traitors should die," said Emma. And her voice had the cold edge of finality about it.

For a moment the colour drained from Aethelred's face.

"Eadric," he said at last, "have both my sons locked securely in a cellar to cool their heels until they agree to acknowledge Edward as my heir."

"I'll never bend the knee to young Edward while my brother lives!"

"Defy me, boy, and you will die," said Aethelred with exasperation. "Take him away."

417

"You have always been too soft with traitors!" Emma hissed and swept out of the chamber.

Eadric smiled as Edmund was led away and he left Aethelred staring blankly out of the windhole.

Several minutes later he returned with Beorhtric.

"Pardon me, my lord, but my brother and I wish to speak on behalf of Prince Edmund."

Surprise took away Aethelred's irritation at having his thoughts interrupted. Then he shook his head sadly. "If my son persists in his treason I shall have no alternative. He will have to die."

"Your son is young, my lord. The young act foolishly He has been led astray by older heads."

"Who is it you mean?" In the shock of his son's act of betrayal Aethelred had forgotten how their earlier conversation had started.

"The bowman told us that Prince Edmund arrived at Stamford in *The Godgifu*."

The king looked blank.

"It is a South Saxon vessel," said Beorhtric triumphantly, "from Bosham!"

"One of Wulfnoth's vessels?"

"Yes I'm afraid so, my lord. It would seem that Wulfnoth was using the prince to cover up his own unlawful association with the rebels of the Danelaw."

"If what you say is true it smells of treachery. You spoke of a list of accusations. "What other charges do you make against the thegn?"

"He took a Danish prisoner as his wife without the blessing of the church, but according to the tradition of the Danelaw," Beorhtric blurted savagely.

"That is hardly a crime."

"You will remember, my lord," said Eadric quickly, "that Ealdorman Aelfric called him insubordinate and accused him of appropriating war booty to his own use."

"Yes, but that is no more than many a victorious thegn has done. It's said that he shared such things among his men."

"I heard that he gave a magnificent sword to a mere fisherman," said Beorhtric, "showering gifts like a Welsh tribal ruler."

"Such actions," said Aethelred shaking his head and holding his palms upwards, "speak of generosity, not treason."

"True, my lord, they are insignificant in themselves," admitted Eadric, "but to my knowledge he has also murdered at least seven people and committed four acts of gross treason against your royal person."

The scale of the charges clearly shocked Aethelred and he demanded to know the details.

"You remember the Danish moneyer Torgrim who attempted to defraud you by issuing debased coinage. He was a friend of Wulfnoth."

"I was aware of that. He asked me to intercede for the man."

"My spies have proof that our Sussex thegn arranged the old man's escape to the Danelaw and two Mercians were killed trying to stop them. Eye witnesses and letters show that he and his family now lodge with Wulfnoth's whore in Bruges."

Gradually the case that Eadric had built up against Wulfnoth was laid before the king: his long association with factions within the Danelaw, the secret meeting at Compton, his attempts to disrupt the purging of the

Danes in Exeter, details of the letters intercepted and of the bodies discovered, his refusal to take the oath of allegiance to Prince Edward at the council of 1004, his attendance at the meeting of the rebel northern lords in 1006, his persistent support for Aethelstan and finally his subornation of Prince Edmund.

"It is clear, my lord," concluded Eadric, "the Thegn of Compton is now the instigator of a plot against your royal person."

Faced with the wealth of evidence that Eadric had compiled, Aethelred's sense of outrage could no longer be contained, his jaw hardened and he immediately summoned Aethelstan and Edmund to attend him.

A Message from Prince Edmund   June 1009

The stranger arrived by horse mid afternoon and had clearly been riding hard for several hours. "I must speak with Lord Wulfnoth at once," he shouted to a dark-haired, thick set middle-aged man in the stable yard as he handed him the rein. "See that my horse is rubbed down and fed for I may need him again by nightfall."

"You're talking to him, young man," said Wulfnoth grinning at being taken for a servant, but it was hardly surprising as he was dressed in a coarse tunic, smelt of manure and had been cleaning the hooves of a sturdy old brood mare.

"Forgive me, my lord," said the stranger, covered in confusion and trying to take back the reins.

"What's to forgive," chuckled Wulfnoth "Let's both deal with your horse and you can tell me what's so urgent that won't wait till suppertime and he tied the horse to a metal ring in the wall, gathering up a twist of straw and began rubbing down the sweating horse.

"I come with a warning from Prince Edmund."

Wulfnoth was immediately alert and, although he continued to work a fresh twist of hay down the horse's flanks, his eyes narrowed and his face hardened.

"Well spit it out boy. What does the king's son wish to warn me about?"

"You are in grave danger, my lord. Prince Edmund is arrested in the Palace."

"Arrested?" Wulfnoth dropped the hay and all pretence of grooming.

"Yes, my lord, He and Prince Athelstan were summoned to attend a meeting at which you were accused of leading a plot to depose the king and put Prince Athelstan on the throne. You have been declared 'nithing'. Your estate is forfeit..... and your life is in danger."

Wulfnoth felt numb. He was the king's thegn and now the king had cast him aside without a hearing. All he had worked for in England was bound up in the Compton Estate and now it was to be taken from him. All who had worked for him would become destitute. The lives of all who had associated with him would be at risk.

"And what is to happen to the princes?" he whispered hoarsely.

"They will remain in the cellar until news of your death reaches Winchester. Then Prince Athelstan has been ordered to lay waste your manor of Compton. Prince Edmund, however, will remain locked up under threat of death to make sure that his brother obeys the order and swears to give up all claim to the throne."

"Then there is still hope."

"Yes, my lord."

"And how do you come to know all this?"

"Prince Edmund was permitted only one servant. He chose me. This morning Beorhtric, came down to the cellar gloating that by the end of the week he would be commander of the king's ship army and that you would be a dead man. Prince Edmund ordered me to ride at once to warn you. I came as soon as Beorhtric and his brother left for London."

"For London? Are you sure?"

"Oh yes. They think that you are already aboard *The Black Wolf* and with the fleet. Beorhtric intends to sail down the Thames and surprise you while you ride at anchor off Sandwic."

"So we have a little time to spare. You have served your master well. Come we'll finish drying this creature."

Once the horse had stopped sweating they shook down a fresh bed of straw in an empty stable, put sweet smelling hay in the wooden cradle and filled a bucket of water from the well.

Then the thegn stripped off his tunic and stood while Edmund's servant drew another bucket of water and tipped it over him. Towelling himself dry with the discarded tunic, Wulfnoth led the young man into the manor, called for refreshments and disappeared to dress.

The transformation was remarkable. The man who joined him for supper was still built like an oak pillar and yet elegantly dressed and fully equipped for action. There was still the trace of a twinkle in the grey eyes, but the jaw portrayed a steely quality that bespoke power and durability.

"Tonight, after I've settled matters here," he said, "I'll ride to Sandwic and join my ships and then we'll wait for master Beorhtric to show his hand. You can ride back to the palace unless you fancy chancing your arm with an old pirate."

"I was warned not to return to Winchester for if Ealdorman Streona discovers my identity, it will not go well with me."

"'Ealdorman Stroena'. I like that. He is avaricious I know, but don't use that name except among his enemies. Ealdorman Eadric is safer. He's Aethelred's axeman, an evil bastard, who'll murder or maim any one who crosses him."

"Prince Edmund told me the king would probably have him put out my eyes just like they did to Ealdorman Aelfhelm's sons and that when I leave Compton I should try to make my way back home to Stamford."

"Does the Prince think that the king ordered the death of Ealdorman Aelfhelm and the maiming of his sons?"

"Oh yes he is convinced the queen ordered it and the king condoned it. My father and the people of Stamford have always suspected it and now they have proof."

For a moment Wulnoth seemed to be gazing into another world. "Then it is finished!" he said quietly. "All my life I have stood for king and honour; now only honour remains."

With a great effort he dragged himself back to the present and staring hard at his guest as if he had not seen him before, he exclaimed, "Your father! Then you must be Siferth's son. I should have known."

"Yes, sir, and my father asked me to give you this letter. It contains a witness account stating that Beorhtric was present when Porthund, the hangman of Shrewsbury, murdered the old man and tore out the eyes of his sons."

"Porthund? I know that name," said Wulfnoth and he read through the letter before folding it and slipping it inside his tunic.

When he had finished he summoned Swithred and then after supper the rest of the household to inform them of the disaster that was about to affect them all, but promised that none would suffer as a consequence.

"I have sent Swithred in *The Godgifu* to Bruges to fetch one of Mistress Alena's trading vessels. It should arrive within three or four days," he told them. "There will be room on board for you Estrith and any of the estate workers who wish to start a new life with their families in Flanders. Everything of value in the manor will go with you. Those who wish to stay and return to their villages take what timber you need to build new homes and Alfred will divide up the livestock and the contents of the grain stores among you. When you finally leave set fire to the manor itself. Within five days only the land must remain. Now go to bed. You have much to think about and much to do in the next few days."

After they had all left he turned once again to his visitor, "My son Godwin is with the Fleet at Sandwic. I must join him to prepare my own surprise for Commander Beorhtric. However, there is no moon tonight so I shall ride at first light. Do you still fancy a life of piracy, Sigewith?"

"Prince Edmund has released me from his service and my father gave me his blessing when I left Stamford, so if you will have me, sir, I will fight at your side."

Wulfnoth smiled as he had done when the stranger first arrived at Compton.

At crack of dawn, before the estate cock birds were strutting their stuff among the bleary-eyed domestic fowl, Wulfnoth and Sigewith rode out of Compton and up onto the South Downs following the ancient flint pedlar's route from beacon to beacon and barrow to barrow before turning north-east across the high ridges of the Weald to Hawkhurst. . On the third morning they reached the North Downs and giving Canterbury a wide birth they cantered into Sandwic in the late afternoon.

He signalled to *The Black Wolf* and once the crew had hauled up the stone anchor Oswy brought the vessel to the jetty to welcome the fleet commander. With night fast approaching it was clear that Beorhtric would not reach Sandwic that day so, after speaking briefly to Godwin and Oswy, Wulfnoth wrapped his cloak tightly round him, curled up on the aft deck and promptly fell asleep.

Soon after day break the following morning Wulfnoth summoned all his captains to a meeting on the jetty. Then standing before them with Godwin on his right and Sigewith on his left he spoke frankly to them.

"I have always served the king and I've made no secret of my support for the Aetheling, Prince Athelstan, as the legitimate heir to the English crown when, God forbid, Aethelred is taken from us.

I now learn, however, that Beorhtric has brought false evidence against me, accusing me of plotting to have Aethelred murdered. Unfortunately, the misguided king has believed him and I have been declared "nithing". Beorhtric will arrive here soon to take over command of the fleet. No doubt his rapacious brother plans that I suffer the same fate as Ealdorman Aelfhelm and my son, Godwin, will have his eyes torn out. I, therefore, free you of all obligation to me. I do not ask you to desert your king, but *The Black Wolf* will slip her anchor before the axe falls." His stark announcement was met by angry cries of disgust.

"If the king believes you are a traitor then his mind is addled."

"The Norman queen must be behind this."

"He relies on favourites and believes anything they tell him."

"Nobody's safe in England."

"If the king thinks that Beorhtric could win a seabattle against the Danes he is a fool and not worthy of our loyalty."

"Beorhtric's no seaman."

"He couldn't sail a trading vessel."

Wulfnoth let them vent their feelings, until one of his senior captains stepped forward and summed up the mood of the others. "Aethelred may be our king, my lord, but he has repeatedly rejected the wise council of the Witan. He's listened only to those who seek to feather their own nests and he's sold us out more than once to the Danes. If loyal thegns are condemned without trial, he no longer deserves our loyalty. You've always protected us, Lord Wulfnoth. You're the lord, here. We'll follow you and take our chances."

"If you do that you too will be outside the law. I cannot let you risk all for me."

"You cannot stop us, my lord. Have you not just freed us from obedience to you?

Wulfnoth sighed, but was visibly moved by their reactions. "What you say is true, enough," he said. "However, I couldn't have defended your communities without your loyalty and support. Together we repelled the Danes and with your help I can outwit this Mercian thegn."

"God preserve us from all Mercians and from all Danes!" shouted a voice from the crowd and there were general cheers, but Wulfnoth raised his hand for silence once again.

"Don't judge all men by their origins. Aelfhelm was a Mercian by birth and a wise councillor and the thegns of the Five Boroughs, though of Danish descent, are men of honour. It is the son of Lord Siferth we have to thank for bringing us warning." Much to Sigewith's embarrassment he drew the young man forward. "He has chosen to fight at my side. If you choose to step outside the law and join us, we'll fight for honour and resist these murdering upstarts that poison the king's ear against us."

There was another cheer and then the captains returned to their own ships and Oswy joined the crew of *The Godgifu*.

When Beorhtric had not arrived by lunchtime and scouts, who had been sent out early to ride to the northern Kent coast, reported no sign of his ships reaching the mouth of the Thames, Wulfnoth had an uncomfortable thought that Beorhtric or his brother might have decided to head overland straight for Compton or Bosham before the estate could be evacuated. He recalled his captains and proposed a number diversionary tactics to protect the people and their homes.

That night the Bosham fleet dispersed and with the identifying carvings on their stem and stern posts covered sailed along the coast setting fire to all the beacons between Ramsgate and Hythe as well as any empty houses and disused boats that they found between. This process began a chain reaction and beacon after beacon spread the word inland across Kent towards London raising the spectre that a new Danish invasion had begun. Panic gripped the walled town and, while the king rode to Sandwic, Eadric ordered his brother to set sail even though many of the large warships were undermanned. Gradually twenty seven vessels were rowed passed the palace and made their way slowly down towards the sea.

Meanwhile *The Godgifu* had caught up with rest of the Bosham fleet now drawn up on the sand a few miles south of the Wantsum Channel. Cerdic, who had returned with Swithred as soon as he heard that Wulfnoth was in danger, brought the news that that Captain Arnulf had successfully picked up Estrith and a cargo of goods from Compton and that *La Pie Bavarde* had been last seen heading safely back across the Channel south of Dover.

"Thank God for that," said Wulfnoth relieved. "And how is your mistress?"

"She's well and busy making arrangements to receive your people. She said it will take her mind off missing you, my lord."

The thegn smiled sadly. She may have more than enough of my company in the years to come, he thought.

"She also asked me to tell you that she has received three letters from Lord Aethelmaer in as many weeks. She says they contain interesting confessions and are safely locked in the box that lies beside her bed."

"Then all's not lost after all!" The twinkle had returned to Wulfnoth's eyes.

Two days later as the weather was deteriorating the first warships of Beorhtric's fleet entered Sandwic harbourl and tied up against the quay. Within minutes the crews were clambering on shore anxious to feel the security of the firm earth beneath their feet. Gradually ship by ship another eight arrived, were moored in similar fashion and each vessel was lashed to its neighbour for good measure. They were followed by one of the two largest warships carrying Ealdorman Eadric which took the only remaining birth. Then half-an-hour before sunset its sister ship finally reached port but there was no room inside the harbour and she was left with no choice but to turn into the wind, lower her large sail and drop anchor in the Wantsum Channel. There followed frenetic activity on board as the raw seamen struggled to stow the voluminous material while others tried to ship their sixty-four oars.

With the shadows lengthening Wulfnoth gave orders for *The Black Wolf* to be launched. Slowly in the gathering gloom he brought the sixty-foot warship into the channel and began to circle behind the recent arrival.

On board Beorhtric could be seen waving his arms wildly as he shouted instructions above the confusion "Well well! So you've brought your contribution to my fleet at last," Wulfnoth called out over the din.

Beorhtric stared open-mouthed.

Struggling to find his voice he screamed, "You! You have been found guilty of treason! You will surrender your commission to me at once!" And then, when he realised that his own crew were staring at him, he added importantly, "I command here."

"We shall see," shouted Wulfnoth and at his signal the sixteen oars pulled *The Black Wolf* ahead of the Mercian vessel and with the wolf banner trailing behind her she headed south.

"Won't the other ships be able to follow us?" asked Sigewith. "There must be over thirty of them in the harbour."

"No, Sigewith. The more: the better! That lot are so tightly packed in and in various states of preparation that any attempt to follow us now would cause chaos. Remember there's hardly a real seaman among them. Most are land ceorls from Shropshire forced to risk their lives on the searoads by Beorhtric and his brother. Besides, fireships caused panic even among hardened seamen. Look!" and he pointed as Swithred released a small fireship in the harbour entrance.

PART SIX

The Storm

"A wind came against them such as no man remembered earlier."

Anglo-Saxon Chronicle 1009

A Lesson in Seamanship

The Islands of Lamoa lay six miles off the Kent coast. According to folk memory it had always lain there like some dormant marine monster, but some who had out lived their biblical three score years and ten swore that there had been times when it disappeared altogether for months on end. Even in the early years of the new millennium there were days when its vast back and thin trailing tail seemed to lie a mere half league from the shore; days when it was a blur on the horizon; and days when it hid beneath the waves. In truth it had spent the latter part of its life making and remaking itself, its shifting sands forever at the whim of the sea.

Due west of this massive bank of shingle and golden sand lay the thriving port of Deal and it was to this refuge that Wulfnoth's twenty ships sailed after they left Sandwic. Here they were able to take on board fresh food and water. Most of the crew spent the night ashore and Wulfnoth himself sought out the leading burgess of the town to whom he confessed his falling out with the king. He impressed on the old man that great harm might come to the people of Deal if it were to be discovered that they had given help to a man outside the law. It was agreed, therefore, that as soon as Wulfnoth's ships were ready to leave fires should be lit and word passed to the agents of Eadric Streona that the Sussex thegn had raided the town and that his ships could be easily surrounded if the ship army were to give chase.

Wulfnoth planned to give Aethelred's fledgling ship army the chance to taste the dangers and hardships of life at sea. At the same time he intended to teach the Mercian a final lesson. He would wait in Deal until the last minute and then slip out and lure Beorhtric and his fleet into the deep waters of the North Sea. Then he would sail due south with the outgoing tide before heading west to the port of Rye. The experience, he hoped, would give the land ceorls their sea legs stand them in good stead when they eventually had to face Swegen and his Danish sea stallions. Only then did he intend to disappear from history forever.

* * * * *

When Eadric's agents reported that Wulfnoth was holed up in Deal, the ealdorman summoned his brother and offered him the opportunity to save face and make a reputation for himself. Beorhtric swore to the king that he would capture Wulfnoth dead or alive and, taking advantage of an improvement in the weather, he gathered the remaining eighty ships that had eventually reached Sandwic and hugging the shore headed for Deal.

The little wind that there was came from the south so the sails were useless, but once the crews had got into a rhythm the huge fleet swept majestically through the sheltered waters of the bay past the smooth bleached beaches and Beorhtric gazed over the oarwale at the glitter of the sun's reflections on the lazy surface of the coastal waters with a sense of pride and power.

As soon as the masts were sighted, Wulfnoth led his twenty warships out of the harbour in a north-easterly direction so that they could benefit from the breeze and be seen clearly sailing across the bows of the advancing ship army. This strategy forced Beorhtric's vessels to change direction and hoist sail, a manoeuvre that clearly demonstrated the clumsiness of their crews and lost them valuable time. As each vessel turned it seemed as if the sea disapproved of their actions and sought to deliver them a corrective slap in the face. The waves, barely visible before, struck the veering bows a series of buffets sending spray over the bent backs of the oarsmen until the steeroar forced the head round onto the new course. For two or three minutes they were riding a see-saw as each successive wave lifted the bows into the air only for it to drop sharply down into the following trough. Then as the crews became accustomed to the new motion and settled into some sort of rhythm boat after boat began to move forward once again. However, by this time Wulfnoth had built up a considerable lead over his pursuers and was forced to reduce his own speed to offer them some hope of eventually overtaking their quarry.

Gradually, as they lost touch with the coastline, apprehension grew among the Mercian land ceorls, but they were cowed by Beorhtric's ship-army captains each of whom had been promised a reward of twenty pounds if their vessel should be the one to capture or sink one of Wulfnoth's warships. They were not likely to pass up the chance of such riches and in turn threatened that any man not pulling his weight on the oar would be summarily tossed over the side.

Tantalisingly, only half a mile ahead *The Black Wolf* was ploughing on making slow but steady progress with the tide that was still running up from the straits of Dover to the North Sea. "They'll not learn much seamanship without more wind," observed Wulfnoth looking up at the clear sky. "Can you handle her for a while, Godwin? I've not had a decent night's sleep in the last week. I want to have my wits about me when the tide turns and the weather freshens so that I can give Beorhtric a lesson in sailing."

Godwin leaped at the chance and took over the steering oar. "When shall I wake you, Father?"

"When the sun reaches its highest point in the sky unless the wind gets up or Beorhtric appears to be catching us. And keep an eye out for other sails. Your eye-sight is better than mine and we don't want Swegen creeping up on us without warning."

Godwin dutifully looked around and, in order to demonstrate the thoroughness of his inspection, he called Wulfnoth's attention to a smudge that had suddenly appeared on the horizon."

"Keep an eye on it," said the thegn. "It's probably nothing, but if it's more than one sail be sure to wake me." And with that he curled up with his head resting against the stern post and closed his eyes.

The smudge, however, proved to be nothing worse than a bank of cloud and Godwin thought no more of it, spending the next two hours or so taking turn and turn about on the steeroar with Sigewith. The young man from the Danelaw, who had had little previous experience of the sea, was eager to make the most of the opportunity and Godwin found pleasure in tutoring him while of course demonstrating his own skill.

It was only when the sun disappeared behind the cloud that Godwin became aware of the change in the weather. The light breeze, the assistance of which they had enjoyed all morning, had swung round so that it now came from the north and was increasing. As it blew the sail back on itself the bow lurched to starboard, leaving *The Black Wolf* momentarily wallowing between the waves.

The sudden change of motion woke Wulfnoth and several of the rowers found themselves pulling the air as the vessel rolled into a trough and their oars missed the water, but years of experience averted disaster and by the time the thegn had reached the steeroar the crew had regained control of their blades and were pulling the warship round onto a southerly course.

Much to Wulfnoth's relief and to Godwin's embarrassment the other captains of the Bosham Fleet had sensed the potential danger minutes earlier and altered course accordingly.

Forewarned, most of the ship army had miraculously managed to complete the turn successfully, avoiding each other as they did so and her crews were now rowing parallel with the South Saxons in a south-westerly direction.

Keeping an eye on the distance that separated the two fleets, Wulfnoth held the same course for several minutes. The sea was like a dying spirit heaving itself up the channel, rolling its shoulders and arching its back. The motion was not an unpleasant one when you got used to the bow rising with each wave, veering slightly to port and then rolling to starboard before dipping down into the yawning trough. It was like cantering on a sway-backed mare across the valleys of the South Downs, he thought.

A rapid deterioration in the light eventually brought his reverie to an end. The dark bank of cloud now stretched from horizon to horizon and beneath this ominous curtain the air seemed oppressive while the unfathomable green sea had turned slate grey, hard and unforgiving. It seemed clear now to Wulfnoth that a summer storm was brewing and, while he knew that his own warships had every chance of riding it out, he wondered how many vessels in the ship army would survive. It had never been his intention to endanger Aethelred's fleet, but now his impetuous gesture to teach Beorhtric a lesson could have disastrous consequences. The prospect of storm winds and a racing tide did not bode well for the unseasoned sailor.

He was left with no choice but to attempt to warn the Mercian of his imminent danger and persuade him to head for the nearest land.

Lowering the sail and signalling to Oswy to hold station he explained his intentions to his own crew and ordered them to fix shields to the oarwales and then waited for Beorhtric's vessel to draw level. When they did, Beorhtric, who had been signalling hard for one of the other larger warships to catch up and close in on the other side of *The Black Wolf*, ordered his men to stop rowing and form a boarding party.

Wulfnoth called across to the Mercian "Give up chasing us. There's a storm closing in. We shall ride it out farther east in the North Sea .Do not try to follow us. Head due west and seek shelter in Sandwic, he shouted."

Beorhtric, pretended that he couldn't hear.

Wulfnoth shouted again. "You'll risk losing every ship in the king's fleet if you don't head for the north

440

coast of Kent at once" and he pointed frantically beyond the Mercian warship.

"Do you think I'll fall for trick like that?" scoffed Beorhtric and he signalled for a handful of selfbowmen to fire a volley, but the unusual motion of the ship sent the arrows flying well wide of their mark.

"Whatever you do steer clear of the Island of Lamoa!" called Wulfnoth and when he had no response he shrugged his shoulders and nodded to his seamen who immediately picked up the stroke and *The Black Wolf* pulled away just before the other two vessels could hem her in.

Beorthtric cursed and ordered the ship army to take up the chase once again.

"I've done my best," said Wulfnoth and both Godwin and Sigewith let out a sigh of relief as *The Black Wolf* headed back to rejoin *The Godgifu*.

Riding It Out

Just as each keel in the Bosham fleet had been cut from a single piece of oak by a craftsman who understood the living qualities of the material he fashioned, so too each crew member had been especially selected to provide a unique blend of skill, strength and comradeship.

No one, therefore, had been unduly concerned when Wulfnoth ordered the Sussexmen to head due East for they knew that when the full force of the impending storm was unleashed they could run before it and no obstacle would lie in their path.

Not long afterwards they were hit by a squall and with the tide on the turn and the weather from the north freshening by the minute, two seamen on each warship hauled on the halyards to raise the sails and others set about trimming them to maintain maximum benefit from what was virtually an unpredictable cross wind.

In the flurry of activity no one aboard *The Black Wolf* had given a moment's thought to the plight of the pursuing ship army. Now as they looked back they could see a picture of confusion. About half of the vessels, presumably those from East Anglia or Northumberland, appeared unscathed. However, the rest of the battle fleet was in various states of disarray. Some were wallowing in the heavy seas, some dismasted and several had capsized and lay with their keels in the air and their crews gasping for breath as they thrashed about in the water.

The sight of men drowning had never affected Wulfnoth before, but then they had been Danes in raiding parties when it was a case of kill or be killed. Now he felt a pang of guilt as he thought of the men forced into service from the fields of Mercia, incapable of sustaining their own body weight in this strange and violent element, slipping beneath the waves only to reappear elsewhere days later floating face down on the surface of the sea.

If he had remained in command of the ship army as the king had promised, they would have been his crews, his men and his loss. He would have seen that their bodies were burned in great pyres after the battle had been won.

Unable to offer any meaningful assistance, Wulfnoth, who was determined to maintain a southeasterly course for as long as possible, turned his attention to the preservation of his own fleet. In order to manage and not be overwhelmed by the wind, the sails had to be shortened and the width of the sail foot reduced by passing the main sheets through cleats in the stern. The oars were shipped, the oarholes closed and leather skins were stretched from the foredeck to the mast giving shelter to the seamen huddled between the thwarts. Finally several shields were slotted into the stern sections of the oarwale to afford some protection to those clustered round the steeroar.

Rain was on its way and he was well aware that in the poor light things were only going to get worse when the heavens opened. Visibility might conceivably drop to a matter of yards and it would become all too easy for vessels in close formation to drift off course and collide with each other. He knew of course that if they were engulfed in rain a man would be stationed at the sternpost of each warship with an ox horn and ordered to blow a series of blasts to alert other vessels of their position. Satisfied that he had taken all possible precautions, he gave orders for the fleet to spread out, head southwest and allow the storm to carry them down the channel.

On board *The Black Wolf* conditions were such that Wulfnoth had to rotate his crew in order to conserve strength and maintain morale. Controlling the steering oar required the skill and power of at least two of the more experienced seamen while he or the captain, whose eyes remained focused on the narrow stretch of water immediately ahead, could provide additional pressure to make any necessary finer adjustments. Other crewmen shared the task of handling the slippery rain-soaked sheets to ensure that the sails held a constant volume of air. At the same time with water rising in the hold bailing had to take place almost continuously and everyone took his turn with the leather bucket.

No one on board, apart from Godwin and Sigewith perhaps, envisaged the prospect of disaster concentrating exclusively on the task in hand or closing their eyes and emptying their minds during periods of respite.

"And the sea flint-flake, black-backed in the regular blow,
   Sitting Eastnortheast, in cursed quarter, the wind."
                                        Gerard Manley Hopkins

Beorhtric, whose own vessel had miraculously come
through the first sudden violent squall unscathed,
stared for several minutes in disbelief at the devastation
around him before he could bring himself to admit to
his failure and give the signal for the ship army to head
for home.

Not long after, the first jagged forks of lightning lit
up the sky and reverberating thunder put the fear of
God into those in the ship army who had never
previously sailed out of sight of land. Many shut their
eyes and begged for forgiveness with one breath and
then cursed Beorhtric with the next.

The more experienced captains, those from East Anglia
and Northumberland, were no longer prepared to follow
his lead and concentrated their efforts on the survival of
their own vessels. Occasional shafts of sunlight pierced the
dark canopy and seemed to confirm that they were heading
in a westerly direction and the seamen, bent over their oars
like cowled monks rocking back and forth at prayer, had
to put their trust in the lookouts and the men at the
steeroar as they tried to ride each wave. Fearful as they
were, the fact that they were still afloat gave them a faint
glimmer of hope that they would eventually see land and
reach a safe haven somewhere on the English coast.

Then the rains came.

First heavy spots landed on the aft deck planking.
Then driving rain like sharpened arrow-heads ripped
into the exposed faces of the men at the oars and the
lookouts stared round in disbelief. One minute visibility

was several hundred yards, but the next a veil was sweeping across the surface of the sea swallowing boat after boat and each captain found himself alone and vulnerable. As some ordered their crews to stop rowing others did not and soon the disembodied screams of men and splintering of timber were heard around them. Then nothing but the howling of the wind! These conditions seemed to last interminably, but eventually the rain squall passed revealing that many of the surviving vessels had managed to keep in touch with each other.

To maintain some sort of formation was still fraught with difficulty for the wind which had been backing since midday now blew strongly from an eastnortheasterly direction filling each sail to capacity. The inexperienced crews, however, failed to maintain the best angle at which to harvest the wind and were often left hanging on desperately to the sheets for fear they would be torn from their grasp.

Even when one of Beorhtric's lookouts swore that he had spotted land off the starboard beam, struggle as they might the three men wrestling with the steeroar were unable to turn the great vessel back onto a westerly bearing across the path of the gale that was pushing them farther up the coast and another ray of hope vanished.

Sometime later, however, there was real excitement and relief when sightings of breakers were confirmed off the starboard bow. Suddenly men who moments before had resigned themselves to an eternity of wandering the seabeds began to believe that against all the odds they might once again feel the soil of England under their feet. Oars were engaged with renewed vigour and backs bent with revived hope.

It even seemed that the elements themselves were responding to their sense of urgency as the wind, now increased to storm force, and the tide anxious to return to its ocean home drove Beorhtric's flagship and what remained of Aethelred's ship army relentlessly westsouthwest towards the line of breakers.

Little more than an hour after high tide the first of Aethelred's warships struck the sand bar that formed the most northerly tip of the thrashing tail of the sea monster men called the island of Lamoa.

Half-an-hour earlier and those more westerly vessels might have passed safely over and been carried onward to the real beaches of Kent. As it was the impact and the mud-like consistency of the sand contrived to trap their keels and when the seamen leapt out to haul them clear of the water they found they were knee-deep in a morass and had to cling to the oarwales to prevent themselves from being sucked under. Some who had been more cautious made for the bows where the sand was firmer only to find that they were stranded on a short narrow ridge still at the mercy of the storm and any rogue waves determined enough to sweep them off into the sea beyond. Few survived.

Passing these scenes of disaster the other warships in Aethelred's fleet struck land at various points along the tail of the monster. Unlike their comrades, however, they were caught like stranded whales and each vessel was flung violently up the shelving beach by the first twenty-foot wave only to be sucked backwards in its wake into the path of the next. Oars were swept away, masts snapped and sails ripped to shreds while the hulls were eventually pounded into their component parts. Most of the crew shared the same fate, sent cartwheeling through the surf. Necks were broken, skin flayed raw against the shingle, their bodies reduced to sacrificial offerings at the altar of an ancient sea god.

A few lucky enough to be hurled beyond the sea's grasp did indeed find solid earth beneath their feet and seeing higher ground strove to reach it only to find that it was separated from them by some twenty yards of fast moving open water. A number clung to the earth and begged for the storm to blow itself out. Others, however, attempted to wade across, but found the seabed itself being continually cut away from beneath their feet by undercurrents. Only a dozen or so reached the comparative safety of the main island.

Beorhtric's own vessel for all its unwieldiness initially fared better than most. From its higher decking the captain had witnessed the savage punishment inflicted on the other vessels and using a combination of threats and the whip he made sure that the sixty-four seamen continued to drive their blades through the waves keeping the flagship in deep water as long as possible. Then he steered directly for what he took to be a substantial beach of sand, only to discover that that he had run the hundred and twenty foot vessel aground leaving her straddling the first sand bar at a relatively high point. Stuck fast it seemed that the warship was no longer in immediate danger. However, bad design and the continual erosion of sand from under the bow caused it eventually to break its back and the unsupported bow section was swept away down the channel that separated the tail from the body of the monster.

Aftermath

The greatest storm in living memory continued to savage the Kent coast for most of the afternoon. Lookouts had been sent out along the coastal paths to report if any of the vessels in the great ship army were to be seen heading for shelter, but no word of comfort reached those watching from the royal burh above the town of Sandwic. By early evening the king and the ealdorman, who had witnessed the two fleets sailing away earlier that morning, now watched in horror as those warships left behind on the beaches were lifted bodily in the air and tossed inland while those inside the seaport itself were herded like cattle and swept ignominiously into a heap one on top of the other against the old Roman wall where they continued to be pounded by the relentless waves.

Eadric was the first to break the uncomfortable silence that had grown between them. "If a storm can cause such destruction in harbour," he said, "surely no one could possibly be expected to have survived it at sea."

"Perhaps one man could," said Aethelred whistfully before curtly dismissing his ealdorman. "You can return to Shrewsbury. If your presence is required at Court you will be informed." Turning his back on the Mercian, he left with a mere handful of his closest retainers and returned to Winchester, alone.

* * * * *

It was the best part of three hours before the storm blew itself out and as the dark canopy of cloud gradually dispersed one by one all twenty of the Sussex warships emerged from the gloom into bright sunshine. Their ordeal was over. Once they had regrouped Wulfnoth led them back up the coast and they entered the harbour at Sandwic just before sunset much to the amazement of the citizens who were attempting to salvage what they could from the chaos wrought by the storm.

That night, accompanied by Godwin and Sigewith, he visited one of Prince Edmund's estates where he learnt not only of the king's dismissal of Eadric, but also that there were no reports of any other vessels making landfall on the Kent coast. There seemed little doubt in men's minds that the whole of the king's ship army had either foundered in the storm or that the great sea monster had devoured them.

At low tide the following morning, Wulfnoth's fleet began a sweep of the sand banks that formed the island of Lamoa. In the sunlight its beaches seemed peaceful, the highest point of its broad back standing some thirty or so feet above sea level and its tail curving graciously to the north. However, as they approached, it was soon evident that its swirling coils had claimed several dozen victims during the storm. Barely recognisable the ribs of once proud warships thrust out grotesquely from the golden sand like the broken limbs of primeval trees. All around lay scattered debris and in the water hundreds

450

of corpses drifted helplessly among the half submerged timbers, strakes, masts, sails and broken oars.

While the rest of the Bosham fleet set about the grim task of collecting the bodies, *The Black Wolf* headed for the main island, the only place where anyone might conceivably have survived. It was a two mile walk to the summit, so Wulfnoth sent the warship back to assist the rest of the fleet while he, Godwin and Sigewith began the trek across the treacherous sands. Most was flat and firm, but occasionally there were places that could swallow a man. The telltale signs were usually depressions, sometimes half full of water, often the result of inroads made by the sea during spring tides. Anything suspicious they avoided and soon they could see sparse vegetation.

"How on earth does anything grow out here?" asked Godwin.

"They say there used to be trees on that hill, but over the centuries the sea has begun to claim more and more washing away the soil, leaving only scurvy grass and seakale. In winter storms the waves have been known to cover everything, but in summer the high tide rarely reaches this far."

"One day I'll have a great church bell set up here that will ring out when the water reaches it to warn seamen of the danger," said Godwin.

"Then it will become known as Godwin's island," suggested Sigewith.

"I doubt it would last long," said Wulfnoth. "A storm like yesterday's on a rising spring tide in winter and everything would be washed away."

They had just reached the line that marked the extent of the previous night's tide and the sand became soft and undulating where the wind had carved a series of hollows and ridges that made their progress slower, but eventually they reached the highest part of the main island and could see the tree-lined coast of Kent in the far distance. Then several feet below them they spotted half a dozen men from one of Ulfkytel's ships huddled together round the remains of a small fire.

Although as East Anglian fishermen they had all learnt to swim their captain had insisted that they rope themselves together and in that way they had managed to cross the channel between the line of small sand banks to what they thought was the coast only to find themselves still marooned on the body of the monster. Somehow they had endured the storm, and in the brief respite before the next high tide approached they had made their way to higher ground. After a night in the open they were exhausted, but relieved that their ordeal was nearly over.

"Are there no other survivors?" asked Wulfnoth.

"None," said the captain, shaking his head. "There was an injured man sheltering in the wreck of a vessel, but he would not risk the deep water and we had no choice but to leave him. I doubt he will have survived."

"If you show us the place on our way back to the ships, we'll check before we leave. The tide will soon be on its way in and I want to be clear of these waters as soon as we have honoured the dead."

As they approached the shore line they could see the great timber pyres that the men from Bosham had built, the piles of bodies and the smaller heaps of shields and weapons that would be shared out before they finally left the island of Lomoa.

Conscious that there was still much to do Wulfnoth asked for four volunteers to make a final search for the injured man. Two of the East Anglian seamen stepped forward at once and Godwin, eager to make up for his earlier failure to warn his father of the approaching storm, begged to go too and it was agreed that Sigewith would make up the fourth. Taking a length of rope they set off at once in the direction indicated by the captain.

When they reached the channel they could see the wreck perched on a sandbank the other side of the fast flowing water. At first it seemed deserted but Godwin caught sight of a movement and, when they called out, a man could be seen waving a shred of sail. Godwin insisted that as he was a strong swimmer and the lightest member of the group he should be the one to swim across to the wreck. Before the others could argue he had removed his cloak and dropped his axe and sword belt onto the sand. The seamen, seeing no point in arguing with the thegn's son, expertly tied the rope under his arms and they waded out into the channel paying out the line as the young man struck out for the opposite bank. Once on the other side he helped the injured man down to the water's edge and the others began to haul the pair back to safety.

As soon as Godwin felt the sand under his feet he untied the rope, turned and, supporting the man, began to walk up the beach towards the cheering seamen. "You were lucky, my friend," called one of them. "If it hadn't been for the sharp eyes of Lord Wulfnoth's son we might not have spotted you."

However, before he reached them, Godwin staggered and fell to his knees. The supposedly injured man had wrapped his long arms around his rescuer and held a hand-seax at his throat.

For a second everyone froze.

"The blond hair! I should have known," hissed the long-armed man menacingly, "and where is 'Lord' Wulfnoth?"

"Organising the funeral pyres on the beach," said one of the seamen hoarsely.

"Good! I am Beorhtric of Shrewsbury and Commander of the King's Ship Army. The Thegn of Compton is a traitor and has been declared 'nithing'. The king will reward anyone who puts him to death. When you return with his body I will release the boy."

"Lord Wulfnoth is no traitor," shouted Sigewith. "After the loss of the ship army, King Aethelred has dismissed your brother, Eadric Streona. It is you and he who are nithing. No one will ever dare to make false accusations against the Thegn of Compton again."

"I hold the King's commission," screamed Beorhtric. "If you refuse to do your duty, you put yourselves outside the law and will suffer the same fate. I order you to kill him."

"We'll not do that, Beorhtric of Shrewsbury," said the older of the two seamen. "Lord Wulfnoth saved our lives and here the odds are at least three to one in our favour."

Beorhtric felt sure they would not risk Godwin's life by rushing him. On the other hand, although he had managed to drag his prisoner to within easy reach of the sword and axe, he realised that he would stand little chance if he slit the boy's throat. Sigewith was fully armed and the seamen could clearly handle themselves well.

"All right," he said after a brief stand off. "I will not harm the boy if you all leave at once. Go and tell 'Lord' Wulfnoth that if he wants to see his Danish spawn alive he must return alone and fight me first. If you don't and he doesn't then I'll slit the boy's throat anyway and take my chance."

Despite their misgivings the others agreed to leave, reasoning that any attempt by them to rescue Godwin might easily provoke the Mercian to kill his hostage leaving them indirectly responsible for the boy's death. At least if they told Lord Wulfnoth the decision would be his.

As they left Beorhtric shouted after them, "And tell the Thegn of Compton to bring me a spear and shield and I'll show him who is best fitted to serve the king."

Wulfnoth's jawline hardened when Sigewith gave him Beorhtric's message and described how the Mercian held a hand-seax at Godwin's throat. Then he summoned Cerdic, Oswy and the other captains, acquainted them with the situation and ordered them to continue with the funeral preparations while he dealt with matters alone.

"At least let one of us go with you, my lord," said Oswy.

"No," said Wulfnoth emphatically. He has threatened my son's life if I am not alone. If he sees anyone with me he will take great delight in killing Godwin before my eyes. I don't doubt that it is in his mind to kill us both if he gets the chance, but I will not take unnecessary risks. This is my fight. You will all remain here. You all once sworn to serve me and I charge you to do so this last time."

With that he strode down to a pile of weapons and selected two shields and three spears.

"He is not to be trusted, my lord," persisted Oswy. "At least let me follow you at a discrete distance, so that he cannot try any tricks."

"No, Oswy. You are my huscarl. You have sworn to obey me in everything and I order you to remain here."

Cerdic and the East Anglian captain exchanged glances.

"Remember, all of you," the thegn said as he thrust one of the spears into the sand, "set light to the funeral pyres as soon as the water reaches this point. It may serve as a distraction." And with that he turned and eventually disappeared among the sand dunes.

* * * * *

Meanwhile Beorhtric had knocked Godwin unconscious with a vicious blow to the side of the temple and proceeded to bind his hands and feet. Then he slipped his hand-seax into its scabbard and collected Godwin's weapons, put on the sword, tucked the axe and Godwin's hand-seax into his belt and waited.

As soon as Wulfnoth appeared he hauled the now semi-conscious Godwin to his feet to act as a human shield and held the handseax to his throat. "That's far enough," he shouted. "Hurl the spear so that it lands a few paces to my right. Take careful aim. We wouldn't want it to injure the son you bred out of that Danegirl would we."

Wulfnoth said nothing, but hefted one of the spears and watched as it flew in a graceful arc and landed no more than a pace from the Beorhtric's left foot. While it was in the air, he took several paces forward knowing that the Mercian's eyes would also be fixed on the missile.

"Careless! It would have amused me if it had struck your precious son!" He pushed Godwin to the floor, slipped his handseax into his belt and held the spear over his prostrate captive. "Now throw me a shield."

Wulfnoth curled his arm round one of the light wicker-framed bucklers and skimmed it in a low curve towards his adversary making sure that it landed several feet ahead of him. Beorhtric was forced to walk forward to reach it.

As he bent down Wulfnoth flung the remaining spear, twisting his wrist at the last moment so that the shaft spun as it hurtled towards the crouching figure. Beorhtric was straightening up when he sensed the danger and brought the shield up instinctively to protect his body. The spear flew under the rim and passed through the splayed legs of the Mercian striking the sand a foot behind him. Although he sustained no injury he was unbalanced with the spear shaft quivering between his knees and staggered awkwardly to his left.

Seizing the initiative Wulfnoth charged at his opponent giving him no time to aim his own spear which he dropped in order to wield his axe. Wulfnoth's intention was to knock the man off balance by clashing shields, but Beorhtric managed to brace himself before the impact and seconds later both were facing each other with axe and shield.

At least Wulfnoth had achieved his first objective in drawing the Mercian some distance away from his prisoner and neither adversary could reach the discarded spears without leaving themselves vulnerable to attack. For a while they traded blows, but both managed to absorb most of the impact of the axe heads by angling their shields and deflecting the force sideways. Both, however, were conscious that their fingers gripping the iron strips riveted inside the cone-shaped shield bosses were suffering from the repeated compressions and that their wrists could not continue to take the sustained pounding. Their attacks became less ferocious, both eager to ease the pain in their throbbing hands and catch their breath for a final assault.

Making use of his longer reach, Beorhtric managed to strike Wulfnoth's shield from above and the axe cut deeply through the leather covering splitting off a section of the wooden frame. However, the axe-head had also bitten into the metal boss and stuck fast. Wulfnoth staggered under the onslaught, but Beorhtric, trying to retrieve his weapon, stumbled off balance, allowing the Sussex thegn precious seconds to recover. Unable to dislodge his opponent's axe he flung his own at Beorhtric's head, only to see it deflected harmlessly by the Mercian's shield and land several feet away.

Both now faced each other sword in hand, but Wulfnoth was still hampered by the other's axe. Beorhtric circled him ominously making a number of deliberate feints confident that, if he could land several blows on Wulfnoth's shield, the wicker frame which was already weakened would eventually begin to break up.

As splinter after splinter was hacked away Wulfnoth was aware that that he would not be able to defend himself indefinitely. Then one stroke missed the shield altogether and the point of the blade sliced down his left thigh ripping an eight-inch gash in the flesh. "This gets better and better," mocked the Mercian savouring the moment. Wulfnoth realised that only a direct assault on his opponent, the Danish way, could save him now.

For some time he had been conscious of feint wisps of smoke rising from the funeral pyres so he waited until Beorhtric had his back to the channel and was facing the ridge. "Look, Beorhtric," he shouted, waving his sword in the air and pointed to plumes of black smoke and flames shooting up into the sky, "the end of Aethelred's ship army and the end of your dreams of glory going up in smoke." Then throwing caution to the wind he charged.

Beorhtric, who had been enjoying the cat and mouse game of whittling down the size of Wulfnoth's shield, looked up at the ridge and hesitated a fraction too long before refocusing on his opponent. By that time, brandishing his sword aloft, the Thegn of Compton had run full tilt into him carrying his adversary several feet in the air before pinning him to the ground and laying his sword across the Mercian's throat.

Wulfnoth looked him at him contemptuously.

Feeling the sharp edge of the blade against his windpipe, Beorhtric's eyes bulged with fear and he whispered hoarsely. "I cannot breathe."

"You should have thought of that before threatening my son," said Wulfnoth coldly.

"Spare my life and I'll admit we lied about you," gasped Beorhtric.

Wulfnoth was exhausted and had neither the strength to dispatch his opponent nor to climb off him.

*****

Meanwhile, as the tide continued to rise the salt water in the narrow channel that separated the monster from its tail became more turbulent leaching through secret tunnels under the sand and sweeping over its banks so that parts of the island of Lomoa changed from compacted sun-baked sand to loose salty granular soup.

Cerdic and the captain, who had waited until Wulfnoth disappeared beyond the ridge before attempting to follow him, had originally intended to swim down the channel and approach obliquely to render any necessary assistance, but the water was too rough and the bank looked treacherous. Consequently they had to make for the ridge and crawl the last few feet before peering over the top. Below them to the right they could see Godwin trussed up on the sand and the two thegns some distance away trading blows. When it seemed that Wulfnoth's shield was likely to be reduced to little more than its metal boss, Cerdic was all for rushing to his former master's rescue, but the captain held him back, "He will not thank you for interfering. This is a fight that he must win alone. I saw it in his eyes when he knew that his son was that devil's clutches."

"But my mistress will never forgive me if I do not go to his aid."

"Release the boy first. Then if Lord Wulfnoth cannot defend himself those two spears will come in useful."

Together they scrambled across the sand and swiftly cut Godwin free. Then as the crackle of the funeral pyres reached them all three watched as the Thegn of Compton charged and flung himself upon the momentarily distracted Mercian. Both fell to the ground and remained locked together for what seemed an age.

Covering the ground rapidly Godwin was able to help his father to his feet, while Cerdic and the captain each planted a foot firmly on Beorhtric's arms and stood over him brandishing spears.

"Shall we kill him, my lord?"

"He's not worth the trouble," said Wulfnoth. "Search him for weapons and release him. He can do no more harm to anyone. He can stay here and starve to death or return as my prisoner to Winchester."

"But I hold the king's commission," Beorhtric snivelled feebly."

"If I had my way I would strike off your head right here." said the captain." You cost me my ship and the lives of fifty of my companions." and he drew his axe.

Beorhtric did not wait to see if the man would carry out his threat, but turned and fled along the bank of the channel. However, he hadn't gone more than a hundred yards before he stumbled as the sand gave way under his feet and he found himself up to his knees in a morass.

Attempting to pull one leg free and return to more solid ground he only succeeded in pushing the other deeper and sinking further into the quagmire. By the time the others had caught up with him he was almost up to his hips in it.

"You planned this from the start," he cried irrationally. You planned to drown me in this....this....bog."

"Relax. Quicksand is rarely more than three or four feet deep," called Wulfnoth.

"I hold the king's commission," retorted the Mercian, still desperately struggling to extricate himself. "I'll see you all hanged for this."

"Keep still. The more you struggle, the more you'll sink," but Beorhtric in his panic ignored the advice and continued to thrash about. As he pumped the liquid gel with his feet he sank lower.

461

"Help me!" he screamed, his long arms flailing wildly. "This monster is sucking me into its belly."

"Can we not simply pull him out?" suggested Godwin staring in horror at the plight of the man who had so recently threatened to kill him.

"No!" said Wulfnoth sharply. "Don't anyone attempt to approach him or we'll have two of you to rescue." He turned to Cerdic, "Get me that shield and the rope."

"The tide is getting dangerously close, Lord Wulfnoth," observed the captain, "We shall have to work very fast if he is to stand any chance at all."

"I know," said the thegn, "but we have to try."

The incoming tide was barely a dozen feet away and Beorhtric was chest-deep in the viscous mixture when Cerdic returned, so, while the captain was tying a noose in the end of the rope, Wulfnoth tossed the shield to the Mercian. "Put your arms on that. It will help to keep you afloat."

Seconds later the captain threw the rope so that it landed beyond the stricken man and slowly drew it in. "Loop it under your arms and we'll pull you to safety," he called, but Beorhtric was too petrified to let go of the shield.

"It's your only chance," shouted Wulfnoth. "This whole area will be covered with several feet of water soon. Show some honest courage for a change."

Stung by the words, Beorhtric glared at him with real venom, but eventually managed to work the noose over his shoulders.

By the time they took the strain the water was lapping round their sandals. Even with their feet on solid ground they would have been lucky to overcome the pressure of the sand that now held him. As it was, the instability of the grit beneath them reduced the force that they could exert. Time and again they took the strain, but their feet slithered forward into the separating particles and they fell backwards achieving nothing for their pains but failure and a string of abuse.

"This is hopeless," said the captain.

"The tide has beaten us." shouted the thegn. "There's nothing more we can do."

"Damn you, Wulfnoth. I don't want to die. May you all rot in hell!" screamed Beorhtric as the first wavelet reached him.

Seconds later Wulfnoth stood watching as successive waves raced across the sands until the sea covered the last hairs of his bitter adversary and the wicker-framed shield floated away on the tide.

* * * * *

The sand had staunched the flow of blood from Wulfnoth's thigh, but now his exertions had opened up the injury again and the gash was bleeding profusely.

"There are seamen on the shore who can sew such wounds together, my lord," said the captain. "Let us return to the ships."

Later as they stood watching the funeral pyres and the bodies of some three hundred seamen being consumed by fire and smoke the expert hands of a seaman stitched Wulfnoth's wound and bound it tightly with strips from the thegn's own linen shirt. Although there was a considerable quantity of blood lost, it did not seem as if any major damage had been done.

"We are finished here," said Wulfnoth. "The sea will soon reclaim what's left of them."

Finally, before leaving the island of Lomoa, it was decided that Oswy, Swithred and the others should take nineteen of the ships back to Bosham and submit to Prince Athelstan, offering their services to the king, who would need every available ship and experienced seaman to defend the coast in the event of a Danish invasion. Meanwhile, Wulfnoth would set sail for Bruges to collect the letters that would not only clear the name of Torgrim, but also restore the fortunes of the Thegn of Compton and cleanse the kingdom after a decade of Mercian domination.

As they headed out once more into the channel the great sea monster that had claimed so many ships and lives was gradually sinking beneath the waves with the last rays of the setting sun reflecting on its thrashing tail. Wulfnoth watched for a while and then turned away leaning back against the sternpost.

"Does your wound still trouble you, my lord?" asked Cerdic noticing that the thegn looked exhausted.

"Not greatly."

"My mother will cure him," said Godwin. "She always does."

"Don't remind me, boy. The one thing I'm not looking forward to is the daily agony of the hot knife and those sharp sweet-smelling herbs. However, I am looking forward to a good night's sleep in clean sheets when we reach the Woolhouse."

Notes

Witan

Abbreviated form of Witenagemot (the supreme council of Anglo-Saxon England which not only advised the king, but chose his successor)

Ragnar Shaggy Breeches

Ninth Century Viking invader of fearsome reputation

Le Mascaret

Famous tidal surge on the River Seine much reduced since the opening of the Tancarville canal in 1963. The bore crest could reach a height of up to 7.3 metres and travel as far as Rouen some 80 kilometres up stream. Records show that 217 ships were lost on the lower reaches of the river between 1789 and 1829

King Ella

Ninth Century King of Northumbria between 863 and 867. According legend King Ella had Ragnar Shaggy Breeches thrown into a snake-infested pit and was later flayed alive by Ragnar's son, Ivar the Boneless

Isle of Scape

The Isle of Sheppey

St. Pedrog's Church

There is no mention of such an atrocity happening in Exeter, but many Danish settlers were burnt to death in St. Frideswide's Church in Oxford during the St. Brice Day Massacre

Julius Work Calendar

A late Anglo-Saxon religious calendar whose illustrations depict the monthly tasks to be undertaken in an agricultural society

Lamoa

Name of former island off the Kent coast owned by Earl Godwin in the eleventh century. Now known as the Goodwin Sands

Glossary

Aetheling   The title usually given to the eldest son of an Anglo-Saxon king

bordar   Middle level of peasant cultivator

ceorl   A general term for a peasant

cottars   Lowest level of peasant cultivator

Danegeld   A Tenth Century tax raised to buy off Danish invaders

fyrd   A levy of the common people to serve in time of war

geld   A land tax raised in Anglo-Saxon times

hide   A unit of land about 120 acres

Hold   A Scandinavian title given to important thegns from Holderness in south east Yorkshire

huscarl   A household warrior-servant

metseax   A knife used for cutting meat

nithing   Outlawed traitor with a price on his head

oarwale   A word coined to describe top strake of a ship's side (cp gunwale)

oubliette	A deep castle dungeon with a single opening at the top
riglines	A word coined to describe ropes that held the mast of a longship
seax	A single-edged sword or knife
self bow	A hunting bow about five and a half to six feet in length
soke	Land owned by freemen of peasant status owing dues to a manor
steeroar	A word coined to describe the wide-bladed steering oar
villein	Highest level of peasant cultivator
windhole	An original form of the word 'window'
wininga	Long fabric strips used to protect the legs
eavesdrip	Water that falls from the eaves

Historical Note and Acknowledgements

While a writer of fiction may occasionally stray from facts recorded in historical documents, I must acknowledge a huge debt to the scribes, translators, writers, commentators, editors and publishers of the following works.

The Anglo Saxon Chronicles Translated and Edited by Michael Swanton

Anglo-Saxon England by Sir Frank Stenton

The Death of Anglo-Saxon England by N.J.Higham

The Year 1000 by Robert Lacey and Danny Danziger

The Godwins by Frank Barlow

Medieval Women by Henrietta Leyser

Harold The last Anglo-Saxon King by Ian W. Walker

The Diplomas of King Aethelred The Unready 978-1016 by Simon Keynes

Anglo-Saxon Thegn 449-1066 AD by Mark Harrison and Gerry Embleton

Hastings 1066 by Christopher Gravett

Guide to Winchester by W.T. Warren

The Anglo-Saxons by David Wilson

The Vikings by Johannes Brondsted

The Life of King Edward who rests at Westminster translated and edited by Frank Barlow

The History of Barnburgh by J. Stanley Large

Domesday Book edited by Dr Ann Williams and Professor G.H.Martin

Domesday A search for the Roots of England by Michael Woods